Diary of a Wedding Planner
in Love

VIOLET HOWE

This is a work of fiction. The characters, incidents, events, and dialogues in this book are of the author's imagination and are not to be construed as real. Any resemblance to actual events or persons, living or dead, is completely coincidental.

No part of this book may be reproduced or transmitted in any form or by any means electronic or mechanical, including photocopying, recording, or by any information storage & retrieval system, without prior permission in writing from the author.

www.violethowe.com

Cover Design: Robin Ludwig Design, Inc.

www.gobookcoverdesign.com

Published by Charbar Productions, LLC

(p-v7)

Copyright © 2015 Violet Howe/LM Howe/Charbar Productions, LLC

All rights reserved.

ISBN: 0996496831
ISBN-13: 978-0-9964968-3-4

Dedication

For Bev, the best cheerleader anyone could ever ask for.

Books by Violet Howe

Tales Behind the Veils
Diary of a Single Wedding Planner
Diary of a Wedding Planner in Love
Diary of an Engaged Wedding Planner
Maggie

The Cedar Creek Series
The Ghost in the Curve
The Glow in the Woods

The Cedar Creek Family Collection
Building Fences

Short Story Anthology Contributor
Pieces of the Heart

Acknowledgments

I took up two whole pages with acknowledgments in book one, and I still missed very important people who were crucial to the book existing. So I'm gonna try to thank all the key contributors this time around, but if I miss you, it's not because I didn't appreciate you!

My sincerest thanks and heartfelt gratitude to:

Bonnie and Sandy: You came through this time in the biggest way imaginable and saved the day when the sky was dark. Thank you, thank you, thank you. A million times thank you. You rock, and your input is invaluable. I would not want to do this without you!

Beth: Your friendship continues to be the most amazing gift. Your support, your guidance, and your enthusiastic input have made this entire experience more enjoyable. One day we'll find my Jimmy Kimmel, but until then, I already feel like I've won the lottery with you on my team!

Lesley: Thanks for taking a last-minute request and rolling with it so fabulously. You are my audience, and your feedback is crucial, so I am so glad you had long layovers and don't buy designer purses. Thanks for saying yes even though you may not have realized what all was involved!

Roberta and Angie: Sorry this got deleted from book one, but I thank you for reading, for printing, for feedback, and for love & encouragement. I was lucky to be your neighbor, I am honored to be your friend, and I am blessed to call you family!

Heather: You continue to be my most trusted source of information, my go-to guru for all things publishing, and my favorite conference sidekick. No one else knows how fun the commentary is behind the scenes making fairy tales, and I can't wait until our next adventure together!

Annie: You rock! I am so happy to have found you (Thanks Ava!) and I look forward to working with you again in the future. Thank you!

Donna, Lisa, and Melissa: Thank you for your careful eyes and valued feedback!

Ava: Your positive voice in my ear gave me strength and encouragement when it seemed the sky was falling, and I am so happy we connected!

Sandra: Thank you for the expert advice on commitment issues, men in relationships, and what fear can do to love.

Michael: Thanks for providing just the right amount of trouble to get the jail time I needed. Your knowledge, your patience, and your enthusiasm were all very much appreciated.

Bree: My best take-home from RWA was my accountability partner. I so enjoy our chats, and I appreciate your support getting this baby birthed.

Ultra Violets: Best street team ever! Thanks for jumping in on the ground floor. Can't wait to see where this journey takes us!!

To my family---immediate, extended, adopted, and in law: I've been overwhelmed and blown away by the support, love and encouragement I've received. I have no words, so I'll just say thanks.

To Dad and Aunt Zona: I am so happy we have unlimited calling plans. I can't imagine life without your pep talks and the laughs we share together.

Last but certainly not least, to My Knight and Dr. Smooth: You are the reason. The reason I'm able to do this, the reason I want to succeed, and the reason my life is complete. I love you both.

.

January

Wednesday, January 1st

You'd think a deputy sheriff could catch a fifty-two-year-old woman running in three-inch-heels. Now granted, he was wearing full gear and a bulletproof vest while she wore only a thin, slinky evening gown, but still. She was pretty far ahead of him before she ever kicked off her heels and ran barefoot. In all, twenty-six people ran. The cops caught two of them. I'm not sure if that says more about the sheriff's deputies or the bride's family.

Beth and Toby told us about their family feud in the initial planning session for the wedding. It had started decades before they were born, so long ago no one on either side seems to remember exactly how it began. Toby wanted to elope, but Beth felt certain they could prevent their wedding becoming a full-blown Montagues and Capulets showdown. Hmmph.

She counted on New Year's Eve hangovers working in her favor when she booked a midday brunch with a limited bar on January 1st. Unfortunately, I think her family subscribed more to the "hair of the dog" methodology.

Tonight's fiasco started on the dance floor when a heated exchange between two guests quickly escalated into a full-on eruption of flying fists, bodies slammed to the floor, kicks to the gut, and bloody noses. Family members from both sides rushed to join the melee, and it took seven security guards to break it up.

Beth got on the microphone, pleading with both sides to allow her and Toby to enjoy their day in peace. A grumbling truce settled uncomfortably over the room, but we pulled the bars as a precaution. No need to add more alcohol as fuel to simmering fires. Beth's father flipped out when he saw the bartenders rolling out, getting right up in Laura's face to express his displeasure.

True to Laura's reputation as the calm one of my two bosses, she never lost her cool. She did, however, seem a bit relieved when security stepped between them and asked him to leave. Beth's mother and two sisters went with him, along with several extended family members.

With most of Beth's family gone, the rest were too outnumbered to wreak much havoc, and Toby's family surprised me by settling down without taunting or gloating. Everyone grumbled about the lack of alcohol, but Beth and Toby were fine with it being pulled. They only had eyes for each other as they danced to song after song together.

Things seemed almost peaceful for the next half hour or so. The calm before the storm, I suppose, looking back on it all.

Laura and I stood talking near the patio doors when a flash of pink whirled past outside. I nearly broke my neck with the double-take when I saw Beth's sister, the maid of honor, riding the shoulders of one of Toby's cousins. She pulled his hair and scratched at his eyes as he spun in circles trying to buck her off. The seams of her tight pink satin dress had given way at some point, leaving her right butt cheek completely exposed.

I opened my mouth to yell for security, but the sound of glass shattering on the patio behind me drowned out my call for help. I grabbed Laura's arm and ducked instinctively. Beth's mother was standing over Toby's uncle, waving the stolen vodka bottle she'd broken over his head. Her pearls swung from left to right, and her hair flew loose from its once elegant chignon as she wheeled around looking for her next victim.

The entire room stampeded past us and out onto the patio as we stood in a state of disbelief and watched the whole disaster unfold. Father of the groom pitted against father of the bride as they scuffled on the ground. Beth's grandmother tripping people with her cane. Random cousins wielding stiletto heels like prison shanks.

Only Beth and Toby stayed on the dance floor, locked in a swaying embrace, seemingly oblivious to the apocalypse outside.

Laura and I pressed our faces to the glass as security fought their way onto the patio. I wasn't about to step outside. I harbored no grand delusions about breaking up any fights or putting myself anywhere in the vicinity of harm's way. Call me a coward, but these people had hidden in the bushes of a five-star resort in evening gowns and tuxedos to spring forth and attack smokers on the patio. Definitely out of my league and far outside the parameters of my job description. Besides, I've never been a fan of pain or blood. Especially when it's my own.

Eventually, the overwhelmed hotel security force called the cops. Deserters on both sides of the battle scattered at the first sound of sirens, jumping over shrubbery or bolting back through the convention center to exit from the other side. I think the scrappers in the center of the pile were too enthralled to hear the cops coming.

They sure heard them when the sirens came under the hotel entrance, though. They took off like rabbits in a greyhound race. Beth's dad swung by near the patio to let her sister jump in the back of the truck, but I never saw her mother again after she shucked her heels and left the deputy in her dust. They probably picked her up somewhere out on the highway.

Luckily, only three people needed medical attention. Well, I say that, but I should say only three people *who stayed to be examined* needed medical attention. I can't speak for the idiots who ran.

Beth and Toby just danced. Never left the ballroom the rest of the afternoon. If they noticed over half their guests had disappeared or been arrested, they didn't let on. After the final dance, they thanked Laura for a perfect event and told her to send them a bill for any destroyed property. Nice couple. I hope their love can survive without anyone getting killed.

There was a note from Cabe on my pillow when I got home.

Woke up in your bed. Don't remember much, so I hope I don't owe you any apologies. Let me take you to dinner tomorrow night either way. C.

Crazy boy. He fell asleep soon after the ball dropped last night. I slept curled up in his arms, finally happy and at peace. I can't believe I didn't realize that Prince Charming, The One I'd been searching for, had been right here the whole time. My best friend. My confidante. My dance partner. My love.

Thursday, January 2nd

Cabe and I agreed he'd pick me up for dinner after work. My stomach fluttered all day with excitement, but a bit of trepidation slipped in there, too. He'd been asleep when I left yesterday, so I hadn't seen him since I threw both arms around him and locked lips at midnight New Year's Eve. He definitely hadn't protested. In fact, I clearly remember him saying he'd waited a long time for me to do just that, but it didn't stop me from feeling awkward about seeing him at dinner.

I think part of the reason I hadn't realized my feelings for Cabe before was fear of losing our friendship. Of it changing. He means the world to me, and I would never do anything to jeopardize our relationship.

Once I initiated the kiss, it was pretty much a slobber fest of groping, kissing, and panting. We didn't have time to get into any discussions of what it all meant, and in his intoxicated frame of mind, he may not have fully comprehended what was happening. So I wasn't sure what to expect tonight. Would he greet me with open arms and pick up where we left off when he started snoring? Or would he be normal Cabe and act like nothing had happened?

In the past couple months, he's made more than one passionate play on me, but afterwards we've not once talked about what happened or why. I wondered if he would ignore it again tonight, or if we would finally acknowledge the big ole elephant in the room.

For me, it definitely feels different. You would've thought I was going on a first date with a stranger instead of hanging out with Cabe. I left work early so I could shower and get ready. Not something I'd normally do to grab dinner with my buddy.

I feel like now that I've seen him for who he is to me, I want to make sure he sees me, too. So I pulled out all the stops. I shaved my legs all the way up—not the usual just below the knee like I make do with in winter months. I didn't have hours to straighten my hair, but I did style it and put it up with a few tendrils floating around my face. *Floating?* Did I really just write *floating?* See what I mean? I'm putting way too much thought and expectation into this now. Good grief!

Of course, I couldn't find a thing to wear, despite a closet filled to overflowing. I mean, what's an appropriate outfit for seducing someone who's been your best friend for years, and obviously enjoys kissing you, but may not be aware you've suddenly realized you're in love with him?

Discarded options littered my bed when he called to say he was starving and could I meet him in the parking lot. I freaked out. I ran from closet to mirror to bed and back a hundred times before he called again to reiterate he was waiting downstairs hungry enough to eat a bear. So I threw on a red dress with a pair of boots and my denim jacket and hurried down.

My heart pounded as I descended the stairs, and I wondered if we would greet each other differently. Would he lean over and kiss me? Would he hold my hand on the way to the restaurant? It's not like he's never held my hand. He's always been affectionate with me, even as friends. But I couldn't stop my mind from racing in all directions with what may have changed.

He jumped out of the car and held the door open for me, as he always has, and he whistled long and loud as I walked to the car.

"Wow. You look adorable. Did you have something special at work you're dressed up for? Or did I screw up and forget something? I thought we were just grabbing pizza."

I had thought he might welcome me with a kiss, but he stood there with an obvious impatient expectation for me to get in the car.

Disappointment rose in my throat, but I tried to tell myself the man was hungry. Nothing else mattered to Cabe when he was hungry.

I told him about the gang fight yesterday as we drove. He laughed as I recounted one woman throwing punches with strands of someone's hair extensions still clutched in her fist and the groom's cousin using the silver tip from his cowboy boots to pop someone in the back of the head. Their behavior was horrid, really, but the absurdity of it all made it impossible not to laugh.

Any awkwardness melted away by the time we got our pizza. I relaxed into enjoying his company without obsessing too much. By the end of the night, I had begun to think he might not bring it up at all and it would go unacknowledged like the other passionate encounters we'd had recently. He walked me to my apartment door, and I casually asked if he wanted to come in, the same way I've asked a million times before.

He took my hand as I unlocked the door, bending my fingers over his and raising them to his lips to kiss my knuckles one by one. Goose bumps popped out all over me, and butterflies swarmed in my stomach. He didn't let go of my hand, but slid his other arm around my back and pulled me in close, his nose almost touching mine. A slight shiver rippled over my skin, and I held my breath, anticipating his kiss and wanting it more than I'd ever wanted anything.

Cabe took his time, though. He leaned in so slowly I almost lurched forward and took over. His lips barely brushed against mine and then pulled back not even an inch before coming back a little firmer. He did it again, this time with a soft, tentative touch of his tongue against my bottom lip, and I swayed against him, dizzy as could be.

He chuckled deep in his throat as I swayed, wrapping both his arms around me as he explored the kiss a little further. My head spun, my thoughts giddy and light as if I'd never been kissed before. Like I suddenly had no idea what to do. I stood there limp in his arms, not even kissing him back, simply reveling in the sensations he created with light flicks of his tongue against mine. His warm hands caressed my back underneath my jacket, the silkiness of my dress providing a sensual barrier between us.

When his lips left mine, he laughed again, a seductive, teasing rumble that told me he knew exactly what effect he had on me.

"I fear I owe you an apology for the other night," he said. "I'm just not sure for what."

I shook my head slightly to try and regain my senses. "What do you mean?"

Cabe opened my door and led me inside to the couch, sitting down and drawing me into his lap with such ease I scarcely felt the movement. He brushed back the tendrils I had carefully left hanging—oh, yeah—I forgot, *floating*—around my face and tucked them behind my ears.

"You have the cutest ears I've ever seen." He grinned while his thumb lightly traced the outer rim of one.

"Ears? Really? Well, that's what every girl wants to hear." I smiled and fought off the shiver caused by his thumb. "I think I've obsessed over nearly every other visible body part, but not my ears. Who knew they were my most attractive quality?"

"I never said they were your most attractive quality. I said they were the cutest I'd ever seen. I don't know what I'd pick as your most attractive quality."

He traced my jawline with one finger, lingered across my lips, and then tapped my nose. "I love the way your nose turns up a tiny bit on the end. The way your forehead scrunches right here when you're mad or really focused on something." He tapped my forehead and tipped his head to one side.

"Your eyes are beautiful. The green broken with little flecks of brown and gold. They change, too. Sometimes a brilliant emerald, but they can be a deep sage. Beautiful, though. Green's been my favorite color since I first saw your eyes."

I giggled like a schoolgirl, unable to believe the whirlwind of emotions swirling inside me. I'd been here with him so many times before, but not like this. This was all new.

Cabe didn't stop there. His finger ran the length of my neck, and then he slid his hand inside my jacket to slide it off my shoulder as I shrugged out of the other side.

"You have exquisite shoulders, Ty. Your neck, the little curve of your collarbone," he whispered as he nestled his thumb in the hollow there and leaned forward to place his lips against my shoulder. I moaned a little without meaning to, and he laughed again.

"Are you laughing at me?" I asked him, sitting up straight.

"Oh, no ma'am. Just enjoying you, Buttercup. Appreciating you. Trying to decide which quality is your most attractive and having trouble narrowing it down."

"Well, aren't you the smooth talker?" I stood and walked to the kitchen, suddenly uncomfortable. Maybe too much too soon, or perhaps I didn't believe it yet. The tingling sensations coursing through me threatened to explode, and I needed space to catch my breath and regain a little control.

"Want something to drink?" I opened the fridge even though I knew it held no options. I glanced up at the wine rack and wondered if I was ready for the consequences of opening a bottle of wine in the current atmosphere.

Cabe followed and stood behind me, brushing my hair aside to plant small kisses along my neckline and across my shoulder. That boy had me fired up like a race car on the starting line. No wine was needed to make me toss any consequences out the window and press forward, but he spoke before I could put my desire into action.

"So about the other night..." he started, turning me to face him as he leaned back against the kitchen counter. His hands grasped my hips to pull me against him. "I don't remember a helluva lot after you came through the door and tried to jump my bones."

"Tried to? What? I didn't..." I couldn't protest much, because that was pretty much what had happened, but I wasn't about to let him hold that over me.

Cabe laughed and slid his hands up my back, leaning down to kiss me again, effectively shutting me up and making me forget to protest.

"I'm not complaining, Ty. To the contrary, I'm apologizing. I'm just not sure what for. I don't know if I need to apologize for passing out in a drunken stupor and not being up to the challenge, or if I actually went through with it and don't remember. In which case, I need to apologize for not only what was likely a poor performance, but also for being a drunken ass and not remembering the first time you jumped my bones. So which is it? I mean, obviously you took advantage of me either way, but I'm willing to apologize."

His eyes twinkled with teasing mischief, and I resisted the urge to playfully raise my knee between his legs in retaliation.

"First of all, I did not *jump your bones,* and does anyone even say that anymore? Really? I kissed you, Cabe Shaw. For New Year's. Then you slobbered all over me a bit, and the next thing I knew you were snoring. So no apology needed. No harm done. Sorry to disappoint you." I lifted my chin in smug defiance, but I couldn't keep a smile from spreading across my face.

He didn't miss a beat. He pulled me to him and crushed his lips against mine until I swayed like a limp noodle again and quite possibly made that moaning noise I mentioned before. He leaned back slowly, and despite the grin plastered on his face, I could tell by his breathing I wasn't the only one affected.

"Oh, well. Then I guess my apology is that I'm sorry you have no idea what you missed out on." He cocked one eyebrow.

"Oh, really? Well, I'd say that's your loss, sir." I nodded and crossed my arms, my hips still firmly against his.

He laughed and pushed me up and away from the counter as he stood to his full height, looking down at me with that smile I adore. He leaned down and kissed me again, this time a brief encounter of the lips before he moved toward the door, still holding my hand. I followed him, debating whether I should ask him to stay. I didn't want him to leave, but I didn't want to push us farther along either. My warning lights were still flashing caution to take things slow. He turned to face me before he walked outside.

"Galen has tickets to a comedy show tomorrow night. What time's your rehearsal done?"

"I should probably be out around seven if it starts on time." He still held my hand as we stood there, but I felt the shift from our newfound intimacy back to the old familiar roles we were used to playing.

"Okay, great. Show starts at 8:30. Want to meet us downtown? Or I could swing by here and get you?" He squeezed my hand lightly, and I shook my head.

"No, I can meet you there. I'm sure your sister plans on getting something to eat."

"Alright. Talk to you tomorrow."

He kissed me again and was gone, leaving me alone to contemplate my heart and my body both aflame.

Friday, January 3rd

I seriously have no idea what happened.

I met up with Cabe, Galen, and her boyfriend, Tate, to see the comedy show after my rehearsal. I thought we were having a great time. Everyone in great spirits. Good times. Hilarious jokes. Cabe especially seemed downright jovial, happier than I've seen him in a while.

My heart soared. I relished the comfort of being with him, snuggled under his arm draped around my shoulders, sharing an occasional kiss, and enjoying the company of his sister and Tate. Life was good.

Well, until Galen broadsided me in the ladies' room from out of nowhere.

"What kind of game are you playing, Tyler?"

She stood there by the sink with both hands on her hips and murder in her eyes. We've always gotten along pretty well, I thought. We both have a sarcastic sense of humor and a quick wit that allows us to play off each other well.

But I've seen that girl go off on people. She has a temper like a penned-up rattlesnake, ready to strike at a moment's notice. I wondered what on earth I'd done to provoke her.

"What do you mean?" I asked as I ran my hands back and forth under the dryer.

"Don't play stupid, Ty. I see how you're fawning all over my brother and giving him puppy-dog eyes. Flirting all sugar-sweet. What are you up to?"

I pulled back in surprise at the hostility billowing out from her like an angry cloak that threatened to envelop me in its folds.

"Galen, I don't know—"

"Look here. I watched my brother flop around at your beck and call for the past five years, hoping you'd give him even the slightest encouragement.

I stood by while you used him for your emotional security blanket, all the while tearing his heart out bit by bit."

My mouth dropped open. "What the hell are you talking about?"

She held her hand up to indicate I wasn't to speak while she had the floor.

"I really liked you, Ty, and I saw how much Cabe loved you, so I hoped it would work out. But you never gave him a chance. Too caught up on some loser back home to see this incredible man busting his ass to be there for you."

I blinked hard, perhaps hoping she'd disappear or I'd suddenly understand her rampage, but it didn't help.

"Galen, Cabe and I were just friends."

"Yeah, I give you credit for that, I must say. You always professed friendship. Didn't pretend to be interested. But you still snagged him on your hook, and he couldn't get loose. Which is why I introduced him to Monica, hoping he'd finally look somewhere beyond you. Obviously, that went bust and between the two of you, you've nearly destroyed my brother."

She took a step closer to me and poked her finger in my chest.

"He's starting to breathe again, Tyler, and I won't have you playing games with his head. So I don't know why you're suddenly all affectionate and acting love struck, but I'm telling you it stops now. He needs to heal, and I'll be damned if you're going to screw him over again. Stay away from my brother."

She spun on her heel and left the bathroom as I stood there trembling. Completely in overload. My knees wobbled, but the only available seats were public toilets, so I leaned against the wall and bent over to try and catch my breath.

What the hell?

Cabe in love with me? Since we met?

No way. How often had we discussed it? How many times had we talked about how comfortable our friendship was and laughed at people who insinuated there was more?

Galen had to be mistaken. Right? I mean, she came across pretty pissed tonight. How long has she felt that way? Why wouldn't she have mentioned this sooner? I thought she liked me. I haven't seen her in a long time, though. In fact, tonight was the first time I'd seen Galen since Cabe moved to Seattle over a year ago to pursue Monica and eventually marry her. And divorce her.

Wait—did she really say she introduced him to Monica to get him away from me?

Even now as I write, I keep replaying the conversation in my head as my thoughts and feelings zing around like a pinball machine on a multi-ball run.

Did Cabe know she felt this way? Had they discussed it? Did he agree with her?

No. That couldn't be. We were on the same page. Weren't we?

My stomach churned, and I fought the urge to throw up. A few minutes earlier, I'd been on top of the world. So happy to be in Cabe's arms and feeling like finally the tides had turned for me.

But he seemed happy, too. It wasn't just me. Cabe was in the best mood tonight. He couldn't take his eyes off me. Or his hands.

And I guess that's when it dawned on me.

New Year's Eve, I crossed the floor and threw my arms around Cabe and kissed him. For me, it was like I saw him for the first time and realized I loved him.

But he never questioned it.

He never asked why his best friend suddenly kissed him. He certainly never resisted. Granted, he'd been drinking and actually passed out cold a few minutes later, but what about last night? Or tonight? Stone-cold sober and he never once questioned the change in our relationship. Quite the opposite, in fact. He hadn't let go of me since I got downtown. Touching, kissing, hugging, and looking at me so intensely my heart beat faster and my body quivered in response.

Could I have been so blind that I had no idea?

I sank down the wall as the past replayed in my head in vivid snippets.

I thought about his kiss on the couch the night his divorce was final. The passionate embrace that took my breath away the night I told him I was going back home for Christmas.

What had he said when I kissed him? "*You have no idea how long I've been waiting for you to do that.*"

Suddenly, it all made sense and yet none of it made sense. Flashbacks fired through my mind in rapid succession. I ran to the nearest toilet and gave up the contents of my stomach before sinking to my knees on the filthy bathroom floor. Dizziness forced me to clutch the bottom of the toilet stall for stability. Scenes of the two of us, tidbits of conversations, memories morphed together and distorted through this new lens.

It was all too much to sort through.

Some drunk chick came into the bathroom and offered to help me up, but I could stand up on my own. I wasn't drunk. Just blindsided. I knew I couldn't go back to the table and act like nothing was wrong.

I couldn't sit there with Galen's eyes boring a hole through in me. Cabe would know something was up, and I needed more time to process this before I mentioned it to him. I was positive he had no idea his sister had played bodyguard in the bathroom and threatened me. The last thing I wanted to do was cause a problem between them.

I splashed water on my face and rinsed the puke taste from my mouth. I wished I could just leave and go home without going back to the table. But I couldn't do that to him. Not on top of everything else I'd evidently already done.

I made my way back amid the guffaws of laughter erupting around me. I couldn't make out the comedian's words, and it seemed for a moment the audience was laughing at me.

"How could you not know? How could you be so stupid? Best friends, huh? Poor guy!"

I tried not to make eye contact with anyone, even though I knew the remarks were only in my imagination.

Cabe stood when I got back to our booth, but I shook my head and reached to grab my purse. I very carefully avoided any glance in Galen's direction at all.

"What's wrong?" He leaned down to ask me, his hand lightly stroking my back. I wanted to throw myself in his arms and beg his forgiveness. I wanted to go back to the happiness of a few minutes before.

"I don't feel well. I got sick in the bathroom, and I want to go home."

"Okay, let me drive you."

I shook my head again.

"No. I have my car. I'll be fine."

"I don't want you to drive if you're not feeling well. Let me take you home, and we'll come back and get your car in the morning."

Tears welled up in my eyes and threatened to spill down my cheeks. I knew he'd never let me go if he saw me crying. I swallowed hard and shook my head back and forth, getting dizzier with each movement.

"No, I have the wedding tomorrow. I don't want to risk being late. I'm fine. Just something I ate probably. I'll text you to let you know I made it home."

He stared at me intently, and I prayed the lights were dim enough that he couldn't see my face well. He knew me. He'd know I was lying. That I wasn't fine. At all.

I reached up on tiptoe and placed my lips gingerly against his cheek, wanting to remain there for as long as it took to figure out everything, but the people behind us were already starting to comment about us blocking their view.

"Ty, let me tell Galen we're leaving, and I'll follow you home."

My stomach revolted at the sound of her name, and I laid my hand across my belly to calm it.

"No! You stay here. Enjoy the rest of the show. I just want to get home and go to bed. I'll be fine."

He frowned and looked away. Guilt racked me. I'd let him down. For much more than just this.

"Let her go," Galen said behind him. "She's a big girl. She can handle herself. Sit down so the people behind you can see."

Anger sparked within me, and I resisted the urge to reach around Cabe and slap his sister across her smug face. Regardless of how badly I may have screwed everything up, none of it was intentional. I cared for Cabe deeply. I loved him. It had just taken me a while to acknowledge it. Whatever happened between us now would be for us to decide, not Galen.

I told Cabe goodbye and stumbled my way through the crowd, hoping he wouldn't follow me almost as much as I was praying he would.

I drove home in a blur of tears as I sorted through the chaos in my mind.

I wondered how much Cabe had discussed with Galen. Was she just going by her own gut instincts, or had he admitted his feelings to her? Lamented over my seeming lack of interest? She came across pretty damned certain of what she was asserting, so they must have talked at some point.

But had he told her about New Year's Eve? I mean, we hadn't discussed it between the two of us. Had they? Was that why she suddenly turned so venomous toward me? Or did she see us tonight and notice the difference? I mean, Cabe and I had been close. But we had certainly never snuggled up and shared kisses in public, whispering and acting all goo-goo over each other.

I don't know what set her off, but she had rocked my perception of everything. Of what it had been. What it was becoming.

Was I the bad guy Galen made me out to be? Had I strung Cabe along all these years without knowing it?

Cabe dated other girls while we were friends. It wasn't like he sat at home like a monk waiting for me.

What about Monica? He'd married her! They were in love. I had nothing to do with their break-up. Hell, I'd even encouraged him to go. Told him he should follow her. That definitely wasn't stringing him along or—how did Galen put it?—snagging him on my hook?

Good Lord! She made me sound like a movie villain who poisoned her brother with mind control and made him do my bidding.

This was Cabe. My best friend. I didn't make him do anything.

I'm not sure how I made it home in the state I was in, but I did. I texted him that I was going to sleep and would call him in the morning. I can't sleep, though. I keep staring at the phone willing it to ring and praying it doesn't.

I think I knew.

Somewhere in my gut, I think I knew. Somewhere deep down inside, Galen's words resonated truth I didn't want to face. I had an inkling all along, but I didn't want it to be true, because then I would've had to give up his friendship. I would've needed to acknowledge my own feelings and risk losing him. Risk him betraying me, or leaving me, or not loving me anymore.

I think I knew how Cabe felt about me. How we felt each other. But I denied it because it was safer just being Cabe's friend.

What had I done? To Cabe? To me? To us?

An image of Maggie popped in my head, and I wondered if she knew, too. I adored Cabe's mom, and I hated to think she might feel the same anger toward me as Galen. Did she think I had strung her son along all these years? Did she resent me, too?

I just want to go to sleep. Please just let me sleep. And please let me know what I should do next when I wake up.

Saturday, January 4th

I went to bed so rattled I completely forgot to plug the phone in to charge. It died in the night so I overslept and got to Mel's wedding twenty minutes late. Thank God it was a Melanie event instead of Lillian's. Mel never gets uptight. I swear the bride could run away with the best man and Mel would just shrug and say, "Oh well. Let's go eat the cake."

My phone came back on after a few minutes on the car charger, and I had two missed texts from Cabe last night and a voice mail this morning checking on me.

I texted him I was fine but running very late. I didn't dare call him back. I had no idea what to say.

The hectic pace pre-ceremony meant there was no time to talk to Mel. Besides, part of me knew she would say I told you so, and I wasn't sure I wanted to hear it. She had insisted all along that Cabe and I were more than friends. That we belonged together and just needed to admit it. Melanie didn't often gloat, but I knew she'd revel in being right about this one.

By the time the wedding reception was underway, the confusion in my head had built to a raging maelstrom, and I feared I may explode into hysterics if I didn't get it out.

"Can we step outside?" I asked Mel as she slid her wedding binder under the cake table.

"I wondered how long it was gonna take you."

"What do you mean?"

"You've been walking around all day hovering between a zombie and a hysterical manic on the verge of tears. You put the cake knife beside the groom's plate on the head table, and you nearly ripped the DJ's head off his shoulders when he asked if you were having a bad day."

"I'm sorry, Mel." I teared up again, and I silently prayed I could lean more toward zombie than hysterical manic with so many people nearby.

"No harm done. I moved the cake knife, and the DJ needed to be taken down a notch. Thinks he's God's gift, ya know? But I wondered when you were going to tell me what's eating you."

We had barely gotten outside the reception room when it all came spewing forth, words and tears and sobs and snots in an incredibly unattractive mess.

Mel stood there calmly throughout my verbal vomit. She continued to stand there silently for a couple of minutes after I finished, an awkward pause that allowed me to catch my breath but almost made me wish she'd go ahead and say I told you so.

Instead, she looked at me without any emotion at all. "I don't see the problem."

"What? What do you mean you don't see the problem?"

"You finally figured out you love Cabe. Great. You also found out Cabe loves you. Great. And when you made a move to take the friendship to the next level, he went with you without any protest. What's the problem?"

I jerked my head back and looked at her as if she had two heads, neither of which was making sense to me.

"What's the problem? I've been completely oblivious."

"So?"

"So, his sister hates me."

"So?"

"But, but—"

"Tyler, you're in love with your best friend. He's in love with you. You don't need his sister's permission."

"But she said I hurt him and I led him on-"

"Did *he* say that? Did he in any way whatsoever make you think he was angry with you or felt misled or mistreated?" Mel crossed her arms and arched both eyebrows high above her confident smirk.

"Well, no, but—"

"Then there's not a problem. His sister may have a problem, but you're not in love with his sister. This is between you and Cabe."

"So what do I do? What do I say? It's so awkward. Do I just tell him what Galen said and apologize?" I swiped the back of my hand across my drippy nose, wishing I had a tissue.

"No! Screw her!" Mel scrunched her face up like she'd tasted something nasty. "I wouldn't say anything. He doesn't seem to be upset about it, so why bring it up and cause a problem when there's not one? The past is the past. You guys are moving forward now, and I wouldn't embarrass him or you by getting all *I didn't know you liked me like that*. Just leave it alone. He's a grown man. If he didn't say anything to you about his feelings, that's on him. Don't cause drama where there isn't any. Come on, it's almost time for cake cutting."

She turned to go and I stared after her amazed. It couldn't be that easy. I couldn't just ignore what Galen told me. I had to confront it.

Or did I?

I mean, after all, I didn't confront it when he asked me to sleep with him the day his divorce was final. I didn't confront it when he landed a big ole smooch on me after I told him I was going back home for Christmas and he thought it was because of my ex-boyfriend.

Was it possible to just let this go, too?

I followed Mel back inside and stood on the perimeter of the room as she went through the motions required for the rest of the event. As an assistant, I normally left weddings right after cake cutting. I wasn't needed once the guests finished eating and settled in for talking and dancing. But I didn't want to go home yet, and I wanted to put off calling Cabe back until I knew what I should do.

"Are you sure I shouldn't say something?" I asked Mel as we walked to our cars around midnight. "I mean, it can't be good to just keep ignoring things and not discuss what's going on. Shouldn't we get it all out on the table?"

"Good Lord, Tyler. You want to freak the man out completely? No guy wants to have the 'let's define the relationship' talk less than a week in. Granted, this isn't exactly a normal just-started-dating situation, but just let it be. When he's ready to talk to you about his feelings, he will. Guys don't like to be pushed into those conversations. Chill. Enjoy his company. Enjoy his kisses. Don't freak over everything."

The whole drive home I flip-flopped back and forth between agreeing with Mel or convinced I should call Cabe and apologize for the last five years. I'm not sure which side I had landed on when I finally dialed his number, but it went straight to voice mail, so I didn't have to decide. I just left a message saying good night. I'll decide tomorrow, I guess. After all, in the words of Scarlett O'Hara, tomorrow is another day.

Sunday, January 5th

Well, it didn't come up today.

I tried. Sort of. There just wasn't a good time. There didn't seem to be a break in conversation where I could say, "Hey! So Galen says you've been in love with me for several years now. Cool! Sorry I didn't catch that."

Cabe called this morning to say his cousin Danny was playing drums for a music festival in Ybor City, so we headed over there for the day. He was in such a good mood I didn't want to bring up anything and make it awkward.

He greeted me at the door with a huge hug and a kiss that said he'd definitely missed me since Friday night.

"What's up, Buttercup? I packed a small cooler with some drinks so I need to grab some ice." He let me go and headed to the fridge.

Emotions rushed through me in rapid fire. Joy at seeing him. The thrill of being in his arms. Guilt for what I've put him through. And a teensy bit of shyness that came out of nowhere. I'd never flung open the door to Cabe and had him immediately lock lips with mine.

I opened my mouth to say I was sorry, but he turned to me with the hugest grin on his face, and my heart melted. I didn't want anything to take that grin away. I figured we had the whole day. I could apologize for being oblivious at any point. We didn't have to start off the day with it.

But the point never came.

We sat on a blanket for hours listening to the music. Holding hands. Nuzzling each other. Laughing. Kissing. It was like every comfortable, incredible day I've ever had with Cabe, except now his hands glided slowly over my shoulders, leaving goosebumps and shivers in their wake. He casually stroked my skin, his fingers like feathers driving me insane with desire. The same desire that darkened his eyes when we leaned together for

18

a kiss.

It was like our friendship remained at its core. The joking, the camaraderie, the shared interests. Being completely at ease. But we'd shifted to another level. A subtle shift. The casual touch meant more. The spark had been lit beneath the surface, and I was more aware of Cabe physically than I had ever been when we were 'just friends.' I couldn't help but wonder if it had been like this for him all along, and I'd somehow never seen it.

After his cousin's band finished, we went backstage to say hello. Danny stood a good six inches shorter than Cabe. They shared no family resemblance at all, but their greeting revealed a closeness often reserved for cousins.

"Cabe!" Danny rushed forward to meet us, and they did the classic man-hug thing where they bumped chests and clapped backs.

"Dan, my man!" Cabe laughed and turned to put his arm around me as he nudged me forward. "This is my friend, Tyler. Ty, my cousin Danny."

I flinched a little at the introduction. I mean, obviously I'm his friend. And now as I write this, I realize it's a little childish or premature to think he would introduce me as his girlfriend or something. It's not like I need a label or a title to know Cabe cares about me. But I sort of wanted one. I wanted him to acknowledge me as something more than a friend. I realize we haven't had some big conversation establishing that we're going steady or something. If that's even what you call it at this point in life.

In high school, it was easy. The guy gave you some token personal belonging, and you treasured it like it was the Hope Diamond, entrusted to your care for an indefinite period of time. You counted each day as some sign of progress toward love everlasting, sharing small celebrations with great fanfare.

"Happy two-week anniversary!" All the while praying the day would never come when he asked for his stuff back and you went back to the mundane passage of time.

I didn't think Cabe was gonna dig some memento out of a box for me to wear on a chain around my neck, but I thought we'd crossed a definitive line. Swapping spit consistently throughout the day should have earned a bit more than a friend introduction, I thought. But I could be wrong.

Danny scooped me up in a giant hug; he clearly didn't care what label I'd been given. Any friend of Cabe's was a friend of his.

"Hey girl! So nice to meet you. I've heard a lot about you. Did you enjoy the show?"

My paranoia kicked in. What had he heard? Was it the big family topic of conversation that Cabe's friend Tyler was stringing him along? Did everyone know that Cabe had been in love with me and I was clueless? Was the whole family mad at me or just Galen?

I stumbled out of the hug and nodded, mumbling something eloquent, such as 'nice to meet you, too.'

The two of them talked about the band, the festival, and how things were progressing for Danny. Cabe's hand never left my back. He held me close as he listened to Danny, stroking my back with his thumb. To any outsiders or drum-playing cousins looking on, we were obviously 'together,' so maybe I was overreacting. It's not like he took three steps away from me and pretended we'd just met. I don't know why it bothered me. Why it still bothers me.

We took the cooler and blanket back to the car and walked hand in hand through Ybor to check out the shops. Cabe veered off when he saw a side street lined with carnival games, one of his favorite pastimes. The vendors came alive shouting for Cabe to win a prize for the lady.

"Does the lady want a prize?" he asked me with a grin, stopping in the middle of the street amid the laughter of children and the distant strains of music from the concert stage.

I perused the stuffed animal offerings. A rather large pink pig wearing a tutu, a few college mascot animals, and a green frog holding a daisy. Nothing I needed to complete my home décor, but I knew how much he loved winning this stuff.

I shrugged and looked at the basketball toss with its curved rims, the stacked milk jugs, and the walls of balloons interspersed with darts. I spied the water pistols and grinned.

"What do you say we have a little contest? The lady might win her own prize." I crossed my arms and nodded toward the pistols.

He followed my gaze and broke into laughter. I knew he would take the bait. We were both suckers for competition, and it didn't matter that this took no talent. As long as you kept your water stream on the bullseye without wavering, your car raced to the top and rang the bell. Luck in picking the seat with the strongest stream more than anything.

I plopped down on seat seven and he took six.

"May the best aim win," Cabe said. "I may have a slight advantage over you here. Aiming my stream." He winked at me as he paid the smirking carnival vendor.

"I might surprise you!" I grasped my pistol with both hands and stared down its tiny barrel toward the target.

"Oh really? Well, bring it on!" Cabe settled onto his elbows to aim, his massive height unsuited for the low stools.

Water dripped onto my hands as I waited to hear the vendor count us off. Suddenly, the buzzer rang and I squeezed as hard as I could, willing the water to come out faster and the car to move higher. I stole a glance at Cabe's car next to mine, and let out a mischievous laugh as it fell behind.

I had almost reached the bell at the top when Cabe put his hand over my eyes.

"Stop! What are you doing? Cabe!" I jerked out from under his hand just in time to see his car hit the bell seconds before mine. He sprang from his stool, waving his arms in the air victorious.

"Yes! I won! In the final lap!"

"You did *not* win! You cheated. You covered my eyes. I couldn't see!"

"Sometimes you have to overcome adversities, Ty. The road isn't always straight and narrow."

I looked to the vendor chuckling beneath his stubbly beard.

"That's not fair. We need a rematch."

"The lady can pick her prize." Cabe swept his arm toward the plethora of brightly-hued stuffed animals hanging from the tent.

"Oh, hell no! I want a rematch."

"I'm not gonna let you win."

"Why not?"

He sat on the stool next to me and put his hands on my thighs. "Because I want to win the prize for you."

"But you didn't. You cheated."

He considered that for a moment and shook his head. "Okay, rematch." He paid the man, and we assumed our firing positions again.

I swear the old dude behind the counter turned down my water pressure or stepped on the hose or something. It barely trickled out this time, and Cabe easily beat me. I think I even saw a conspiratorial glance shared between them.

Whatever. I have to admit that a teensy-weensy part of me is happy he wanted to win the stupid frog for me. I don't know that shooting a water stream into a bullseye to win a stuffed animal is necessarily a gallant act, but it was sweet, nonetheless. The frog is staring at me now from his perch on the rocking chair in the corner of my bedroom.

We never did have the talk. I didn't bring it up at dinner because I figured we'd have more privacy when we got back here. But then his mother called to say she'd locked herself out of the house and needed him to come home. So he dropped me off with a kiss in the car and drove away into the night.

Maybe Mel is right. He doesn't seem to be bothered by the past that brought us here, so why should I?

I got up and brought the frog back to bed with me. The faint scent of Cabe on him is comforting, but the frog is just a stand-in. Cabe is the real prize.

Monday, January 6ᵗʰ

"Wanna go to a work thing with me?" Cabe asked. We had just finished dinner and were washing dishes together. I had this momentary vision of us ten years down the line having the same kind of night and the same kind of conversation. Oddly enough, the thought made me smile.

"Sure, what is it?" I took each dish as he rinsed it, drying it and putting it away.

"Volunteering at an animal shelter."

"Oh wow. I figured you meant some cocktail reception with a bunch of computer geeks standing around talking in a code I didn't understand. An animal shelter sounds like way more fun. How is that a work thing?"

"We have this service initiative to get employees out in the community helping others. Each of us had to sign up for a project, and I thought you might like the animal shelter."

"Well, yeah! What's not to like about playing with adorable puppies and kittens?"

"Cleaning up poop and being covered in hair and slobber?"

I flicked my hand in the dishwater and splashed him. "It'll be fun!"

"I'm sure it will. As long as you don't bring anything home."

"I can't. I know that. I'd love to have a dog, but I'm never home."

He drained the sink and dried his hands on the towel I held. "Too much work. Too much responsibility."

"That's not it." I frowned as I hung the towel on its rack. "I don't think they're too much work at all. We always had dogs growing up, but I can't leave a dog home alone all the time while I'm working crazy wedding hours. Not to mention traipsing all over town with you to movies and festivals."

"Exactly what I mean. If you have a dog, you have no life. You can't go anywhere. Can't do anything. You always have to be home for the dog. No thanks."

He wrapped his arms around me and leaned in to kiss me, but I resisted.

"Wait, so you're saying you wouldn't ever want a dog? Like, never?" I leaned further back as I asked, his arms still encircling my waist as I tried to get a better look at his face. "Never?"

The thought was disconcerting to me. I'd always assumed at some point I'd have a dog. Like, when I grew up and had a real house and a family and stuff. Not just me living alone in my apartment with the dog by itself, but I figured at some point I wouldn't live alone. Of course I'd have a dog then. Wouldn't I?

In my vision of future us, I hadn't necessarily seen a dog in the picture, but I assumed there would be or could be. It may have been a trivial thing, but it mattered to me. We hadn't discussed the future. Our future.

"I don't know," he said. "*Never* seems harsh. But I just can't see me wanting to be tied down with a dog. It's a big time commitment. A big money commitment. I don't know. It's not something I've ever wanted."

"What if I wanted it?" I asked, leaning in closer this time. Wanting to bring us together on the issue, I suppose.

Cabe smiled down at me and planted a light kiss on my forehead. "Do I need to change our service project to beach clean-up?"

"No. I want to go to the animal shelter." But I also wanted him to tell me I could have a dog. That *we* could have a dog. That there would be a *we*.

He changed the subject and we moved on, but it bugged me in the back of my mind. I had come to some sort of peace about not bringing up the past and his feelings for me. To listen to Mel and not need the 'let's define the relationship' talk. But I wanted to know what he was thinking. What he was expecting. Did he see us ten years down the line drying dishes and attending work functions? Did he see us in the same house at some point? With a dog? I didn't want to ask, but I certainly wanted to know.

I think it's still bothering me that he didn't introduce me as his girlfriend yesterday. Which is stupid. Completely stupid. Why should I need a label to establish what I already know? I mean, if his sister was right and Cabe has been in love with me all this time, then surely now that I realize how I feel about him, we're just *together*. Right? I shouldn't need to have a conversation about it. Obviously we have a future. We love each other. We haven't said those words yet, but I know we do. We'll be fine. Cabe's The One. I know it. And one day, we'll have a dog.

Wednesday, January 8th

Cabe came over tonight to cook dinner and watch a movie. Dinner wasn't the only thing that ended up cooking, though. We had finished eating and were maybe a third of the way through the movie. Some stupid, slapstick comedy easily ignored. I had been lying against Cabe, my head on his chest and his arm wrapped around my shoulders as he reclined against the back of the couch. He kissed the top of my head and I turned to look up at him, and that was all she wrote.

We tore into each other like we'd been stranded in a jungle for days and suddenly wandered upon a feast. Nothing tentative, shy, or polite about it. I'm talking covering half your face, tongues and lips and teeth kind of kissing. I sat up to face him and give the task at hand my undivided attention, and he literally just lifted me up and settled me in a straddle over his lap. More like unsettled me, really. After all, there is nothing at all settling about straddling a hot guy right across the hottest part of him while he strokes his hands up and down your back underneath your shirt and gives you the most erotic dental inspection of your life with his tongue.

I slid my knees a little wider apart, grinding against him as my teeth nipped at his bottom lip. He responded with a deep groan as he pulled me closer and slid his thumbs around the front of my stomach. I arched toward him as he trailed kisses down my neck and inside the collar of my shirt. I shuddered as though a chill had run across my skin, but no part of me felt remotely cold. Quite the opposite, in fact.

I wouldn't say I have a ton of experience, but I'm no prude either. I've made out on some couches in my day, and I can tell you I've usually had my mind elsewhere while it was happening. Maybe I felt uncomfortable because I was on bottom and being smushed into a couch with my arm trapped on one side. I might have been self-conscious about my weight if I was on top of the guy, or my breath as we went at it face-to-face. Sometimes I obsessed over how far things would go and when and how to shut it down. Or something would happen like the hooks of my bra getting stuck and the guy couldn't get them undone without help. It's never as smooth and romantic in real life as it appears to be in the movies. Or so I thought.

Let me tell you, there was absolutely none of that chatter going on in my head tonight. My sole thought and purpose was entirely consumed with Cabe.

Touching him, tasting him, feeling him, needing him. I couldn't get enough of him. I wanted to pull him inside me. Not just in the literal sex sense of inside me—although that was certainly on my radar—but like all of him and all of me coming together. No separation, no division, no holding back. Just melting into each other until there was no more him and no more me. Just us. I wanted to completely surround him, envelop him, and never let him go.

When I write it, it sounds like a bad scene in a body-snatching alien movie, but it's how I felt. I wanted to just wrap him up until he became a part of me. I couldn't hold him tight enough. Couldn't kiss him deep enough. Couldn't press myself against him hard enough.

I'm sure we bumped elbows and smashed noses. Struggled with a zipper or hook here or there. But I honestly have no memories other than just the passion of wanting Cabe. None of the rest of it mattered.

He flipped me over on my back and stretched out on top of me, his long body surpassing the length of the couch. My shirt had long ago been tossed aside with my bra, and heat emanated from our bare chests pressed together with a light sheen of perspiration. We both had been unzipped and undone, and I thought I knew where we were headed and what was coming next. But then Cabe raised himself up on his elbows and looked down at me smiling.

I leaned forward and kissed him again, but when he didn't follow me back down, I laid my head back on the couch and grinned at him.

"What?" I asked, never comfortable with awkward silences. Especially when I was lying half-nude beneath a guy with my heart and pulse racing uncontrollably in anticipation of his next touch.

"Just looking at you." He propped his chin in his palm and stared at me, the smile never leaving his face.

"Umm. Okay. Why?"

"I just think you're beautiful, and I wanted to take a moment to look at you. To see you. To appreciate you."

"Thanks?" It came out as a question because I was asking a lot of them in my head.

Granted, it was an awesome, wonderful statement for a guy to make.

Kudos to him. But in that moment, it wasn't what I wanted to hear. Doubts and chatter immediately filled my head. I thought we'd been headed *there*. I thought we were of the same mind and purpose. What had stopped him? Had he changed his mind? Did I do something wrong? I could tell by the bulge between us he was still interested, so why the sudden change in pace and the need to stop and stare?

His weight was heavy as it pressed me into the couch, even though I hadn't felt it moments before. I couldn't take a full breath, but I didn't dare move or shift because I didn't want him to stand up. I didn't understand why he had applied the brakes so abruptly.

Cabe kissed me again, but gently. Softly. Tenderly. Completely removed from the insane frenetic pace we'd engaged in moments before.

His tongue pressed against my lips, ever so easily nudging them apart. He teased with it, a little flick here, a little plunge there, and the fire reignited in me, begging to rage out of control.

"I want you, Tyler." His voice was deep. Guttural. Barely above a whisper, and yet I heard it with every fiber of my being.

I arched up against him and sighed, wondering if it could be possible he wasn't aware of how I felt.

"I want you, too."

He pulled his lips from mine and smiled again, our faces so close I couldn't focus on his expression. His lips opened, closed for a brief second, and then opened again as he spoke.

"I'm going to go."

Okay, that is so *not* what I thought he was going to say. It was like a needle had skipped across a record player and stopped the music.

"What? Go? Go where?" I tried to lean back so I could see him clearly, but I could only push my head so far into the couch.

Cabe chuckled and rolled off of me and onto his knees on the floor next to the couch. I struggled to sit up and he extended his hand to help me, conveniently planting a kiss on my breast as it passed him on my way up. He didn't let go of my hand and instead kissed my palm and all five fingers as I reached for my shirt, suddenly self-conscious of being nude from the waist up.

He took my hand as soon as I had my shirt over my head, kissing my palm again and holding it against his cheek.

"I'm going home, Beautiful."

"Why?" I didn't understand why he had changed gears so suddenly. Was it something I did? Something I said? No, couldn't be that. I hadn't said anything.

"Because I want you more than I've ever wanted anything in my life, Tyler Warren. I want to take you back there to that bedroom and devour you and never come up for air. And if I don't leave right now, that's what'll happen and there'll be no going back."

Okay, and that's a problem because? Why on earth would we want to go back? I thought it, but couldn't get my mouth to form the words. I stared at him, willing him to change his mind and get back to the devouring part. Or at least to say something that made more sense.

"I don't understand," I finally whispered.

"I don't want any regrets between us, Tyler. I can wait."

"What regrets? What if I don't want you to wait?"

He took me in his arms and squeezed me against him as he kissed the top of my head.

"I don't want to wait either, Buttercup. But I want to do the right thing. I want it to be right for us."

"And this is wrong?" I pushed against him to make him look at me.

"Not wrong. But not the way I want it to be. It's been a long road for us to get to this point. I don't want to rush anything. You mean too much to me to do that."

I started to tell him five years wasn't exactly rushing things, but I didn't want to beg him to stay. I wasn't at all sure what he meant by the way he wanted it to be. But he had said no, and I needed to respect that. I also needed a cold shower as soon as he left.

I don't know if I have ever had the guy be the one to put on the brakes and say he didn't want to rush things. Am I in some alternate universe here? Have we switched roles? Because tonight, I would have so jumped that man's bones in a heartbeat, to use his words.

After all, we were already in the process of some mutual bone-jumping. One minute we were on the couch half undressed and kissing, petting, fondling and groping, and the next minute he's walking out the door with a smile on his face. A bit of a strained smile, and I'm sure a set of brilliant blue ones in his jeans, but he chose to walk away. I don't get it. Is this his weird concept of being a gentleman? Because I think I would have rather had the knave tonight.

Thursday, January 9th

We met at the animal shelter after work, and I probably should have agreed to change the service project to beach clean-up. So many adorable doggies. I wanted to bring them all home with me. We bathed a few and played with some others. A couple just wanted to be held. One made it very clear he didn't want us to come near him at all.

It was dirty work, and we left covered in hair and doggy smell. But I loved every minute of it. I've missed having a pet so much. I can't believe I haven't volunteered there sooner.

We signed up to go back next month and left behind wagging tails and inquisitive noses along with a little piece of my heart.

"You were great with the dogs," I said to Cabe as we stood by our cars in the shelter parking lot.

"They were awesome. Especially Kipper. Did you see the way he kept taking the ball from Laila? So freakin' funny. He didn't want to go catch the ball and bring it back. But if she got it, he took it immediately. Just to hide it from her. Cracked me up."

"So you still think you wouldn't want a dog?" I asked.

"Tyler, it's not that I don't like dogs. I just think it's too big of a commitment. I wouldn't want to be tied down or plan my entire schedule around a dog. That's all."

"But it's not like your entire life shuts down because you get a dog. You can still go places. Do things."

"Look here, Buttercup. If you want a dog, get a dog. I don't want a dog. I'm happy to come here. Play with them. Help take care of them. Donate money to get what they need. But I don't want a dog. I don't want the commitment."

Now, right there I should have just shut my mouth. I don't know why I was taking it so personally that Cabe didn't want a dog. I mean, hell, it's not like I was ready to take a dog home, either. With my schedule I'd never see the poor thing, and it would be crossing its legs by the door on my long wedding days.

But it irked me that he was so adamant about not wanting it. I don't know if in my head he was somehow refusing our future dog and therefore our future life, but I got pissed. I didn't drop it.

"Fine. God forbid you have a commitment you have to actually stick to." I regretted it as soon as I said it. He flinched and looked at me with hurt evident in the blue depths of his eyes.

"Wow. Let me just pull this little dagger out of my back. I didn't see that coming."

"I'm sorry, Cabe. I didn't mean that. I don't know why I said it." Which was actually true for the most part. Looking back on the conversation as I write this, I don't know why the dog thing bothered me so much. Or why I felt the need to jab him about the commitment thing. I guess I was just being a bitch.

He didn't say anything else but just stood there looking at me. Wondering what my deal was, I'm sure.

I tried to laugh it off and make a joke about it, but the damage was done and the words were out there. The mood had changed.

"I'm gonna head home and take a shower," he said. "You have a rehearsal tomorrow night, right? I'm probably going to catch a movie with Mom."

"Okay. I'll talk to you tomorrow, then." I leaned in to kiss him, and it turned out all awkward. He leaned the same time I did. We bonked foreheads, and then barely touched lips before we pulled apart laughing.

He opened my car door for me, and I started to get in but knew I couldn't leave it alone.

"Cabe, I'm really sorry I said that. I had such a good time today. Thanks for bringing me."

He slid his arms around me and lifted me to him, covering my lips with his and then setting me back down on my toes as he kissed my forehead. "No worries, Buttercup. I had a good time, too. I'll talk to you tomorrow."

I have to get myself under control. I don't know why I'm pushing his buttons. It's not about the dog, really. Not at all. I just feel like I want him to declare something. To say he loves me. To say we'll be together. He's here. He obviously cares. He's not going anywhere. So why do I feel the need to push him? Why do I need something more?

Saturday, January 11th

So I suppose the universe gave me a lesson in patience today. A little reminder about good things coming to those who wait.

My bride, Rosaline, was from the Dominican Republic, and her groom, Thomas, was Jamaican. Knowing many of their guests would be on 'island time' and therefore tardy, Rosaline printed her invitations with a start time an hour earlier than the actual ceremony. Even with that, she reasoned most of them would fail to make it for the ceremony at all, so she only ordered thirty chairs. For two hundred invited guests.

Talk about making your wedding planner nervous. I knew from past weddings that certain cultural groups practice a more relaxed attitude toward time, but I kept envisioning two hundred people yelling at me to get the ceremony started and find them more chairs.

Rosaline laughed and told me not to worry, but I did.

At four o'clock—the ceremony time stated on the invitation, mind you—I had not one single soul there except the minister and the guitarist.

Two guests arrived at twenty after four, both apologizing for being late and neither from the islands.

By the time five o'clock rolled around—the actual ceremony start time—nine co-workers and four neighbors had showed up, but no one else. Not even the bride or groom.

To say I was freaking out is an understatement. I've never drank at work, but I was sorely tempted to ask the bartender to crack open a bottle of wine.

Rosaline finally arrived about a quarter after five with ten family members. By the time Thomas got there twenty minutes later, we had a total of forty-seven guests. Out of two hundred.

So when we started the ceremony an hour and forty-five minutes after the start time on the invitation, we had roughly one-fourth of the invited guests in attendance.

It is possible I have bald spots from pulling out my hair in frustration. Rosaline laughed at me. "Don't worry, Tyler. They will come."

We extended the cocktail reception until seven, by which time we had about sixty guests. I needed Valium, but Rosaline and Thomas took it all in stride. Like it was the most normal thing ever.

"Don't worry, Tyler. They'll come." Rosaline patted my arm with a smile. "I told you. Island time."

At seven-fifteen, the caterer demanded to serve dinner. It could sit idle on the stoves no longer.

"That's fine," Rosaline said. "They'll eat when they get here. Don't worry, Tyler."

Seventy guests went through the buffet meant for two hundred. The caterer nearly fainted.

"What are we going to do with all this food?" she asked. I shook my head in disbelief. I had no answers.

The pastry chef arrived with the cake around eight, and I gasped at the size of it. Six towering layers of cake. Enough to feed an army. Way too much for the eighty guests I had on hand.

"Here's a box for leftover cake, and a box for the topper," said the pastry chef. "She wants to save it for her anniversary."

"I think I'm going to need more boxes," I told her. "There's no way these people are going to eat all that cake."

The chef laughed and shook her head. "I've worked for this family before. Don't worry. They'll come."

That seemed to be the mantra of the night.

I asked several times if they were ready for first dance and toast, but Rosaline and Thomas put me off each time.

She would laugh and say, "Don't worry, Tyler. They'll come. We'll do it when they get here."

I began to feel sorry for the poor, delusional girl. She had invited all these people, bought a cake twice the size she needed, and less than half of her invited list came.

But she never wavered in her certainty that they were coming. Never showed any doubt or disappointment.

"Don't worry, Tyler" was all she would say.

The caterer came to me sometime after nine to say she needed to pull the food soon due to the time it had been out.

Rosaline was adamant the buffet should remain intact. "They'll be hungry when they come. Don't worry, Tyler."

"Are you ready to do cake cutting?" I asked.

She laughed at me. "You're so impatient. You must learn to wait. Other people don't live on our schedule. They live on their own. If we love them, we wait. Don't worry, Tyler."

It sounded like sage advice on my own life, but it came from a girl who'd invited two hundred people to her wedding and only had eighty show, so I wasn't too sure how much faith I should put in it.

But then, it happened. They came.

It must have been around nine thirty when it started. A seemingly never-ending line of guests streamed in as if a bus—or on second thought, a train—had pulled up outside and unloaded its passengers. The noise level in the room tripled as they hugged and high-fived, filling the dance floor and every corner of the room.

I stood to one side frazzled with exhaustion.

Rosaline shouted as she whirled past me on the dance floor. "I told you not to worry, Tyler. I told you they'd come."

They wiped out the buffet in less than twenty minutes. We had to hide the top anniversary layer when the cake ran out, and by midnight the caterer had sent someone to get additional ice and alcohol for a guest count hovering around two hundred and fifty.

It is now a little after two in the morning, and I just dragged my tired ass in the door and collapsed across my bed to find the cutest little stuffed animal. A precious white doggie with a tag reading 'Roscoe' attached to a bright red collar. He had a note between his front paws.

Hope your wedding went well. I waited for you for a while, but I guess you're having a late night. I left Roscoe here to keep you company. Hope you can handle the commitment.

Talk to you tomorrow. C.

I went to sleep with Roscoe in my arms, a smile on my face, and Rosaline's words in my head.

"Don't worry, Tyler."

Cabe is definitely worth waiting for.

Sunday, January 12th

Cabe and I went to Ybor City again today. No music festival going on, so the streets were much quieter than last weekend. We took our time meandering through the quaint shops and admiring the old architecture left behind by the Cuban and Spanish influences of the area's cigar history. We found a funky little vintage clothing shop, and he patiently waited as I tried on outfit after outfit, offering his appreciation for the ones he liked and laughing hysterically at the more outlandish ones.

We drank mojitos and listened to live music at sidewalk cafes, walking along hand in hand. Sometimes stopping to steal a kiss. I felt like a million bucks walking alongside him. I have always seen the way girls cast appreciative glances his way, and a mingle of pride and possessiveness filled me when they looked at him today.

I know this sounds like a voiceover in a cheesy movie, but today was a good day to be alive. The crisp air filled my lungs and the cool breeze tickled my skin. The sky was an unbelievably clear blue, so deep and alluring I couldn't help staring up into it. The sun bathed the buildings and the trees in a golden brightness that made every color vividly clear. Like watching a really well-done 3D movie with layers of complex scenery.

And Cabe. Oh Cabe. I cannot believe my good fortune. He's still my best friend. Still laughing and joking the same way we always have. Still having the same intense debates about whatever topics came to mind. Still interested in the same music, the same art. But now it's different. It's deeper. It's better than I could have ever imagined. Not only do I have my very best friend walking by my side, but I am hyper aware of the incredible hotness of the man.

His broad, muscular shoulders. His biceps so strong beneath my fingers on his arm. And those legs, so long and lean I have to take three steps for one of his to match his relaxed stride.

And those eyes. God, I could just stare into his eyes all day. So clear and light today they looked more silver or grey than blue. But always sparkling with mischief, and occasionally deepening with desire.

Speaking of desire. Wow. It is amazing that I have walked side by side with this man, slept by him, woken up next to him, laid across him on beach and couch and bed, and have never experienced the surges I have coursing through me now whenever he is near. I get goosebumps when he looks at me. Sometimes I can't look away, and my insides bubble up all warm and tingly when he smiles and says, 'What?'

I shake my head and say 'Nothing' because I don't dare tell him how giddy I am inside.

Even the most casual contact tingles and sparks. Which probably explains why I can't keep my hands off him, and vice-versa. He touches me every chance he gets. His hand always on my back. A little squeeze of my hand. A brief kiss brushed against my cheek or the top of my head. A light caress of my rear end as I brush past him in a store.

And the looks he gives me. God, the come-hither look when I emerge from the dressing room is enough to make me want to pull him back in there with me.

It's like I just hit puberty or something. I can't think about anything but being with him. Wondering what it will be like. When it will happen. How it will happen. I am obsessed. With Cabe. Who would have ever thought it possible?

We ended up on the couch again tonight, elbows and knees akimbo as we twisted and writhed and moved against one another instinctively.

But then he did it again.

He went from panting breathless, pursuing a goal with a concerted effort, to suddenly looking at me with that goofy grin and telling me how beautiful I am. It's maddening. I have sworn to myself that I won't pressure him about the past or the future, what to call our relationship, or whether or not we'll ever get a real dog without a 'made in Taiwan' label on its butt.

This, however, needed addressing.

"Why do you do this?" I pushed his long curls off his forehead and tousled his hair as I smiled up at him.

"Do what?" He smiled, fully aware of what I meant. He traced my jawline with his pinkie finger and then put his hand behind my head and pulled me forward for a kiss so passionate I almost forgot what I needed to know.

I remembered when he let go.

"This. You come onto me like I'm water in the desert, and you get me all revved up and ready to go, and then boom. You just pull back like it all means nothing and announce you're leaving. What's up with that?"

"I've told you. I want to wait. I want it to be right." He didn't stop stroking his fingers along my forearm as he talked. Could he really be so oblivious to what he was doing to me?

"Wait for what? When will it be right?"

He chuckled. "Tyler, you know I want you. I think it's rather obvious." He grinned and pulled me tighter against the evidence. "But I don't know. I feel like we were friends for so long, and I just don't want to go anywhere we can't come back from."

Shock numbed me like I'd been doused in cold water.

"Okay, so what does that mean? Do you want us to just be friends?" I cocked my head to the side and tried to fight the fear welling up inside me.

"We still are friends, Ty. And we're exploring that deeper and further. I just want to make sure we don't go too fast and make any decisions we regret."

Whoa, Nelly. What did that mean? We still are friends? Does he somehow think none of this meant anything? That we're just friends? I know I said before I didn't need a label or a definition, but I changed my mind.

"So we're still just friends?"

"You're putting words in my mouth. We *are* friends. And no matter what else we become and where this goes, I hope we will always be friends. Obviously, we've gone beyond that, but I don't want us to rush into anything."

I moved to sit up.

"I don't get it. Your hands are all over me all day. You're kissing me every chance you get. We're all up in each other's business on the couch. How do you just shut that down and say you don't want to go any further?"

"Again, you're putting words in my mouth. I never said I didn't *want* to go any further. But what I want and what I think is best are two different things. A lot has changed between us in the last couple of weeks, but it's only been that. A couple of weeks. I just feel like we need to put on the brakes a little. That's all."

I heard him. And I suppose on some level I understood him. I know I should have, like, admired him for it or something. Being a gentleman. Being chivalrous. Being cautious.

But I had never wanted anyone like I wanted Cabe. I felt like every doubt I'd ever had—about him, about love, about sex, any of it—was gone. I just wanted to be with him. His resistance conflicted with that and compounded my frustration.

What if I didn't want to wait? What if I wanted him to take me right then and there? What did that make me?

I've never been one to jump into bed with every guy I've dated, but surely this meant more than just a casual fling. In my mind, we had wasted so much time already. Why wait longer? If we both knew what we knew, then why not just go all in?

I felt frustrated. Physically. Emotionally. Mentally. I sighed in frustration and got up to pace the floor.

"Would you rather I just didn't touch you?" Cabe asked.

"No! Why would I rather that?" I flung my arms to the side and looked at him with an expression I am sure said "Idiot!"

He laughed and came to me, wrapping his arms around me and pulling me close.

"Ty, patience has never been your virtue."

"I don't think I have any virtues." I knew just my saying that probably jolted my mother awake from a deep sleep without a clue as to why.

He pressed his lips against mine and held them there. No tongue action, no groping, no panting. Just a simple physical connection of tenderness that melted my anger away.

When he pulled back, I smiled at him. And I let him go without any further argument.

I still think he's worth the wait, but I don't like it. Not one bit.

Wednesday, January 15th

Cabe texted this afternoon to say he had great news and wanted to celebrate. To wear something fancy and be ready by six. I can count on one hand the number of times he's requested fancy in the five years I've known him, so I knew it must be something good.

He buzzed with excitement as we drove to the restaurant, singing at the top of his lungs and playing piano, guitar and drums simultaneously on the steering wheel. He teased me with hints about his news, but then insisted on waiting until we were seated to spill the beans. I practically shoved the seating hostess away from our table as soon as we sat down so he could finally tell me.

"February marks six months that I've been back in Orlando."

I hoped the news was going to get better than that. A bittersweet reminder that he didn't call me as soon as he got back from his ill-fated move to Seattle and the short-lived marriage that happened there. I forced the smile to stay pasted on my face as he continued.

"Wade, my old boss, has been trying to move me back into his team, but they told him he had to wait six months after my transfer."

Cabe had taken a step down in order to move to Seattle with Monica, which he'd been willing to do since he thought she was the love of his life. Then he had taken another demotion in order to move back here to Orlando when Monica decided *he* wasn't the love of *her* life. It was nice of the company to work with him on both moves, but I knew he didn't enjoy the new position as much as his old job. On top of that, along with the two pay cuts, he had also given up some of the perks of his former position. Namely, working from any remote location of his choosing, extra weeks of vacation time, and a sizable annual bonus.

"Starting the second week of February, I will be completely reinstated to my old status with full pay and benefits." He laid his palm across his chest as he spoke, bowing his head slightly after his announcement.

I clapped my hands and laughed, my eyes filled with tears of happiness and pride. I knew the entire Seattle situation had been a huge blow to Cabe's ego. The divorce. Monica leaving him for another woman. Moving back home with his mom. And, of course, returning to the old office building two steps lower than he had left it. So having his former job restored marked a huge step in his recovery and healing from the whole fiasco.

"That's wonderful! Cabe, I'm so happy for you!"

"Thanks, Buttercup. I'm pretty happy myself. I missed working with my old team and being on the inside of the new projects think tank. I know you probably think computers are computers and it's all pretty boring, but there really is a difference in what I've been doing and I missed the work."

"No, I know that. I won't pretend I understand what you do, but I know you were much happier before. I think you used to come up with new stuff and how to make it work, and I guess now you've just been typing all day."

Cabe laughed as the waitress poured our water. "That's a pretty watered-down description of what I do, Ty. I was a program manager, and I've moved back down to being a developer since I've been home. Now I'll be a program manager again."

Greek to me. I had no better idea what he did for a living than before he explained it, but oh well. I was happy for him, and he was happy. That's all that mattered.

He ordered a few appetizers and a rather expensive bottle of champagne. I raised an eyebrow at him, and he laughed again. "We're celebrating!"

"Wow, you must be happy. You don't even like champagne," I said.

"I don't like *cheap* champagne, Buttercup. There's a difference."

I nodded and smiled at him. I swear he was glowing. He carried himself differently, with his head held high and his shoulders relaxed, like a huge weight had been lifted from him. The tension I'd grown accustomed to seeing in his face was gone, replaced with an easy smile that crinkled the edges of his eyes with soft lines. Seeing him so happy swelled my heart to near bursting, and I reached my hand across the table to take his. He squeezed my hand in return, leaning over the table to meet me for a kiss.

I have no idea what will happen in our lives, and I have no idea if Cabe and I will get a happily ever after ending. But in that moment, at that table, gazing into those blue eyes and basking in his sweet smile, I know I have never been happier in my life. I have never felt more completely at peace. To be sitting with him, hand in hand, sharing kisses and celebrating the future, filled me with such joy and contentment I thought I was going to be a total dork and cry. My throat felt constricted, and I struggled to swallow as I blinked back tears.

"Are you gonna cry?" Cabe leaned forward and grinned, taking my chin in his and kissing me again.

"I'm just happy for you. Shut up."

"I'm happy, too, but I'm not crying."

Warmth spread across my cheeks as I blushed. I wanted so much to tell him I loved him. To say how sorry I was it took me so long to know it. To apologize for any time he felt it or wanted to say it and couldn't. For any time I hurt him—or rejected him. I wanted to say I didn't mean to rush things, and I would wait however long he needed. To tell him I would never leave his side, and that I wanted us to celebrate every milestone together from here on out. But then our champagne arrived, and the words stuck in my throat as I reached for my glass.

"To happy days ahead." Cabe raised his glass in a toast.

"Happy days ahead." I clinked my glass against his and savored the tickle of bubbles sliding down my throat and chasing the tears away.

"And now, for the best part." He drained his glass and shifted in his seat, obviously excited to tell me the rest of his news.

"There's more?" I asked as he refilled our glasses.

"Wade petitioned the board to reinstate my share of the bonus for the projects my team completed last year. It's only a portion based on my work in the upstart of each project, but they've approved his request, and I will be receiving a rather sizable check at the end of the month. So I'm thinking we should plan a trip for your birthday. Anywhere you want to go!"

"What?" My mouth dropped open and then closed again as I squealed in delight. "Seriously?"

"Yep. You pick the destination, and we'll do it. Where do you want to go?"

"Oh my gosh, Cabe. I don't know. I'd have to think about it. Are you sure that's what you want to do? I mean, do you want to take that money and use it to move out of the pool house?"

"Tyler, it's not like I'm broke or I can't afford to move out of Mom's. I just haven't been motivated to find a place. The pool house was an easy solution when I came back from Seattle, and I haven't thought much about packing up and moving again. Not that there's much to pack this time around. But still. This is a bonus I wasn't expecting, so I want to do something special. With you. I want to take you somewhere for your birthday weekend. You just tell me where. The Caribbean. New York. Paris."

"Paris? Oh my God, Cabe. You're not kidding around. Holy crap. We can't do that in a weekend."

"Why not?"

"Well, because. I mean, we just . . . I mean, well . . ."

"Why not? You don't have a wedding on your birthday. I already checked your calendar, and I called Melanie to see if you were scheduled for rehearsals or anything, and she said you could be off if you needed to."

"Wait, you called Mel? When?"

"Yesterday. I wanted to surprise you with the trip already planned out and give you tickets tonight, but then I figured it might be best to let you pick where you wanted to go."

"Oh wow. You're completely serious. But what about your work?"

"I talked to Wade when we met about the new position. I have to hit the ground running with a new project as soon as I transition over in February. But he's willing to give me Thursday, Friday, and Monday off the weekend of your birthday. I would love for it to be longer, but we can at least take a long weekend away. So whaddya say? Weekend in Paris?"

I couldn't formulate coherent thoughts. I was stunned.

Paris? With Cabe? For my birthday? A few short moments earlier I had thought to myself that I had never been happier in my life. And then this? Blown away. Completely blown away. Happier than I could ever have imagined.

"Wow, Cabe. Okay. Yes! Yes, a weekend in Paris. But wait. My birthday's only like two months away. How are we going to plan a trip to Paris in two months? Maybe we should go someplace closer."

"No, Mom's best friend is a travel planner. I already called her and asked her to start scouting out locations. I'll tell her Paris. If that's definitely where you want to go."

"Sure. But I don't speak French."

"It's okay. I do. And a lot of Parisians speak English. If you're not rude to them, they're pretty much not rude to you."

"Oh wow. I think I'm in shock."

He laughed. "That's good, I hope. I want you to be happy. Are you happy?"

"Oh yes. Yes. A million times yes. Wow. I keep saying wow, don't I?"

So obviously I need to just chill on the relationship thing. He's happy. I'm happy. We're going to Paris. I need to just relax and trust that things are going to happen in their own time.

Thursday, January 16th

My happiness from last night spilled over into this morning. Mama called and I actually answered the phone with a cheerful, "Good morning, Mama!"

"Well, good morning, baby! You're awful chipper this morning."

"Just having a good day, Mama." A good day. A good month. A good year. Looks like the tides *have* turned and I'll be having a good life.

"I sure am glad to hear that. I love when my young'uns are happy. Your sister Tanya got a new minivan. One of those fancy ones where the doors just open up when you push the button and then close by themselves once you get in. Takes forever for them to close, though. You could just shut it yourself and be out the driveway in the time it takes, but she likes it. It's got TV screens in the back for the kids, so I guess they'll be glued to the tube every time they're in the car. I swear those kids wouldn't know what to do without a TV or an iPad in their hands. They're talking about getting Eric a phone. Now what in tarnation he needs with a phone, I don't know. He's eight years old. Who's he gonna call? I mean, really. But if that's how they want to spend their money, then who am I to judge? I'm just her mother, you know."

"Yes ma'am." I struggled to hold onto my euphoria.

"Your brother made the honor roll. I don't think you ever did make honor roll at college, did you? Course, you quit. So I'm sure you would have made it eventually, you know, if you had stuck it out. He's still dating that huzzy of a girl. She don't like me none. And I don't care not one bit. He'll see through her eventually. Lord, I hope he don't marry her. I can't even imagine—"

"I'm going to Paris, Mama!" I blurted out my news without really thinking it through.

41

"What? Paris? Like Paris, France? Well, Lord have mercy on my soul! When did this come about?"

"Last night. Cabe is taking me to Paris for my birthday." I realized I may have just handed her a grenade that could blow up in my face, but it was too late. I had already pulled the pin.

"What? He's taking you to Paris? You mean he's paying for the trip? Well, that surely doesn't sound like just a friend to me."

"Well, we've sort of been…dating." Even if I didn't have a definition for it, what we had been doing would constitute dating to my mama. Although I didn't know if she would take me going to Paris with a man better if she thought we were dating or if she thought we were just friends. I cringed in anticipation of her response.

"I knew it! I knew it! I told your Aunt Debbie all along you was dating him. I knew it!"

"No, we weren't. It's just kind of happened since New Year's."

"And all this time you telling me you weren't interested. But I knew it. I didn't have any doubt. I knew in my heart he was the one for you."

"Mama, you've been telling me the man was gay for five years."

"Why, I did no such thing! Tyler Lorraine, how dare you. I have said no such thing."

I didn't want to argue with her, and I knew it would do no good if I did. "So his mom's friend is a travel agent, and she's going to find us a good hotel and stuff. We're gonna leave the Thursday before my birthday and come back on Sunday. Just a weekend trip."

"Well, a weekend in Paris sure sounds romantic. Are you using protection?"

"Mama!"

"Like you're gonna tell me you're going to Paris with this man and y'all ain't having sex."

"Oh, my Lord. We are not having this conversation."

There would never ever be a day that I wanted to have this conversation with my mother. She had never so much as mentioned sex to me my entire life, and I surely didn't want to change that now.

"You can't be naive, Tyler, and neither can I. The world is a scary place and you need to make wise choices."

"Mama, it's not like that. We're not sleeping together." Why I felt the need to prolong the conversation in the slightest by giving her that information I will never know.

"Well, what are you waiting for?"

"What? Oh good grief. I'm gonna hang up now."

"You listen to me, missie. I loved your daddy like he hung the moon, but between you and me it wasn't all that."

"La-la-la-la-la. I so do not want to hear this, Mother." Just the thought of her and Daddy doing the nasty caused instant nausea.

"I'm just saying. I watch all these movies and hear all these songs, and I have to think there wouldn't be so many people going crazy about it if there wasn't more to it than what I've experienced. Your daddy was a good man, honey, but I've read a lot of romance novels, and I can tell you right now I've never spiraled to the heights of ecstasy and floated back down seeing stars. So I ain't saying you need to throw your ankles behind ya ears for any ole Joe walkin' by, but if you've got feelings for this man enough to fly across the ocean with him, you might want to make sure he knows what he's doing in that department."

I couldn't believe my devoutly religious mother was actually telling me to sleep with a man I wasn't married to. It wasn't something I cared to discuss, though. Nor was I going to mention I'd basically thrown myself at the man and begged only to have him tell me no.

"Baby Girl, if I had it to do over again, I'd a roller skated, and danced, and smoked. I'd a worn short skirts and slept with every man that wanted to."

"Mama, I'm gonna puke. Please stop talking about sex!"

She cackled. "What? You think your mama didn't ever turn a head? Where you think you and your sisters got those looks of yours? I was a stunner in my day."

"I know you were. And this has been a real eye-opener for me, but I'm gonna hang up now. And go join a convent, I do believe."

She laughed again. "Aw, honey, don't be like that. Make sure you let me know where you're staying. Flight numbers, too. I won't be able to sleep between now and then thinking about you crashing in the ocean."

"Why, thank you. That's exactly what I wanted to hear. Bye now. I gotta go."

"When can I meet him?"

I shook my head violently from side to side in immediate resistance to that idea.

"I don't know. We'll have to see. Bye. Love you."

I don't know what got into my mama, but if she's going to start asking details about my sex life, that may be the best reason yet to put off sleeping with Cabe.

Saturday, January 18th

I had a small wedding this morning. Only fifty guests. Ceremony at a church and then brunch at a small golf club. For the first time probably ever, I didn't want to be there. Cabe and I fell asleep on the couch last night, and he woke me up carrying me to bed sometime in the wee hours of the morning.

I left him sleeping this morning, and I so didn't want to leave. Didn't want to be away from him. He was off today, and I had to be at work, which irritated me beyond belief. I just wanted this wedding to be done and over with.

When the bride and groom came back down the aisle as husband and wife, I waved them into the holding room and told them I'd be back to get them shortly.

I grabbed the basket of white rose petals that would be tossed for their exit and thrust it in front of the wedding party as they came through the double doors, blocking them long enough to give them directions.

"I want you to line up on either side of the sidewalk outside as you go toward the limo. Take a handful of these and then toss them as the bride and groom exit."

We actually call it a 'staged exit' in the office because the bride and groom aren't really leaving. They just get in the limo and take a ride around the block so I can herd all the well-wishers into their own cars and send them to the reception. Pictures go much faster if you don't have fifty people standing around flashing their own camera bulbs and offering suggestions to the professional photographer about who should be in photos and how they should be posed.

I repeated my spiel over and over today as the guests filed out of the church, trying not to sound like a pre-recorded robot voice. I smiled and made eye contact and pretended to be thrilled to be a part of their day.

"Please take a handful and line up on either side of the pathway to celebrate our bride and groom as they exit."

Some people daintily picked up about five rose petals. Others dug in and snatched fistfuls like it was free money and they had one shot to get all they could.

A few people refused to take any at all. That usually happens any time we pass out something for a staged exit, whether it's bubbles, rose petals, birdseed, whatever. They act like it's a scam, and they're wary of participation. Like there's a fine-print catch and it's going to cost them something in the end if they take a handful. Or maybe I just look untrustworthy.

It's not a big deal if they don't take any, but it irks me. That need to go against the process and throw a kink in the carefully laid plans irritates me. I want to tell them I'm not standing there for my own health and profit, and that I'm actually passing out stuff because it's what the bride and groom wanted.

Today, my basket had nearly emptied of petals as I passed through the guests lined up along the sidewalk. A tall, slender empty-handed guest in a navy suit reached toward the basket, his expression somewhat tentative and uncertain. He'd refused my offer before, and I held full eye contact to drive home that I knew he thought I was selling oceanfront property in Kansas when he passed me by with a suspicious glance.

"Can I get some?" He hesitated and pulled his hand back a teensy bit as he asked, put off, I'm sure, by the arrogant, knowing look I shot him. I nodded slightly as I extended the basket toward him, like a queen granting a pardon. Yes, I can acknowledge the inherent bitchiness in my attitude, but sometimes working with the public just brings it out of you. And since it happens *every single time* we do an exit, it has long since gotten old.

He smiled a bit wider as his face turned red. "I thought they were potato chips before, so I didn't take any."

What the hell?

Why would I stand at the exit of a wedding ceremony and pass out potato chips? No napkin or plate. Just reach on into this fancy white wicker basket and grab yourself a handful of greasy potato chips.

Like, here's your chips. There's dip in the parking lot.

Why?

Why would I have a random basket of potato chips? At a freakin' wedding ceremony? And why on God's green earth would I be asking people to toss potato chips at the bride and groom as they exited?

I honestly think working in customer-service-oriented fields can make you hate people. Especially the dumb ones. Every time I begin to chastise myself for thinking such nasty thoughts, someone comes along like Potato

Chip Guy and does or says something so stupid I just can't get past it.

Cabe had left by the time I got home, and when I called he was at his buddy Dean's playing video games. So I went to Carmen's for dinner. I've really missed our trusty office assistant since she went out on maternity leave, so I had fun playing with baby Lila and catching up with Carmen, but my thoughts never strayed far from Cabe.

When we're apart now, I feel like a piece of me is missing. I wonder if he feels the same way.

He texted me to call him when I got home, but he was still out playing when I called, so we'll talk tomorrow. Looks like it's just me and Roscoe in the bed tonight. At least it still smells like Cabe's cologne.

I'm so pathetically in love.

Sunday, January 19th

Spent the day at his mom's house today. I worried Galen might be there, but she and Tate had gone to Miami for the weekend. If Maggie shares her daughter's vehement disapproval of me, she didn't let on today. If it shocked her to see us kissing and nuzzling on the couch, she never showed it. She acted the same as always. Fussing over whether or not we had enough to eat, cracking jokes, ribbing Cabe, and providing her unique commentaries on whatever movies we watched.

The day was comfortable. Natural. Like I was part of the family.

We had gone back to the pool house after the last movie, and I was sitting on the bar counter with Cabe standing between my knees, sliding his hands up and down my back as we kissed. The counter put me at a perfect height for us to be face to face with my arms draped around his neck.

"Do you have any idea how happy you make me?" Cabe asked.

I shrugged and shook my head. "No."

He laughed and wrapped me in his arms. "I just can't get enough of you."

"Really?" I grinned, my face just inches from his.

"Yes, really! Are you kidding me? I have truly never been happier than I am right now."

I arched my eyebrows and smirked, his admission catching me off-guard and filling me with a shy giddiness.

He lifted his hands through my hair and cupped my cheeks. "You're happy, right?"

"Yes." I grinned from ear to ear. "Blissfully so."

He kissed me again, soft and sweet this time, and when he pulled back to look at me, I just knew he was going to tell me he loved me. It was like the perfect time. I was all ready to say it back, too, but instead of professing undying love, he asked if I wanted to stay over. I should have said yes. Everything in me screamed yes, but my head couldn't get past his mom being in the house next door with my car in her driveway all night. My mama may be telling me it's okay to sleep with him, but I don't know that his mama would be on board with that. I still remember how mortified I was when Maggie walked in the pool house and found me in Cabe's bed a couple of months ago. Fully clothed, of course, but I still felt like a skank slipping out past her. We may be grown adults, but she's still his mama.

So I'm home alone in my own bed tonight. Again. Happy and content, though. Happy to know I make him happy.

Thursday, January 23rd

Well, I guess statistically it had to happen. I mean, if you keep doing weddings, eventually you're gonna have one, right?

They were a nice enough couple. Priscilla seemed a bit dominating. Neal seemed a bit dominated. It was just a small ceremony with the two of them, her parents, and her two teenage kids, who could not have acted more bored if they tried.

When I met them last night at the rehearsal, nothing seemed out of the ordinary. Laidback. Easy-going. No frou-frou.

I got to the lake early this morning to make sure the flowers were set and the sand had been raked. I admit I was dragging. Cabe and I went dancing after my rehearsal last night and didn't come in until almost three. A stupid choice, I know, but I was having a blast at the time and didn't want it to end. He ended up sleeping over, which he's done the last three nights. I still don't sleep well when he's in bed next to me, laying there all sensually male. So at some point, I really need to get some rest.

Or some relief, whichever comes first.

I sent the limo back for Neal while I tucked Priscilla and her dad out of sight in the ladies room and took her mom and the kids down to the ceremony area.

Neal's hotel was a five-minute drive, tops, and I had already spoken with him and confirmed he would be out front waiting. So when twenty minutes had passed without the limo, I started to worry.

I called the driver twice but got no answer. I tried Neal's phone. No answer. Ten more minutes went by and Priscilla's dad came out of the ladies room and found me in the parking lot.

"What's the hold-up?"

"Just waiting for the limo," I answered. I smiled and gave what I hoped was a reassuring nod. "Must be tied up in traffic."

"Traffic? The hotel's at the light. Where would there be traffic between here and there?"

There wouldn't.

"Um, maybe the limo had to go down and make a U-turn at the next light."

I was grasping at straws and he knew it. He arched an eyebrow at me and said, "And why, pray tell, would he do that?"

I shook my head and smiled again. "Not sure."

"Have you called him?"

I nodded. "Maybe I'll call him again, though. If you'll excuse me." I took a couple of steps away from him, but he tagged right along behind me. It didn't matter since I got no answer.

Priscilla yelled behind us. "What's going on, Dad?"

"He ain't here yet," her father bellowed.

Her mother came across the grass and into the parking lot.

"Where is he?" They all looked to me like I knew the answer and was just hiding it from them.

"I don't know."

"Can't you call the limo driver?"

"I have. He's not answering."

Priscilla's dad shoved his hands in his pockets and spit on the ground. I didn't know if he had tobacco in his mouth or if it was his statement on the turn of events.

"So call the limo company!" Priscilla's mom turned to her husband and back to me, her hands spread out in exasperation. "Do something."

I dialed the main number for the transportation company and asked if they had another number for the driver. Nope.

"This is ridiculous," Priscilla yelled from the bathroom door. "You lost my groom. How on earth does someone lose a groom?"

"We don't know if they're lost. The limo driver is just not answering. There could be a perfectly good explanation."

"Oh yeah?" her dad asked. "And what would that be?"

I turned toward Priscilla, who was heading our way. "Have you checked your phone? Perhaps Neal called."

She screamed at the kids to bring her phone, and they both came running up from the beach.

They had almost reached us when the driver's name came up on my caller ID.

"Quentin! Where are you?"

"Um, it's a long story, Tyler."

"What? Where are you? Where's Neal?" The entire family leaned close behind me straining to hear the other end of the conversation.

"At the airport."

"What? The–" I turned to their shocked faces and smiled. "If you'll excuse me just a minute."

I walked a few steps away and whispered into the phone, "Why the hell is he at the airport, Quentin?"

"He told me he couldn't go through with it. He offered me five hundred dollars to take him to the airport, and I refused. He walked over to the valet and asked for a taxi. I've been trying to talk him out of it, but he just got in a cab and left. He gave me a note for the bride, but I wanted to call and let you know what went down. You want me to bring the note and come pick all them up?"

I was stunned. Not something I wanted to explain to a bride on her wedding day.

"Yes, Quentin. Please come as quickly as you can." I put the phone back in my pocket and sighed. "Um, Priscilla. Can I talk to you for a minute?"

"Whatever you need to say can be said in front of us," her mother said. Priscilla nodded, and I took a deep breath.

"Okay. I'm not sure what's happened, but Neal took a cab to the airport."

Priscilla's dad let loose a streak of curse words that would make a sailor blush. Her mom burst into tears and gathered both teens up into her arms, but they both looked more amused than upset.

Priscilla stood still for a moment and then let loose a wail. Slow and low at the beginning, and then building in pitch and volume as she held it out, sinking to her knees in the beautiful white gown.

I've never been happier to see Quentin and the limo. I wanted nothing more than to load these poor people up and send them on their way. Bless her heart. I couldn't do anything for her now.

Quentin got out of the car and handed me the note, which I in turn offered to Priscilla. She shook her head and looked at me with pained, tortured eyes that gripped at my heart and twisted it in sympathy for her pain.

"Read it to me. I can't," she whispered.

Quentin opened the limo door and I climbed inside the car with Priscilla to convey her groom's words.

My darling Priss,

You know I love you. With all my heart, I do. But I can't do this. I'm not a father. I'm not a husband. It's too much. I thought I could. I'm sorry I let you down.

Neal

Damn. Love can really hurt sometimes.

Saturday, January 25th

It's a miracle I didn't kill anyone today. Divine intervention, I'm sure. The result of my mama praying for me my whole life.

Charlotte worked my wedding with me today. Oh, lucky me. That girl has got to be the most incompetent assistant anyone has ever had. Dumber than dirt, I tell you.

As if her presence grating on my nerves wasn't enough, I also had a five-year-old ring bearer who I'm pretty certain meets all the criteria for a case of demon possession.

I'll probably hear darling little Nathan's name ringing in my ears for days because every five minutes someone yelled, "Nathan, no. Nathan, stop. Nathan, quit. Nathan, don't." Well, everyone except his mother, the bride's sister. She somehow remained strategically enthralled with her make-up and unable to tend to her evil offspring. He probably cast a spell on her or something.

I carefully tied the rings onto the ring-bearer's pillow, ensuring the ribbons were tight enough to withstand the hellion's trip down the aisle, but loose enough to be untied easily by a nervous best man on the altar.

I gave the pillow to Charlotte and told Ms. Brain Trust she needed to put it someplace safe until we were ready for it. Then I sent the mothers and groomsmen down the aisle, and lined up the bridesmaids. When I had only one bridesmaid and the maid-of-honor (Hellspawn's mother) left in the line-up, I told Charlotte to go get the pillow.

"I don't have it," she said.

I cued the bridesmaid to go as I hissed at Charlotte, "Well, go get it!"

"I don't have it," Charlotte snapped back at me. "I gave it to him!" She pointed to Nathan, who was trying to stand on his head in the foyer while his eight-year-old sister Hannah plucked the petals from her flower-girl basket and dropped them on him.

"Hannah, put the petals back in your basket," I said, closing the doors behind their mother, the last in the processional. She never even looked back. "Nathan, buddy, come here. Where'd you put the pillow?"

He ran past me and slapped his hands in the water fountain, and I wished for a moment it was holy water so the truth would be revealed once and for all. Evil of me, I suppose, but this kid was on my last good nerve.

"Nathan, come here. I need to know what you did with the pillow." I don't know why I thought he'd listen to me. He hadn't listened to anyone else.

The organist began the bridesmaids' song again, and panic set in. The kids should have already been down the aisle, and I should have already been on my way to retrieve the bride and her father from the dressing room.

I crouched in front of him and got doused with water flicked from his hands into my face. "Nathan, listen to me." He flicked the remaining drops of water at me, and I grabbed hold of his arm as he tried to make a run for it. "I need the pillow, Nathan."

Before I knew what happened, he punched me right in the nose. Hard enough to make my head swim and my eyes go all dark with twinkly spots for a moment.

"I'm Batman! No one messes with Batman," he said, charging past me and back into the foyer.

"Catch him, Charlotte!"

Ms. Brain Trust stood there dumbfounded, looking back and forth between me and the little tuxedoed beast as he struggled to open the heavy door. He managed to squeeze himself outside just as I got to my feet and in pursuit.

"He threwed it in the lake."

I stopped and looked back at Hannah, who had put her petals back in the basket and was busy shredding them one by one.

"What did you say, Hannah?"

She repeated it without ever looking at me.

"Nathan threwed the pillow in the lake."

I bolted out the door and after Nathan, waving at the bride and father to go back inside the dressing room. "I'll be right there. Just gotta grab Nathan!"

"Nathan! Get your ass over here, boy," the bride's father bellowed at his grandson, who completely ignored him and set out to climb the nearest tree.

"Nathan, I'm gonna get your Daddy! Get off that tree and get over here," the bride yelled, but her nephew kept right on climbing.

I reached the base of the tree just in time to grab his ankle, but he kicked wild, so I let go and ducked. My nose still hurt too much to risk a heel to the face. Nathan perched himself on a limb just out of reach and looked down at me, grinning like the devil himself.

"Nathan, what did you do with the pillow?"

He nodded and pointed to the lake before laughing and clapping his hands in delight.

I scanned the lake near the shore but saw no sign of the small pillow.

The bride's father pushed me aside and easily grabbed his grandson's legs, yanking him down from the tree and planting him on the ground.

"Get yourself inside, boy," he said as Nathan took off running away from him.

I scanned the lake one more time before facing the bride, uncertain how to tell her the wonderful news.

"Um, I think Nathan may have thrown the rings in the lake."

No way to really sugar-coat it or pretty it up much. Especially when the organist was on his third run-through of the bridesmaids' song waiting for the flower girl and ring bearer to enter.

"He what?" She shrieked loud enough that I am sure the guests could hear her over the organ music.

I sent her and her dad back inside the dressing room with Nathan and Hannah, and then I opened the sanctuary door just wide enough to cue the organist to play some filler music and stall. He glared back at me, but I had no fear of him after dealing with the pint-sized prince of the underworld.

It took me almost twenty minutes of wading barefoot in the shallow water along the shore to find that stupid pillow. The tannins in the lake from the tall Cypress trees that lined it had already stained the white satin a deep rust color. Thank God I wore a skirt today. The hem got a little wet, but not as bad as pants would have been.

I'm proud to say both rings stayed firmly attached to the pillow, a credit to the knot badge earned during my illustrious three-month stint as a Girl Scout.

Charlotte did not even so much as apologize. Not that Nathan's behavior was her fault, but who hands a five-year-old demon a pillow with thousands of dollars of diamonds tied on it? Aargh.

No word at all from Cabe today. Texted him three times between weddings and called on my way home from work to tell him about the ring drama. No answer and no call back.

I'm sure he just got tied up doing something, but what? We talked yesterday before my rehearsal, and he didn't mention having plans today. He didn't call me to say goodnight last night, either. Which is odd.

No big deal, I guess. Miss his voice, though.

Sunday, January 26th

Okay.

I haven't heard from Cabe since we talked Friday afternoon. He hasn't returned my calls or texts all weekend. I'm a little freaked out. I thought about calling Maggie, but I figure she would've called me if something had happened to him. I don't want to look like some psycho-girl calling his mom just because I haven't heard from him. Maybe he went fishing or something. Camping with someone. Maybe he is just somewhere he doesn't have cell service, and he didn't realize it until he got there.

I have a sick feeling in the pit of my stomach, but I don't know why.

If I don't hear from him tomorrow, I'll call Maggie.

Monday, January 27th

I didn't hear from him today, either. I'm beyond freaked out now. I couldn't concentrate at all today. I must have checked my phone twenty million times, just in case I'd missed a text or a call. I kept turning up the volume. Turning the silent feature on and off to see if it got stuck somehow. I even called my cell phone from my office phone to make sure the damned thing was working.

I dialed his number every half hour this morning but forced myself to stop when it produced no result.

I feel sick. I don't know what's going on. I want to call his mom, but I don't know what to say. I'm scared. I still think if something had happened to him, Maggie would have called me. I mean, even if she's on the same page as Galen and wants me to leave him alone, I can't imagine she wouldn't let me know if he'd had an accident or something.

So what if I call her and she tells me she hasn't seen him all weekend? Or what if I call her and she tells me he's been home all weekend?

Which sends me down another rabbit hole completely. One I really don't want to venture down. It terrifies me that something could have happened to him. But the alternative also scares me.

What if something happened, and it's just *me* he's not calling??

Even as I write that, my mind reels with the question of what it would be. I don't know.

Did I do something to make him angry?

Did Galen turn him against me?

Did he meet someone else?

My stomach turns at the thought.

I shake my head every time it enters my mind to try and stop it from taking root.

This is Cabe. My best friend. I've known him for five years. Evidently, he's been in love with me for five years even although I didn't know that. He literally just told me days ago he's never been happier in his life. So he wouldn't just meet someone in a bar and then drop off the face of the earth and not call me.

Would he?

I want to throw up.

I want to drive over there.

I want him to call.

I want to cry.

Tuesday, January 28th

I couldn't take the deafening silence. I left work early and drove to his office. Tuesday is usually the only day he has to work from the cubicle due to the morning staff meetings so I figured I had a pretty good chance of finding him there. If he wasn't at work, I had decided I would drive to his mom's and if he wasn't there either, I'd just sit in her driveway until he came home.

I found his car in the parking lot at work right away. I don't know if I was more relieved or pissed.

I marched right into the receptionist and asked to see Cabe Shaw. Probably the first person ever to do so since his job description does not involve direct contact with the outside world. She looked a little hesitant at first, which may have had something to do with the dark circles under my eyes, the crazy puffiness of my face from days of tears, and the slightly crazed vibe I was giving off.

She went and got him though, and when he walked into the reception area, I felt torn between wanting to collapse against him in relief and wanting to tear out his throat with my bare hands.

He didn't look at me. He walked toward me with his head down, hands in his jean pockets. I took it to mean admission of guilt, and I decided to catalog every aspect of his appearance so the moment would be committed to memory forever. His crisp, white linen shirt, casually unbuttoned to reveal just the tips of dark blonde hair peeking up from his chest. His gold chain laying against his neck in the exact spot my tongue had traced mere days before. The top of his tousled head reflecting the sunlight from the window in sparks of gold and bronze with deeper undertones almost brown.

When he lifted his eyes to mine, they took my breath away, the normally

58

clear blue clouded by an expression I didn't want to decipher. His lips, so soft and velvet against mine in these last few weeks, stretched tight into a line across his face, just above the strong, chiseled jawline that takes the edge off his pretty face and secures his masculinity. He stared at me, motionless. Emotionless. Silent.

I stared back. Unable to breathe or speak. I took in a short gasp of air to fight off the lightheaded swirl of darkness that threatened to overtake me, and the breath rushed back out of me with a gargled sigh against my will.

"What the hell, Cabe?"

He looked down again, kicking the toe of his boot against the triangular pattern on the carpet.

"Look at me." I fought to keep my voice from shrieking. The receptionist busied herself with shuffling papers, but I could feel her sonar hearing zoned in on our every word. I trembled all over with the effort to stay calm and not lash out at him with fists and fury.

He looked up, casually, as though he had heard a bird in the distance and thought perhaps he could see it fly. His eyes met mine, but they stared right through me, a force of cold slapping me so hard it almost knocked me back a step.

"Cabe," I said his name again, not sure how much longer I could hold on to any measure of calm.

"We need to talk," he finally whispered, looking down at the carpet again. "I'll call you tonight."

"What? Let's talk now!" My voice came out shrill, crackling with emotion. I knew standing in the office lobby with Rosie Receptionist listening in was not the time or place, but fear of what he had to say gripped me, and I didn't think I'd survive waiting until night. Besides, what if he didn't call? I wanted answers while I had him standing in front of me.

"I can't talk now. I left a meeting to come down here. I know I should have called you. I just didn't know what to say. But I'll call you tonight, okay? I gotta go."

He turned, and I lurched forward to run after him as he walked away. To force him to turn back and talk to me. But Rosie Receptionist's eyes met mine, and I stopped in my tracks. There was no judgment there. Not even pity, really. Just a shared female understanding. I could feel her eyes willing me not to make an ass of myself. Maybe I'll send her a thank you card one day. When all this makes more sense. If it ever does.

He texted me an hour ago. Said he could come over around eight if that's okay. I am on pins and needles. I want to tell him not to come. There is absolutely no way this is going to be good news. No way at all it will be something I want to hear. Maybe I should just leave. Not be here when he gets here. Put off the inevitable.

I can't breathe. Waves of nausea rise and swell within me but I can't throw up. I pick up the phone to call Melanie or Carmen, but then I hang up again. I don't know what to say. I don't want to say anything. Like maybe if I don't say anything this won't be true.

Dark thoughts creep around in my head as I try to reject them all. I keep telling myself to just wait and hear what he has to say, but I already know it's over. I saw that in his eyes. Cabe's gone, and I don't know why. And I don't know how to live without him again. Especially now. Now that I know I've loved him all along.

Wednesday, January 29th

I thought he wasn't going to show last night. It was about twenty minutes after eight when he finally rang my bell, and I had worked myself into a frenzy convinced he wasn't coming.

I flung open the door and burst into tears immediately. And I mean an ugly cry, too. A snot-running, red-faced, spit-hanging-from-my-lips, eyes-squished-shut, hyperventilating kind of ugly cry.

He put his hands on my shoulders and pulled me to his chest, softly saying *sshh* over and over again. I fell against him with the full weight of my emotions. He was the source of my pain and my comfort. I clung to him with desperation even as I felt his torso stiffen against me.

Eventually, he led me over to the couch to sit while he went and got me tissues and a glass of water. I drank it to rinse the taste of snot and tears from my mouth, but it all threatened to come back up almost immediately.

I ran for the bathroom and dry-heaved into the toilet, over and over again, quite aware I was being a complete hot mess before the guy had a chance to even say a word. I couldn't help it, though. It was all different, and I knew. I felt it. He didn't have to say a thing.

He ran a washcloth under the water and knelt on the bathroom floor beside me, wiping my face so tenderly that tears streamed anew.

"You need to calm down, Ty. I can't stand to see you so upset."

Anger sparked then, and the flames caught quick. I shoved his hand away from my face, the washcloth flying to the floor.

"Then why are you upsetting me? Why are you doing this?" I screamed at him, backing away the few inches I could in the tight space between the tub and the toilet.

He rubbed his face with one hand and sighed, running his other hand through his hair.

"I'm not trying to hurt you. I don't want to hurt you. I've never wanted to hurt you."

"Well, you're doing a damned good job of it. Where have you been, Cabe? Why haven't you called? What happened?" I was still screaming, and I didn't care anymore. Raw, throbbing emotions pounded inside me, beating against my resolve and spilling out of my throat in angry words and drops of spit.

He sat back on his butt in the hallway, leaning against the wall on the opposite side and stretching his right leg out toward me. He bent the left one, and stretched his left arm across it, staring at his fingers as he made small movements in the air.

I closed the toilet lid and tried to position myself between it and the tub, but no matter how I tried, I couldn't help touching his foot and leg. The contact burned my skin.

He let out a deep sigh and tilted his head back against the wall as he closed his eyes.

"Answer me!" I screamed like a madwoman. He opened his eyes to the ceiling but didn't look at me.

"Saturday was my wedding anniversary." He said it with no emotion, really. Just a calm, matter-of-fact statement.

I didn't understand at first. I didn't know why he was mentioning it or what it had to do with our situation. Then it dawned on me that his wedding anniversary was the reason I hadn't heard from him. The reason he had disappeared off the face of the earth. The reason he now sat in my hallway cold, calm, collected, and removed from emotion.

I went from distraught to pissed in six seconds flat.

"Are you freaking kidding me? That's why you haven't called me? Why you haven't let me know you weren't dead on the side of the road? *That's* why you're treating me this way?"

He gave a slight shake of his head and closed his eyes again.

"I don't expect you to understand."

"Well, good. Because I don't. If you were upset or something, why couldn't you tell me? If you needed some space to process, or you were having trouble with the day, do you think you couldn't talk to me? I've been worried sick about you, Cabe."

"I'm sorry. I should have called. I just got all caught up in my own head, and I didn't want to talk to anybody."

"That's fine. It's fine to say *I don't want to talk*. But you say that. You give the other person the courtesy of saying you don't want to talk. You don't just disappear."

I started relaxing a bit. Okay. So I forgot they got married the end of January. Shame on me. I guess I should have remembered that, and I should have been more proactive about reaching out to see if he was okay with it. But I really thought he'd gotten over Monica. I mean, he hasn't mentioned her pretty much at all since the divorce became final, and since everything seemed so hunky-dory between us, I assumed he was good. After all, I'm supposedly the one he was in love with for so long, right? She was basically a distraction from me, right? So if he has me, why would he still want her? I tried to cop an attitude and convince myself it was all okay, but it didn't work.

There had to be more to the story. Okay, so maybe he had been upset about the anniversary Saturday. But he hadn't called at all since then, not to mention the way he had acted at his office earlier and even here tonight. Something was wrong. Very wrong.

"Wait, are you still not over Monica? Did she contact you? Did you call her?"

He shook his head. "No. I haven't heard from her since she left our apartment in Seattle to move in with Kristen.

"So help me out here. What's wrong?"

"I don't know how to explain it to you, Ty. You've never been married."

Ouch. That one hurt. He was right, of course. I've never been married. But was there some pain or conflict he was feeling that only married people could relate to?

I stood up and stomped over him to get to the kitchen.

He stayed silently seated in the hallway with his eyes closed while I poured myself more water and stood at the entrance to the hallway staring at him.

I was pissed. Hurt. Confused. Scared.

I wanted to scream at him. I wanted to hold him and beg him to never let me go. I wanted to tell him to go screw himself. I wanted to calm the fear inside me, but only he could do that.

I finally went and knelt beside him. He looked so broken.

Again. Like he did when he first came back from Seattle. My heart tugged, and I wondered if maybe he did have some deep chasm of pain I had no way of understanding. I reached out and touched his hair. Softly, lightly. A gentle caress I hoped would say, "I care."

He turned his face toward me, but his eyes were still closed.

"Will you look at me?" I asked. I needed to see what his eyes held. Would the old Cabe be there? The one from before Monica? The one from last week? Or would it be that scary shell of a person I saw at the lake when he returned in October? Or even more frightening, the cold emptiness from earlier today at his office?

He opened them, but the dark hallway cast no illumination on what they held. I leaned in close, close enough to kiss him. Close enough to feel his breath as he exhaled. He made no move to either pull away or to meet me.

The thought of my breath smelling rank after sobbing and dry-heaving popped into my head, and I pulled away abruptly. He didn't stop me.

His lips parted, but no sound came out. They stayed that way for several seconds before he spoke, each word obviously chosen with much care and thought.

"I don't mean to hurt you, Ty. It's the last thing I want to do. But I don't know if I can do this."

"Do what?" I asked, but I already knew. My heart plummeted. My anger had slipped away, leaving me vulnerable and exposed in its absence.

"Things are just moving so fast between us. I can't get serious right now. I have to think about things, you know? A year ago, I stood in front of a woman and pledged to love her the rest of my life. I don't fully understand all the reasons I did that, or all the reasons it failed, but I do know it's something I need to figure out before I rush in again."

"But it wasn't your fault, Cabe. She fell in love with another woman. You couldn't compete with that. That wasn't something you could have prevented. You just—"

He held up his hand to stop me. "Ty. Listen to me. I made a vow to someone. A promise. But it fell apart, and before I jump into something else, I think I owe it to myself, and to you, to figure out what happened. I've only been divorced for a couple of months. I think I need to take some time."

I refused to hear him.

"This is Galen, isn't it? Galen got to you. She talked to you and told you we shouldn't be dating."

He turned to face me, wide-eyed in confusion. "What? No. What are you talking about? Why would you think that?"

"Galen cornered me in the bathroom the night of the comedy show. She told me to leave you alone and let you heal. She basically said I had…done you wrong…and that—"

"She did what?" He was on his feet then, pacing down the hallway and then back and forth across my living room. "My sister has no business telling anyone how to manage their life. She's a revolving door of messed-up relationships."

I bit my lip, not sure now how much truth Galen had given me. Her words had upset me, but they'd also given me a measure of confidence in the last few weeks that Cabe loved me and had loved me for years in spite of myself. That knowledge had given me a huge bolster in being able to relax and trust my feelings for him. But what if it wasn't true? What if Galen was wrong?

He turned to face me, his face red and his jaw clenched tight. "Why didn't you tell me? Is that why you left that night? Talk about being honest about your feelings. A bit hypocritical, don't you think? Were you ever going to mention my sister jumping you in the bathroom?"

"I wanted to. But ... but I just didn't know what to say or when ... would be a good time," I stammered and stuttered. I'm not sure how things suddenly all got flipped around where I felt like I'd done something wrong, but I sure felt that way.

Cabe turned and went to the sliding glass door, slapping the wall beside the door with an open palm.

"God! That pisses me off. This is exactly what I mean, too. You're having all these thoughts I know nothing about. I'm having all these thoughts you know nothing about. I can't do this. I don't know what it takes to make something work, but at least I'm *aware* that I have no idea. I don't want to fail again. I'm not going to fail again. So before I get deep into this or anything else, I need to figure out how to stop that from happening."

"I'm sorry, Cabe. I should have told you. It's just that everything was so good, and I was so happy. You were happy. You told me you were. I didn't think it was that big of a deal."

Okay, that last part was a lie. I had obsessed over every word Galen said. I definitely thought it was a big deal, but I hadn't wanted to risk sharing it. Which I guess was wrong. I don't know. At that point of the night, I wasn't sure what was up and what was down. I had no idea what to think. I just knew I felt him slipping away, and I desperately wanted to hold onto him.

"Cabe, I don't know how to keep something from failing either. But we can figure it out together. We can be honest with each other. Talk. Get it all out in the open. We can make this work."

The whole time I talked he shook his head, his hand over his eyes. The more he shook, the faster I talked. I could feel my heart pounding in my chest.

"I just need some time, Ty. I don't want you to get hurt. You've had enough of that. I just need to take a breath and be on my own for a little bit, you know? I was so beat up after Monica left, and then trying to move back here and get settled in. I just feel like it's too fast. I want to make sure it's what's right for both of us. The last thing I want to do is lose you. Lose your friendship. You're so important to me, Ty. I don't want to risk that when I can't be sure how it will turn out."

I felt like I'd been thrown into the Twilight Zone. The man I loved was standing in front of me, saying he needed time and space. Basically the same words my first love had uttered to me a month before he married another woman. He was also saying he didn't want to risk our friendship by pursuing it further, which had been my mantra keeping us apart for the last five years.

What the hell? I finally decided to take the leap and jump all in and now *he* had cold feet? It just didn't make sense to me. If Galen was right...but what if Galen wasn't right? What if my original concept of our friendship had been true all along? What if he'd always thought we were just friends?

To be honest, Cabe had never professed his love for me. Sure, we'd gotten closer in the last few weeks. Definitely become more than friends. But he didn't introduce me as his girlfriend that day to his cousin. He hadn't said he loved me. Plus, no matter how intimately we'd fooled around, he'd never actually had sex with me.

My whole world spun backwards, sucking the oxygen out of the room as it turned.

"Wait, Cabe. Don't do this. Don't walk away. We can—"

He cut me off. "Tyler. I need to sort my thoughts. For you and for me. Please don't make this harder than it has to be. I truly do not want to hurt you."

Tears streamed silently down my face. How could he stand there and say he didn't want to hurt me when he was ripping my heart from my body?

"Cabe, I love you."

His head popped up, and his eyes met mine. For a brief second, I thought I saw a light there. A glimmer. A hope. But then he shook his head and walked toward the door.

"Don't do that, Tyler. Don't say that to manipulate me or force something to happen."

"I'm not. I do love you."

He turned back to face me, his hand on the doorknob.

"Tyler, don't. Just don't. If we share those words, I want it to be because we're sure of what we're saying. What we're promising. I need to be sure. I need you to be sure. Can you please just give me some time? I'm not Dwayne. I'm not getting married to anyone else next month. I'm not saying I don't care about you or I never want to see you again. I just need some time. Okay?"

What could I say? What option did I have? No? No, you can't have time? You have to love me right now? You have to know right this minute that we're supposed to be together, and you need to be fine with it.

I had no choice but to let him go. To let the last pieces of my heart shred away from me as he carried it with him down the stairs.

I crumpled into a heap on the floor and stayed there until I woke up about an hour ago. Late for work and not really giving one hot damn.

Well, that's not true. I give a damn. I'm taking a shower now and getting ready to go in. I called Laura and told her I wasn't feeling well and would be late. So, I give a damn, but in the grand scheme of life, none of it matters as much as it did before last night.

February

Sunday, February 2nd

I spent the entire weekend curled up in a ball in Melanie's guest bed. The first weekend I've had off over in a month and I was completely bedridden with grief. I don't give a damn how old you are and how much life experience you've acquired, break-ups suck.

I haven't heard from Cabe since he left my apartment on Tuesday night, and it's like an eclipse completely blocked out the sun.

I spent Wednesday, Thursday, and Friday dodging client phone calls, staring at my computer screen, and crying behind my closed office door.

At first, Chaz gave me a hard time, but it took exactly one complete hysterical breakdown in his presence to shut him the hell up. He even brought me a cheap bouquet of flowers on Friday. One of those they sell in the grocery store check-out line, but it was the thought (and the apology) that counted.

Mel seemed almost as devastated as I was. She had practically planned the wedding and named the babies Cabe and I would have. She even teared up right along with me when I told her what had happened. Well, as much as I could. I don't even fully understand it, so how could I tell her?

She insisted I come home with her for the weekend. I didn't even bother to go pack clothes. I stopped and bought a toothbrush on the way to her house and moved into the guest room, emerging only to use the bathroom and refill my water glass.

Mel and Paul pretty much tiptoed around the house all weekend. They whispered in hushed tones just outside my door, and occasionally they would knock and offer me food, but I couldn't eat. I just pulled the shades, flung a blanket over the curtain rod to block out more light, and slept every minute I could.

I woke up every couple of hours. The first few seconds I would be disoriented, unsure of where I was. But then I would remember, and the whole situation would come rushing back and I'd start wailing again.

Finally, I reached a point this afternoon where I wanted a shower more than I wanted sleep. So I climbed out of my dungeon and ventured down the hall to the living room.

"Mel." Paul said, looking at me like I was an escaped quarantine patient. "Mel!" Louder this time.

"What?" Melanie came through the swinging half door from the kitchen scowling at him. Her expression changed as soon as she saw me, and she rushed over to wrap me in a hug. "Oh honey. Do you want something to eat? Something to drink? What can I get you? Paul, get her something to drink. Fix her something to eat. What do you want, honey? Paul, go make her something."

Paul stood and took a couple of steps toward the kitchen, but his gaze never left me and it never lost that wary 'what the hell is she going to do next?' look.

"I'm fine," I croaked, my voice hoarse from crying so much and not talking for so long. "I don't want anything." I cleared my throat and coughed. "Maybe a glass of water."

"Paul, get her water! Go! Why are you standing there? Go! Come here, honey. Sit on the couch."

She led me by the arm as she would an invalid, and I suppose in some ways I was. Paul brought me the water and then took two steps back. I wondered if he thought heartbreak was contagious. I took several gulps of water and looked up at him, nodding thanks. He nodded back and disappeared down the hallway.

"He doesn't know what to do with tears. Never been his strong suit." Mel rolled her eyes and smiled.

"Thanks for letting me stay here."

"Oh honey. It's no problem at all. You stay here just as long as you like. You're always welcome, you know that."

I did know that, and the thought comforted me. Pain stabbed behind my eyes, and I drank a couple more swallows of water.

"I think I'm gonna go home. I want to take a shower. Wash my hair."

"You can do that here," Mel said. "There's shampoo, toothpaste, deodorant. Whatever you need. It's in a little basket underneath the sink in the bathroom. I can get you a robe."

I smiled and shook my head, the movement causing waves of pain to reverberate across my skull.

"Thanks, Mel. I really appreciate everything. But I need to go home."

She hugged me again, and I felt like I wanted to cry but had no tears. Dried up. Empty inside. And the emptiness left a hole that burned and ached.

I drove home in silence, the colors whizzing past me in a blur of madness. I had no conscious thought of anything I passed or saw, just a magnetic pull to get home. Alone with my own thoughts. My own pain.

I had turned my phone off after work on Friday, and I couldn't bring myself to turn it back on yet. I would have to do it tomorrow, to address the irate messages from brides, but they could wait.

Part of me was scared I would turn it back on and find a missed message from Cabe. Part of me was scared there'd be none.

My apartment echoed in empty silence as I entered. A stark contrast from Melanie's house, with its bustle of color, sounds, and smells. Her bright hues splashed across the upholstery and walls. Three dogs yipping and yapping and climbing all over the furniture. Paul's obsession with car shows playing non-stop on TV. Melanie banging pots and pans in the kitchen and yelling at Paul to turn the TV down.

I welcomed the silence of home, and yet I felt engulfed by it. The air too heavy to breathe. Too dense.

The cleansing waters of the shower washed away a portion of the funk, both on my skin and in my head, but after fifteen minutes standing under the stream, my eyes had started to pour out tears again. I collapsed into the tub with loud, racking sobs that would have terrified Paul. I cried until my sides hurt and the water grew cold.

I stripped the cologne-tainted sheets from my bed and washed them. I hid the stuffed frog and Roscoe the dog underneath the bed so they wouldn't stare at me, and then I lay on the fresh sheets and stared at the ceiling, praying the morning would soon come.

Tuesday, February 4th

It completely caught me off guard when he called after a week of silence. I wasn't expecting it, and my heart skipped beats, raced, and stopped, all at the same time. I jumped out of my chair to close my office door, but then I got nervous he would hang up before I answered and cracked my knee on my desk trying to rush back to the phone.

"Hello?"

"Hey there, Buttercup."

I sucked in a quick gasp of air and fought the tears that sprang to my eyes. Partly from my throbbing knee, but mostly from the pain of hearing his voice, much more quiet and subdued than normal. "Hey."

"How ya doin'?"

"I'm hanging in there." I declined to mention I'd lost nine pounds in the past week, hadn't had solid food since last Monday, and had cried so much I'd acquired what seemed to be a permanent fog filter over my vision.

We were both silent for a long pause, and then we spoke at the same time.

"Go ahead," Cabe said.

"No, no. You go."

We were silent again, and then we both spoke together again. We laughed, and I told him I would listen and he should go first.

"I need to talk to you about something. Could we meet somewhere?"

My heart screamed '*Yes!*' pretty much before he finished asking, but my battered self-defense system shrieked '*Oh hell no!*' in the back of my head. I paused to decide which voice to go with.

"Ty?"

My heart won out. "Yeah. Where do you wanna meet?"

He picked a restaurant near my house, one we'd been to several times. I went home first to change clothes, but I couldn't decide on an appropriate outfit for the occasion. I don't own heart-protecting armor or a straitjacket.

He looked awful, and I'm not just saying that because I was hoping he would. There were dark circles under his bloodshot eyes, his hair was tangled mess, and his shirt looked like he'd slept in it. For days. He was seated at the bar, and he rose to give me a half-assed hug when I walked up to him.

"Hey, Ty. You okay?"

I glared at him and swallowed the vile string of words that came to mind in answer. *Why would I be okay, jerk? You broke up with me a week ago, haven't called since then, and now you casually ask if I'm okay?*

I liked the strength the anger gave me, so I decided to try and focus on that instead of throwing myself in his arms and begging him to never let go.

They seated us right away, and we both stared at the menu and laid it aside.

"Hungry?" he asked.

"Nope."

"Me neither. So I guess I'll get right to it. I'm not sure what to do with this, but I got the travel packet for Paris on Friday."

My heart fluttered, and my stomach flipped. I'd forgotten all about Paris. How does anyone forget about Paris? Tears sprang to my eyes, and I dabbed at them with the linen napkin as he talked.

"I need to know what you wanna do. Do you want me to cancel the whole thing? Do you want to take someone else? I'll pay to transfer my tickets over."

The napkin proved completely ineffective at keeping the steady stream of tears from seeping down my face. "I don't want to go with anyone else."

"Okay. I'll tell her to cancel it then."

I nodded and swallowed hard. "Will you be able to get your money back?"

"I don't know. Don't worry about that. It's my problem."

I nodded again and more tears flowed. Was this why he called? To tell me he would cancel the trip? Did I need to know that? Did he really think I would just up and take someone else on our trip to Paris? I grabbed hold of the anger and used it to push myself from the table and stand up. "I can't do this, Cabe. I'm gonna go."

He followed me to my car. He walked silently behind me, his presence pulling the pressure from the air around me like a storm system. He grabbed my elbow as I reached the car door, spinning me to face him and lifting me into his arms and against his mouth before I knew what was happening.

His lips covered mine, rough and demanding, as his tongue plundered and his hips pushed me back against the car. I clung to the front of his shirt, hanging on for dear life as my knees weakened and my heart soared. Just when I thought I may actually pass out, he released my mouth and held me tight against his chest.

"I'm sorry, Ty. I'm so sorry."

I stood motionless, afraid if I moved he would pull away and the moment would be gone. I could have stood there forever. Cabe's arms around me, his voice against my hair, his heart beating against mine. Both pounding faster than I ever thought possible.

"It kills me to see you in pain, Ty. I'm sorry. I don't know what to do. I can't stand being away from you."

His voice cracked, and I looked up. Tears shimmered in his eyes and one huge drop rolled slowly down his cheek as he looked toward the sky. My shattered, wounded heart exploded into a million jagged pieces.

"Then don't," I pleaded, my voice so quiet I'm surprised he heard me at all.

More tears rolled as he shook his head. "I know I need to slow this down. That makes sense in my head, but my heart just wants to be with you. I'm sorry."

He leaned forward and kissed me again, slower this time. Gentler. The tip of his tongue rolled against mine, and any straggling shreds of anger I had mustered up before deserted me. But I had to ask the question raging in my head.

"So what do we do now?"

He brushed my hair behind my ear and caressed my cheek. "I don't know." His eyes were clouded, troubled, and I feared he might turn and walk away at any minute.

I struggled to think of a solution. Anything to keep him from bolting and shutting me out again.

"Well, let's slow it down if that's what you need."

He sighed and let his head flop forward to meet mine. "Can we do that? Are we able to see each other and talk to each other without it going all nuts?"

I didn't know what he meant by nuts, but I didn't really care as long as I could see him and talk to him.

"I don't see why not. Just communicate with me, dude. Let me know what the hell's going on in your head."

He nodded and swallowed, his Adam's apple rolling against the collar of his shirt. Amazing what weird-ass details you notice when you're trying to freeze everything happening and commit it to memory.

"You have no idea what you do to me, girl."

I had no response for that. The way he said it could have gone either way as to a good effect or a bad one. He let go of me and dropped his hands down to hold mine. His thumbs slowly caressed the backs of my hands, and I shivered at the sensations it caused.

"You're cold. Here, get in your car. I'm sorry. I should have realized it was cold out here." He kissed me once more and then brought each of my hands to his lips as well. "Have a good night, Buttercup."

I wish I could have told him I wasn't cold at all. In fact, quite the opposite.

He opened my car door and waited until I was buckled in before shutting it. He backed away, and his eyes didn't leave mine until he was dangerously close to bumping into another car across the parking lane.

I feel numb now. Like I should be relieved or happy or something. I mean, he wants to see me. To talk to me. He obviously wants to kiss me. But we're not okay.

Friday, February 7th

I am so damned confused. I have no idea what to do about this man.

We had that tearful, sappy-ass moment in the parking lot of the restaurant Tuesday night where he asked if we could slow things down, and then he ends up coming over the past two nights.

What the hell?

Am *I* supposed to be policing our speed limit? Should I be telling him to stay at home and reminding him he had a problem with everything moving too fast?

Wednesday he called to say he had free movie tickets for an advanced screening. Then last night he called to say his buddy Dean had brought him a bunch of shrimp from the coast and asked if I wanted to boil shrimp and cook together.

Luckily, I have a rehearsal dinner and dessert party I'm helping Chaz with tonight and then the wedding tomorrow night. Otherwise I may have to say, "Look dude, for someone who wants to slow down, you sure are showing up a lot."

Not that I'm complaining. Not at all. I don't mind him being here everyday. I don't want to go anywhere near the pain I felt last week without him. But that's exactly the reason I'm concerned. If he keeps coming over every night, isn't he just going to wig out again like he did last time?

I'd rather see him less than not see him at all. So should I say something?

It's so nerve-wracking. Like I'm scared I'm going to make a mistake or do something wrong and he's going to bolt. I'm on edge, and I have so many questions I want to ask him, but I don't dare. Not yet.

Saturday, February 8th

Let me just start by saying I don't think Chaz Bryant could plan his way out of a paper bag. Why that man has the title of Senior Event Planner is beyond my understanding. I get that he worked with Lillian back in her hotel days, and they're tight. But I swear he couldn't find his ass with both hands and a flashlight. Even if Lillian has blinders on when it comes to Chaz, I don't see how Laura could possibly not see through him. They're equal partners and owners in the business. Shouldn't both of them need to approve of an employee?

Oh, he's a charmer and a half in the office, though. Sugar wouldn't melt in his mouth he's so sweet. I've never seen anyone so skilled in the finer arts of ass-kissery. He can't trip over himself fast enough to bring Lillian her tea every morning, or to drop the latest Vera Bradley bag on Laura's desk. He volunteers for coffee runs, brings in brownies he supposedly bakes himself, and he is an absolute whiz at creating complex PowerPoint demonstrations for the various plans and ideas he proposes. Of course, I'd like to point out that if he was actually servicing his clients and taking care of the necessary paperwork for their weddings, he wouldn't have time to be doing PowerPoints and running out for coffee. He'd be sitting at his desk working like the rest of us.

I cannot even count the number of times I have covered for that imbecile on wedding days. Like the time he forgot to send the limo company the itinerary and I had to call up a driver on his day off and beg him to come pick up the wedding party. Or the day he forgot to order a cake and I talked the bakery supervisor at Publix into giving me a display cake to use with a real bottom layer for the bride and groom to cut into and a sheet cake in the back to serve to guests. Or the time he failed to realize the menu cards Charlotte printed in the office had the wrong groom's name on them and I had to scramble to run to Staples and pay a fortune to have more printed. (Which, by the way, I just realized I forgot to expense. Dang it!)

But today, today just took the cake and the plate it was sitting on. He had a huge wedding ceremony planned at a nature park in Orlando, a ludicrous location for such a large party since there's no rain back-up. But Chaz doesn't like confrontation, so he didn't want to talk the bride out of it. The forecast this morning said thirty percent chance of rain, so we should have been fine. But sure enough, just as the rental company finished unloading the ceremony chairs, the sky darkened and the wind picked up. We had an hour and half to go, plenty of time to call the wedding to a back-up location if we had one. The hallmark of good planning is to always have a Plan B. Especially when you have an outdoor ceremony location and the B stands for back-up.

Did I mention Chaz had no back-up?

I was pinning on corsages and distributing bouquets in the bride's dressing room at the reception hall when the videographer came in and asked to speak with me. I excused myself and followed him into the hallway.

"You might want to head over to the ceremony site and check on your buddy."

"What do you mean? My buddy?"

"Um, yeah. Chase or Chaz or whatever his name is. He's crying in the men's room and refusing to come out."

"What?" I immediately dialed Chaz's cell phone but it went straight to voice mail. "Did he say what was wrong?"

The videographer shook his head and chuckled. "He mumbled something, but I couldn't make it out. He's sitting on the floor in the men's room. Just thought you should know."

"Okay, thanks." I told the bride I needed to check on a few things and then promptly broke several traffic laws to get to the ceremony site as quickly as possible.

The temperature had dropped noticeably between the time I got in my car and the time I got out ten minutes later. Trees swayed to and fro at the mercy of the wind, and loose limbs and branches torpedoed through the air like projectile missiles as dark clouds swirled and churned above the treetops. The cold air sat damp and heavy on my skin, and I could tell it wouldn't be long before the sky could no longer contain the moisture and it would have to open up.

I tried Chaz's cell phone again with the same result. I got no answer to my knock on the men's room door, so I glanced around to find any available male to send in for reconnaissance. There wasn't a soul in sight, and time being of the essence, I had no choice but to barge in. I did hold my hand up to shield my eyes just in case someone occupied it other than a tearful Chaz.

I found him just as the videographer said I would. Sitting on the bathroom floor with his back against the wall between two urinals, his head bowed in his hands.

"Chaz?" I asked, carefully looking around to make sure we were alone. The two stall doors were closed with no feet visible beneath, so I dropped my hand shield and relaxed.

I tried to kneel beside him, which pretty much put my face at eye level with the basin of the urinal, so I stood back up and bent at the waist. Which also put my face closer to a urinal than I've ever thought it would be. I stifled a cough at the stench of urine and air freshener and called his name again.

He didn't look up at me, but when I spoke he started crying again. Mumbling something about the rain, weddings, and how he should have taken the job offer in Colorado.

I bit the bullet and knelt on the bathroom floor, praying the impending wedding had prompted the custodians to mop and my bare knees wouldn't catch some terrible bathroom fungus.

"Chaz, buddy, what's wrong? Did something happen?"

Now, let me just add here I am not a cold and heartless person. If I truly thought something was wrong with Chaz, or that something terrible had happened to him, I would have been showing the compassion, empathy, and concern it warranted. But from the moment the videographer told me Chaz was crying in the men's room, I knew what was going on. I've seen him sit on the floor and cry before. Any time life, or work, or responsibility became overwhelming. Which happened more often than you might think with Chaz.

He looked up at me, his face red and splotchy, his eyes puffy and swollen with tears. "I can't, Tyler. I can't. It's going to rain. It's going to pour. It's never rained on one of my weddings before."

"Never?" I asked, sure he was exaggerating.

"No! Never! I don't know what to do. I can't tell her. I can't. I never should have taken this job. I had a job offer, for more money even, out in Colorado at a big ski resort. But I hate snow. I hate cold. I couldn't leave Florida. And now it's going to rain." He wailed loudly and buried his face in his hands again.

I rubbed my hand across my face and resisted the urge to tell him to man up and get his ass off the bathroom floor.

"Chaz, honey. We can't do anything about the rain, but we can figure out another way to have the ceremony. It'll be fine."

"No, it won't! She wanted her wedding in the gardens, surrounded by nature and blue skies. Now it's all ruined. Her pictures won't be as pretty, and her guests won't see her walking down the pathway through the trees. I just can't." Sobs overcame him again, wearing my patience thin. I mean, you would have thought *he* was the bride, and it was *his* wedding that was ruined.

"Did you really say it's *never* rained on one of your weddings? How is that even possible?"

"I know. It's crazy. But I've just had this incredible luck, and it's never happened. I always tell my brides they'll have sunny weather because it doesn't rain on my weddings."

He sniffled, and I got up to get him a handful of paper towels. I tried not to gag as he blew a mountain of snot from his nose and wiped his tears.

"Until today, buddy. 'Cause it's gonna rain. No doubt about it. In fact, it may be raining already, so you've got to pull yourself together. That bride is counting on you to have a plan in place. It sucks, but we have no control over the weather. We have to work with what we *can* control. If she sees you falling apart, how the hell is she going to hold it together? You need to be calm and tell her everything will be okay. She needs to *believe* you."

He tossed the nasty tissue in the trashcan but made no move to get up.

"You don't understand, Tyler. I'm not cut out for this. This ain't my thing. I never wanted to be a wedding planner. I didn't want to deal with crazy brides and their emotions and their expectations. I can't do this."

I squatted beside him and sighed. "Chaz, we all feel like that sometimes. This job carries a lot of responsibility. A lot of stress. It's kind of like the pack mule position, ya know? We don't bake the cake, we don't play the music, and we don't make the bouquets. But if any of it goes wrong—even the weather—we get blamed for it. It's just the nature of the business. But you wouldn't be this upset if you didn't care about the bride and her special day. Look, we do whatever we can to make it absolutely perfect. But when something goes wrong, the bride depends on us to be behind the scenes fixing it or working around it. Making it right. You owe it to your bride to get up and figure out the next best thing for her. So she doesn't get the gardens and the blue skies! What else can we do to make it just as memorable and just as fantastic?"

He cocked his head to the side and arched a thin eyebrow. "Tyler, there ain't a thing you or I can do to make this mess fantastic. We have no ceremony back-up. We're screwed."

Oh, how badly I wanted to tell him that *we* weren't screwed. *He* was screwed because he believed his own hype and didn't book a back-up plan. But we're a team. A reluctant team, but a team. My mind had already been churning all the possibilities since last night when I found out today's forecast and learned he had no back-up. I tossed out my best idea to him.

"Okay. The reception hall has a stage on one end. Let's just have the caterer adjust the tables to give us a center aisle, and we'll go ahead and seat all the guests at the tables and have the ceremony on the stage. We have about an hour before ceremony time, so if we call the caterer now, they should be able to have all the tables set with linens. They can always place silverware and water glasses after the guests are seated if need be. Wine glasses can be poured and passed. So we just need to get the florist to move everything from here to there, and we need to have someone stationed here to direct arriving guests over to the reception area. Maybe a park staff member could do that for us. I'll call the minister and let him know. He's probably already in the parking lot, actually. I saw the violinist in her car, so I'll tell her on my way out. I've got to try to find the chair guys to get them to load those chairs before they get soaked. Now, you have to get up off your ass and dry your tears so you can go present a big ole smile to the bride and let her know the new plan."

He sat there with his mouth open just a bit, his eyes wide with amazement.

"Holy shit, Tyler. How do you do that? You see, that's why you should be doing this job, and I shouldn't. I would never have thought of that in the first place, and if I did think of it, I wouldn't have remembered all those other details. Wow."

I smiled as I extended my hand and pulled him up.

"I tell you what, dude. You go do what you do best and schmooze the bride, and I'll do what I do best and solve problems behind the scenes."

"Deal."

Chaz bent to splash his face as I exited the bathroom, nearly scaring the crap out of some poor man who assumed he had entered the ladies room when he saw me.

Senior event planner, my ass. What a joke.

Tuesday, February 11th

Lillian and Laura invited us to come to Lakeside Gardens tonight for a cocktail reception and a big announcement. They told us we could bring dates, so I asked Cabe. Since I started working weddings he has pretty much accompanied me to every social work function we've had, so everyone in the office knows who he is. Well, except Chaz and Charlotte have never met him.

I felt strange about asking now that we're doing the whole 'slow down' thing, but when I asked, he simply said, "Sure! What time?"

Wow. No big deal, and here I was obsessing about it.

He nearly took my breath away when I opened my door. He wore a dark purple button-down shirt with a purple and gray paisley tie and dark gray slacks. His curls were slicked back away from his forehead, which only served to accentuate those incredible baby blues of his. He had a bit of a goatee happening, which I've seen him do before and have always liked. Although I have to admit when I saw it tonight, my first thought was whether or not it would tickle. Boy, the myriad of sensations that mental image caused.

Our arrival caused quite a stir, and it seemed everyone had a comment to share with me.

"Oh honey," Chaz said the moment we were alone together. "You did not mention the absolute divineness of this specimen when we talked before. Girl, you let *that* move cross country with another woman? You need your head examined."

Next it was Lillian when we ended up in the restroom at the same time. "So, you two seem back to being cozy. Patch things up, did you?" I nodded and exited quickly to avoid another session of Lillian's relationship advice.

"You look so happy, sweetheart," Laura whispered into my ear as she hugged me. "I'm so glad it all worked out."

I felt like the entire office had been following my dating life like a bunch of soap opera groupies.

Mel was the worst of all. She followed Cabe around all night, constantly making little innuendos with clever double meanings. I could have killed her. She is my best friend, but the woman sometimes has no tact and not a clue how to be discreet.

Carmen was there with her husband, Omar, and baby, Lila, excited and upset about returning to the office from maternity leave at the end of this month. She treated Cabe with indifference that borderlined on hostility, still pissed at him for leaving me to marry Monica.

Then, of course, there was Charlotte. She couldn't keep her eyes off Cabe, and the minute he stepped away to use the restroom, she made a beeline for me.

"Oh my Gawd! He is so hot. I mean, like he is off the charts. Is that who you're dating? Because if not, I would totally give him my number. I mean, not if you're dating him or anything. But are you? 'Cause he is definitely my type."

Luckily, I knew I wouldn't look good in orange or horizontal stripes, and I'd be claustrophobic as all hell in jail, so I just walked away from her without responding the way I wanted to.

I hoped the big announcement would be that Charlotte was leaving us now that Carmen was returning, but Mel seemed to think it had something to do with Chaz. Maybe they had fabricated a title higher than senior event planner just to bestow another promotion on the golden boy. Hell, maybe they were going to make him partner.

Karen and Mitch, Lakeside's owners, circulated among the crowd greeting each new arrival. I could tell Karen had been crying, but she smiled graciously as she hugged everyone and remarked on the snazzy attires.

Cabe rarely left my side, although I am sure it had as much to do with avoiding Mel and Chaz as staying next to me. His hand either stroked the small of my back or intertwined with mine the whole night. His touch coursed through me like adrenaline. My nerves jittered on edge with the anticipation of the big announcement, anxiety over the state of our relationship, and bitchiness over Charlotte's constant ogling of Cabe. I couldn't stand still for long and found it hard to smile and make small talk with the various industry peers who had been invited.

I felt relieved when Lillian and Laura finally took the stage and called everyone to attention as Karen and Mitch joined them.

Laura took the microphone and spoke while Lillian looked on with a rare beaming smile. "Since Karen and Mitch built Lakeside Gardens, it has been the premiere ceremony destination in Central Florida. We have been privileged to be the event planning company of choice for their brides, and now we are excited to announce we have purchased the property and business from Karen and Mitch. Welcome to the beginning of a new chapter for Lillian and Laura, Inc."

Shock and applause rippled through the crowd as Lillian and Laura hugged Karen and Mitch and accepted the crowd's words of congratulations.

Karen wiped her eyes with a tissue and took the microphone Laura offered.

"It's been an amazing journey to build this property and watch it grow. Mitch and I had a dream to create a place of beauty and serenity where brides and grooms could start their lives together. We've fulfilled our dream, and it's time for us to move on. As many of you know, we have two adorable grandbabies in Oregon, and we will be moving there this spring to be full-time Nonna and Papa. We will miss you all, but we know we are leaving Lakeside Gardens in the best possible hands with these ladies and their team."

The rest of the night flew by in a blur of champagne toasts, congratulations, shared laughter and work stories. I was quite tipsy as Cabe walked me to his car, and I was relieved he had chosen not to drink since I was in no shape to drive.

He walked me to my door and unlocked it for me as I wrapped both arms around his neck, my stilettos slapping the back of his neck from where they dangled on my thumb.

"Cabe, will you stay with me tonight?" I asked.

He closed his eyes and leaned his forehead against mine.

"I'll probably be asleep in five minutes anyway," I said. "I just want to be with you. I want to fall asleep in your arms and wake up next to you. Please?"

He kissed me then, the familiar fire sparking deep within me and unfurling at his touch. Somehow he reached down and swept me off my feet, carrying me through the door in his arms without ever letting his lips leave mine.

He carried me straight to my bed, laying me down gently before straightening to loosen his tie. I moved to kneel in front of him, nudging his hands aside to tug the silk free from his neck.

My head swam with dizziness, in part from the alcohol but more from the absolute intoxication of his touch. His taste. The scent of him. His warmth against me.

The residual pain of losing him intensified my need to connect. To be close. I didn't want anything to separate us. I unbuttoned his shirt and pushed it from his shoulders before pulling my dress over my head and leaning forward to mold my skin against his body.

He inhaled with a bit of a groan as he slid his arms around me, his touch blazing a trail of fire on my bare skin. With a quick flick of his thumb, he unfastened my bra, removing the lacy barrier from between us.

I moved to press against him again, my nipples taut from the sudden exposure to the air and yet warmed by the heat from his chest. I twisted my fingers into the long curls at the back of his neck and pulled him to me, but our mouths only met for the briefest of moments before he bent his head to nuzzle behind my ear. Anticipation coursed through me as he kissed along the curve of my neck, and I thought I would explode by the time he finally closed his mouth over my breast. His tongue teased at my nipple—nibbling, licking, tugging, and releasing. Creating sensations that emanated out across my body like wildfire. I buried my hands deeper in his curls and arched toward him, whispering his name in a moan and a plea.

He tensed for a moment, and I thought he might pull away. Shut us down again and put the wall between us. But then he groaned, and his touch grew more frantic, more urgent. In that moment, he surrendered. I felt it. I knew I could push him wherever I wanted to go tonight.

But somehow knowing that calmed me. It eased my fears. Cabe still wanted me. He still needed me. I was certain of that. But he had wanted to wait. He needed time, and I knew that, too.

Without a doubt, he was worth waiting for, and I would do anything to keep from losing him again.

"I'll wait," I whispered as he kissed his way down my stomach, his hands on my hips caressing my skin. He didn't stop at first, so I tugged at him and said it again, a bit louder this time. "I'll wait, Cabe."

He looked up then, and the desire I saw burning in his eyes sent shockwaves tingling through me. It matched my own desire, an ache desperate to be satisfied. I could feel my pulse pounding between my legs.

He pushed me back onto the pillows and eased himself onto the bed.

"God, I want you, Tyler," he whispered against my skin as he bent over me.

His tongue. His mouth. His hands. It was torture and pleasure all at the same time. He tasted and teased his way across my ribs, plundered my bellybutton, and nearly drove me insane with his feather-light kisses along the lacy edge of my panties, lingering on each hip bone as I writhed beneath his touch.

I moaned as he slid the lace down, his tongue following his fingers as he went. He continued his journey of kisses down my leg as he took the panties off and tossed them aside. He paused for a moment to look at me.

I swear if he had said he was going home right then, I may have killed the man. Luckily for him, he didn't. A slow, seductive grin played across his face, and his voice was husky when he spoke.

"You are so damned beautiful. You have no idea what you do to me. What you mean to me."

He dipped his head between my thighs then, and I nearly lost my mind. I swear this man has talents I never knew existed.

I'd have to say I reached ecstasy in record time. It felt like he'd been there for mere seconds before I screamed out, arching my back and allowing the deep spasms to wash over my body. I fell limp back to the bed, my hands grasping at his curls as he rose from between my legs and kissed his way across my hipbones and back up my stomach. I yelped and pulled away when his lips tugged at my nipple, too sensitive for any further sensations. He chuckled and buried his face in my neck, wrapping his arms around me while I trembled against him and breathed deeply to slow my racing heart.

He shifted onto his back, pulling me with him so that I lay somewhat across him with my head on his chest. I wanted to just drift away into the most completely relaxed state I'd been in for years, but I couldn't. I desperately wanted to give him the same intense pleasure he'd given me.

I traced the line of hair down the middle of his stomach, circling his navel with my finger as his heartbeat quickened beneath me. I ventured just beneath the waistband of his pants, dragging my fingertip slowly across his abdomen. His sharp inhale empowered me, and I dipped my finger even lower the second time across. The bulge in his pants moved slightly in response to my touch, and I watched it in fascination as I unhooked the waistband and slowly pulled the zipper down.

It was Cabe's turn to moan as I moved my tongue down the path my finger had taken, pausing here and there when I hit a particularly sensitive spot. With every tremble and every groan, my efforts intensified. I wanted him shaking. I wanted him aching. I wanted him to cry out my name, to lose his mind in the moment because of me. I wanted there to be no doubt of whether or not we had crossed the friendship line.

My hands shook as I knelt beside him to pull his pants over his hips. I couldn't help but think how stupid I'd been all this time. How could I have not noticed this man? How could I have spent so much time with him and never seen the beauty of his body?

The perfectly chiseled abs honed from years of surfing. The strong biceps and pecs from paddling out through the waves. The long, lean thighs and tight, muscular calves. The tantalizing V between his hipbones inviting me to explore.

And explore I did. I took my time, too. My every movement was focused on appreciating him, pleasuring him, and telling him with my mouth what my words had failed to say all these years. I moved slowly at first, reveling in the intimacy of the act, my tongue alternating the rhythm and adjusting ever so slightly to match his reactions. But then he began to move with me, and I quickened my pace until his entire body tightened and convulsed in release. He cried out my name, just as I'd hoped he would.

I can't deny I experienced a small twinge of pride in knowing I could make him react that way, and I crawled back up his body like a satisfied cat who's caught her prey. I settled myself on top of him with his arms wrapped around me, my head nestled under his chin, and the length of our bodies interwined.

Our weeks of starting and stopping had brought us both to the edge, and we trembled in the aftermath of the pent-up tension, completely spent and unwilling to move.

I marveled at the depth of the emotions flowing through me. I had never experienced anything like the passion between us. I had no idea physical intimacy could be so intense. So fiery. So all-encompassing. It was as if every feeling I had for Cabe, every emotion I'd been wrestling with, was intensified and centered in the pleasure we'd given each other.

I snuggled closer to him, and he tightened his arms around me, kissing the top of my head. Had it had been the same for Cabe? After all, he'd wanted to wait, to slow down. I knew I'd probably pushed him tonight, even though I offered to wait before desire swept us away.

"You okay?" I asked, wanting to be assured I hadn't screwed anything up.

He opened his eyes and smiled at me. "More than okay. Pretty freakin' fantastic. And you?"

"No complaints here," I said, refraining from adding '*why the hell haven't you done that sooner?*'

He leaned forward to kiss me, and I stretched against him so our lips could touch.

"You're going to be the death of me, girl."

I pulled back to look at him, doubts creeping in to cloud my serenity in the aftermath of ecstasy. "I'm sorry."

Surprise crossed his face and then he squeezed me tighter to him, covering my lips with his before he lifted his head and kissed my forehead gently. "Don't be, Ty. I *do* want things to be right between us before we go too far. But I'm also human. Red-blooded male, if you will. I can only resist your temptation for so long. Tonight, I wanted you more than I wanted what's right. I needed you. To touch you. To taste you. To give you some inkling of how much you mean to me."

I smiled at his words and how closely they echoed my own thoughts.

"Well, you certainly accomplished that," I whispered, and he kissed me again.

He yawned, and I weighed whether I wanted to ask questions or allow him peace. I chose the latter when he reached to turn off the lamp.

The alcohol combined with the orgasm had made me drowsy and relaxed, but I don't think I ever really went to sleep. I drifted in and out of consciousness, unable to ignore Cabe's presence next to me.

I wanted to stay there with him forever, but eventually I had to get up to pee and brush my teeth. So now I'm watching him sleep as I write this. Mesmerized by the steady rise and fall of his chest in the moonlight through the window. The relaxed, peaceful expression of his face in sleep. The curve of his abs and the thin, dark blond line of hair trailing down his stomach and disappearing beneath the sheet. The stray curl splayed across his forehead, and the others safely tucked behind his ears.

I love him so much it hurts.

I am his. Completely his. I don't think I can ever let go.

Wednesday, February 12th

Cabe texted me around noon to remind me we have animal shelter duty this evening. I had totally forgotten about it, and I think he may have, too. He didn't mention it last night or this morning before he left.

It would have been awesome to be prepared and have a change of clothes. A two-piece suit and a pair of pumps is not exactly the best attire for bathing dogs.

We were on our third dog bath, a huge St. Bernard mix named Hank. I was pretty much already soaked to the bone from the first two baths, but at least my heels had been safely stowed in the car. I had crouched beside Hank holding his leash, whispering what I thought were calming words while Cabe held the water hose and applied the shampoo. Just when we got him completely lathered, Hank gave a huge, enthusiastic shake to rid himself of the suds. The shock of being doused with cold water and soap suds stunned me, and I stood and covered my face instinctively.

Unfortunately, I dropped the leash in the process, and Hank took off like greased lightning. Who knew a dog that size could move so fast? As if it wasn't bad enough that I'd let the leash go, it turns out I'd failed to latch the gate securely when I put my shoes in the car. So Hank had escaped and was running full speed ahead down the narrow two-lane road with Cabe in hot pursuit.

"He'll come to your car," the shelter volunteer yelled from behind me. "If you run after him, he just runs faster. Take your car!"

I sprang to action and jumped into my car, oblivious to the sopping wet mess I created on my seat. I peeled out of the parking lot and passed Cabe, whose athletic build proved no match for Hank when it came to running.

I saw Hank veer into the large yard on the corner of the upcoming intersection. I turned right after a slow roll through the stop sign and searched for the big soapy mutt on either side of the road. He was behind a bush a few houses down, and I pulled off the road and jumped out to catch him. I recoiled in my pain when my bare feet hit the sharp stones along the edge of the highway, and my loud, high-pitched yelp caused Hank to run again.

I got back in the car and followed him to the next house, where he stopped to take a massively huge dump on their lawn. I figured I could get him while he was pooping, but just as I opened my door, he turned and headed straight toward the car. I leaned over and opened the passenger door in time for him to leap inside.

Hank quickly realized the passenger side wasn't big enough for him, so he squeezed his huge, wet, soapy body over the console and proceeded to dance in circles in the back seat. His wet fur had collected dirt and mud all along his escape route, and as he flopped around the back of my car, bits and pieces of it flung against the windows, doors, and even the headliner where he used his height to rub his head back and forth. It wasn't until I reached across the passenger seat to pull the door closed that I realized dirt and mud wasn't all he was slinging.

Hank's bowel movement had not been clean cut, and the fragrant aroma filling my car triggered my gag reflex and made my eyes water.

Cabe reached the car and opened the passenger door as I screamed in outrage at the disgusting destruction of my vehicle. He had already climbed in to sit down before the stench hit him.

"Whoa, what the hell?" He immediately got back out, as did I. We both stood outside the car staring at Hank in the back seat, happily panting away as he licked dirt off the window and gazed out at me.

"What am I going to do about my car?"

Cabe cracked up laughing, though I failed to see the humor in the situation. "I don't know, but I'm damned sure walking back to the shelter."

"Cabe! My car is covered in dirt, mud, water, and shit! What am I going to do?"

He couldn't stop laughing long enough to answer me.

"Here," I said. "I'm going to open the door to grab his leash and walk him back. You drive my car."

He stopped laughing then. "No way. I'm not riding in there. I'll walk him back."

"Cabe, I can't get back in there. I'll puke. I swear."

He wiped tears from his eyes as he bent over in another fit of laughter.

"It's not funny! My car is seriously messed up."

Hank jumped from the back seat to the front seat as we discussed the situation.

"No! Not my driver's seat!"

Cabe was laughing so hard he could barely stand. I didn't find it so funny. Not then and not now.

"Look, Ty. He's already in your car. It's already messed up. Let's just take him back and we'll go clean out your car." He tried to keep a straight face but failed. I had no choice. It had to be done.

With Hank in the back, we drove together with the windows down, coughing and gagging the whole way. We hosed him down and got him settled in his kennel. The staff members apologized and offered me cleaners to use in my car, which still reeks after two hours of scrubbing, vacuuming, and disinfecting.

I finally made it home and took off the wet, stanky, mud-and-feces-encrusted suit and threw it in a plastic bag, which I promptly carried to the dumpster downstairs. No amount of dry cleaning would have helped that outfit.

I took a hot shower, allowing the warmth to cleanse my skin of the afternoon's funk, but it became a bit of overkill after being wet for the last several hours.

Maybe I need to concede on this one. A dog may not be a good idea after all.

Friday, February 14ᵗʰ
Valentine's Day

I get that Valentine's Day is a made-up holiday probably invented by companies who sell cards and candy. But in my line of work, it's kind of a big deal. We had seven weddings today back-to-back: two ceremonies only, three ceremonies and receptions, and two receptions only. I was pretty much involved in some aspect of all of them. I did the four ceremonies at Lakeside, then raced across town to help set up Laura's reception while she did her ceremony, and then came back to this side of town for the last two receptions. Throughout the entire day of hearts, cupids, and lovey-dovey smoochfests, I heard not one single word from the man in my life. No text. No call. No card. No flowers. Not a single balloon or hand-scribbled note.

Now granted, he came and got my car while I was at the office yesterday and drove it to the dealership to be professionally cleaned and disinfected, which I appreciated.

But today was freakin' Valentine's Day.

He coulda called. He coulda texted. He could have let himself into my apartment and been waiting for me to crawl home from work exhausted, only to find him waiting with a nice, hot bath and maybe champagne and chocolates. Perhaps a foot massage and a carnal favor or two.

But no.

Not a word.

I guess this is where the whole slowing down kicks in?

Are we slowing down for Valentine's Day?

So you can kiss me, hold me, hug me, taste me, sleep next to me, and wake up in my bed any other night, but today necessitates radio silence?

I'm sorry, but I'm pissed. I'd like to be a big enough person to say the holiday means nothing, or to acknowledge that in some weird-ass technical sense of the word, we're not actually in a dating relationship.

But let's consider for a moment that every year that I've known this man, he's given me something for Valentine's Day. Well, except last year when he lived in Seattle. With Monica.

But other than that, *every single Valentine's Day* since I met Cabe, I've gotten chocolates or balloons or a stuffed animal or something. Even flowers one year if memory serves me right. Plus he has *always* given me a card.

All those years, we were just friends. Not dating. Not smooching and hugging and groping each other's private parts or kissing the most intimate of places. Nope. Just friends, and yet we were Valentines.

So how in the hell does it make sense to not hear one peep from the son-of-a-bitch today?

I get he needs time. I get he needs space.

Okay, you know what? No, I don't. I wrote that because I felt like I'm supposed to get it, but I don't. It makes no sense to me in any way whatsoever that he could supposedly have feelings for me all this time, and obviously have some sort of feelings for me now, but yet not be sure if he wants to act on those feelings or pursue them. And at the same time, not want to abandon it or let it go.

So no, I don't get it. But I'm trying to.

What I really don't get is how I'm supposed to just keep reacting to whatever bullshit he throws out without losing my freakin' mind!

He loves me, he loves me not. Except he's never even said he loves me at all.

You know what? Screw Valentine's Day. And screw Cabe. I'm sick of this whole situation.

But I really wish he'd call.

Saturday, February 15th

I don't think I've ever wanted to quit my job before today. I mean, there may have been days I was frustrated, or a particular bride may have pushed me over the edge. But I seriously was ready to just walk away from it today.

I realize part of this stems from still being tired from yesterday, and then having five more weddings back-to-back today, along with knowing I have three more tomorrow. So physical exhaustion is definitely a factor.

Then there's the mental and emotional crap I have going on with Cabe's hot and cold emotions and the fact that he didn't call or text again today. Didn't answer my texts or the voice mail I left earlier tonight. He's pulled another one of those drop off the face of the earth moves, and I don't know whether to be scared or mad. I guess I'm both.

But the final bride of the evening topped it all off for me and made me want to tell the entire world to screw off.

It rained all day today. A rare, weather anomaly where it pretty much poured non-stop all day. Never happens in February in Florida. But it happened today. On the Saturday of Valentine's Weekend. The equivalent of Wedding Hell Day Two. Happy-happy-joy-joy.

I had shuffled umbrellas back and forth from the chapel to the parking lot before and after every wedding. Escorting people from their cars or buses inside before each ceremony and then escorting them back out afterward. Does no one ever pack an umbrella for vacation or think to pick one up in the hotel gift shop? I mean, I get that you're coming to the Sunshine State, but come on, people. It rains here, too.

The downside of all this escorting back and forth—besides my feet and shoes being soaked beyond measure all damned day—is that while I'm walking alongside wedding guests and members of the wedding party, I'm holding the umbrella over *them*. Which means I am fully exposed to the weather and soaking wet. All damned day.

My hair dripped and hung in my eyes. My mascara ran down my face and left what may end up being a permanent smudge on my cheeks. My wet bra chafed against my wet skin and rubbed it raw underneath my breasts. My feet wrinkled and shriveled and turned that sickly white color like when you've been in the tub too long. Oh, and did I mention I was freezing cold all day? We had the heat running inside, but when you're soaking-flipping-wet and spending so much time outside in the rain, you just never really get warm.

So the last wedding of the day became a goal I worked toward with a coal miner's determination. Just keep digging. Keep walking. Keep going, and there'll be light at the end of the tunnel.

Glenda was Melanie's bride. The train of her gown stretched so long it literally needed its own umbrella. The wind had picked up as we escorted her down the sidewalk from the parking lot, so we had one umbrella on each side of her one shielding her back in addition to the one over her train. Melanie held the one over the train as she followed the bride; Renee the florist and her assistant Addie held the ones on each side with Renee also balancing the one over the back of the dress. I walked in front of the bride holding one over her head and veil and the other at an angle to keep the wind from blowing rain in her face or on the front of her gown. Drops of cold rain pelted my face as I walked, and I sputtered and blinked trying to breathe and see where I was going.

It worked, and thanks to the efforts of our amazing team juggling six umbrellas over her, Glenda went down the aisle as dry as a bone. Even her shoes had been protected from the water in a plastic bag her mother carried, so once we dried her feet with a towel, she had nary a damp spot head to toe.

The rain lightened up by the end of her ceremony, and I could send a couple of guests out to the waiting bus on their own and then collect the umbrellas from the bus driver each time I went across.

By the time the photographer finished pictures, the rain stopped altogether, and I had already completed all my closing duties except turning out the lights and locking the doors. I was literally counting down the minutes until they were out of there and I could come home, take off my wet suit, peel off my wet panties, and wrap myself up in a nice, warm robe with a glass of wine.

Glenda stood touching up her make-up in the foyer mirror as she waited for her groom to exit the restroom, and she turned to me and asked if I was coming to the reception. In my head, I shouted, "Lord, no!" and whispered prayers of thanks that my day was done and I was about to go home. But my outward self smiled politely and said, "No, I'm headed home to take a shower and get out of these wet clothes. But thank you for asking."

"Oh, I wasn't asking you to come," she said as she applied her blood-red lipstick. "I was hoping you weren't. You look horrible. It's bad enough my guests had to see you here. I didn't want you at my reception."

My mouth dropped open, and I let it. I couldn't believe the nerve of the bitch to say that to me after I, along with my co-workers, had slopped through the rain to protect her gown, her hair, and her guests. After I sat there dripping water on the carpet and shivering while I dried her freakin' feet so they wouldn't be damp when she put her shoes on.

Ugh. It makes my blood boil again just thinking about it.

I wanted to tell her exactly what I thought of her. I wanted to go off on her with all the vehemence, anger, frustration, and angst I have bottled up inside me right now. It's not just her, but rather a combination of everything that's been going on.

I am sick of feeling unappreciated, unvalued, unwanted, unseen, unloved. I am about ready to tell all these ungrateful, disrespectful, self-absorbed people where they can stick it. The brides, the guests, Cabe, Chaz, even the idiot who went inside to get food and shoot the breeze with the cashier while I was waiting to pump gas on the way home tonight. All of them can just kiss my fat patootie.

I came this close to quitting and walking away from that bride tonight. But I knew that would affect me volumes more than it would affect her. She'd just go to her party and fly home in a few days. I'd end up broke and homeless.

Why do they always seem to get their way? Why can the tide never just turn my way and stay there? Even once!

Sunday, February 16th

I finished my wedding shifts a little before six tonight (without any rain, thank you, Lord!) and went straight to bed without even eating dinner. I dozed on and off, watching bad reality television between snoozes.

Cabe finally called around nine. My anger had built over the weekend, starting with the no-call no-show from him on Valentine's Day, increasing with the rain-fueled day of misery on Saturday, and reaching a pinnacle with Glenda the Witch Bride on Saturday night. I was irritable and short-tempered all day today, which I'm sure came across to at least some of my unfortunate wedding guests.

I was so mad I actually hit the ignore button and let Cabe's call go to voice mail. My hands shook as I dialed to retrieve his message, seething inside with hurt and anger.

Hey, Ty. Look, I'm really sorry about this weekend. I had some family members come into town unexpected. It kind of messed up the whole weekend, and I'm sorry. I know you're probably pissed at me, and you have every right to be, but I just wanted to let you know I didn't mean to disappear again. I know I said I'd communicate with you, and I meant it. I just…well, this family thing just hit me out of nowhere. I want to talk to you. Tell you about it. Call me back.

I didn't, which, I must say, felt extremely satisfying and empowering.

I mean, come on. You didn't call me all weekend because you had *family in town?* Really? You couldn't even return a text? Make a quick call to say you had company?

I've never known him to lie, so I believe he had something going on with family, but talk about rude, inconsiderate and disrespectful. To just blow me off without a word because he had family in town?

I'm sick of being on the crap end of the stick. Let him sit there and wonder where I am and why I'm not calling for a change.

Monday, February 17th

He called again this morning before I left for work, and again about twenty minutes after I got to the office. I didn't answer.

I planned to call him back once I got settled in, but Lillian came in the kitchen area while I was fixing my coffee and asked me to follow her to the conference room.

My curiosity turned to worry when I saw Laura sitting at the conference table with paperwork on the table in front of them. When Lillian closed the door behind us, my stomach flipped and twisted into a knot. I first thought maybe Glenda had complained about me or maybe I'd been ruder to guests on Sunday than I thought.

My shoulders slumped as I took the seat they offered and prepared to take my reprimand. I reminded myself not to cry and to be respectful. I couldn't help but think this felt like one more straw on the camel's back. My temper simmered, ready to blow, but my bosses' office wasn't the time, the place, or the audience for it.

"Don't look so scared, sweetie." Laura smiled. "We didn't call you in here for bad news."

I forced a grin and nodded, but I know my eyes still looked like a deer caught in crosshairs.

"We have been planning to talk to you for some time," Lillian said, "but we thought perhaps we would get everyone past Valentine's weekend and then talk if we all survived."

They both laughed and I tried hard to join them, but I just couldn't muster it up. I think something may be seriously wrong with me. I may have flipped on a bitch switch I don't know how to turn off.

Laura's next words surprised me and caught me off-guard.

"We've been so impressed with your performance, Tyler. You do so well thinking on your feet, rolling with the punches. You have a knack for seeing the big picture and at the same time being able to focus on the smallest of details, and that is a gift."

"You can't teach that," Lillian added.

"No, you can't," Laura agreed. "You either have it or you don't. You do. You've shown us you're able to perform well under pressure, especially under the tremendous circumstances of this past weekend, although we had already made our decision long before that."

Decision? What decision? It sounded like something good, but I'm always a little wary of people making decisions about me without actually including me in the process.

"As you know, Laura and I have just purchased Lakeside Gardens, and we feel to ensure the best experience for our couples and their guests, we need to have one person in place to manage the property and its ceremonies. Someone who knows the building inside and out—the logistics, the best processes. Someone who can manage people in such a way that we can maximize the number of ceremonies produced in a day without overlap and delays."

I nodded as my brain raced ahead of their words and guessed the outcome. They were going to offer the position to me, and I already knew I didn't want it.

I mean, any time your bosses are offering you a position and lavishing praise upon you in the process, it's a good thing, right? But I just spent an absolutely miserable three-day weekend at Lakeside Gardens. I had been assigned most of the ceremonies there for the past year. They were right about me knowing the property inside and out. I had more experience at Lakeside than anyone else in the office.

But they weren't necessarily good experiences.

"Lillian and I would like for you to be that manager," Laura said. She smiled like she was presenting me with the biggest blue ribbon at the fair. "It would be a salary increase, of course, and we'd need to look at how we'd reassign any files you have now which conflict with bookings already made. But we feel this would be a great fit for your skills."

My brain fired in seventy different directions, and I hoped one of those signals had reached my mouth and formed a smile.

I didn't want to appear ungrateful or uninterested, but I definitely needed to process what they were offering me before I replied.

"Can I think about it?"

"Well, sure you can. We'd like to have you in place when you come back from your birthday trip, so if you could give us an answer by the end of the week, that would be great. Do you have any questions?" Laura smiled, and I saw concern in her face that indicated I may not have pulled off a convincing smile.

"I'm sure I do, but it's just all so unexpected. I think I have to get my thoughts together before I know what to ask." I realized after I spoke that my Southern accent had kicked in full-on, which says a lot about the condition of my brain at the time. I don't revert to those speech patterns unless I'm in extreme situations. Drunk. Or mad. Or stressed beyond normal levels.

"Of course, of course." Laura nodded and glanced to Lillian, who was looking at me like I'd just refused to curtsy to the queen.

"I mean, I'm really grateful. Thank you so much for considering me. For your kind words about my performance." I scrambled to do damage control. "I'm just a little overwhelmed coming off the weekend and getting this news. I'm honored, really. I am. Thank you so much. I'll figure out if I have any questions and get back to you before the end of the week. Thank you again."

I stood and backed my way out of the room, smiling the whole way. My mind raced as I walked back to my office in a daze. Then without any thought or consideration as to whether or not I was still mad at him, I called Cabe and asked him to meet me for dinner. He's so good at laying out pros and cons and helping me see an issue from different angles. Whether he's acted like an ass or not, I trust him and I need his opinion.

Okay, maybe that was an excuse. Maybe I just wanted a reason to see him despite all that's happened. Who knows?

Tuesday, February 18th

My nerves damned near crackled with excitement at the anticipation of seeing Cabe last night, due in part to the job offer stress, I'm sure, but also because I hadn't seen him in almost a week, and I missed him. My anger at him had subsided quite a bit with the whole work thing occupying all available channels in my brain.

"So it's a promotion?" he asked when we'd gotten our appetizers and I'd explained their offer.

"I think so? I'm not sure. I mean, it's more money, yeah. But I'd just be doing the ceremonies. So to me, it's *not*, really, because it's almost like a demotion from handling entire events."

"They've been giving you more full weddings on your own, right?"

"Yeah. I thought I was working my way up to being a senior and eventually I wouldn't be assisting at all, just working my own files. But now I guess I'm sidelined." I broke off a piece of bread and shoved it in my mouth. My appetite had been almost non-existent since Valentine's Day, but it was like being with Cabe suddenly signaled my body that we'd survived a drought and sustenance was available. I was ravenous. Like I couldn't get enough food and get it fast enough.

"Well, do you *want* this job? Do you even like doing just ceremonies? You've always sounded like you enjoy the planning aspect. How much of that would you be doing?" He motioned the waitress to bring more bread and poured me another glass of wine.

"For the ones with only a ceremony, they may have me book and confirm vendors, which is minimal. But the event manager would plan everything for the full-scale weddings, even with me doing the ceremony. I don't know if I'd be included in any planning sessions at all. Good question to ask."

I wrote it down in the notebook I'd brought for that purpose.

"Ask how this affects your line of growth for future positions. Will it help you reach senior planner, or would this essentially pull you out of that path and stick you somewhere else? Where do you go from this position?"

I wrote as he spoke, and I mentally gave thanks for his calm, logical nature. I knew all these things, but he could lay them out so clearly.

We talked throughout the entree service and until they cleared our meal. By the end of the evening, I had several questions outlined to bring to Laura and Lillian, along with a well-defined pros and cons list. I knew I was leaning against accepting the position already, but with Cabe's help I had valid arguments and reasoning I could present to my bosses. Now I just needed the courage to stand up to them and not allow myself to be talked into a job I didn't want.

We walked to our cars silently, each deep in our own thoughts. Just as we reached my car, it dawned on me Cabe hadn't told me about the family visit or why he was AWOL all weekend. I'd been so pissed when he blew me off, but with my focus and worry consumed with the job offer, I'd forgotten to ask about it.

"Oh, what were you going to tell me about the weekend? You wanted to explain about your family?"

He frowned and stuffed his hands in his pockets, shaking his head ever so slightly as he replied. "It can wait. I know you have a lot on your mind, and it's kind of a long story. Another time. Just know I'm sorry and I didn't mean to be an ass. It was just…well, again. It's a long story."

It obviously bothered him, and I felt guilty for monopolizing the conversation all night. It never occurred to me *he* might need to discuss what had happened.

"I'm sorry, Cabe. I didn't mean to be self-absorbed. We can talk now."

"No, it's okay. I'll tell you later."

"You sure? I don't mind listening now."

He shook his head again. "No. Thanks, though. For not being mad and all."

I didn't say anything. After all, I had been mad. I'd been furious. And if it hadn't been for all the work drama, I still would be. The awkward silence stretched until he spoke again.

"So when do you have to give them an answer?"

Smart move on his part. Switch the conversation's focus back on my issue and off his.

"By Friday. They said they want me in place after my birthday trip, which I guess I need to tell them is canceled."

I cringed when I realized I'd just brought up Paris. Neither of us had mentioned the trip since the night at the restaurant when he said he'd cancel it. It was like a healing wound we avoided so it didn't reopen and hurt us both.

Cabe looked down at his shoes and kicked at a non-existent rock on the pavement. I opened my car door and threw my purse inside, cursing myself for bringing it up just as we were leaving. I'd been so focused on the work aspect that it came barreling out of my mouth without much thought for the consequences. More tension added onto everything else.

"I have a confession to make," Cabe said without looking up from the ground.

I leaned against the door frame and braced myself for whatever was about to come. The word confession is rarely followed by something good.

He finally met my eyes and held the stare for a moment. Silent. A little shiver ran across my skin as I squared my shoulders and prepared to hear him out.

"I never canceled Paris."

My eyes flew wide open. "What?"

He shrugged and gave the little half-smile he does when he's embarrassed about something.

"I just couldn't do it. I know it sounds really stupid, but I didn't want to cancel it. I booked it for your birthday. I wanted to take you. To see Paris with you. It just didn't seem right to cancel it."

I didn't know what to say. So I didn't say anything.

He cleared his throat before he continued. "I mean, it was too late to get any money back, you know? Either way, I'd already paid for it. So I guess I just figured maybe...well, I don't know. Again, it's stupid."

"You figured maybe what, Cabe? What were you going to say?"

I held my breath as I waited. I realize it was irrational of me to want him to say what I was thinking, but the heart isn't known to be logical. Obviously some part of him still wanted to go, or he would have canceled the trip. So if he hadn't, we could still go. I could still go to Paris with Cabe for my birthday.

"Cabe, what were you going to say?" I pushed, hoping he'd say what I wanted to hear.

He looked down again. "Maybe we could just go. You know. It won't be like it was gonna be before, but we're still hanging out and stuff. So maybe it wouldn't be so different if we hung out there instead of hanging out here. I mean, if you still wanted to."

I threw both arms around his neck and kissed him with everything I had. I know it's probably a terrible idea to go. I know I probably should have told him no. I probably should have remained calm and not nearly knocked the man down with enthusiasm.

But here's where my heart went with this. If he still wants to take me to Paris, he still wants *this*. *Us*. Which means we have time to work things out before we go. Then I realized how little time that was.

I pulled back so abruptly he nearly lost his balance.

"Cabe! It's only two weeks away!"

"I know. Everything's planned, though. I already had the museum passes and the transportation cards. The hotel and the airfare are booked. The only thing I hadn't done was the Eiffel Tower, and we can book it online. But if we're really gonna do this, we have to take care of that quick. It sells out."

I took his hands into mine and held them there.

"Are you sure you want to do this, Cabe? Are you really sure? Because we don't have to. You don't have to do this for me or because it's my birthday. Or for any reason. We can just not go. I'm fine with that. You being okay is more important to me than going."

He smiled and kissed my hands.

"I want to take you to Paris for your birthday."

So there you have it. I'm going to Paris. For my birthday. With Cabe. My on-again, off-again, might be, may be, could be boyfriend who's somehow not my boyfriend. I'm excited, I think. But nervous, too. I sure hope this turns out to be a good thing.

Friday, February 21st

I marched right into the office today armed with my notes on why the Lakeside management position did not further my interests. Well-rehearsed in how to explain the benefits I offered the company in my present position. Confident in my ability to offer solutions that could help us all achieve our goals.

It took one arch of Lillian's eyebrow and one curt question from her to unnerve me, and before I knew what had happened, I'd accepted the job.

I even ended up thanking them for the opportunity after she explained why it was such a great role for me and how I should be honored to have it.

I don't think you're supposed to feel this discouraged after getting a promotion. I could be wrong, but I thought a promotion was supposed to be a good thing. Maybe somehow it will be. Right?

Saturday, February 22nd

Talk about a first-class royal ass of a bitch. Definitely not one of my favorite brides. Victoria's been a thorn in my side since our very first meeting, and I'm just relieved this wedding day is over. I don't understand what Wyatt sees in her or why he wanted to marry her.

Wyatt's mom, Andrea, refused to come to the wedding for a while in protest of this union, but I guess Wyatt talked her into it.

Victoria retaliated by insisting Andrea not be included in the ceremony processional. Victoria's dad passed away a couple of years ago, and she only had her mother walking her down the aisle behind one maid of honor. Veronica decided Andrea could just be seated with the other guests, but Wyatt disagreed. He wanted his mom involved, so he told Victoria to let her walk by herself in front of the maid of honor.

You could cut the tension with a knife during pre-ceremony pictures. It got so bad the photographer ended early just to escape without bloodshed.

I sent Wyatt and the best man to the altar area with the minister and tried to corral the ladies with no cat fights. I cued the violinist to start the music, but as I told Andrea to start walking, Victoria leaned forward and grabbed her by the arm. She leaned in close to her future mother-in-law and spat her venom so quietly I barely heard the words above the hissing.

"You go ahead and walk down the aisle, and I'll be right behind you. When I get there, I'm gonna marry your son, and you will no longer have any say-so at all, you miserable hag. I will be first in his life, and he will be mine. All mine."

Victoria let go, and Andrea turned to make her way toward her smiling son. He had no way of knowing what words had transpired. For all he knew, his beautiful bride had extended a peacemaking olive branch.

Poor Wyatt. Stuck in the middle between his wife and his mom. That must suck. I feel sorry for him and for Andrea, who cried her way through the ceremony. I feel pretty confident Victoria will be a temporary problem. I don't see this marriage lasting long.

Wednesday, February 26th

Maggie called me around ten this morning to invite me to lunch. I immediately went to Melanie's office.

"Maggie wants to take me to lunch."

Mel gasped and put her hand over her mouth. "Oh wow. Did she say why?"

I shook my head.

"Okay. Well, maybe she misses you and just happens to be in the neighborhood."

I cocked one eyebrow and screwed up my lips to show her how ridiculous that concept was.

"Why on earth would she possibly be in this neighborhood? I've known the woman five years, and she has *never* asked me to lunch before."

"Okay, okay. Don't panic. Wait and hear her out."

"But what if she's going to go off on me like Galen? What if she's mad at me or something? What's she going to say?"

Mel sat back and crossed her arms. "You won't know until you go. Doesn't seem like Maggie's style from what you've told me about her. I don't think she'll be ugly to you."

"Should I tell Cabe? He got really pissed when I didn't tell him about Galen."

"Not until after you hear what she has to say. It may be nothing."

I walked outside when Maggie texted to say she was waiting in the parking lot.

"Hi there! Get in and I'll drive," she called out the window.

My stomach fluttered as I climbed into her Lexus, but she smiled and extended a hug across the console, immediately putting me at ease.

She asked me how work was going, told me about a charity function she

108

was coordinating with the symphony, and asked if I was okay with a nearby French cafe for lunch.

By the time we'd received our salads, I had relaxed, feeling pretty silly for questioning her motives. She'd been nothing but nice since I got in the car. The same old Maggie. No tension, no discomfort. But the moment I let my guard down, it happened.

"So about this Paris trip." She smiled and took a sip of water before continuing. "Are you dead-set on going?"

My lettuce suddenly felt solid in my throat and I couldn't swallow. I gulped several swallows of water, but the lump in my throat lodged tighter. Maybe it wasn't the lettuce.

"Dead-set? I don't know if I'd say that, but we're planning on going."

"Do you think that's a good idea?"

I sat back in my chair and stared at her. Other than Maggie's eyes being green where Galen's were blue—the same blue as Cabe's—Maggie looked like an older version of her daughter. She shared Galen's dark red hair, though Maggie's framed her slender face in soft waves whereas Galen's hung ramrod straight. Maggie's face was softer. Her jawline not as rigid. Her eyes were more compassionate. More soulful. Even now as her challenge radiated across the table at me, it didn't assault me like Galen's. She was protecting her son, just as Galen wanted to protect her brother, but Maggie's approach held more kindness. I sensed a concern for my feelings as well.

"I don't know. What do you think I should do?" She'd obviously brought me here to tell me, so I gave her the floor.

"Well, I can't really answer that, Tyler. I think it's a difficult decision, and I think you both have a lot to consider. I don't pretend to know how you feel or what you want in this situation, but I can tell you I'm worried about Cabe."

I shifted in my seat. I'd been mentally preparing for her anger just in case she went on the attack, but she didn't come across angry. She seemed genuinely worried, which unsettled me more.

"Worried about him? Why?"

"Well, I'm certain he wouldn't be happy to know I'm having this conversation. Especially not with him so angry about Galen right now. So I will leave it to you as to what you choose to share with him. I would never ask you to hide anything from my son."

Did his anger at Galen have anything to do with me? It sounded like it, but I didn't think it would be appropriate for me to ask. I nodded instead and drained the last sip of water from my glass, scanning the room for someone who could get me a refill.

"I've watched the two of you tango for years, Ty. I've seen him pursue you, and I've seen you pursue him. I think you two have a powerful connection, and I think it scares you both. For quite a while, you weren't in a place to fully receive what Cabe was ready to offer. You needed time. You needed healing. Growth. Now, I think the tables have turned and Cabe is not in a place to fully receive what you want to offer. He's dealing with a lot."

Moisture glistened in her eyes, but she looked away and blinked rapidly. When she looked back at me, it had gone, and a fresh determination filled her face.

"Give him time, Tyler. Give him space. I can't make you any promises of what will happen between the two of you, but I can tell you he needs space right now. He needs to breathe without the fear of losing you. This trip is a mistake. It's too much right now."

"I told him he could cancel the trip, Maggie." I crossed my arms and struggled not to feel defensive. Did she think somehow I was making him go? That I was pushing him?

She waited for the waitress to fill my water glass and leave. "I don't think he'd ever back out of it because he knows you want it, and he gave it to you. But I'm telling you, it's a mistake. I know my son very well, Ty. Not as well as you in some areas, I'm sure, but better than you in others. Cabe needs to work on himself. He needs to be alone and process some things. If you love him, and I believe you do, then give him space. Give him room."

"He says he wants to go, Maggie. I'm not forcing him."

She smiled at me, but I could sense frustration hiding behind the curve of her lips. Her eyes didn't even try to fake the smile.

"He wants to make you happy. He wants to keep from hurting you. It doesn't mean he should go."

I wondered how much of this they had discussed. What had he told her that he couldn't tell me?

"Did he tell you this?" I asked.

"We've talked. I don't intend to share details, but suffice to say I wouldn't have called you and asked for this meeting behind my son's back if I didn't feel certain about what I'm sharing with you. I'm fond of you, Tyler. I think you care a great deal for my son, and I know Cabe cares deeply for you. I don't want to see either one of you hurt, and I'm willing to reach out to you to try and prevent it."

What was I supposed to say to that? I didn't want either one of us hurt either. I had my own apprehensions about going to Paris under the circumstances. Was I supposed to tell him I didn't want to go?

I didn't know if I could do that. I wanted to go. I wanted to get him away from here. From Galen. From Maggie, even. They both seemed to be against us being together. I just felt like if we were alone, if we went away together, we could escape all the background noise and connect. Without all the pressure.

Was I wrong? Was she right? Was the trip going to be too much for him, or was it what he needed to see how it could be between us? Why should his mom and his sister get to decide what Cabe and I should do?

I squared my shoulders and forced my voice to sound nonchalant despite the growing burn in my throat. "I appreciate your concern, and I'll think about what you've said. But ultimately, it's up to Cabe what he wants to do."

I wanted to get up and walk out. To get out of there. Her eyes pleaded with me and condemned me at the same time. I couldn't take her stare, and I just wanted to be gone. But I had no car. I had no way back to the office, and we still needed to get the check and pay before we could go. Minutes dragged interminably as we sat in silence.

Finally, she spoke.

"Okay. Well, I tried. You're both adults. Your decisions are your own. Dessert?"

I almost laughed. Her clipped manner belied her disappointment and the offer of dessert provided a mask of politeness which I in turn politely refused.

We rode back to my office without talking, but she reached across the car and gave me another hug before I got out.

Her eyes glistened again, and she smiled at me. "I hope everything works out for the best."

So now the ball is in my court. What do I do? And what do I tell Cabe?

Friday, February 28th

Cabe and I went shopping tonight for cold weather clothes and a few other items for the trip. I wavered all night over whether or not to tell him about my lunch with Maggie. He was in such a great mood, and he seemed genuinely excited. He had been to Paris twice before. Once with his mom and Galen, and again when he took a year off college to backpack across Europe and India.

All night, he described things he wanted to show me, his passionate enthusiasm so contagious I found myself getting pumped up for Paris. But the whole time, Maggie's warnings and the fact Cabe didn't know we talked weighed in the back of my mind, like a slow, blinking red light cautioning me not to fully engage in his excitement.

As we unloaded the shopping bags in my living room and separated out our purchases and receipts, I couldn't hold it in any longer. I felt like a traitor hiding something from him and pretending everything was alright.

"I have something I need to tell you, and I want you to promise you'll stay calm and not get upset."

He froze in the act of folding a shirt and looked at me with confusion. His voice was taut with tension. "I've never understood why people say that. How am I supposed to promise you I won't get upset if I don't even know what you're going to tell me? Not to mention obviously it's going to upset me, otherwise you wouldn't preface it by saying that."

He was right, of course.

"I just don't want you to get all mad or something and it ruin the mood. I've had a really good time with you tonight. I don't want to end it on a bad note, but I also feel like I want to be upfront with you."

He sat down on the edge of the chair, the shirt rumpled and forgotten in his hands. "Go ahead. Shoot."

He was already upset.

"I want you to promise me what I tell you will stay between us, and you won't mention it to anyone."

"You're asking for a helluva lot of promises when I don't have any idea what you're talking about. Just tell me, Tyler."

I took a deep breath and prayed he would take it okay.

"Your mom asked me to lunch on Wednesday."

I could tell he didn't know. It caught him off-guard, and his facial expression changed right away.

"She said she doesn't think we should go to Paris." I exhaled as I said it, the words running together as I rushed to get them all out before he reacted. I barely made it. He stood to his feet pretty much immediately and tossed the shirt aside.

"You're kidding me. Tell me you're kidding. I swear to God if I could just get my family to stay out of my damned life." His jaw tightened in anger, and I could see his pulse pumping at his temple.

I tried to reason with him, although I don't know why I felt the need to defend Maggie. "I think she was just concerned because we haven't been getting along so well, and—"

"I don't care what she was concerned about. She has no business talking to you about my life. She has no business playing puppet master and trying to have other people make my decisions for me. I'm sick of it."

He gathered up his purchases and shoved everything back in the bags.

"Cabe, please don't tell her I told you. I don't want her to be mad at me, and I don't want any tension between the two of you."

"Well, it's a little bit late for that. She's gone too far, and she knows it. But by God, her and Galen are going to learn to stay out of my life. I'm going to make sure of it."

I walked between him and the door, desperate to stop him from leaving that way.

"Wait, Cabe. This is exactly what I didn't want. I don't want you leaving all upset and being mad at your mom. I honestly think she wanted to help. Can you please not say anything to her?"

"No, Tyler. I can't. I'm going to say something to her. I'm going to say a lot to her. You don't even know what all is going on."

I put my hand on his arm but he flinched and jerked it away.

"Then tell me. Tell me what's going on. Let's talk about it. Don't leave upset. Talk to me."

"We're going to Paris. I'm not letting her tell me, or you for that matter, what I can do with my life. Now please step out of the way. I'll call you tomorrow."

Did I do the right thing? Should I have just not told him? He got so mad when I didn't tell him about Galen at the comedy club. I feel like if my mom went behind my back to talk to him, I'd want to know. He got so upset. I knew he wouldn't be happy about it, but I had no idea he'd be so angry.

He commented about Maggie playing puppet master and going too far. He lumped her in with Galen as though the two of them did something to him. What happened? He said I didn't know what all is going on, but I don't know because he hasn't told me! What else has she done? Maybe it has something to do with Valentine's weekend. The long story he never got around to telling. We're supposed to go dancing tomorrow night. Maybe I need to insist he clues me in.

March

Saturday, March 1st

My morning wedding with Lillian went well, and I got done in plenty of time to catch a nap and be showered and ready when Cabe got here.

He was still on edge. I could tell from the moment he walked in the door. I assumed it stemmed from last night and whatever drama may have transpired between him and his mom today. He refused to talk about it, though.

"Are you okay?" I asked as soon as I saw the scowl darkening his face.

"Oh, I'm fine." The sarcasm dripped from his voice.

"You want to talk about it?"

"Nope." He went straight to the pantry, got out the bottle of gin, and immediately mixed a gin and tonic. Not a good sign.

"Maybe we should just get a movie and stay in tonight."

"No. You have a Saturday night with no wedding. We're going dancing. Cheers." He lifted his glass to me and then drained it.

I sat and watched him for a moment, trying to choose my words carefully.

"Maybe going out's not a good idea. Let's just hang here." I added a bit of extra cheer for encouragement.

"I want to go out. You ready?"

I was, before he stormed in and changed the forecast for the evening. His current mood didn't bode well for a great night out.

"Cabe, I think we need to talk. Why don't you tell me what's going on? With Maggie? With your family?"

"My *family*—", he stressed the word with such vehemence that I flinched, "is a dysfunctional, twisted and toxic situation right now. It's not something I care to discuss."

"Okay, but I think it might do you good to talk about it. To get it out. I mean, obviously you're upset. Tell me what happened. I want to understand so I can help."

He laughed, but it held no joy. "To help? Yeah. They're beyond help. *I'm* beyond help. Maybe we're all beyond help."

Wow. Whatever it was had to be serious. To hear him talk like that about his family—about himself—broke my heart and frightened me.

"I wish you'd talk to me, Cabe. I know I've been self-absorbed with the job stuff, and maybe with everything happening between us, I've kind of been oblivious to what you're dealing with, but I'm here. I'm listening. Please tell me why you're so upset."

He looked at me for a few seconds, and I could almost see the wheels churning in his head, deciding whether or not to talk. I thought for a minute he had decided to speak, but then he walked to the door and opened it.

"I want to go dance. Let's go."

In hindsight, I should have refused. I should have insisted we stay in and pushed him to talk. I definitely should have kept him from drinking any more, but I didn't know how it was all going to turn out.

He made a beeline for the bar as soon as we arrived, and he drained a drink and hit the dance floor with a vengeance. I've always been a little bit in awe of Cabe's dance skills. I think he inherited his mom's dancer genes. The man has moves on the dance floor which must be seen to be believed.

So fluid, so natural, so sexy. He exudes confidence and charisma, and it only takes a few moments for him to be completely surrounded. Likes bees to honey. Moths to a flame.

We usually dance tight to each other, though, so when girls try to elbow in, there's not a way to get between us. Even before we started swapping spit these last couple months, we've always pretty much danced with only each other. We have moves. We have steps. We know each other's rhythm, and we move well together.

I mean, we've definitely had nights in the past where one of us had someone else on our radar so we flirted or pursued our own interests. But since things turned more intimate between us, there'd been none of that. The few times we'd been out dancing as a 'couple', he'd had eyes only for me, and his roving hands along with his body moving against mine left no doubt to anyone watching that neither of us was available.

Tonight was different. Cabe danced wild, a man tormented by his own demons. Alone on the crowded dance floor in his own internal world. He stayed near me, but we didn't connect. In fact, I sometimes wondered if he knew I was there. He had turned his back to me for a short portion of the song, and the space between us allowed a guy to step in.

"Hello," the dancing man said loudly. He gave me the appreciative perusal of a man on the prowl and moved in a little closer.

I took a step back as I danced, looking to make eye contact with Cabe, but he kept his back turned as he moved to the beat with his head down. I twisted sideways to ignore the dancing man, but he moved with me.

"What's your name?" he asked. I spun back around with the music, intending to move closer to Cabe, but he was gone. I searched the dance floor for him, but he was nowhere to be found. I made my way through wild elbows and head tosses until I broke free of the dancers. Cabe was standing at the bar, tossing down another drink. I knew I needed to get him to slow down.

"Hey, where'd you go?" I asked him.

"I got thirsty, and you looked busy." He took another swallow and looked away toward the dance floor.

Whoa. I'd never known him to exhibit jealousy. It surprised me and unnerved me. This wasn't the Cabe I knew. I was in uncharted territory.

I didn't see Dancing Man approach until he was already standing between us.

"Hey, I would love to have just one dance with your girlfriend," he said to Cabe. "May I?"

Cabe stared past me and answered Dancing Guy without looking at him.

"She's not my girlfriend. We're just friends. Be my guest." And with that, he drained his drink and walked away.

I couldn't move or speak. Pain ripped through my gut like I'd been sucker punched. Which I guess symbolically I had been. Cabe had just basically denied my existence in his life. My importance. He had denied any feelings he had for me. Any intimacy we had shared. He had pretty much just handed me over to some other guy without so much as even making eye contact with me.

Talk about being hurt. Humiliated. Embarrassed. And pissed.

I didn't know what the hell he had going on in his head. Obviously he was upset. Angry. In pain about something. But since he had neglected to deem me worthy of hearing about it, I had no idea what it was.

Besides, regardless of what was wrong with him tonight, how could it possibly justify him just tossing me aside? Maybe I had been a bit slow on the uptake of realizing my feelings for him, but I had stood by him through thick and thin for years. I'd done everything I could to be supportive and understanding since he started wigging out about our relationship and what it all meant. Even when he pulled away from me and it cut like a knife.

But this? This was bullshit. It was rude. Hurtful. Disrespectful. Demeaning. Degrading.

I realized Dancing Man was still standing there, his hand outstretched to take mine, and I grabbed it wholeheartedly.

"I didn't catch your name," he said as we entered the dance floor.

"Tyler," I growled back at him. Poor man. He had no idea what the hell he had just got caught up in. Now, I admit I probably could have handled the situation differently, but I reacted based on my wounded pride and my battered heart without giving much thought to all the outcomes.

I rocked Dancing Man's world. I made sure to grind against him. I swayed against him. I teased and flirted and tantalized. I never once made eye contact with him, and I never smiled or spoke, but he didn't care. It probably added to the allure.

I knew Cabe was watching. I could feel it. I didn't know why he'd done what he did, but I knew with everything in me he was somewhere watching me and Dancing Man. I casually scanned the crowd, not wanting him to catch me looking. I didn't see him, but I could feel his eyes on me.

So I put on a show. I'm not proud of it, and in hindsight, it only added fuel to a combustible situation, but I was a woman rejected. I exacted my revenge.

Dancing Man never knew what hit him, and he never knew he didn't have a chance in hell of closing the deal dangling in front of him. He was an enthusiastic, unfortunate pawn in my endeavor to punish Cabe for giving me away.

After a while, I had grown tired of the game and repulsed by Dancing Man's advances. Granted, he was only reacting to the signals I gave him, but it was never about him anyway.

I left the floor without even saying goodbye and began to search the club for Cabe. I circled the entire ground floor twice but saw no sign of him. I headed upstairs and looped the balcony area but didn't find him there. My anger battled my fear to see which would dominate my mind.

Had he left me here without a ride home? At first, I rejected that as impossible, but I never thought he would hand me over to a stranger, either.

The thought crossed my mind that perhaps he had taken the whole game a step farther and tucked himself away in a dark alcove making out with some other girl. My stomach turned at the thought, and I became just as wary of finding him as I was of not finding him.

I ended up almost running right into him as he careened out of the men's room, sloshing his drink all over me, him, and anyone else in the vicinity.

"Whoa there," he yelled. "It's Buttercup. What's up, Buttercup?"

He was wasted. Messy, sloppy, beyond drunk wasted.

"Where's your guy, Buttercup? Your dance partner?" He sneered the words and grabbed onto a chair to remain upright.

"You're drunk," I stated.

"No shit, Sherlock." The S's slurred and he sputtered spit.

"Come on," I said. "We're leaving."

"Oh, really? Last time I checked, we came in my car. So I don't think you get to tell me when we're leaving. I'm a little sick of all of you telling me what to do."

"There you are!" Dancing Man came up and put his arms around my waist from behind, and I jabbed an elbow in his ribs without a moment's hesitation.

"What the hell did you do that for?" Dancing Man bent over holding his ribs as he glared at me. "You crazy bitch!"

Cabe lunged for him and slammed him to the ground. At least, I think he did. In all honesty, he may have just fallen on top of the guy.

I pulled at Cabe and begged him to stop as he drew his fist back to punch the stunned Dancing Man. Other club goers grabbed him as well and pulled him to his feet, where he wobbled and put out both hands to try and steady himself.

"I'm sorry," I said to Dancing Man. "I'm just dealing with a situation. Please just leave us alone."

Dancing Man looked for a moment like he had no intention of backing down, but then Cabe stumbled and almost fell flat on his face. I think the dude realized there was no fight to be had. He glared at me again before he walked away, and I truly felt bad for the guy's unwitting role in my drama.

I struggled to get Cabe down the stairs, sure a couple of times he was going to tumble us both ass over teakettle. We were almost to the door when he announced they had his credit card at the bar for his tab.

"I need you to stand right here, okay? Cabe? Are you listening? I need you to stay here. I'm going to get your card, but they're not going to give it to me without you letting them know it's okay. So stand right here, please?" I worried he would freak out over me telling him what to do again, but instead he smiled and took my face in his hands. His breath reeked enough to intoxicate me, and I turned my head to dodge a drunken kiss. "Stay here."

"Yes, ma'am, Buttercup. Whatever you say. I don't want you to elbow me in the ribs." He made a noise that sounded somewhat like his laugh.

I managed to get the bartender to give me his card, but Cabe had to come and sign the tab. I was shocked to see he had consumed six drinks in the past hour. I'd seen him put away a few here and there over the years, but nothing like this. What the hell was he trying to do? I looked at the check again, hoping the bartender had charged him for someone else's drinks by mistake. But there were six gin and tonics. Maybe he had spilled them. Or sat them down and walked away. Undoubtedly, he hadn't consumed that much.

But his condition made it seem highly likely that he had.

The trip to the car took forever, laborious and slow. I couldn't bear his entire weight, and his height made it difficult for me to hold him upright to walk. We had to stop and sit for a few minutes every time we saw a bench, and by the time we got to his car, I was exhausted and aching from head to toe.

I worried the whole time he would refuse to give me the keys, but he handed them over without question and spilled himself into the passenger seat. I couldn't reach the pedals at all, and he laughed as I waited for the BMW's driver seat to move all the way forward.

"You're short." He hiccuped as he said it, and I chose to just ignore him. Just as I had ignored his comments and outbursts of singing the whole way to the car.

He let the window down and leaned his entire upper body out of it as I drove, and I prayed he wouldn't fall out.

"Are you gonna be sick?" I asked when he got quiet and laid his head on the window's edge. He didn't answer me, but I didn't hear any gagging noises so I hoped for the best.

I knew I couldn't get him up the stairs to my apartment, so I went to his place. He had fallen asleep in the car, and I swear his body weighed twice as much as before when he leaned against me. Getting him out of the car and into the pool house nearly killed me. It's a miracle we made it inside without waking Maggie up.

He collapsed across the bed, and I got his shoes off and swung his legs onto the bed, pulling the sheet over him. I thought he had fallen back asleep, but he suddenly opened his eyes and looked right at me. For possibly the first time all night.

"I don't want anyone else to have you, Tyler. I can't bear the thought of it."

Words sprang to my throat in argument about his behavior earlier with Dancing Man, but I swallowed them back down. He was in no condition to argue, and his voice trembled with too much pain for me to attack him.

"No one else has me, Cabe."

"I can't do this. It hurts, and it scares me. I don't deserve you."

My anger ebbed as my heart clenched in response to him. I moved to sit beside him on the bed and pushed his hair off his forehead.

"You're not making any sense."

"No, you have to listen to me, Tyler. You need to stay away from me. I'm messed up."

"Don't say that."

He turned his head away from me. "You don't understand. I'm not good enough for you. You deserve so much better. One day you'll figure that out and be gone."

I knew it was futile to try and make sense of drunken ramblings, but I also desperately wanted to understand what was happening. Obviously, something much bigger than tonight.

"What are you talking about? Talk to me."

He looked back at me with a lopsided smile, his eyes unfocused and bloodshot. "I want to take you to Paris. I want to see Paris with you."

"You will. We're going to Paris next week."

"I can't wait for you to see Notre Dame. I want to take a river cruise with you. I want to see your face when you watch the lights dance on the Eiffel Tower. I want to do everything with you. I want us to do it all." His speech slurred even worse, the words running together like slow molasses.

"We will, Cabe. We will."

"I wish you understood. I wish I could make you understand." He closed his eyes as he said it.

"So tell me. Make me understand. Cabe? Cabe?"

He snored, fast asleep. I repositioned myself to stretch out next to him on the mattress and tried to pull the sheet over my legs.

I heard a deep intake of his breath, and then he turned and kissed the top of my head.

"Don't leave me, Ty. I don't want to lose you." He spoke in barely a whisper, and I would have thought he was talking in his sleep had it not been for the kiss.

"I'm right here, Cabe. You're not going to lose me."

"I can't lose you, and I can't have you." His words drifted off and almost immediately he started snoring again. The loud, grizzly bear snores of someone who has had too much to drink when they finally succumb to sleep.

I lay beside him replaying the entire night in my head. Analyzing every decision. Every word. Every action. What I could have done differently. What I could have said. But no matter how I replayed it, I couldn't get his words out of my head. Why didn't he think he was good enough for me? Why did he think he was going to lose me? Or couldn't have me?

I stayed until just before sunrise without ever falling asleep and slipped out to avoid any morning encounters with Maggie. I left him a note saying I had his car and would bring it back when I woke up.

It's almost seven in the morning now, and I've just showered and am going to try to sleep. What am I supposed to do with all this?

Sunday, March 2nd

I woke up a little after two in the afternoon with a raging headache and a sour stomach. Considering I didn't even drink last night, I hated to think how bad Cabe must be feeling. I shuffled to the kitchen and found my phone dead on the counter, so I plugged it in and considered going back to bed.

The phone beeped as soon as it powered back up. Cabe had texted a couple of times asking if I was awake, and he had left a voice mail.

Hey Ty. Sorry about last night. Thanks for getting me home. Don't know how you managed that, and I hope I wasn't too much of an ass to deal with. At some point, you'll probably need to fill me in on what happened. Although based on what I do remember at the club, I'm not sure I want to know. Your phone's going straight to voice mail, so I don't know if you're sleeping or mad at me. I'm hoping sleeping. I asked Dean to bring me to my car, so don't freak out if you go outside and it's gone. Call me, okay?

My stomach roiled. I wasn't ready to call him. I called Mel instead and asked if I could come over.

"You don't look so good," she said when I walked through her front door.

"Thanks, Mel. Just what I wanted to hear."

"Have you eaten?"

I shook my head.

"You need to eat. Let me fix you something. What do you want?"

"Nothing."

She ignored me and made toast with peanut butter and honey. I ate it like a wild boar, so I guess I was hungry after all.

When I'd poured out the details from last night, she scrunched her face up and said, "Poor Cabe."

"Poor Cabe? What? Really, Mel?"

"Tyler, the guy is obviously dealing with something huge. Surely you can see he's hurting."

"Well, yeah. But so am I. Except he's the one hurting me. I don't know if I can keep doing this, Mel. It's like being on a ride at the fair that makes you sick and thrills you at the same time. One minute you think it's fun, and then the next minute you're begging them to stop the ride and let you off. I think I want off."

"Love doesn't come easy, babe. It's work. Why do you think they vow for better and for worse?"

"I haven't made any vows, Mel. He's never even said the L word. I realize he's going through something, but he won't talk to me. He's always talked to me, told me what was bothering him, or what he was thinking. But I feel like since he came back from Seattle, and especially since we kind of took this a step further. It's so frustrating. I get that it's something with his family, and obviously he's got lingering divorce stuff, but damn, Mel, what am I supposed to do? I want to support him, but at what point do I just say this hurts too much and stop the ride? I can't help him if he won't talk to me."

She sighed and kicked back in her recliner. "He needs to talk to you, for sure. Do you think you could talk to Maggie?"

I shook my head. "Oh, hell to the no! He would be furious. Not only that, but I don't think she'd tell me anything. I think it may have something to do with Galen talking to me at the comedy club, or Maggie taking me to lunch, but I don't get the whole bit about him not being good enough for me and him not deserving me. What's that all about?"

"I don't know. Poor guy."

"Poor guy nothing! Stop saying that! He needs to talk to me. He needs to let me in on whatever's going on instead of pulling me close and then shoving me away. Passing me off to some other guy and then telling me he doesn't want to lose me. Or drinking himself into oblivion. He's lucky he didn't end up in the hospital with alcohol poisoning. What was he thinking?"

Mel put the recliner back down and came to sit on the couch beside me.

"Look, Ty. You've known this guy for how long now? He's never treated you this way before. He's never acted like this before. Something's going on. He's in pain. Men can't talk about their feelings the way we do. It's hard for them to open up."

"But he's always talked to me!"

"Yeah, when you guys were just friends. Now that you've gone beyond that, it makes him more vulnerable. He has something to lose now. You gotta cut him some slack until you know what's going on. You guys are going to Paris this week, right?"

"I don't know, Mel. I'm thinking maybe it's not such a great idea. I mean, what if he acts like this over there? Or what if he decides once we get there he wants to pull the disappearing act again? I don't speak French. How will I find my way around? What about Maggie saying we shouldn't go?"

"Cabe told you he wants to go, right? I say you try not to bring any of this up in the next few days. Take the pressure off, and just leave him be. When you guys get to Paris, you'll have lots of time alone. Away from his family and their crap. It'll be romantic. You'll be staying in a hotel room. Eating croissants. Drinking wine. Who knows? Maybe he'll even finally go all the way. Probably what the man needs. He's got the batter on the brain, messing him up. You just need to throw him down in that hotel room and make him forget all his troubles. Ride him, cowgirl!"

"Oh my God, Mel! Batter on the brain? You kill me!" We both laughed. "It's not like we haven't been doing *anything*, you know? We've fooled around. There's been other…sexual activities. We've both had our share of some happy-ending sessions."

Mel shook her head and smiled at me. "Not the same thing."

"What do you mean, not the same thing? We didn't do any of this stuff when we were friends. I definitely don't pass out any of those types of favors for any of my other friends. We just haven't had actual *intercourse*. For some reason he seems to draw the line at that."

"Because it's different," Mel said. "I'm telling you, intercourse means something more to some guys. It's the grand prize. Everything else is just consolation. Cabe's a tender-hearted guy. A romantic. It's gonna mean something to him."

I rolled my eyes and exhaled.

"Think about this, Ty. You guys have both been dealing with commitment issues since you met. I mean, if me and his sister are right and this guy's been in love with you for five years without having sex with you, it says a lot. It tells me he got companionship, friendship, and fun from you. It was safe. He could love you without any risk and without any commitment. He got his physical needs met with other people he dated, but never really committed to any of them. Well, until Monica."

I flinched at the thought of Cabe's needs being met by other girls, despite the fact I'd been in his life during each of those short-lived romances. My stomach turned at the thought of him with Monica. Now that I'd given into my feelings for him and been intimate with him, it bothered me greatly to think of him being with anyone else.

"Since you guys have acted on your feelings, it opens him up to get hurt. It's a risk."

"But it's a risk for me, too!"

"Yes, but you're ready. He's not. I think by holding back on sex, he's holding onto the last thing he hasn't already given you. You have his heart. You have his time. His companionship. His trust. If he has to go all in physically, then there's nothing left that you don't have. You have him by the balls, then. Literally and figuratively. I'd be willing to bet whatever's going on with Cabe has to do with commitment. He's told you he wants to wait to have sex. He's told you he needs time before he can go any deeper into this. He's backed off when you guys get close. I think the whole thing centers around his commitment issues."

I ran my fingers through my hair and sighed with frustration.

"Listen Ty, I don't think he's gonna go there until he's decided he's all in. Ready to lay his claim. Like, okay, now you're mine. I think that's where the *just friends* comment came in last night. He's not sure he's ready to claim anything yet, but based on what he said later about not wanting to lose you, he doesn't want to let you go, either. He's scared."

I considered her words. Not any great revelation, of course. I knew Cabe had commitment issues. We both did. Hell, how long had it taken me to be able to even acknowledge my feelings for him? But it hurt to think he didn't want to commit to me, or that he was holding back from me to keep from being all in. Fear and anxiety mingled with my frustration and anger in an uneasy cocktail.

"So what if he decides it's not worth it, and he doesn't want to stay?"

"Cabe loves you, Tyler. I've been telling you this for how long? He just needs time. He needs space. Whatever this family thing is just adds to the pressure he's struggling with right now. He's hurting. You gotta be patient." She wrapped her arms around my shoulders and hugged me to her. "I'm sorry, honey. I want you to be happy," she whispered against my ear.

I pulled back. "Me too, Mel. Me too. I thought I'd found The One. That everything would finally work out. But ever since I figured out how I felt about Cabe, it seems like it's gone all wrong." Tears rolled down my face, and I didn't even bother to wipe them away.

"Oh, Tyler. A lot happens between Once Upon A Time and Happily Ever After. I've never yet read a fairy tale where she met the prince and they immediately rode off into the sunset. There's usually dragons or witches or evil curses. You can't give up on him, though."

"I'm not giving up on him. Yet. But how do you know when you need to keep being supportive and loving versus when you need to cut your losses and walk away? This hurts."

"Get to Paris. It'll be just the two of you. No family. No pressure. Wait and see what happens in Paris. In the city of love. Don't try and make him talk before then. Just get to Paris and take it from there."

I called him on my way back home.

The concern in his voice when he answered made me feel guilty for not calling earlier. "Hey, Buttercup! Did you just get up? Are you okay?"

"I'm fine. I've been at Mel's."

He was silent for a moment, probably digesting the fact that I had been up and out of the house without calling him back.

"I'm really sorry about last night, Ty."

I refused to say it was okay, because it wasn't. But I figured I might as well follow Mel's advice and not push it. I'd wait for Paris.

"Yeah, you really tied one on. How you feeling today?"

"I've felt better, for sure. I haven't moved off the couch much since I got back from picking up my car. Thanks for getting me home. For taking care of me."

I grimaced. "Anytime, buddy. That's what *friends* are for, right?" Snarky, I know. I probably shouldn't have said it. But the *we're just friends* comment still stung.

He hesitated a minute. "You wanna come over?"

I was surprised to realize I really didn't. I didn't want to see him. I didn't want to talk to him. I didn't want to worry about what I said or what he said or what he was thinking or how he felt. I just wanted to be alone.

"Nah, I'm gonna head home. I'm tired."

A slight pause on his end before he spoke. "We still going to the Mardi Gras parade on Tuesday? It's tradition."

The Mardi Gras parade. Our tradition. Other than last year when he was in Seattle, we'd been every year since we met. I've always loved the elaborate costumes and floats—so much purple!—but what makes me ridiculously happy is to catch beads. Stupid, plastic, ugly-ass beads I will never wear anywhere. Maybe it's my competitive nature along with the thrill of getting something for free, but we have a blast laughing together as Cabe jumps high and fields everything I can't reach and I end up laden down with plastic. It's always a good time. We could sure use a good time right now.

"Yep. Wouldn't miss it." I couldn't muster excitement into my voice, and I'm sure he noticed. It was taking all I had to hold my tongue and not spew forth everything I was thinking and feeling.

Just get to Paris. Just get to Paris. Just get to Paris. We'll talk everything out when we get to Paris.

Tuesday, March 4th

I knew he didn't feel well as soon as I opened the door. His face was flushed, his eyes glassy.

"Are you okay?"

He stumbled into the living room and collapsed onto the couch. "Yeah, I'm fine. Just coming down with something I think."

"That's not good. We fly in two days."

He waved his hand in my direction as if to shut me up. "I'll be fine."

"Well, let's just stay home tonight."

"Are you kidding me? And miss the parade? No way. I know how much you love this."

"Don't be ridiculous. If you're running a fever, you don't need to be out in the night air."

"I'm fine. I took some meds. They just haven't kicked in yet. You drive."

That's when I knew how sick he was. He never lets me drive. He still wouldn't budge on not going, though.

We found a spot right on the parade route. I stayed on the edge of the road, but Cabe leaned against a fence post back behind me, still close enough to talk but not like we were standing together. The medicine had helped some, but I could tell he still didn't feel well.

Just as the music reached us and the parade came into view, a big ole burly dude stepped right in front of me and completely blocked my view.

Definitely one of those times I wished I was bigger and male.

I tried to edge around him but couldn't, so I leaned forward and very politely said, "Excuse me, sir. I've been standing in this spot for quite a while, and I can't see with you in front of me. If you could just..."

He glanced over his shoulder at me and then back toward the approaching parade as he placed his hands on his hips and widened his stance, his elbows blocking me on both sides.

I was shocked and pissed. Why would a grown man purposely block my parade view?

The first float tossed a handful of beads toward us. The kids scrambled for the ones hitting the ground while I reached high to catch a strand. But Burly stuck up his arm and grabbed the necklace right before it reached me. Then he did it again—for every strand of beads that float threw.

"Dude!"

Burly said nothing, just smiled. Which pissed me off even more.

I felt Cabe's hands on my waist and his breath in my ear. "I'm happy to step in if you need me, but keep in mind I'm not one hundred percent tonight. Not sure how this would all turn out if it came to a fight."

I met Cabe's eyes for a brief second, and my heart tugged at the glassiness there. "You wanna go home?"

"No. Get your beads. Let me know if you need me."

I moved forward again, pushing my weight against Burly Dude to jump as the next set of beads flew. He reached above me again, blocking me and catching the beads. Then he laughed. The jerk actually laughed.

"Look, dude, I just want some beads. They'll throw enough for both of us. Can you not just let me catch a few?"

He looked at me with a sneering grin. "Back off, bitch."

Cabe grabbed Burly Dude's shoulder and jerked him away from the road before I even had time to react to what he'd said. The man stumbled backwards one step and drew back to swing at Cabe.

Cabe spread his feet wide with his fists curled at his sides. Locked and loaded.

"You wanna hit me in front of all these people, buddy?" Cabe asked him. "Go right ahead."

With Cabe drawn up to his full height, he had at least five inches on Burly Dude. Despite the guy's bulk, Cabe's shoulders were broader by quite a bit, and with his glassed-over eyes glaring and flashing, he made quite the formidable figure. The guy hesitated and looked around at the crowd surrounding us. Cabe leaned closer to him and lowered his voice. "Look here. Nobody disrespects my girl. So she's gonna stand there and catch some beads, and you're going to show her the respect she deserves. Otherwise, we'll probably both go to jail. Whaddya say?"

Burly Dude looked from Cabe to me and back again before turning to leave through the throng of people.

Cabe motioned for me to go back to bead-catching and then went to sit down on the bench behind the crowd. The next float sailed a huge mess of beads my way, and I caught them with one jump.

I couldn't concentrate on my haul, though. My mind focused on analyzing what he'd said. *My girl.* He'd called me his girl. Stood there in the midst of a raging fever and defended my ridiculous passion for beads. Why? Why must he be so damned confusing?

He slept as I drove us home, and he didn't protest when I led him back to my room and tucked him into bed. I made him drink a dose of cold medicine and brought some water for the nightstand.

His eyes were closed, but he reached his hand out and touched my leg as I stood there.

"I feel like shit," he said.

"You look like shit. I'm not sure you're gonna be able to fly anywhere."

"I'll be fine by then. I promise." He tugged at my jeans. "Come lay down with me, Buttercup."

My heart skipped at the tenderness in his voice. Gets me every time. I can't resist him.

I lay down beside him, and he curled his fevered body around me. The heat was stifling, so once I heard him breathing steady in deep sleep, I extricated myself from his tangled limbs and went to brush my teeth and turn out the lights.

I'm on the couch now and in a funk. I don't know what to do with this. I don't know how this will turn out. If Paris will be the best thing ever or the biggest mistake.

I wish I knew what's in his head. What he truly feels for me.

Am I *your girl* or are we *just friends?* Make up your mind.

Wednesday, March 5th

I wanted to leave work early today to pick up a few last-minute things before the trip, but by the time I'd finished the mound of paperwork and emails, it was a little after six.

Mama called soon after I got in the car, and I realized I never sent her the flight and hotel info. With all the *we're going-we're not going-we're going* over the last few weeks, I never got around to updating her. She didn't even know we almost canceled the trip.

"Bone jewer!" Her attempt at French with her thick, Southern accent was painful to the ears.

"*Bonjour*, Mama!"

"Well, are you gettin' excited? I'm excited, and I ain't even going."

I had a lot of feelings swirling around, but I don't know where excited came in on the list. Nervous seemed much higher at the moment. No need to share that with Mama, though.

"Yeah, this time tomorrow I'll be in the air." I tried to sound enthusiastic for her benefit, and a couple of tingly butterflies did a little dance when I realized what I'd said was true.

"I can't believe you'll be in Paris for your birthday. Am I gone talk to you? I've never not talked to ya on your birthday."

"I'll call you. Or you can call me. I'll have my cell phone."

"You all packed?"

"No ma'am. I pretty much know what I'm packing, but I still have to do laundry and get it all in the suitcase. Cabe says we should just share one suitcase since it's only a weekend. But I've gotta figure out how to get it all to fit. Or how to condense it down."

I wanted to take daytime and night-time outfits, and I'd need several layers for each because of the cold. I had no idea how to fit it all in half a

132

suitcase.

"Take comfortable walking shoes. You'll probably be doing a lot of walking. Did you pack protection?"

When did this become a normal topic of conversation for my mother? Twice in a row? We've *never* discussed anything sexually-related unless you count her telling me my clothes were too revealing in high school and college. And yet, here she was asking if I'd packed protection in the same sentence with comfortable walking shoes. Both sensible, practical items, but still.

"Mama, don't."

"Now, Tyler, I'm not naive enough to believe you're gonna fly off to Paris with this man and not have sex with him. So just put my mind at ease and promise me you'll take some protection."

"I'm on the pill." I'd been on the pill since age eighteen, but I'd never told her. I braced myself for the torrent sure to follow, but she didn't break stride.

"Well, the pill don't do squat about diseases. This ain't no more comfortable for me to talk about than it is for you, but I'm not taking no for an answer. Promise me you'll take some condoms."

I really didn't think it would be necessary. One, I know Cabe had medical exams done soon after he found out Monica had been unfaithful, and two, based on his reluctance to have sex when we were getting along great, I didn't foresee it happening now.

But I told Mama I'd go buy some in order to appease her and make her stop talking about sex.

I decided that along those lines if I was going to have condoms in the suitcase 'just in case', I might as well have some sexy lingerie. I mean, how much would it suck if we get to Paris—the most romantic city on the planet—and everything's going great, Cabe professes his undying love, but we get back to the hotel and all I have is a box of condoms, a t-shirt and a pair of boxers?

So now my wallet is a couple hundred dollars lighter, but I have some beautiful intimates and matching bras and panties for every outfit I'm taking. Oh, and condoms.

Now I just have to stop writing in my diary and go figure out how to get all this stuff in half a suitcase.

Thursday, March 6th

Well, the people at Gate 23 got a little added entertainment just now. I can still feel their stares pricking me as I write.

Cabe and I had bickered back and forth all morning. Snippy. Snappy. Irritable. I know for my part, I got no sleep at all last night. I stayed up much too late doing laundry and packing. I should have started the whole process earlier in the week, but I think in the back of my head I wasn't certain we were actually going until last night. I didn't want the heartache of having to unpack if he changed his mind.

I'm pretty sure he still felt under the weather, despite his fever breaking yesterday. From the time he picked me up at my apartment, he was already bitching. He complained my clothes took up too much space in the suitcase. He complained the suitcase weighed too much. He got irate because I wanted to bring an extra carry-on for shoes. Then he got irritated that he had to wait while I tried to stuff my shoes into the overflowing suitcase to eliminate the carry-on. I knew it was frivolous to bring different shoes for every outfit, but I wanted to look cute. I can't wear boots or heels to walk all day, and I am not going out for dinner in sneakers.

Right from the start, this trip has been ill-fated, and if this morning gave any indication, it may not turn out quite the way I'd hoped.

We had just settled in at the gate when I remembered I didn't go online to book the Eiffel Tower like he'd asked me to.

"Damn, Tyler. I told you we had to book it in advance. That line will take hours. Great, just great. We have basically two days to see everything, and we'll be standing in line for half of one."

"So we skip the Eiffel Tower."

He whirled to face me like I'd just said we should hijack the plane. "It's the Eiffel Tower. The symbol of Paris. We're not going to skip it."

I cocked my head from side to side in agitation. "Well, fine. I'll go online and book it now. Oh, awesome. My phone has no signal."

"Use mine." He flung his phone at me and sat forward in his seat, resting his elbows on his knees and twisting his hands together as his left leg bounced up and down.

I pulled up the Tower site on his phone, only to find no available times during our trip. Great.

"They're sold out, but it's okay. We'll just see it from the bottom. We can't see everything in two days anyway."

"This sucks," he said. "We shouldn't even be going." He ran his hands through his hair and leaned back in the chair, his left leg still bouncing. Up and down, up and down, up and down.

"What is your problem? I've never seen you act like this, and I can't say I'm excited to sit next to you for the next ten hours if this is how you're going to be."

"Well, that makes two of us."

My mouth dropped open. "What did I do? Okay, so I wasn't ready when you got to my place and I forgot to book the Eiffel Tower, but at least I'm not acting like a total ass."

"You're an event planner, Tyler. How did you forget to book the one event I asked you to handle? I took care of the hotel, the flights, the museum passes. You had one thing to take care of. Well, two if you count packing. Three, if you count being ready on time. You struck out on all three."

All my stress and tension of the last few weeks boiled right up to the surface. I didn't care if people could hear us. I didn't even bother to whisper.

"Are you kidding me right now? You are so out of line. First of all, you had a travel agent book all that stuff for you, so it's not like you went to great lengths to make it happen. Maybe I have been a bit forgetful lately, but it's probably because I've been riding the Cabe merry-go-round. One day you can't get enough of me and the next you want me out of your sight. One minute you're all over me, and the next we're *just friends*. It's kind of hard to keep everything else straight when I'm being spun around in circles."

"Nice, Tyler. Nice. This is bullshit." He stood up, and I stood with him.

"Bullshit? You want to know what's bullshit? You offered me this trip for my birthday. I didn't ask for it. Then you had your momentary freak-out whatever the hell it was, but you came back and said you never canceled the trip because you still wanted to go. I offered to back out, but nooo. You wanted to take me to Paris. And now you're being a complete asshole and ruining the trip. Ruining my birthday."

"I should have canceled this damned trip. I knew this was a bad idea. "

"Then why didn't you?"

"Because I knew you wanted it, Tyler."

"*I* wanted it? This was your idea!"

"Because I know you. You want *this*. The sweep-you-off-your-feet grand romantic gestures. The warm, fuzzy movie moments that don't happen in real life. You want some prince to ride in on a white horse and rescue you. Well, that's not me. Hell, I can't even help myself right now, much less rescue you."

My mouth opened and closed a few times as I fought to find words and swallow tears. "I never asked you to rescue me. I never said I needed this."

He grabbed his backpack and slung it over his arms onto his back as he spoke. "Sure you did. A million times in conversations over the years. You have this guy built up in your head who will do all the right things and say all the right things. I'm not him. I can't be him. I want to make you happy. But I don't even know who I am right now. Where I belong. I can't do this."

His words stabbed through me like sharp daggers I didn't see coming. I was vaguely aware of the sudden silence of the people around us, but then they disappeared into peripheral darkness and all I saw was Cabe.

"Cabe, I know you're under a lot of pressure right now. But I'm not asking you—"

"I gotta get outta here."

I opened my mouth to protest, and he shook his head. "Just leave me alone. Please, Tyler."

He walked away, and I paused a moment, unsure of what to do next. I gathered up my bags to follow him, but I could hear Mel and Maggie's words in my head telling me to give him space.

I cannot believe he just stormed off. What the hell? I didn't ask him for this freakin' trip. I thought he canceled it. Which was fine with me. Where does he get off acting like I need him to take me to Paris? To rescue me? Give me a break. I didn't ask to be rescued.

This is ridiculous. I'm tired of dealing with it. He needs to figure out what the hell he wants and stop being all Jekyll and Hyde on me.

What if he acts like this in Paris? I don't even want to go if he's going to totally ruin the trip.

He better calm down before he gets back. We have a long flight to get through. If he comes back nice, I'll be nice. I can wait to talk later. At the hotel. When we have privacy. We have the whole weekend to talk things out. Even if we don't see a damned thing while we're in Paris.

Take-Off

Oh holy shit. What do I do now?

I got nervous when they started boarding and he hadn't returned, but it just fueled my anger more at him for acting like an ass and ruining everything. My angry facade had cracked a bit when they called his name on the PA system for final boarding, especially when I reached for my phone to call him and saw his in the top of my bag. I'd tossed it there when the argument began. I had no way to reach him.

I decided I'd be damned if he'd come back and see me sitting there all by myself waiting for him. He thought I needed rescuing? I'd show him I could take care of myself. I didn't need him.

So I said to hell with it, and I got on the plane. By myself. Now we're in the freakin' air, and I'm still sitting here by myself. On the way to Paris. By myself.

He didn't get on the plane.

He didn't come back.

WTH.

The pop of the cabin door sealing shut had clamped down tight on my heart and took my breath away. I unbuckled my belt and stood, ready to grab my things and run, but then I realized I didn't want to get off. I didn't want to wander around the airport looking for him. To walk back to the car in the lot and find he'd driven away without me. To go back to the office and tell them I'd been abandoned at the airport. Or to call my mama on my birthday and tell her I was in Orlando after all. I most definitely didn't want to spend my birthday crying all day because I was supposed to be in Paris. With Cabe. Wearing my matching bras and panties, checking out Notre Dame, and taking river cruises.

So I sat back down and struggled to buckle my seatbelt with shaking hands.

Waves of nausea threatened to overtake me as they went through the emergency procedures. I waited to turn my phone off until the very last second possible in case he tried to call.

But he didn't. He left me. Cabe left me.

Disbelief and shock numbed me throughout take-off and the first few minutes of flight. But when the cold truth of the situation set in, I sobbed a good ole ugly cry without a care in the world who saw or what they thought. After all, it ain't like they didn't see us going at it before take-off. They knew I didn't start this trip alone.

But I'm alone now.

What was I thinking? I don't speak French. I know nothing about Paris. I don't even know where the hotel is. Or how to get there from the airport. I trusted Cabe to take care of all that.

Thank God all the paperwork and vouchers ended up in my carry-on bag. Now I just hope the hotel will let me check in without him.

I'd say this ranks up there with one of the dumbest decisions I've ever made.

In a couple of hours, I will step off this plane in a foreign country where I don't speak the language and have no idea where to go or what to do.

I will be completely and utterly alone.

Oh holy hell.

Friday, March 7th

Well, I survived so far. Woohoo. Way to go me, right?

Thankfully, some compassionate soul put English on enough signs in the Paris airport that I found my way to baggage claim. Not that it did me much good, since our suitcase somehow didn't arrive in Paris.

I stood there at the luggage carousel, watching as one by one my fellow passengers claimed their bags and walked away. I felt a little more panicked as each one left me.

When the last family picked up their bags to go, I almost clung to them and begged them not to leave without me.

There I was, the only one left as the empty carousel circled around and around without my bag. I have never felt so alone in my life.

An airline employee directed me to the luggage help desk, where I joined a group of twenty or thirty disgruntled passengers from various flights who were also seeking their luggage. I heard bits and pieces of several different languages, but no English. An odd sensation to be sure. One I'd never experienced before.

My ears perked up when I heard a tall gentleman in a long, black pea coat say his name to the attendant behind the counter. He'd been speaking to her in French, but his American accent clearly came through when he said his name and flight details in English. It was like hearing the cavalry coming across the hill. Someone spoke my language!

He was alone like me, which I noticed immediately since everyone else seemed to be traveling in pairs or with their family.

He didn't seem upset like the others, though. He conversed with the attendant casually, calmly. Almost like he was buying tickets for a movie or a museum instead of demanding the return of his personal belongings.

He turned back once, and his eyes stopped briefly when they met mine before he looked away and faced the attendant again. The color caught me by surprise. Not quite blue. Not quite green. Teal, I guess, except people don't have teal eyes. They were striking, especially against the black fringe of bangs that fell low across his brow.

"You're American?" I asked as he walked past me.

"Yeah." He smiled, but it was clear I'd startled him. "Ohio, and you?"

"Florida." I grinned like a mule eating briers, ridiculously happy to be conversing with someone.

He cocked his head to one side. "I detect a Southern accent."

I nodded. "Georgia, originally."

He smiled and found a seat to fill out his paperwork. When I'd finished at the counter, I took the seat next to him to fill out mine. Ohio might be nowhere near Georgia or Florida, but in the grand scheme of life and the globe, we were from the same place. Practically neighbors from across the ocean. I needed to be near him and feel connected to home.

"So you speak French?" I asked the obvious.

"Yeah. Some. Enough to get by. And you?"

I smiled and shook my head. I fought back fear as I considered again the overwhelming prospect of navigating the city without the language.

"Oh, you'll do fine," he said. "You'd be surprised how many people here speak English. A lot of the signs have it, too."

I nodded again and turned back to the forms in front of me, willing myself not to cry.

He finished his papers and took them back to the counter, stopping near me when he returned.

"Alright, well, I hope you enjoy your trip. It's got to get better from here."

"What?" I asked, wondering if he somehow knew what had happened.

"Lost luggage. Not a great start to a trip."

"Oh, right." I nodded.

He paused for a moment and then extended his hand. "Jack Rainey."

I shook the hand he offered. "Tyler Warren."

"Enjoy Paris, Tyler Warren. It's a magical place."

He walked away, and I immediately felt alone again.

Damn Cabe.

I finished the paperwork, and the attendant lady told me they'd deliver my luggage to the hotel. Well, if they find it. I thought maybe Cabe had gotten it back when he left, but she assured me it was on the plane at take-off. Not sure how they lost it between there and here, but my luck, it's bobbing around in the Atlantic.

At least the Metro station proved easy enough to find. I must say I felt relieved I didn't have the bulky suitcase to maneuver through the turnstiles on top of figuring out the ticket system.

I studied the guidebook I'd bought at the airport for pretty much the entire train ride, looking up every few minutes to make sure I didn't miss my stop for the hotel. The train filled more with each stop, and by the time we reached my station, I had to fight my way through the crowd to get out the door.

Cold air blasted me in the face as I came up from the Metro and out into the bustling city. I shivered against the light mist of frigid rain as it settled over me, chilling my bones and making my eyes water under its stinging assault. I dug my gloves and scarf out with trembling hands, thankful for the first time that I'd carried my heavy coat with me since it wouldn't fit in the suitcase.

The map I'd memorized on the train didn't translate well above ground, which resulted in a few wrong turns before finding the hotel. In the first stroke of luck I'd had all day, the room was ready and they let me check in without even asking about Cabe. Thank you, Lord, that the reservation was in both names.

I've checked my phone a hundred times since I landed, but no call. No text. He really did leave me stranded at the airport.

I bet he never thought in a million years I'd get on that plane without him.

I'm sure he thought I'd just sulk my way back to the car when I realized he wasn't coming back.

Well, he was wrong. My stubborn ass waltzed right onto that plane and right off into the unknown. And now I'm sitting here in this hotel room looking out the window at Paris, and I'm terrified.

I can't believe I'm here alone. All by myself.

Part of me wants to burrow down under the covers and sleep until it's time to go back to the airport on Sunday. But part of me wants to show him, and me, that I can do this.

I mean, I'm in *Paris*. I can think of a helluva lot worse places to be abandoned. Even now as I stare out at the city, I feel adrenaline and excitement coursing through my veins underneath the fear. This is not how I planned to be here, but I'm here. I might as well enjoy it.

Still March 7th
Later that night

So when I said earlier I'd survived so far, I was being a bit dramatic. After tonight, it holds a bit more truth. I have to say for the most part it was a pretty good day. Despite the disastrous start with Cabe and tonight's scary finish here.

I allowed myself a much-needed nap before venturing out with my handy guidebook in hand. I found a crepe wagon a couple of blocks from the hotel and wolfed down a ham and swiss crepe like a stray dog who's been tossed a meaty bone.

I figured I'd start with the Eiffel Tower, it being the biggest, most well-known landmark, and therefore easy to find.

None of the pictures or movies I've seen do it justice. It is even more commanding, more regal, and more breathtaking in person. I probably could have sat there for hours just staring at it, but the rain started up again, so I sought out the Louvre as an indoor haven.

I meandered through Greek and Roman history and then fought the crowds to catch a glimpse of the Mona Lisa. After a couple of hours, all of history began to blur together, and the outside world beckoned to me once again.

Thankfully, the rain had stopped, but that didn't keep the cold from cutting right through my thin Florida skin. My coat provided sufficient warmth for the rare cold day in the Sunshine State, but it was no match for such a blustery European day. If only I'd had the extra layers of clothes from my suitcase.

I drifted in and out of boutiques to try and stay warm on my way up to Sacré-Cœur perched on the tallest point of the city, high atop Montmartre.

The nuns were finishing their evening performance as I entered the church, and I wished I had arrived sooner to hear more of their angelic voices lifted to the heavens. I don't know how long I sat afterward on the low walls in front of Sacré-Cœur, gazing out over Paris beneath the gloomy sky. The gray clouds lent a vintage filter to the Paris skyline, and I probably took a million pictures, none of which could possibly convey the scenery laid out before me.

As the falling temperatures and darkening sky signaled the inevitable end of day, I made my way back to the Eiffel Tower, eager to see it at night. It didn't disappoint. In fact, it seemed even more impressive with its massive pillars bathed in a golden glow against the darkness. I waited breathless with the crowd for the first twinkle light display, all of us gasping in unison as the entire tower went dark and then began to shimmer all over with sparkling white lights. Truly the most magical thing I've ever witnessed. In fact, it so enthralled me that I forgot to take pictures during the five-minute display. Thank goodness they repeat it every hour.

I snapped shots of the tower from every angle, even one from underneath staring straight up into it. I had just stepped out of the crowd a little to playback the pictures on my camera when I saw Jack from Ohio. He was sipping a coffee and looking up at the tower, maybe four feet from me.

You would've thought I'd seen an old friend from high school. I got ridiculously excited to see someone I knew, even if I only *knew* him from a five minute encounter at the airport.

"Jack!" I yelled above the crowd.

He turned in surprise and smiled as he saw me. I walked toward him, not even considering how forward that may be. I hadn't talked to anyone in hours, and I feared I may self-combust if I couldn't have a conversation.

"Isn't this thing incredible?" I motioned to the massive structure above us.

"Yes, it is. This is your first time, then?"

I nodded, still grinning like I'd won the lottery.

"I can't believe how big it is," I said, looking back up at the tower.

"Much larger in life, for sure. Did you go up today? To the top?"

I shuddered just thinking about it. "No. I was supposed to get tickets before I came"—the memory of the airport argument momentarily clouded my thoughts—"but I'm kind of glad I didn't. It's so high up. I don't think I could have done it."

"Oh, you have to. The view is just incredible. You can see the whole city up there."

"I'll take your word for it."

"So what did you see today?"

"I spent some time at the Louvre, and went up to Sacré-Cœur, but I think I've pretty much sampled food more than anything. Macarons, crepes, croissants. I've eaten my way through the city."

"The food in Paris is like no place else. Have you tried the crepes right over there?" He pointed toward one of the huge pillar bases. "I was considering getting something sweet to go with my coffee. If you'd like to join me?"

I nodded even though I wasn't hungry. I had no desire to part company with conversation so quickly.

"So what brings you to Paris?" I asked as we joined the line for crepes.

"I'm a clinical trial director for a pharmaceutical company. We're doing some drug trials in a research facility here in Paris. And what about you?"

"I'm a wedding planner."

He laughed and looked at me like he thought I was joking. "Really? Okay. I never met a wedding planner before. That must be an interesting job."

"It is. Most people always say they think it's glamorous. Which, it's not. Or they say it must be nice to work around happy people all the time. Which, they're not. They're probably more stressed than at any other times in their lives. But you said interesting. That it is."

"I bet."

He ordered a cinnamon and vanilla crème crepe, and I ordered one with hazelnut filling and strawberries. The warm, gooey sweetness filled my belly and gave me a momentary sugar buzz.

We stepped out from under the tower as we ate, going upstream against the never-ending onslaught of people beneath it.

"So you didn't say what brings you to Paris. Are you doing a wedding, or just here on vacation?"

His eyes sparkled with reflections of the lights behind me as he talked, which only served to enhance their unique color.

"I'm here to celebrate my birthday tomorrow." My insides twisted as I said it, remembering who booked the trip and wasn't here with me to celebrate. The crepe felt heavy in my stomach, and I swallowed hard to force the emotions down. The last thing I wanted to do was cry in front of the only person in the city I could talk to.

"Well, happy birthday! Paris is a great place to celebrate it. Would it be rude to ask how old you'll be?"

I struggled to push thoughts of Cabe out of my head and smiled. "Not at all. Twenty-six. Officially closer to thirty than twenty."

Jack laughed and covered his mouth to chew before he spoke. "Well, I turned twenty-nine not too long ago. Officially closer to thirty than twenty-six."

We talked more as we ate, and I found myself enjoying his company for more than just his language. It felt great to talk and laugh after so many hours alone, but the cold wind cut right through me as the hour grew later, and I couldn't stand still without shivering.

"I guess it's a lot colder here than Florida, huh?" Jack asked as I adjusted my scarf and tucked my hands in my pockets.

I nodded. "Definitely. I dressed for the trip to the airport, figuring I could add more layers once I got here. I wasn't planning on not having my suitcase, though." I also wasn't planning on not having my traveling companion, but I didn't mention that.

"Hopefully it will be there when you get back to your hotel. I've been lucky. Only lost luggage twice before in all my travels. One other time landing in Paris, ironically. But both times I had my suitcase the first night so it wasn't so bad."

"I hope so. Otherwise I may have to stay indoors at night. This wind is brutal!" I stamped my feet back and forth to try and generate warmth.

Jack smiled. "Well, don't let me keep you out here. I need to be moving along anyway. I want to get an early start tomorrow and jet lag's catching up with me. It's been nice talking with you. Always good to meet a fellow American abroad. So...happy birthday, and enjoy the rest of your trip."

I wanted to ask him not to go, to delay parting a little longer. I wasn't looking forward to being alone again. But I didn't want to seem like some weird stalker, and it was colder than a witch's brassiere in a blizzard. The thought of my nice, warm hotel room enticed me enough to say goodbye.

"Nice talking to you, too. Maybe I'll see you around." Part of me hoped I would. Someone familiar in the crowd.

"You never know. It's a big city, but a small world." Jack smiled again and tipped his hat to me, his black hair falling forward over his face before he tossed it back out of his eyes. "Good night."

He turned and disappeared into the crowd, and a melancholy loneliness settled over me. I walked to the Metro entrance bundled against the bitter bite of the wind that chafed mercilessly against my cheeks.

As I descended into the depths of the subway station, I should have been paying more attention to my surroundings. But my thoughts were consumed with Cabe, with Jack, with being alone, and with the uncontrollable shivers racking my body. I crashed right into a guy as I walked along the platform.

He grabbed my arms lightly, although I don't know if it was to steady me or to assault me. Either way I jumped back like he'd burned me. He said something in French, obviously a question by his tone, but he didn't release my arms. He reeked of alcohol, and his bloodshot eyes leered up and down me like he could see right through my coat.

Panic raced through me as I tried to pull my arms free and found them firmly held. He repeated his question, along with a few other words. Another man stepped up from behind him, saying something to me in

French as he licked his lips in exaggerated lewdness. They both laughed. Not a pleasant laugh, by any means. My stomach turned as I pulled again to try and free my arms.

His buddy said something else, and French Man repeated what sounded like his original question, but in a tone that definitely came across more sinister. They laughed again.

I couldn't decide if saying I didn't speak French would help or hurt my situation.

He pushed me back a step, and every terrible scene I'd ever seen in movies flashed through my mind. I'd be kidnapped. Sold as a sex slave.

"*Ne parler pas.*" I stuttered out one of the only French phrases I knew, letting him know I didn't understand his request. I jerked at his grip and pulled free for a second, but he caught my right arm again, twisting it this time as he pushed me backwards toward the stairs.

I opened my mouth to scream, but my body slammed back against someone, effectively knocking all air from my lungs and sandwiching me between French Man and whoever blocked our path.

"There you are, honey," Jack said behind me. "Come on, we don't want to miss our train." I twisted to see him smile at French Man and his companion, noticing his eyes held no humor at all. He spoke to them briskly in French as he took my left arm and guided me around them. French Man released me and backed up a step, spewing angry French at us both.

Jack didn't respond but kept walking me toward the benches at the far end of the platform. He released my arm, but his hand stayed at the small of my back as we walked.

"I see you made new friends," Jack said as my knees wobbled out from underneath me, and I practically fell onto the bench.

"No. Oh my God. I am so freaked out right now. What was he saying?" I kept my eyes on Jack, not daring to look back at French Man. Jack stared over my head, and I knew he was either watching them or watching for them.

"He made you an offer of his company for the evening. It wasn't one I thought you'd like, so I provided an escape route. Hope you didn't mind."

"Not at all. Holy crap. I can't stop shaking. I thought I was a goner. Kidnapped and sold into slavery."

"I think he was considering a bit more personal encounter." He looked at me then and smiled as I leaned forward to rest my elbows on my knees and my head in my hands. "You okay?"

"Yeah, thanks. *Honey.*" I glanced back at him and forced what I hoped looked like a smile, my stomach still flipping in loops from the anxiety of the encounter.

"Sorry about that. It was the quickest plan that came to mind."

"Oh, no complaints. I was glad to see you. *Honey.*"

Jack chuckled. "Good thing I arrived when I did."

"Why did you? Arrive here, I mean. Is this your train?"

He nodded as wind whooshed through the platform with the arriving train. We got up together to board, and I exhaled and risked a glance back toward French Man, but he and his friend had gone. The experience had left me shaken and grateful for Jack's presence in the car with me.

"So which stop is yours?" I asked, hoping he'd be on the train until after I got off.

"St. Michel."

"Me too!"

We laughed to discover we were staying within a block of each other, which worked out great for me. He escorted me all the way to my hotel entrance before wishing me a happy birthday and a safer day tomorrow.

No suitcase awaited me, but the front desk clerk offered me a toothbrush and toothpaste, which I greatly appreciated. A shower rinses away the grunge of the city, but teeth that haven't been brushed in over twenty-four hours need something a little stronger than water. Yuck.

Still no word from Cabe. I tried not to think about him today, but that proved impossible. Everything reminded me of him. The architecture. The people. The food. Every experience brought to mind that he should have been there with me, experiencing it alongside me. But he chose not to.

I still can't believe he *chose* not to come. The pain of it overwhelms me and infuriates me all at the same time. His absence burns like a hole in my gut, but every time I think about it I get madder about the whole thing. How could he do this to me? After all we've been through together? I've never purposely done anything so hurtful to him. If anything, I've tried to be supportive and understanding through all his crap.

The anger helps. It buffers me from the desire to ball myself up and cry the whole time I'm here. I refuse to do that. It's his fault I'm here by myself, so I'm determined not to allow him to ruin the whole trip. I'm gonna make the best of it. There'll be plenty of time to cry once I'm back home.

Saturday, March 8th
My Birthday

The sun came out in full force for a gorgeous birthday! Gone was the misty rain of yesterday, and the brilliant blue skies and golden sunshine I saw through my window lifted my heart and gave me hope for a great day. I hopped out of bed ready to start exploring as soon as possible before my heart bogged down in mourning what might have been.

I made it maybe two blocks from the hotel when I saw Jack sitting at a sidewalk cafe. I couldn't contain my smile at seeing him, and I stopped just short of hugging the poor man. I never realized before this trip how much I need human contact and conversation throughout my day. I probably should have kept walking and left the man in peace to eat and read his newspaper, but that would be like seeing your neighbor in the grocery store and not speaking. A neighbor who had saved you from creepy drunk people in the subway. I couldn't just walk by. It wouldn't have been proper. Downright rude, in fact.

"Hey!" I tapped him on the shoulder as I stood on the other side of the restaurant's rail.

"Well, hello. Happy birthday, Birthday Girl. Have you eaten?" Jack folded his paper and indicated the empty seat across from him.

"I grabbed a croissant at the hotel."

"One croissant? That's not enough fuel for Paris. Here, have a seat. I was just about to order."

"I don't want to intrude," I said, hoping the whole time he'd insist. Which he did.

"So what's on your birthday agenda today?" He asked once we'd ordered our breakfast.

"I thought I'd check out the Rodin Museum, and maybe the Opera House."

"Ah, both great choices."

I wondered if it would be inappropriate to ask him to come with me. I didn't want to spend my birthday alone, scared I might give in to the self-pity-party hovering just beneath the surface of my emotions. I weighed coming across too forward against trekking all over the city by myself and found I was willing to take the risk. "What about you? Do you have plans for the day?"

"I'm gonna start with Notre Dame. Thought I'd get there before the crowds get too crazy. Have you been yet?"

I shook my head.

"Oh, it's only a couple a blocks from here," Jack said. "Just across the river. If you want, you could check out Notre Dame with me and then be on your way to visit Rodin. If it won't take you too far off schedule."

"Sure!" Yeah, probably a bit too eager. But, oh well.

We finished our exquisite omelettes and made our way to Notre Dame. The grand cathedral loomed high and noble in front of us, and we both stood in silence as we stared up at the intricate carvings gracing its facade. My mind struggled to conceive something so old, not to mention how on earth the builders had accomplished such great feats without the technology and tools of our modern times.

Inside proved even more awe-inspiring. The height of the ceilings with their curved buttresses. The sunlight filtering through the myriad of colors in the stained glass windows. The sheer immensity of the stones. The smell of things ancient. And the quiet . . . an eerie, reverent quiet no one dared to break. As I looked around me, people milled about in all areas, but all quiet. No laughter. No conversation. An occasional whisper close to ears, but nothing more.

It was the most sacred, holy place I've ever been. Like I could literally feel the presence of God surrounding us in the silence.

A gentle peace settled over me. A quiet stillness inside. Whether it came from the silent environment around me or from the heavens above, I don't know. I'd never felt anything like it before.

Jack led me to a row of wooden chairs facing the massive altar where we sat for probably ten minutes, maybe more. The peace still held me, and I felt at ease sharing the silence with Jack. Probably the longest span of time I've ever been silent, come to think of it.

Eventually, Jack stood and motioned toward the door. I nodded and stood with him, but stopped as I caught sight of the enormous organ pipes.

"Oh my God!" I whispered to Jack, pointing up to the pipes above the cathedral doors.

He chuckled silently and leaned in close. "I don't think you're supposed to say that here. Unless you're actually speaking *to* Him."

"Oh, right. My bad!" I felt guilty for being so irreverent after my moment of solemn peace, but I'd never seen an organ like that before. I hoped God understood.

We stepped out into the sunlight and squinted against the contrast from the dim halls of Notre Dame.

"Bright light! Bright light!" Jack shrieked playfully, shielding his eyes and pretending to stumble.

I laughed at him and buttoned my coat back up, adjusting my scarf around my neck.

Jack looked to the top of the cathedral and back to me, squinting with one eye against the sun. "Let's go to the top. The line's pretty short right now."

I followed his eyes back up to the tiny figures walking around so high above me and then shuddered all over.

"Oh no. Not me. You go right ahead. I'll be standing right here cheering for ya. You can wave to me from up there."

"Come on. The view is incredible. Especially on a clear day like this. You can see the Eiffel Tower. Sacré-Cœur on top of Montmartre."

"I've seen the Eiffel Tower, and I saw Sacré-Cœur yesterday while standing firmly on the ground, thank you very much. You go right ahead!"

"C'mon, Birthday Girl. You only live once. If you go up, and you hate it, you don't ever have to go again. You can always say you tried it and didn't care for it. But if you don't go up, you won't ever know what you missed."

"I'm okay with that." I glanced up in disbelief at the insane people waving and taking pictures from the walkway above.

"Tyler," Jack said as he took my hands in his. "You'll only get today one time. It's your birthday. You're in Paris. Live it up!" He widened those weird-ass teal eyes of his and offered me a smile anyone would be hard-pressed to resist. It occurred to me that I'd never fully realized how handsome Jack was. His dark black hair tousled by the wind. His easy smile carving out dimples beneath his cheekbones. Broad shoulders blocking the sun from my eyes.

Guilt tightened in my chest, and I flexed against it. I had chosen Cabe, but he didn't want me. So I didn't owe him anything. I could find someone else handsome if I wanted to. To hell with him.

"What do you say? You gonna go for it?" Jack tugged softly at my hands. I knew he meant climbing the steps of Notre Dame, but the question dug so much deeper for me. Something in my heart screamed *yes.* Go for it. Do something daring. Out of character. Something to remember this trip to Paris by other than the rough beginning and Cabe's rejection. I wanted to have fun. To enjoy my birthday. In spite of Cabe. Because of Cabe. Without Cabe.

So I squeezed Jack's hands and nodded, pushing aside my fear of heights and the aching in my heart for the one I loved.

Four hundred and two steep, circular steps to the top inside a small, claustrophobic stone tower sent my stomach and my mind into knots of panic. I stopped a couple of times—okay, maybe more than a couple—to catch my breath and protest to Jack that I couldn't go any farther. With every step, I knew we grew closer to the moment we'd step out into the sunshine so high above the ground. My stomach flips again just writing this, despite the fact I obviously survived doing it.

Throughout the entire journey upward, Jack proved to be the epitome of patience. He quietly encouraged and praised me, comforted me when I stopped, and playfully taunted me just enough to make me want to prove to him I could achieve the goal at hand.

And achieve it, I did. I climbed to the top of Notre Dame.

It was worth it, too. Worth every step. Worth every gurgle of my stomach and shake of my knees. From the top of Notre Dame, I could gaze down into the streets of St. Michel and watch the people going their merry way through the cavorting patterns of streets and alleyways. I took way too many pictures of the myriad of roofs below us and of the gargoyles on their perches high above the city where they'd kept watch over its inhabitants for centuries.

Thankfully, the high walls and complicated structures of the cathedral kept me from looking straight down, and Jack's firm grip on my hand steadied me in the moments I felt dizzy from the thought of the distance between me and the ground.

As I gazed across the cityscape, it was like Paris was frozen in time. If it weren't for the sound of traffic beneath us, I might've believed we'd traveled back to an older day. The architecture and the skyline portraying a city of a much older era.

In some ways, time had suspended for me. Like the real world and my real life existed in some parallel universe not affected by the one I was in. Like Paris was a separate life from the one I lived. Perhaps that made it easier to enjoy.

Still My Birthday
Picnic Lunch

When we came back down, I couldn't stop giggling. Facing and overcoming my fear had lightened my heart and filled me with a euphoria unlike anything I remembered experiencing. I felt ready to take on the world. I also felt like I could eat a horse. (Okay, not a *real* horse. I feel like I should clarify since the French considered horse meat a delicacy for quite some time. Maybe still today. I have no idea.)

Jack recommended a sandwich cart nearby, and we sat on a bench to eat a yummy *Croque Monsieur* as I consulted my guidebook. Well, until Jack grabbed it from me and pretended to toss it.

"What are you doing?" I wrenched it back from him as he laughed.

He spread his arms wide as he looked up to the sky. "It's a gorgeous day, Birthday Girl. Look at this sky, feel this sun. You don't need a guidebook. We should just go where the city takes us."

I rolled my eyes. "Jack, I'm a planner. I plan things for a living. There's no way I can just walk around and see where the city takes us. I'll go nuts. I have to at least look at the map and figure out where we're headed."

He considered this for a moment as he finished his sandwich, then clapped his hands together and said, "Okay. Tell you what. Let's compromise. You find your next tourist stop, and we'll head towards it so you have a target. But along the way, we'll meander and see where the streets take us. Deal?"

He looked so excited by the prospect it was hard not to be intrigued.

"Okay, deal."

We spent the next two hours making our way through the maze of twisted streets and crooked buildings throughout the *arrondissements* of St.

Germain and St. Michel, the Latin Quarter of Paris. Along the way, we found vintage shops and antique stores and plenty of places to stop.

It was hard not to think of Cabe as we walked through the neighborhoods. His love of Paris had inspired this trip. I could hear his voice in my head and imagine his blue eyes dancing when my eyes lit on a bit of scenery I knew he would love. Every sight and sound emphasized the emptiness inside me. The absence of the man I loved experiencing the most incredible place I'd ever been. The deep, gnawing acceptance of the fact that he left me. Possibly for good.

Thank God for Jack. I don't know if this dude fell from the sky in answer to prayers or what, but he was an excellent travel companion. His brain held a multitude of trivial tidbits—history, culture, architecture, art. No matter what topic we encountered, he had input. I soaked it up like a sponge, completely inspired and wide open to the environment around me. He waited patiently as I snapped photos of details that caught my eye, even posing without protest now and then. Without him, I never would have seen so much of Paris. I would've stuck to the most well-known landmarks in the guidebook. The back streets and tiny shops we encountered would have been lost to me.

When we finally reached the Rodin Museum, I was almost sad I had given him an endpoint. The spontaneity of drifting from street to street, following whatever sound, smell or sight caught our eye, engaged me in a way I'd never experienced before.

"Do you always just wing it when you visit someplace new?" I asked Jack after we left the museum, destined for a market street I'd seen in the guidebook.

He shrugged and nodded. "Yeah, pretty much. I mean, I like seeing the landmarks. You know, the Eiffel Tower. Notre Dame. But if you want to really explore a place, you have to hit the ground without knowing everything about it before you get there."

I shook my head in disagreement. "But I see value in knowing the history and background. I can walk right by any number of buildings and meander down any number of streets, but I want to know what happened there. I want the stories."

"Well, I like stories, too. We've been sharing stories. I would rather just find them out by chance discovery. Meeting a local and asking questions. Reading the plaques on the sides of buildings. Seeing something interesting and then looking it up on my phone. I don't want to know only what the guidebooks tell me."

The cool breeze lifted my hair across my face, and I shivered as I shook it back in place.

"Well, then I guess we tour well together. I'll share the history and background I learn from the guidebook, and you pepper it with spontaneous discoveries and daring detours."

He laughed and nodded again. "Yes, indeed. We are the perfect traveling companions. Are you cold?" Jack asked as I shivered again.

"I wasn't before, but the wind's picked up, I think." I hugged my arms tight around me and nestled my chin into my scarf.

"Do you want my coat?" he asked, taking his hands from his pockets.

"No, I couldn't. I'll be fine," I said, shivering even as I said it.

He looped his arm through mine and pulled me closer as we walked. Our feet matched each other stride for stride in what seemed to be as natural as walking alone. His nearness gave me wisps of his cologne as the wind whipped across us. I breathed it in deeply, suddenly enjoying his scent, his arms through mine, his maleness. My body reacted in all the right ways in all the right places, but my heart scolded me for being attracted to Jack when I knew I loved Cabe.

The market street bustled with activity and fresh, aromatic foods. The nose-tingling smells of strawberries. The mouth-watering essence of fresh baked bread. The decadent richness of the *chocolatier*.

"Let's have a picnic on the lawn by the Eiffel Tower," Jack said. "Buy some cold cuts, some bread, maybe cheese. A bottle of wine."

"Wine? It's mid-afternoon," I said, laughing.

"We're in France! You drink wine with breakfast here."

I shook my head at him, immersed in the colors and smells bombarding me from the sidewalk bins lining the narrow street. We ended up buying way more food than we needed. It just all looked too delicious to pass up. Pastries from the patisserie, cold cuts from the butcher, cheeses from the cheese shop, strawberries and grapes from the produce stand, and of course, a bottle of French Bordeaux.

"There's no way we're going to eat all of this," I said as we headed toward the Eiffel Tower.

He smiled at me and took the shopping bags from my hands. "We can die trying, and I'd be a happy man. Isn't that one of the things you're supposed to do in France? Eat and eat and eat?"

My heart skipped a beat. Cabe had been so excited about the French food and wine. He researched restaurants for the trip, planning out every meal to maximize our sampling of the city's cuisine. He would have truly been in his element on the market street. Our passion for cooking together had stemmed from his love of food and his knowledge of culinary skills. Had he been with me, we would have lingered in each shop with him conversing in French with the owners and picking up new ideas to bring back home with us. I pictured him going insane over the chocolates, cheeses, wines, and meats. I still couldn't believe he wasn't with me. I closed my eyes and grimaced to try and shoo him from my mind.

"You okay?"

I looked at Jack and swallowed hard, determined not to cry.

"Yep, I'm good." He stared at me for a moment, but I kept my head straight forward, knowing if I made eye contact with him I'd lose it, for sure.

Cabe wasn't here. His choice, not mine. So I clenched my teeth together and shoved him from my mind once more as we reached the crowded lawn. The rare appearance of the sun had brought out Parisians and tourists alike, and people sat on the grass reading, talking, eating, or just basking in the rays.

I followed Jack to an open area in the grass, unable to stop looking at the Eiffel Tower every few seconds. I'm blown away every time I see it. Like it's a mirage. Not even real.

I laughed then, a nervous giggle of happiness welling up within me to drown out the sadness that had threatened my resolve.

"What?" Jack asked.

"I'm just happy. It's my birthday. I'm in Paris about to have a picnic at the Eiffel Tower. Life is good!"

Even as I said it, my brain yelled Cabe's name and reminded me life was not good and I should be sad. But I refused to be. Maybe life back home was sad, but here in my alternate universe, in Paris, things were good.

"Too bad we couldn't get a blanket." Jack looked around at the ground before taking off his coat and spreading it wide on the grass. "Here, take this and sit on it."

"I'm not going to sit on your coat!"

"It's black. Not like it's going to show a grass stain. Just sit on it. It's actually pretty warm here in the sun. I don't need it."

"I can just sit on my jeans," I said. "Or my coat. I can take off my coat."

"Don't be ridiculous. There's room enough for both of us on mine." He patted the coat beside him before emptying the shopping bags on the inner lining.

We spent about an hour there on Jack's coat, finishing the bottle of wine between chunks of fresh, soft bread, salty cheeses, and sweet strawberries. We talked about Paris and traveling. Places I'd never been. Places he had been. Others where we'd each like to go. We talked about religion, politics, and food. I learned Jack is the youngest of three with one older brother and one older sister, and his parents still live in his childhood home.

I shared that I have two sisters and a brother, and that my dad died when I was thirteen.

"So any weddings for you, Ms. Wedding Planner? Ever been married?"

"Nope. I just plan them. I don't participate in them."

"Ahhh, a self-confirmed bachelorette, eh?"

"I guess. What about you?"

"No. I was engaged, once. But she seemed to think I needed to be home in order to be in a relationship. Which I guess I can understand. My job keeps me away a lot. It's okay, though. I mean, I like to do my own thing. Take off when I want to. Go where I want. Do what I want. When you're married, you have to take someone else into consideration. You have to do what they want. Or at the very least, make sure it's something they're okay with you doing. I don't know how well I'd handle that." He peeled the paper from the bottom of a fruit tart and finished it off in one huge bite.

"I guess that's one way of viewing marriage," I said through a mouthful of chocolates. "I'd rather think that if you loved the person enough to marry them, you'd want to take them into consideration. You know, want to spend time doing things they wanted to do?"

He brushed his hands together to rid them of crumbs. "You may be right. I need water, Birthday Girl. Can't wash down the sweet stuff with bitter wine."

He stood and began to gather the remnants of our lunch just as I felt my phone vibrate in my pocket. I looked at the screen with a mixture of dread and excitement, relieved to see it was Mama. I slid to answer it and barely got out "Hey Mama!" before my phone died.

I panicked, knowing that woman would be on the phone with the American Embassy in minutes insisting I'd been abducted if I didn't find a way to call her right back.

"I need your phone," I shouted. Jack immediately handed it over without question.

"Mama, hey! I'm sorry. My phone died."

"Hey, my baby girl! Happy birthday. Are you having the time of your life?"

"Yes, ma'am. I've had an amazing day. I can't wait to tell you all about it, but I can't talk long right now." I felt bad enough using Jack's phone. I definitely didn't want Mama to go off on one of her tangents.

"Okay. I tried to call you earlier, but I got your voice mail. I figured you was living it up in Paris and didn't have time to talk to us country folk back home."

"I had the phone on silent. I was going in museums and churches and stuff. I must not have felt it vibrate."

I mouthed 'sorry' to Jack. He shook his head and waved his hand telling me not to worry about it.

"Is Cabe having a good time?"

Her question was innocent, but I hesitated before answering. I didn't want to lie to my mother, but I also didn't want to tell her Cabe didn't come. Nor did I want to get into that conversation in front of Jack. I chose to be creative with the truth.

"How could anyone be in Paris and not have a good time? It's fabulous, Mama. But I need to go."

"Okay, baby. You have a great time, okay? Take lots of pictures. And don't forget to use protection."

"Good grief, you're a broken record with that. I got it, I got it. Stop telling me."

She laughed, and I cringed again at her sudden preoccupation with my sex life.

We said goodbye, and I rubbed Jack's screen on my leg to wipe away any make-up before handing it back.

"Everyone all good on the home front?"

"Yep. All good." I swallowed against the lump in my throat. Hearing Mama's voice had reminded me how far I was from home.

"You okay?" Jack asked.

I nodded and blinked back tears. "Yeah. Just talking to her, and my birthday and all."

"Awww. Come 'ere." He wrapped his arms around me, comforting and warm as I burrowed deeper into the pine scent of his cologne.

I may have ended up in Paris alone, but I wasn't alone anymore.

Still My Birthday (Long Day!)
On Top of the World

We walked to the refreshment stand underneath the Tower and bought water bottles, which we quickly drained.

"Okay!" Jack said, tossing his empty bottle in the recycle bin. "Let's do this."

"Do what?" I asked, afraid I already knew.

"You conquered Notre Dame and lived to tell about it." He pointed above us. "You can't leave Paris without going to the top of the Eiffel Tower." He grinned, and the dimples in his cheeks deepened beneath those gorgeous teal eyes.

"Oh hell no. You're insane." I shook my head and took a couple of steps backward.

Jack laughed. "Come on! Think about how awesome it felt when we came down. You were so excited! Don't you want to feel that way again?"

"I was excited to have my feet back on solid ground."

He shook his head. "No, you were excited because you faced your fears and challenged yourself to step outside your comfort zone. That was just the beginning, Birthday Girl. The warm-up to the main event. You can do this."

"Can't you find a tunnel or a secret passageway under the city for us to see? Aren't there, like, catacombs?"

"You'd rather go in a dark tunnel filled with skulls than the top of the Eiffel Tower? Really? Besides, you've already been beneath the city. The Metro."

I rolled my eyes. "Yeah, which went oh so well."

Jack laughed. "Come on. You have one shot to make this birthday

158

count."

"That sales spiel already worked on me once. It won't work again." I smiled at him and crossed my arms over my chest.

"But wasn't it worth it? Didn't you love the view? Think how awesome it'll be from here! It's even higher."

"Okay, that is not helping your case." I lifted one finger and wagged it in front of him.

"You're stalling. Let's do this, Birthday Girl."

I shook my head again, but I felt no real resistance. After all, he was right. It was a day for facing my fears and stepping out of my comfort zone. I'd arrived in Paris yesterday morning alone and bereft. But I'd made the best of it and created some pretty incredible memories along the way. I craned my neck back and shielded my eyes against the sun.

"Oh, wow, Jack. How high is it?"

"I don't remember. I think it's like six hundred feet. Want me to look it up or ask someone?"

I smiled and shook my head. "No. It doesn't really matter, and knowing would just make it worse."

He laughed as he wrapped me in another hug. "You can do this," he whispered against my hair.

I knew I could do it, but that didn't stop my stomach from wanting to upchuck lunch.

The sign for the lift said the wait was over two hours. I remembered Cabe's anger at the airport and how upset he'd been at the prospect of standing in the line. Jack seemed undaunted, however, deeming it worth the wait. My stomach turned its flips every time I looked up or thought about how high we'd go, but I also felt excitement building within me. My nerves buzzed with adrenaline. A lingering euphoria from my climb earlier today, perhaps.

We'd been in line about a half hour when I looked up again and shivered against my will.

"Are you cold? Here." Jack rubbed his hands up and down my arms.

"Thanks. I'm okay. Just nervous."

He looked ahead at the line before us, which barely seemed to move at all.

"Come on," he said, taking my hand and pulling the stanchion up for me to go under.

"What are we doing?"

"The line for the stairs is a lot shorter. We can take the stairs to the second level and then take a lift from there. Besides, climbing the stairs will help warm you up."

I pulled back on his arm. "No, no, no. No way. It'd be bad enough in the elevator. I can't climb those stairs and be able to look down and see how far it is. I'll flip out. I won't be able to move!" I stood firmly in my spot as he tugged lightly on my hand.

"Tyler, you can do this," Jack said. "I've got you. I won't let anything happen to you."

I started to tell Jack that climbing the stairs of the Eiffel Tower was nowhere on my bucket list. Like even if you looked all the way down the list, it wasn't there. But the way he looked at me, pleading with me to come with him, melted me a little. He'd made the difference in my birthday being special after Cabe left me high and dry. I didn't want to let Jack down.

"Okay, but if I faint or throw up, it's all on you. Literally!"

"You won't." He laughed and pulled me with him to the stairs. "You want to go in front of me or behind me?"

"Neither" I laughed as the nervous energy inside me bubbled over.

Seven hundred and four steps later, we reached the second level. Every single one terrified me. If it wasn't for Jack, I'd probably still be sitting on one of those damned steps with my head between my knees crying. Of course, then again, if it wasn't for Jack, I wouldn't have gone on the stupid steps to start with.

He was an amazing coach, though. If I ever lose my mind and decide to run a marathon, I will definitely look him up and have him be my trainer. He encouraged me and waited patiently for me, moving aside to let other people pass when I needed to sit. He held my hand and stroked my hair, speaking softly to me the entire climb, instilling me with courage and strength. Jack made me want to reach the top. For him. For me. For my future endeavors and things I may add to my bucket list now.

We walked around the second level and soaked up the view. No pictures or postcards from Paris could ever adequately capture its beauty. I tried to take in every single detail, but with so much to see, it felt impossible to absorb it all.

Jack held onto the rail and leaned back, his face turned up to the sun, and his ever-present smile radiating almost as brightly. I felt a bit guilty about monopolizing his experience with my fears. I'm sure he would have enjoyed the climb up the stairs much more without me alternately crying, cursing, and hyperventilating.

"I'm sorry about the stairs, Jack, I hope I didn't ruin it for you. I really appreciate you making me do this. You were right. It's incredible."

"Don't be sorry! I wouldn't have offered if I didn't want to. Life is usually better when it's shared with someone else. Especially the scary parts. I was honored you let me share it with you, Birthday Girl."

I smiled and turned back to feel the sun on my face. I saw the rays reflecting off *Les Invalides's* golden dome through a film of moisture. I had planned to share Paris with someone. As thankful as I was for Jack's appearance and his presence, it also made me painfully aware someone else should have been here with me. My smile faded as I blinked rapidly against the tears.

"Hey, you okay? Did I say something wrong?" Jack asked.

I shook my head but kept looking straight ahead, scared the tears would come spilling out if I looked at him.

He knew something was wrong. To his credit, he didn't push the matter, although I'm sure his next question was because of my tears.

"So, I don't think I asked you. What made you decide to travel to Paris by yourself?"

He stayed silent while I considered my answer. I didn't trust my voice to speak right away.

"I had originally planned to come with a friend"—pain pricked my heart at the word—"but it didn't work out. I didn't want to miss the experience." And what an experience it had been.

A call for the open lift to the top floor rang out, and Jack took my hand again as we headed toward it. We piled into the crowded lift, and I felt certain I would throw up by the time we got to the top. I had visions of me passing out at the top of the Eiffel Tower. Paramedics rushing to the scene. Tourists snapping photos and posting them on social media. News crews reporting live on the scene. And Jack, standing there embarrassed. Insisting he didn't know me. Had never seen me before in his life. Disappearing into the crowd as they hauled me away.

I didn't want to let him down or make him think less of me. He had put a lot of effort and encouragement into getting me up there. So I gritted my teeth and pushed my paramedic fantasy from my thoughts as I stepped out on top of the world.

I have regrets in my life, to be sure. But taking the hand of a relative stranger and climbing five hundred and ninety feet to the top of the Eiffel Tower will never be one of them. (I looked up the height afterwards.)

It was a once-in-a-lifetime experience. Truly magnificent in its fear-inducing, awe-inspiring, breathtaking, and nausea-defying awesomeness.

A Perfect Ending to
a Damn-Near Perfect Birthday

We took the lifts all the way back down, and once again, I felt euphoria and intense hunger.

We found a cafe near the river, where we sat under an umbrella, a cool breeze chilling us as the sun started its descent. Two hours went by like minutes, and I soaked up every bit of happiness I could pull from the scene. The sunset, the people around us, the conversation, and the magical energy pulsating through Paris.

After we'd eaten and drunk our fill, we meandered along the riverbank in the dark. Jack took my hand in his, and I let him, enjoying his warmth and his company.

"Wanna take a river cruise?" Jack asked. Memories of Cabe flooded to the forefront of my mind after I'd successfully held him at bay for a tiny block of time. I remembered him talking about the river cruise and how much he looked forward to taking me. I clenched my teeth and begged the anger to rise before sadness could take over. I would have loved going down this river with him, but he wasn't here. He chose not to be.

"Let's do it," I said somewhat defiantly. "Let's take a river cruise."

"You sure? You seemed to hesitate."

"I hesitated about climbing over a thousand steps today, too, but that didn't stop you." I stuck my tongue out at him and walked up to the ticket counter.

We sailed the Seine snuggled together underneath the blanket provided as we listened to the guide explain why Paris is known as the city of love. The boat's bright green and yellow lights danced along the river's banks and flooded over the tall buildings built alongside it. After a while, I rested my head against Jack's shoulder and breathed in his pine scent, lulled into a relaxed state by the movement of the boat and the wine I'd had with dinner. A moment so perfect I wished I could freeze time. Just to be there for a bit longer. Wrapped in Jack's arms underneath the blanket as the cold nipped at my nose and cheeks, listening to the guide regale us with love tales, surrounded by the magic and splendor of Paris. I didn't want it to end. I didn't want to go back to my real life and the mess I'd left behind.

We disembarked near the Eiffel Tower and sought out a coffee shop to get some hot java before the nightly light display began. It dazzled me all over again. The sparkling flashes added to the air of magic, another layer of the surreal spell Paris had cast over me where we existed in a different world, far removed from our everyday lives with their stresses and entanglements. I was mesmerized by the cold air, the bright lights, the buzz of the crowd surrounding us, and the warmth of Jack by my side.

I don't know exactly what led up to it, or who started what. I don't know if Jack kissed me or I kissed him. I guess we kissed each other. One minute we were sitting on a bench, huddled close together as we watched the lights sparkle and dance, and then there we were. Lips on lips, tongue against tongue. Hungry and needy. Searching and exploring.

I won't even lie and say I didn't enjoy it. And I won't even try to regret it.

After all, I was in Paris, the City of Lights. The City of Love. I was in the arms of a handsome, successful, well-spoken, well-educated man whose company I enjoyed immensely. It was my birthday. A day that had been incredible from start to finish. Great sights. Great food. Great company. Great accomplishments.

What could be a more perfect ending to a perfect day than a kiss underneath the Eiffel Tower while intoxicated by French wine and the magic of Paris?

Jack pulled back and looked down at me, his teal eyes vivid green in the amber glow of the tower.

"I wish I could stay right here. Right in this very moment," he whispered.

I smiled at his own thoughts so closely echoing my own. I shivered as the wind swirled between us, and Jack pulled me closer in his arms as he kissed me again. Warmth seeped through my body and spread like wildfire. A deep warmth no cold could touch.

We stayed there for over an hour, talking in between kisses. The frigid cold finally got the best of us, though, moving us indoors to a nearby restaurant for dessert and more wine.

The clock had long ago struck midnight when I finally climbed my final stairs of the day up to my room. Jack had left me at the hotel entrance with a rather passionate kiss and a promise to be around early to take me to breakfast.

My calves screamed with each step I climbed, and my mind swirled in a whirlwind of wine and confusion. I liked Jack. A lot. I'd enjoyed spending the day with him. In another world at another time, I'm sure I would've felt like one lucky girl to have found him. I mean, what was not to like? He was sweet. Charming. Intelligent. Funny. Upbeat. Always smiling. Definitely nothing like the maelstrom of depression and doubt I'd been dealing with back home.

All in all, I'd had a wonderful birthday, in large part due to Jack.

Which turned my thoughts back to Cabe.

How would the day have gone if Cabe had been here? Would we have laughed and been crazy like we can be? Or would he have been moody, withdrawn, and sensitive to everything? The Cabe he's been lately? Would I have felt so free and so exhilarated? Or would I have been worried about Cabe? Seeking to make sure he was okay. That *he* was happy.

I entered my room to find our suitcase on my bed with a note from the airport apologizing for the delay.

Our suitcase. A visual, tangible reminder of Cabe. Of his absence. Of his presence.

The illusion of my perfect day shattered, and my emotions went into overdrive as I wavered between guilt for feeling like I'd rather be in Paris with Jack instead of Cabe, and a longing for Cabe that threatened to completely undo me.

It was all so unfair. Why couldn't Cabe have chosen me? Why couldn't he have just gotten on the plane and been here to experience everything by my side? Then I would have never met Jack.

My heart rebelled at the thought even as it fleeted through my mind. I couldn't regret meeting Jack. He'd been a bright spot in the darkness for me. He'd been there for me when Cabe wasn't.

I showered and dug through the suitcase to find something to sleep in. I shoved Cabe's clothes to the side, but then I held his shirt to my face and inhaled deeply, the scent proving more painful than I could bear. I wiped my tears and exchanged the shirt for one of the silky negligees, but that brought forth memories of what might have been.

So I guess I'll just sleep in my birthday suit again tonight. Appropriate to close out my birthday, I suppose.

Sunday, March 9th

Jack rang my room from the front desk bright and early this morning. I took the stairs two at a time on the way down, anxious to see his smile and have him lift my sullen mood. My impending departure had weighed upon me since I woke up. I had no idea what waited for me back home. Hell, I didn't even know how I was getting home from the airport. If Cabe would even show up or if I wanted him to. When my phone charged back up this morning, I saw he'd left two voice mails last night, but I just deleted them without even listening. I didn't want him to ruin my last day. I'll figure out a ride home when I land if I need to.

Jack's smile lit up the entire lobby as he lifted me off the ground in his arms, kissing me soundly on the lips before setting me back down. "Good morning!"

"Well, good morning." I glanced at the front desk clerk and the family checking out, but they didn't seem to notice Jack's exuberance. It was Paris, after all. Frisky behavior is expected there, I suppose.

"Your plane doesn't leave until four, so I was thinking we could take the train out into the countryside, maybe to Versailles? Or we could stay close and head up to the antique markets, browse a little and do more meandering, if you'd like."

I laughed at him. "Who's this making all these plans? What happened to going where the city takes us? Throwing the guidebook out the window? You'll notice I came downstairs without it." I spread my arms wide so he could see I carried no book.

"I see, and I also see you're sporting new clothes. So I guess your suitcase made it after all?"

"At pretty much the last freakin' moment possible," I scoffed. "They may as well have left it at the airport. More of a pain in the ass for me to get it back there than it was worth to have it today. Although, I must admit, there's something to be said for clean panties and clean pants."

That remark garnered a sideways glance from the woman checking in, but I ignored her.

"Versailles sounds intriguing, but it makes me nervous to go so far. I want to get to the airport plenty early. Can you imagine if I missed my plane?"

Jack nodded. "It's only about an hour and a half round trip travel, but it's probably better to wait to see it when you have time to explore the grounds. I just wanted to make sure you had a great time on your last day here."

A wisp of sadness crossed his brow as he said it, and my conscience pricked me regarding Jack. For all he knew, he happened to meet some girl in Paris and ended up spending the weekend with her. Things must have been going pretty well from his point of view, but he had no way of knowing what a tangled web I'd left behind. I'd allowed him to live in my alternate universe, choosing not to share my troubling reality.

It would do him no good for me to explain it all, I reasoned. After today, I'd probably never see Jack again. So what did it matter? The thought pained me, and I reached up to plant a gentle kiss on his lips, one which he accepted and deepened into something much more passionate. The lady at the desk cleared her throat, and I reluctantly pulled away from Jack.

"I'm sure whatever we do will be a great day, but I need to stay close to check out of the hotel and get my luggage."

"They can store it for you," he said. "That way no matter where we end up you won't have to worry about your luggage until later this afternoon. You could check out now."

"Is it safe? To leave my luggage here, I mean?" I leaned close to him as I said it, not wanting to insult the front desk clerk.

Jack laughed. "Yes, people do it every single day."

So we went up to the room to get my suitcase, already packed and zipped on my bed next to the carry-on bag. I never really unpacked the stupid thing, so I only had to stuff my disgusting much-worn outfit in it to be ready to go.

"Wow, spacious room," Jack joked as he edged around the bed to look out the window. He swung open the large shutters and leaned out, the dark blue of his sweater contrasting nicely against the deep orange curtains. I had already put my camera up to take a shot when he turned and looked back at me, the outside light illuminating one side of his face while the other was cast in shadows. He smiled just as I clicked the shutter, the moment captured perfectly and frozen in time. Too bad I couldn't do that with the rest of our day.

It went by so quickly, the ticking countdown always present in our minds as we strolled hand-in-hand through parks, stole kisses in courtyards, and browsed through antique relics of other people's yesterdays gone by. My shoulders fell away from my ears, and I relaxed and gave myself over to the hazy fog suspended over the city. Any time my thoughts drifted to home—Cabe, my job, my real life—I forced myself back to Paris. To stay in the moment. Inside the snow globe existence Jack and I had created. I mean, who knew when I'd be happy again once I got back home? Why not take what happiness I could get while it was offered?

We took a bus to the *Père Lachaise* Cemetery so I could take a picture of Jim Morrison's tombstone for Mel. We lunched at a sidewalk cafe near the Sorbonne University, laughing and talking as if we had all the time in the world. We didn't, though. I realized with each passing moment how much I would miss Jack when I left. Our brief time together had been intense. Magical. I wanted to memorize every feature of his face. Of the cafe. Of everything about Paris. I dreaded leaving and going back to unhappiness.

Our pace slowed the closer we got to the hotel, goodbyes imminent. Jack suddenly pulled me against him and kissed me like the world might end tomorrow.

"I don't want to say goodbye," he said. He brushed my hair away from my face and tucked it behind my ear before grazing his knuckles across my cheek. "I feel like I've had air in my lungs for the first time in a long time. Walking away from you right now would be like walking away from oxygen. I don't know how to do that."

I smiled, conflicted between happiness at what he offered and guilt at the massive amount of crap he wasn't aware of.

He leaned forward to kiss me again, and I wriggled closer against him, which was nearly impossible as tightly as we were pressed together.

I wished again for the umpteenth time that I could freeze the moment. What a wonderful concept. For time to stop right then. To be frozen right there, without consequences, choices, and heartaches. Just me and Jack in the most romantic city in the world.

But time didn't stop. If anything, it sped up. I've been sitting here in the airport almost an hour already, and the weight of home pulls at me like mud stuck to my boots.

I'm not the same girl I was when I left home. This trip has changed me. Molded me. Shaped me. It's been terrifying, intimidating, empowering and meaningful. I've accomplished things on this trip I didn't know I could, and I've experienced things I never planned for. My confidence has increased tenfold after being stranded for these couple of days.

Was I stranded? Really? Stranded at the airport, yes. But I didn't have to board that plane. I could have gotten off when Cabe didn't get on, but I didn't.

I flew to Paris all by myself. I made my way to the hotel and to several areas of the city on my own, without the benefit of speaking the language or having any prior knowledge of the city.

I am stronger and more capable than I have given myself credit for.

Of course, once I met Jack, I was no longer on my own. Meeting him has changed me, too. He pushed me outside my comfort zone and gave me the courage to accomplish those things. He reminded me how much I love to laugh, and how good it feels to be wanted. How good it feels to be happy. Knowing the limit of our time pushed me to be vulnerable, to open myself up and allow him in without the usual bullshit I go through before falling for someone.

My heart aches to think I may never see him again. That this brief encounter is our only allotted time together in the grand scheme of life.

He asked if we could keep in touch, and I wrote my number on the back of a cocktail napkin at the hotel lobby bar and handed it to him. How clichéd. I cannot begin to imagine how any of that would work out, and I am certain it could only serve to complicate my life further, but I do know I couldn't just fly our separate ways and disappear forever. The time we shared meant too much.

I think striving to enjoy each moment this weekend made it painfully clear I haven't been living that way. I've wasted too much time overanalyzing, trapped in the past or paralyzed by fears about what the future may or may not bring with Cabe.

Whatever happens between Cabe and me back home, I know I need to stand up for myself and stop hiding my feelings in order to keep the peace. To keep from ruffling feathers so I wouldn't push him away.

I've tried to say what I thought was the right thing. To be considerate and put him first. To be who he needed me to be. I swallowed my hurt at him not contacting me when he came back because *he* was hurting and he needed *me* to be there for him. I haven't been honest with him since our relationship turned on its head New Year's Eve. Haven't really told him how I feel about him other than blurting out *I love you* as he threatened to leave that night. I've been holding back. Afraid to speak. Afraid to rock the boat. Afraid to upset him. Afraid to lose him.

You can't lose what you don't have, and I can't keep quiet anymore. I have to be open with Cabe. Lay my cards on the table and see how the game plays out.

I accomplished the things I did on this trip because I faced my fears, embraced the unknown, and went for what I wanted. When I get back, I need to tell Laura and Lillian I don't want the Lakeside manager position. I'm going to ask what is needed for my path to lead to senior planner.

It's amazing how many emotions you can feel at one time. Fear. Exhilaration. Inspiration. Grief. Joy. Hope. Sadness. A whirlwind rages within me as I write this. I am both excited and saddened by the changes that must happen as a consequence of what I've learned here.

Of course, part of the whirlwind inside me may be due to exhaustion. I've never walked so much in my life or climbed so many stairs. I'm actually looking forward to this long-ass flight so I can sleep.

Then wake up in Orlando and begin the rest of my life.

Flight Home

Why on earth would you wake someone up to ask if they want juice or water? I'm thinking if their eyes are closed and they're obviously sleeping, then they don't have thirst issues at that exact moment. I get that flight attendants have a schedule to adhere to. I understand they want to do one trip down the aisle for beverage service and it's inconvenient to keep getting requests from all over the plane after service concludes. But I say if someone is sleeping, they just missed their juice.

I'd been asleep about five hours, but I could easily have slept five more. Or ten.

Now I'm awake, and my brain is whirring and spinning. All that confidence and resolve felt great while I was sitting in the Paris airport, still safely ensconced in my snow globe world. But soon, I'll be getting off the plane. To what?

Will Cabe be there to pick me up? What will he say? Will he apologize profusely and beg me to forgive him? Or tell me he's decided we can't see each other anymore?

How will I feel when I see him? I left Orlando certain Cabe was The One and devastated he didn't seem to realize it. My feelings for him haven't changed, but the time I spent with Jack allowed me to see what happy can feel like without the fear. I want that. With Cabe. What if he's not capable of it? He keeps telling me he can't do this. What if he's right and I've just been holding on to the hope that he's wrong? I mean, if the man is telling me he can't, shouldn't I be listening to him?

Can I do that? Can I let him go? I don't know if I can. My heart screams no even as I write that. I love Cabe. He is my best friend. My confidante. My partner in so many ways. We've been through so much together. Weathered so much.

It's easy to be happy-go-lucky and upbeat for a weekend in Paris. It ain't real life. Cabe has been with me for real life.

Everyday life. Heartache and pain. Triumphs and joys. Can I really walk away from him because he doesn't make me laugh all the time? Because he isn't as carefree as some random stranger I met while we were both on vacation with no stress or responsibilities hanging over our shoulders?

Don't I owe Cabe more? Yes, I have to tell him how I feel. Yes, I need to stand up for myself. Loving someone doesn't mean they get a free pass to hurt you and take you for granted. But loving someone also means not giving up just because the going gets tough. Where does the line get drawn?

I'm exhausted again just thinking about it all. I wanted to sleep. To be oblivious for whatever time I had left before real life overtakes me on the ground and fully immerses me into its chaos and messiness. Damn flight attendant. Stupid juice.

I'm so glad I took the day off tomorrow. If I had to talk to a bride or groom right now, I'd probably convince them *not* to get married.

My job. Holy crap. Here I was talking all tough like I'm gonna walk in and tell Lillian Graham what I will and will not do. Ha! Okay. Like that's gonna happen. But I gotta do something. I don't want to hate my job.

I hoped writing my thoughts would make it easier to stop the hurricane blowing in my mind. I think I'm just getting more upset. Maybe I should watch a movie instead. Or maybe I'll push the attendant button and ask for more juice.

Home Again

He was there. Standing at the first available spot past security. My heart leapt at the sight of him, but anger and hurt slapped it back down and threatened it not to leap again. He moved forward to scoop me up in a big bear hug, and I stiffened. It seemed we'd been separated for much longer than a weekend.

He looked like hell. Like he'd been through the wringer.

"Oh my God, Ty. Are you okay? Are you alright?" He released me and held me back to look me up and down, then squeezed me to him again. "I'm sorry. I'm so sorry. I tried to get back to you. I tried to get on the plane. They wouldn't let me. I'm so sorry."

I shoved lightly against his chest. I needed space to breathe. I was tired. My emotions were raw. Anger simmered beneath the surface, battling for air alongside my wounded heart. One minute I wanted to burst into tears and cling to him, and the next I wanted to kick him in the nuts and walk away.

"What do you mean they wouldn't let you? Who's they?"

"Security. TSA. I walked past the security point without realizing what a pain in the ass that would be. I thought they'd let me skip the lines and the scanners since I'd already been through, but no. I tried to explain to them my flight was leaving and I didn't have time to wait. I guess I got a little belligerent."

He'd been belligerent with me that whole day. It took no stretch of the imagination to believe he'd been hostile with other people, too. Especially people standing in his way.

Numbness crept over me as his words sank in. I'd been furious with him all weekend, and the fury was the buffer I needed to get by. Not to mention the reason I made the choices I did while in Paris. But if he'd tried to get back to me—if he hadn't left me to travel alone on purpose—then it was a whole new ballgame. Uh-oh.

"They pulled me out to detain me, which definitely did nothing to improve my mood. When I heard my name announced for final boarding, I pretty much went ballistic. One thing led to another, and I kind of shoved a TSA agent. It appears the authorities don't look too highly on that sort of behavior. They had me in handcuffs before you were even off the ground."

I gasped. "Cabe! Are you okay?"

"I've been better, Buttercup. They held me here for about eleven hours questioning me to determine if I was a terror threat, and then when I passed that test, they arrested me for simple battery and sent me downtown. I couldn't appear before a judge until Saturday morning, and then it was late Saturday afternoon before everything got processed for me to be released. I have to say, I met some really interesting folks in lock-up, and I have a date with a judge coming up, but I'm fine, all things considered. Just happy to see you and finally have you back in my arms. What about you? You okay? Please know I did everything I could to get back to you."

I didn't know what to say. Guilt washed over me as I considered my actions of the last few days. I worried he might see shame written all over my face. At the same time, I was still angry. Obviously I felt bad he'd been arrested, but it was his own damned fault. If he hadn't stormed off at the gate, if he hadn't walked past security, if he hadn't shoved the guy. My head swam just thinking about what a mess he'd made. Not to mention the extension of the mess on my end.

"As soon as I got out and could get to a phone Saturday, I tried to call you. It went straight to voice mail. Oh, do you have my phone, by the way?"

I nodded and fished it out of my purse.

He took it from me and his hand lingered on mine.

"Did you not get my messages? I'm so sorry, Ty. I'll make it up to you, I swear."

I managed a hesitant smile but couldn't muster much more. It made me feel better to know he tried to come back. It felt good to hear him apologize, and I was relieved he came to the airport to pick me up.

But I felt detached. So much had happened since the last time I saw him. I didn't know where to go from there. What to tell him about Paris. About Jack. What to say about his arrest. Being so damned tired didn't help, of course. I just wanted to go home and sleep. Too much to think about.

"So, how was Paris?" he asked once we were settled in the car and out of the garage. His voice was tentative and quiet, his hesitation clear.

"Good." What else was I supposed to say? It was fabulous? Life-changing? I'll never be the same after this trip? I had one of the best experiences of my life. And oh yeah, I met the coolest guy.

"Did you take lots of pictures?" I could hear wistfulness in his voice, and I knew it pained him to know I'd seen Paris without him. The trip he'd planned. The places he'd wanted to show me. Not only wasn't he there, but someone else was. Not that he knew that yet.

Guilt racked me. There I was, enjoying the sights and living it up in Paris, hand in hand with a stranger and writing about my surreal snow globe break from life, and the whole time Cabe had been sitting in a jail cell and worried about getting back to me.

"Yeah, I think I got some good shots." Talk about awkward. What could I tell him about the trip? Anything I talked about, anything I described or got excited about, would only serve to hurt him and make it worse that he wasn't there with me.

My exhilarating, life-altering weekend suddenly seemed less exciting. I waffled between guilt and happy memories. I mean, like I said before, it wasn't my fault he'd gotten mad and stormed away. I didn't make him go past the security checkpoint as he wandered in anger.

Hello?! Duh! They have signs clearly marking the point of no return. It certainly wasn't my fault he'd shoved someone and landed in jail.

I felt guilty that I'd thought Cabe deserted me, though. That I'd tossed him aside on the trip any time my thoughts tried to resurrect him, and then sought comfort from someone else without fully knowing the circumstances or giving Cabe a chance to explain.

How could I love him and turn away from him so easily? If I truly loved him, wouldn't I have given him the benefit of the doubt? Wouldn't I have tried to reach him once I landed in Paris?

My mind sought to put the blame back on him because that was easier. I replayed the airport scene in my head, reminding myself of how angry I'd been and what an ass he'd been.

"What was wrong with you, Cabe? You weren't yourself. You haven't been yourself for a while. You don't normally go around punching people or shoving people, but you've been in, like, three altercations in the past month. Why won't you talk to me? Tell me what's going on."

He sighed, his hands gripping and releasing the steering wheel as he weighed his words.

"It's a long story, Ty. I know you're tired. It can wait."

Frustration and anger sparked immediately as the old familiar tension settled over me.

"Bullshit. You keep saying that, but it can't wait. I need to know what's going on with you. I think you owe me an explanation."

"You're right. But it's late, and we've both had a long weekend. Can we talk tomorrow? I'll answer anything you want to know. Open book."

As much as I wanted to demand he tell me right then, I knew he was right. I was whipped. I'd been up almost twenty-four hours and despite the few hours I dozed on the plane, my body was still on Paris time. I didn't know if I could even stay awake to hear what he had to say, much less be able to process it.

I gave us both a reprieve.

"Okay. Tomorrow then."

We rode in silence the rest of the way to my apartment, and I told him goodbye at the door.

So now here I lay. Unable to sleep and unable to stop wondering what he will tell me tomorrow. Then where do we go from there?

Monday, March 10th

He came over around noon with lunch, which paled in comparison to the rich food I'd grown accustomed to. I'd had a restless night with my body's time clock jet-lagged out of whack and my brain wrestling with the issues at hand. I didn't know what he intended to tell me, but I knew it must be pretty serious to have caused us so many problems.

On top of which, I had some 'fessing up of my own to do. My time with Jack in Paris ate at me. I had no idea what to tell Cabe. I felt dishonest not telling him, but how could I explain without hurting him?

Cabe seemed on edge. Uneasy. Something to do with the talk we were about to have, I'm sure. He ate his lunch standing at the kitchen counter, then he went to the sliding door to look out and then to the couch. No longer had he sat than he was back up and to the sliding door again.

I wanted to put him at ease and make him relax, but I was all keyed up myself in anticipation of what his news might be and what to do with my own confessions.

"Okay, Cable. Let's talk." I settled into the comfy chair with my feet tucked beneath me, my heart pounding as I listened.

He took a deep breath and let it out with a whistle. "Alright. What do you wanna know?"

I smiled at him. "I don't know. Whatever is bothering you. Whatever makes you drop off the face of the earth and not call me. Whatever's making you run hot and cold. Making you want to punch people in bars and parades and airports."

"Where the hell do I start? It's not a simple answer. Not like it's one thing."

"Okay. Something happened Valentine's weekend when you had family in town. You said it was a long story, and you never told me. Start there."

"Right. That. Well, you already know my father left my mother when I was a kid."

"Yeah. When you were three, right?"

He nodded. "And you know he left her because he was already married."

"Yeah." I didn't understand why this would have anything to do with us.

"Well, you also know I don't talk about him a lot because I don't want to have anything to do with the asshole. I've probably told you more than I've ever told anyone else, which isn't much. I prefer not to think of him at all."

He stood and moved to the sliding door, running his hands through his hair in frustration.

"I spent my whole life without a dad, Ty. He left my mother the first time when I was only six months old. He came back when I was about two, just long enough to get her pregnant with Galen and give me a couple of fuzzy memories, and then he took off again just before my sister was born. We were expendable. We weren't his real family, so we didn't matter."

"Which means he's a jackass, and you were better off without him."

"Yeah, but growing up, I didn't know that. I hoped for a while he'd come back. That he'd choose us. But then as I got older, I just got mad. Every ballgame I pitched without a dad in the stands. Every time a friend's dad invited me along on a father-son camping trip or fishing excursion and I felt like a third wheel. At least kids with divorced parents got every other weekend. Or a few days at Christmas. I even told people my father was dead for a while, but that got back to my mom and she said it wasn't right to lie about it. But I was embarrassed. So eventually I clammed up and avoided any conversations where I may have to explain why my dad was a no-show in life."

He walked to the kitchen and poured himself a glass of water.

"I don't remember how much I told you about his other kids. The ones he chose over us. A son born six months after me. Hence him leaving and going back to his wife. A daughter, born two months before Galen. They were his *real* family. They got the father. Ball games, school events, birthdays, Christmases. They got what Galen and I never had. I was his firstborn, Tyler. His firstborn son. He denied my existence and raised his other son in my place. That one got the last name, the ritzy mansion in the Hamptons, the college fund. I got jack shit."

I heard the wounded boy in his voice, and my heart hurt for him. But I didn't understand what this had to do with us. Or him going AWOL on Valentine's.

He spoke again before I could ask.

"I hate him, Tyler. I despise him with every fiber in my being. He ruined my mother's life. He walked out on me and my sister, and he left my mom to fend on her own with two babies and her dancing career in ruins. If he was on fire in the desert, I wouldn't piss in his mouth to put the fire out."

"Okay. That's understandable."

"Galen, on the other hand—" he paused, and I flinched at the venom he used to say his sister's name, "—she doesn't see it that way. She's always held onto the fantasy that one day the old man would come to the door bearing gifts, and he'd take her to his fancy house and introduce her to her other brother and sister. Like she'd be rightfully restored to her throne."

His tone conveyed his view of Galen's fantasy as a betrayal.

"She called me Valentine's Day and asked me to come over for dinner. Said we needed to clear the air. I thought she meant between the two of us. The comedy club thing. But when I got there, it was a set-up. She'd tracked those two down. Been talking to them behind my back to arrange a visit. I walked in and got blindsided. I had no idea. There's my *sister*"—he spat the words through his teeth—"laughing and joking and having a family reunion with these damned people. Sharing freckles and moles and discussing childhoods and life stories. I couldn't believe she did that to me, Ty. To me and our mom. I have *never* wanted anything to do with them. She knew that. Galen knew. We've discussed it so many times. She took it upon herself to decide my life for me. To throw them in my face."

He rubbed his hand roughly cross the stubble on his chin as he stared out the sliding glass door.

"Jeffrey could have been my twin. Same age. Same height. Our faces almost identical. Same eyes. I couldn't help but look at him and hate him. He is who I could have been if I'd had my father. If my father hadn't chosen him over me."

I exhaled and realized I'd been holding my breath, my heart tight with his pain. I couldn't imagine how he must have felt to come face to face with this phantom brother with no warning. "Damn, Cabe. I'm so sorry. What did you say to him?"

"I don't know. Nothing nice. I didn't stay long."

"Cabe, why didn't you tell me? Call me? Or come over? You didn't have to deal with this alone. I would've been there for you."

"It was Valentine's Day. You had a bazillion weddings and were all stressed out. I wanted to tell you, but what kind of boyfriend would I be to lay all that on you for Valentine's? Of course, I ended up screwing up Valentine's anyway, didn't I? I had planned to be here when you got home. Flowers, bubble bath. Instead I ended up driving around by myself for hours, trying to process everything and make sense of it all. I finally drove over to the beach and just sat there in the sand until the sun came up. Then I drove back home and slept."

My heart leapt a little at hearing him say boyfriend, but this was no time to get all silly sentimental.

"What did your mom say? Was she upset?" I couldn't imagine Maggie would be happy with her daughter for betraying her and her son that way.

Cabe scoffed. "She knew. She knew Galen had contacted the daughter, Julie, on Facebook, and she knew Galen had been talking to them both. She even knew they were coming to visit. But no one in the family bothered to tell me. Or to ask if I wanted to be included. Galen took it upon herself to decide what was best for me. Something she and my mother seem to have been doing a lot lately." He sneered and pushed off the wall to turn and go back to the kitchen. He paced like a tiger caged.

"I don't get it. He screwed her over, Ty. My mother was gorgeous. Stunning. At the height of her career when she met him. Do you have any idea how much work it takes for someone to reach the level of a prima ballerina? How good she had to be to achieve that? He took it all away from her. I stood by her all these years. Tried to protect her. To make up for it. For what we cost her by being born. And then she turns around and supports Galen associating with those people."

I stood and went to him. He flinched when I put my hand on his arm, but he didn't pull away.

"Cabe, you can't fault Galen for wanting to know them. I understand your reasoning, but she has to make her own decisions for what's best for her. I'm not saying it was right of her to not tell you, but—"

He jerked his arm away and stepped away from me, whirling to face me in anger. "She had no right. I will never forgive them. Any of them. Not Galen. Not my mother. And never ever will I forgive that man or forget what he did to us. Even if they forget, I won't. I swear to God, Jeffrey will never be my brother. Julie will never be my sister. They can all kiss my ass as far as I'm concerned. The whole lot of them. I grew up without a father. I can go the rest of my life without a mother or a sister. Fine by me."

I gasped. If anyone had ever told me he would say such a thing about Maggie or Galen, I would not have believed it. They'd always been such a tight-knit unit.

"Cabe, you don't mean that. Maggie and Galen mean the world to you."

He shook his head. "Mom called him, Ty. We had a heated conversation when I woke up that Saturday, and I left the house angry. I drove to Lakeside to see you, but a wedding was just ending and it was pouring down rain. I could see you had your hands full so I pulled away. And as I was leaving, my phone rang. It was him. My mother called the son-of-a-bitch and gave him my phone number. She turned on me and sold out to him. Like Galen wasn't enough. I get to answer my phone and hear my father's voice for the first time since I was three years old, only for him to chew my ass for the way I treated his other children. Galen included. Like the three of them were separate from me. They can all go to hell. I won't shed a tear."

I'm very rarely speechless. I talk a lot, and I will break into song and dance to avoid an awkward pause. But I had nothing to say. I knew from the few times he'd discussed it that his dad's abandonment had always screwed with Cabe's head. I also knew he'd always felt like the protector for Maggie and Galen. The man of the house by default. Regardless of the fact he was only a young boy when he assumed the role.

To feel betrayed by them. In conjunction with the one who originally betrayed them all. Wow.

I couldn't believe all this had happened a month ago and I never knew. He hadn't told me. Had I really been so self-absorbed that I didn't sense something was wrong? Well, yeah, I guess I did. But I thought it was all about me. The push and pull. The commitment issues. The anger simmering just underneath the surface. The edginess. It all made more sense now. I wondered how differently the last few weeks would have gone if he had only talked to me.

"Cabe, I can't believe you didn't tell me any of this. I had no idea this was going on. Why haven't you told me?"

"Hell, it's not like I didn't try. I called you that Sunday, but you didn't call me back. I asked you out to dinner to talk, but you had all the work stuff going on. Paris was coming up. We already had tension between us, and I didn't want to add more stress. I guess I thought if I kept it all inside it wouldn't affect us. That didn't really work, huh?" He walked to door again and leaned his forehead and forearm against the glass.

"You used to tell me everything," I said. "I feel like since you came back you don't talk to me anymore."

"No, I do. I don't know. I just feel like…like it's all so screwed up now. Like all you're going to see is my flaws."

"That's ridiculous. I've been seeing your flaws for years. I have no illusions that you're perfect."

"Thanks." He turned back to face me, his face more tired and haggard now than before.

"You know what I mean. I need you to talk to me. Let me back in. I can't stand when you shut me out."

"I'm not. Or I don't mean to. I just feel like everything's caving in on me lately. From all sides. Everywhere I look there's the potential for disaster. Sometimes it seems safer to just retreat inside myself and try to figure it all out. I don't mean to hurt you. I don't want to do anything to lose you."

"You're not, but we've got to work together. I need to know you're in, no matter what comes against us."

He came to me slowly and rubbed his palm against my cheek. I nuzzled my face into his hand and kissed it before he pulled me in his arms and sighed heavily. I could feel the tension release from him, and I clung to him in a fierce determination to help him carry the load. My resolve to never give up on Cabe strengthened tenfold. He may not be able to count on his mom and sister, but he could count on me. I wouldn't let him down, and I'd protect him from all of them.

That's about when it dawned on me I still had to tell him about Jack. About my own betrayal. I cursed myself again for ever doubting Cabe. For tossing him away while I was in Paris.

He took my face in his hands and kissed me so tenderly I thought I would surely cry.

"I'll do better, baby," he said. The first time he'd ever called me that. "I'm sorry. I'm trying."

His eyes held mine, and I hoped he couldn't see me freaking out. There was no way I could tell him. Not tonight. Another time, maybe. I'd find a way. Find a time. He'd promised to do better at being open with me, so I had to be open with him. But not tonight.

Tonight I wanted to do all I could to make him okay. Knowing the entire time I had another bombshell to drop on the poor guy. Galen and Maggie weren't the only ones who had betrayed him. I hadn't meant to, but I wasn't sure he would see it that way.

Tuesday, March 11th

And just like that, it's over.

We'd talked a bit longer last night, and then I took a shower. When I got out, my bedroom was bathed in candlelight. Cabe took me by the hand and led me to the bed. With a touch so gentle it seemed he thought I may break, he began to kiss me. His lips barely grazed my skin as he moved across my forehead and down my jaw, pausing to nibble on my ear lobe before continuing his feather kisses down the side of my neck. He paused for a moment in the hollow at the base of my throat before crossing to the other side to trace the outer rim of my ear with his tongue, his voice barely a whisper.

"You're so beautiful, Ty."

I shivered as he kissed along each shoulder and down each arm, pausing to take each of my fingers in his mouth before coming back up to my neck again. A quiver shot through me as he opened my towel and let it drop to the floor. He lowered his head to linger on each breast, nibbling and kissing, tasting and tugging. I whimpered softly in protest when the warmth of his mouth disappeared, but he only left long enough to ease me onto my back across the bed before returning his lips to my skin, kissing his way across my ribs and over my stomach.

I was disappointed for a moment when he bypassed the part of me that most wanted to be kissed, but then he took my breath away trailing kisses down the soft flesh inside my thigh and flicking his tongue along the inside of my knee. I reached for him, but my hands came up empty as he continued his journey down my calf, caressing my ankle with his tongue before his lips tickled across the top of my foot and each toe.

By the time he made his way back up my other leg and reached my inner thighs again, I thought I would truly go mad if he didn't give my body the release it was screaming for. It was worth the wait. His tongue was every bit as wonderful as I remembered, perhaps even more so.

He cradled me in his arms afterward, stroking my hair and whispering as he kissed me.

"I'm so sorry about Paris. About your birthday. Valentine's. Hell, everything. I'm gonna make it up to you. I swear I will."

I started to lift my head, to tell him he didn't have to make anything up, but he stopped me.

"*Sshh*. Just sleep, baby. Just let me hold you in my arms and be thankful for you. Go to sleep."

He kissed the top of head, and I snuggled into him. We stayed that way the whole night. He never let go of me, even as he murmured and fretted in his sleep.

I couldn't stop thinking about him all day. His childhood issues had to factor into his reluctance to commit. If he felt like he could be abandoned or betrayed again, naturally that would affect his ability to be all in. Was he scared he would be like his father and leave? Or worried I would leave him? Betray him? Like Monica? I felt like I'd been given a hugely important piece of information, but it only led to more questions. Key pieces of the puzzle were missing.

I drove home from work determined to talk through whatever else he was feeling and get to the bottom of the disconnect. In order for us to make it, I'd have to understand what was going on in his head. Scary or not. I mean, hell, we were both scared. Better to face it together, right?

I pushed all thoughts of confessing about Jack to the background. We had more imminent issues to deal with, and it wouldn't help Cabe for me to tell him now on top of everything else he was dealing with.

He was still at my place when I got home, in the kitchen making dinner for the two of us. He seemed to be in better spirits than last night, and though I hated to bring up more serious stuff, I knew I needed answers. I needed to understand how his past and his fear of commitment might be holding us back. I had promised myself in Paris I would start standing up and speaking up. No time like the present.

Cabe cleared the table while I gathered dishes to set it. My satchel wasn't latched all the way, and when he picked it up, the flap came open and spilled the contents. He grabbed the paperwork and slid it back inside but lingered on the photo developing envelope.

"These your Paris pictures?" He hesitated a bit when he asked, like he wasn't sure he wanted to know. I hesitated, too. Froze is more like it. When I picked them up at lunch today, I figured I would weed out the pictures of Jack before showing the others to Cabe. Which I hadn't had time to do yet.

"Yeah." I reached to take them from him, but he pulled his arm back.

"Wait a minute. I wanna see."

I shook my head and reached for them again. "Nah. Let's just eat before it gets cold. We can look at those later." After I went through and removed any incriminating shots of Jack.

"Let's look over dinner," Cabe said, holding the envelope firmly in his hand. For a split second, I wondered if he somehow knew about Jack and meant to trap me. I don't know how he would, but my guilty conscience kicked into overtime.

"So let's see 'em," he said as soon as we were seated. "Show me what you saw, and I'll let you know if it's someplace I've been."

My appetite disappeared completely, and my heart nearly turned inside out. Here he was, being all gallant and giving. I knew it must be bittersweet for him that I'd gone without him, especially since it was his own fault. I appreciated his interest in the photos, but I knew he wouldn't be too happy about what had transpired there.

The first few pictures were fine. They were taken Friday when I was still alone. Cabe looked carefully at each one, sharing his own experiences and questions as we went, complimenting my artistic eye and the quality of the shots. The first photo of Jack was taken at the top of Notre Dame. We'd asked a stranger to snap one of us together.

"Who's this?" Cabe asked.

I so didn't want to be one more nail in the betrayal coffin. Monica. His sister. His mother. His father. How much should one man have to take? But I couldn't lie to him. I wouldn't.

"That's Jack," I said. "A friend I met in Paris."

"You met a friend? You didn't mention that."

I tore off a piece of bread and put it in my mouth, then had to chew it and swallow before I could speak. "We haven't really talked much about the trip. We've been caught up in other conversations."

He continued to flip through the photos, skipping past tons of scenery and landscape shots to pause and linger on any photo of Jack. I cringed. Jack in St. Michel. Jack at the Rodin mimicking The Thinker. Another during our picnic lunch with Jack smiling as he sat on his coat, surrounded by food and wine with the tower in the background. One together at the top of the Eiffel Tower, and another on the river cruise, taken with the captain. Jack standing in the window of my room. Jack smiling at me as he ate a crepe at the cafe Sunday afternoon.

Cabe flipped through them rapid-fire, no longer even focusing on the photos. When he had finished, he slammed the stack down on the table and looked at me, accusation strong in his eyes.

"A friend? You met a friend in Paris? A friend you spent the whole weekend with?"

I felt busted. No words sprang forth in explanation or defense. I had nothing.

He picked up the photos and flipped back to the hotel shot. "Please tell me this isn't your hotel room. *Our* hotel room."

"It's not what it looks like, Cabe." But wasn't it?

"Then tell me what it is, Tyler. Because I booked the reservation online, and I could have sworn this is the brick wall and orange curtains from our hotel room."

I hated him calling it *our* hotel room when he hadn't made the trip, but it was a technicality and I knew it. He had booked it. It was ours. And I had brought another man into it.

"Look, Cabe. I met this guy at the airport and then ran into him again at the Eiffel Tower. We just sort of clicked and hung out. He was alone, and I was alone, so we just kind of banded together." I refrained from adding in my defense that I was alone because Cabe had stormed off at the airport and gotten himself detained by security and arrested.

He took a long drink of his iced tea and wiped his mouth with his napkin before he spoke again. His voice cracked with a slight tremor, and his eyes blazed as they met mine.

"Did you sleep with him?"

"Why is that always a guy's first question? Do you think a girl can't meet someone and hang out without sleeping with him? You think I'm the type of person who would just meet some total stranger in Paris and go to bed with him?" My cheeks flushed hot with shame as I said it, knowing full well even though Jack and I had gotten nowhere near having sex, we'd certainly shared quite a few passionate kisses.

"You didn't answer the question, Tyler." Cabe's words were like barbed steel cutting through me as his eyes glistened cold and hard.

"No, Cabe. I didn't sleep with him." But I'd definitely been attracted to Jack. Wasn't that enough?

He looked away from me and stood to clear his untouched meal. I felt defensive. I felt ashamed. I wanted to lash out at him for putting me in that crazy situation and then judging me for how I dealt with it.

"Might I remind you," I asked, "that I wouldn't have been alone in Paris if you had simply communicated with me about all the crap going on with your family? If you had just told me why you were wigging out, none of this would have happened. You chose to walk away from me that day. You chose to let me get on the plane alone."

He slammed his plate into my sink. "Bullshit! I did everything I could to get back to you. I went to jail trying to get back to you!"

I stood and matched his volume. "But if you hadn't walked away, if you'd just talked to me, then there wouldn't have been a need for you to go to jail. I went to Paris alone because you couldn't let me in, Cabe."

"So you just run into the arms of the first man you meet? You're actually saying it's my fault you hooked up with someone else while I sat my ass in a jail cell trying to figure out how to get back to you?"

"What do you care? As you so easily conveyed to the guy in the dance club, *we're not dating! We're just friends!*" I screamed so loud I'm surprised my neighbors didn't call the cops. I didn't care, though. Every emotion of the Cabe-Tyler roller coaster had come roaring down around me, and the adrenaline of it coursed through me like wildfire.

"You're right," he said with a calmness that gave me chills. "We're not dating. You can be with whomever you choose."

I went to him and put my hands on either side of his face. "I choose you, Cabe. I want to be with you."

He pushed my hands away and crossed past me to the living room.

I spun around and forced my voice to be quiet and calm. "So if we're not dating, then what is this? What are we doing?" I paused to give him time to answer, but he didn't. "I love you, Cabe. You know I do. I believe you love me, too."

Still no response. He stood facing the sliding door again in a silence so deafening I wished he would yell and scream. The air in the room felt heavy. Too heavy to breathe. Like my lungs were working twice as hard with minimum results.

"Cabe? Do you love me?"

He turned slowly, his face strained. His shoulders slumped. He looked utterly defeated. His eyes lifted to meet mine and held there.

"I don't know."

We both stood in the heavy silence for a moment as I unpacked what he had said.

He didn't know.

He did not know if he loved me.

The words hit me like a hammer with a sharply-honed edge that pierced my heart and took my breath away.

I think I always thought if I ever got the courage to ask, he'd have no choice but to tell me the truth. Except I'd believed the truth was he loved me. What if that was my truth, but not his? That would explain everything, wouldn't it?

My breath caught in my throat as I opened my mouth to speak. I swallowed hard and tried again, forcing the air past the constrictions that choked me.

"Then go, and don't come back until you know. I can't do this anymore, Cabe. I can't be your everything one day and your nothing special the next. I can't stand for my body to burn like a fire when you kiss me and touch me, and then starve from the lack of it when you won't. To suffer the consequences of what's going on in your life without being allowed to be privy to it. You either love me or you don't. We either go all in or we don't. You need to figure it out. This hurts."

I walked to the door and pulled it open with shaking hands.

"I want all of you, Cabe. If you can't give me that, then I'm better off alone."

His eyes never looked away from me as he grabbed his coat and his keys. He paused at the door, his face just inches from mine. My mind screamed and pleaded with me to tell him to stay. To reach out and grab him, hold him, and never let him leave. To kiss him and make him realize what I meant to him.

But if he couldn't give it freely, it would never work. He left without a word, and I collapsed on my floor in what has been an all too frequent occurrence. My heart disintegrating as it shattered yet again.

Saturday, March 15th

I don't know if I should be doing weddings in my current state of mind. Everything about them pisses me off. Everyone's gushing about how much in love they are. The bride and groom just can't wait to walk down the aisle into marital bliss. It's disgusting. It turns my stomach until I want to scream at them all. Their guests are all just stupid people who irritate the hell out of me.

Today, we had bubbles for the staged exit. Little, tiny plastic bottles with just enough soapy solution to create a beautiful bubble-filled backdrop for the bride and groom's photos as they exit through their guests.

As I stood there with my basket repeating my spiel to each guest telling them to line up on either side of the sidewalk to blow bubbles as the bride and groom leave, some freakin' idiot asked me if they were supposed to throw the bubbles.

Like, I offered him the basket and said, "Please take a bottle of bubbles to blow as the bride and groom exit."

And he looked back at me and earnestly asked, "Do we throw these?"

It took everything I had in me not to answer, "Why, yes, sir. You just toss these here hard plastic bottles right at the bride and groom. In fact, we'll give you a free drink at the bar if you can peg the bride right between the eyes. And later, we're gonna pass out potato chips in baskets for no damned reason at all."

WTF.

Where do these people come from, and how do they navigate everyday life without killing themselves or others in their ignorance? I mean, really. You got yourself dressed, boarded a plane, made it from the airport to your hotel, then managed to get yourself here for the ceremony, but you have to ask me if I want you to throw something hard and plastic at the bride and groom? Are you kidding me?

Laura put her arm around my shoulders as we walked to the car after the event and asked, "Wanna talk about it?"

"Talk about what?"

She shook her head and chuckled under her breath. "Let's go get a coffee."

"I don't want a coffee," I said, stubbornly refusing to give up my armor of bitchiness. I knew if I let my guard down I would fall all to pieces, and I couldn't do that.

"Then we'll get ice cream, but I'm not taking no for an answer."

I explained the situation to her over a salted caramel sundae, and I marveled again at how easily I pour my heart out to my bosses. I really think I need to pony up for a good therapist. I tell my life story much too often to way too many people. Isn't that what this stupid diary is supposed to be for?

"I just thought I'd finally found The One, and I'd be happy, you know? Happily ever after, they say."

Laura nodded and licked her spoon. "Ah, the inherent fallacy of the fairy tale. Happily Ever After doesn't mean happy every day. They don't tell you that, do they?"

"I know that. But it can't be the right thing if there's this much conflict. If it's this hard to make it work, then he must not be the one for me. Am I right?"

She took another bite of ice cream and rolled the spoon on her tongue. "So, you think there's just one?"

I thought about it for a moment before I answered. "I don't guess. I don't know. I mean, I don't think there's one guy who'll ride in and fix it all. That's unrealistic, but I do believe if he's the right one, it will just click. Like you'll just know it. If I didn't know it for five years, then maybe I don't love him after all. And if he's been through all this with me and he doesn't know whether or not he loves me, then I must not be the one for him. Right?"

"Hard to say. Sometimes it just doesn't work, even if you do love each other, and you have to cut your losses and walk away. I believe in soul mates, but I also believe you can love different people at different times of your life. Or even love the same person in different ways depending on where you're at in life. Take Henry and I. We started dating at seventeen and got married at eighteen. Young. Had our two boys, and then we split. We just couldn't make it work. Fighting all the time. Not agreeing on anything. We had gotten to the point where we had more contempt than anything else. I wasn't in love with him anymore, and I decided I couldn't stay a day longer. We divorced and spent two years apart."

Ice cream dripped from my spoon and onto my hand as I stared at her, open-mouthed. "Wow! I never knew. I thought you guys were rock-solid."

"We are, now. We both dated other people when we went our separate ways. We kept in touch, of course. Saw each other. We had two kids together so we had to. But I thought we were done. I guess our hearts weren't. Eventually we rekindled those flames smoldering somewhere down in there. Hotter and brighter than ever. When we remarried, we had a completely different relationship. I had changed so much. Him, too. We weren't the same people anymore. But our love grew stronger and more mature. We've been married fourteen years this time, and I can't imagine my life without him."

"I'm stunned. I always looked at you guys like the perfect couple. I never would have guessed."

"We're not perfect." She shook her head as she scraped the bottom of her ice cream bowl. "We have our rough spots here and there. Everybody does."

She put the spoon and bowl down and wiped her face with the napkin. "Look, Tyler. I'm not saying you and Cabe will end up together, and I'm not saying you won't. What I *am* saying is don't expect love to be easy. No matter who you're in love with and no matter how much you love 'em, we're dealing with human beings. And we all can be fragile, messed up, broken little creatures. No one is perfect. No relationship is either."

I swirled my spoon in the melted ice cream and cursed love for being so damned difficult.

I haven't heard a word from Cabe all week, which I guess is to be expected since I told him to get out of my house and not come back until he could tell me he loved me for sure.

In related news, I'm a little surprised and a tad bit hurt that I haven't heard from Jack either. I knew it was a weekend fling. Both of us swept away by the location and not wanting to experience it alone. But I would have thought I'd at least get a phone call. Not that I need the added drama. All I need is for Cabe to come back with love declarations and Jack be hanging on the line.

Saturday, March 22nd

Today was my last straw. I knew at the end of four back-to-back weddings at Lakeside Gardens that whether it makes Lillian and Laura mad or not, I have to go in Monday and tell them I can't do this job.

I resorted to calling security during the first wedding because the father of the bride—who was drunk at ten in the morning, I might add—threatened the groom, took a swing at the best man, and shoved his wife into a wall. It was like being in the live studio audience of the Jerry Springer show and then realizing I was supposed to be the stage manager for the crazies.

The second wedding's couple tried to sneak a dog into the chapel. Like I wouldn't see a fluffy little poodle trotting down the aisle in a pink tutu? Or hear it bark every time the organ played? Really, people?

Then lightning struck just as we were getting ready to start the third wedding. Blew out the entire sound system and caused a ringing in my ears that may end up being permanent. We thought for a while it had blown the lighting system too, but the lights blinked a couple of times and came back on. The bride and groom were so gracious about it all, even without microphones and music for their ceremony. They laughed it off and posed for pictures with the firemen sent out as a precaution.

The last wedding, however, is what pushed me over the edge. Due to the horrendous storm earlier, the buses were all late picking up the guests, and it also caused pre-ceremony photos to be delayed. When the limo delivered the mother of the bride, she was completely distraught over timing as well as concerned about the risk to the bride's hair and gown in the nasty weather. She'd already been on edge before the first raindrop fell because the rehearsal dinner location last night had royally messed up the menus and the seating, and the hotel had put her and her husband in a smoking room. I knew all this because she ranted about it all the way down the sidewalk to the chapel as I carried the umbrella over her.

When she finally paused for me to get a word in, I explained about the lightning and having no sound system or microphones.

To say she lost her shit would be an understatement. I have never had anyone speak to me in such a manner, nor have I seen any other human being treat a living soul so poorly.

She screamed at me until her eyes were bloodshot and her lips were purple beneath the spittle that had gathered in the corners. The limo driver tried to come to my rescue, but she wheeled on him like a demon fighting an exorcism, so he quietly retreated back to his car. One of her guests tried to calm her down, but Demon Lady threw him out of the wedding and told him she never wanted to see him again. When her own daughter, the bride, came out of the dressing room to tell her she needed to let it go, I thought her head may explode off the top of her body and shower us all with hot lava-like boiling blood.

Demon Lady motioned for me to follow her inside the restroom, and I tagged along like a loyal puppy, not knowing what else to do. Once inside, she continued to scream and shout obscenities at me as she entered a stall, hiked her skirt to pee, wiped her privates, and then washed her hands. All without taking a breath, missing a beat, or breaking stream.

So here's the deal. I know being a senior planner won't prevent me from having drunk guests, or people who break the rules, or lightning strikes, or rude and irate clients who can pee and yell at the same time without closing the stall door.

But at least as the planner I'm forging a relationship and have some idea what to expect. I'll know from the get-go when I'm dealing with a Demon Lady or an unbalanced bitch. I have some emotional investment in the clients, and they in me. I'd much rather plan the whole event than be resigned to just meeting everyone as they arrive the day of their event while I try to pick up all the loose ends and tie them together.

Surely, Lillian and Laura will understand that.

Monday, March 24th

Well, that went pretty much as I thought it would. I asked Lillian and Laura if I could speak with them in the conference room. I explained that while I certainly enjoyed conducting ceremonies at Lakeside Gardens—which was sort of not true, but I didn't want to start out on a negative note—my career aspirations were to make senior planner and I felt it would be best for me to step down from the management position.

"Well, I certainly don't think holding this position would eliminate you from senior consideration," Laura said, "but the fact of the matter is we don't have any opening for seniors and don't foresee any in the near future."

"Not to mention," added Lillian, "our senior planners have degrees. Correct me if I'm wrong, but didn't you drop out of college without yours?"

The barb stung as I'm sure she knew it would.

"Um, yes, but I'd be happy to work towards a degree. I already looked into it, actually, and depending on what courses would transfer over from my first two years in college, I could probably have my degree in another two years."

Laura smiled. "That's a great idea. Maybe by then we will have increased our file load enough to justify another senior. In the meantime, keep learning and expanding your experience at Lakeside."

Lillian stood to go as if the meeting were over. I knew it was now or never.

"Actually," I said as I licked my lips and willed myself to speak, "I really don't enjoy just doing ceremonies there. I don't feel I'm well suited for it, and I would like to step down."

Lillian sat down again, and frustration set in around the corners of her mouth.

Laura looked at me and blinked a couple of times before she leaned back in her chair, her hands folded in her lap.

"We had no idea you felt that way. You asked for time to think and came back to us saying you wanted the job. Why the change?"

"I realize I agreed to the position, but I've reconsidered. I don't want to be confined to one location or doing only ceremonies. I really enjoy the planning aspect and getting to know the couples ahead of time. I also like the variety of being in several different locations and interacting with different venue staff. I want to go back to being an assistant planner."

The two of them looked at each other for a long, awkward pause and then Laura turned back to me.

"What you're asking is not so simple. We don't have anyone trained who could step in and take the role. Charlotte is certainly not a candidate—"

Lillian harrumphed in agreement and shook her head as she looked heavenward.

Laura continued without acknowledging her. "—and Carmen is fully immersed in her support role. With her new baby at home, she's not interested in any weekend work."

That was what it came down to in the end. No one else in the office could be put in the job. It was mine. Whether I wanted it or not.

I left the meeting discouraged and downtrodden. Combined with everything going on in my head with Cabe, the job situation only compounded my misery and made me even more certain I wanted to run away from home. Again.

When the clock hit five o'clock on the dot, I bolted out the door. No longer able to sit and make niceties with the outside world.

Lillian was getting in her car as I reached mine. As luck would have it, she'd parked right next to me this morning.

"Bye. Have a good night," I offered so she wouldn't think I was mad or bitter about being turned down.

"You should have asked for more money," Lillian said as she ducked into her car.

She disappeared from view just as I turned, so I crouched down and pressed my hands close to her tinted windows so I could see inside. "What did you say?"

She put the passenger window down and leaned into my view.

"I *said* you should have asked for more money."

I shook my head slightly trying to understand what she was telling me.

"We obviously need you to do this position. There's no one else. We don't have the time or labor allocated to find someone and train them moving into April and May wedding season. You may not have gotten what you wanted in stepping down or getting streamlined for a senior, but you certainly could have negotiated for more money to stay in this position.

You had bargaining power, and you didn't use it. It's a management position. It could feasibly be quite a bit more in salary."

"Wait. Are you saying you'll pay me more money to do this job?"

"No. I'm not going to pay you a dime more than I offered you when you accepted. But you should have asked. You should have negotiated. You always have to stand up for yourself, Tyler. What did I tell you before? The day we went to breakfast. Other people will always make their decisions based on what's best for them. You have to make your choices based on what's best for you. Always, always try to negotiate a better deal. Even if you don't get it, it sends the message that you have self-worth. That you value yourself. Have a good night."

The window went up abruptly, and she drove away.

I stood there for a moment after she pulled away. I couldn't tell if I'd been insulted or counseled with good advice. Angry tears sprang to my eyes as I got in my car.

Maybe I should have negotiated better circumstances with Cabe, too. Did I have to kick him out with an ultimatum that said don't come back? Surely we could have worked out a way to still see each other. The man was already freaked out from a million directions. Did I really have to pick that moment to push the issue? I mean, he had every right to be upset with me for Jack. His anger was justified. Would I have pushed him out the door if I hadn't felt so guilty?

But even as I write those words, I hear Lillian's voice coming back to me and telling me to make the decisions that are best for me. I know if Cabe isn't capable of loving me, fully and completely, then it's best for me not to be with him.

But damn, it hurts.

April

Saturday, April 5th

I should have been wary when Mel said today's wedding would make me feel right at home. After all, I left my hometown years ago because it didn't feel like home to me.

They'd booked a private ranch deep within the Green Swamp. Thankfully, the barn for the reception had electricity and running water, but the ceremony was in the middle of a freshly mowed field. You couldn't take a step without bugs swarming up into your nostrils, eyes, and ears, and the possibility of stepping on a snake stayed ever-present in my mind. I saw more than one rat roaming dazed and confused through what used to be its home.

It didn't surprise me when the wedding party arrived in a four-wheel-drive swamp buggy, but the bride riding in behind her daddy on the back of his dirt bike proved a little much even for my country background. She hiked that white dress up around her hips, which gave the guests a glimpse of her horseshoe garter. Her veil flowed out from under her pink cowboy hat, trailing behind the dirt bike to create great shots for the photographer.

The groomsmen, who cleaned up surprisingly well in their tuxedoes, had monogrammed spit cups because the bride wanted everything in her color scheme of black and pink. Because nothing says elegant and put together like groomsmen spitting tobacco during the ceremony in matching black cups with their names painted in pink.

The bridesmaids were equally as elegant in their pink cowboy hats and black satin gowns with hot pink bras underneath. The bride proudly explained when I walked into the stable area they had set up as a dressing room that she chose strapless gowns so the pink bra straps could show. Classy, I tell you.

The reception set-up was eerily familiar to me. And not just because of the barn. She had the traditional country wedding staples of Jordan almonds, salted peanuts, and pastel mints, and the buffet included cocktail sausages in barbecue sauce and homemade pimento and cheese sandwiches. Fancy ones, mind you, with the crust cut off the bread.

"Who catered this?" I asked Mel.

She rolled her eyes in response. "Her aunt, Ethel. She's supposedly done over a hundred weddings. How many you reckon were in a barn?"

"Did you just say reckon? Wow. Look at you blending in with the surroundings. How'd we end up with this one? I mean, technically, we have clients of all budget levels, but with Aunt Ethel at the helm, why'd they need us?"

"The bride wanted a coordinator. I think we cost more than the wedding itself, but she's happy."

Actually, the entire wedding group seemed happy. The groom changed into jeans and a T-shirt, and the bride put on an adorable black sundress with the same pink cowboy boots and pink cowboy hat she wore during the ceremony. They laughed and danced all night, dining on barbecued pork from a huge black iron smoker in the back of a truck and drinking beer from kegs at the bar.

The best man was single, which I know because every member of the wedding party, as well as the mother of the groom, and mother of the bride, made sure to tell me. They even casually mentioned him being quite smitten with me. And that he'd love a date. Or a dance at the very least. He got neither.

He was cute, I guess. Courteous. Country. A gentleman by all appearances. Well, other than the spit can, but in areas of the country where I come from and where this family came from, that's accepted gentlemanly behavior. He came over and talked to me a couple times. Sweet. A little shy.

But I had no interest at all. Mel even suggested maybe I hit the dance floor with him for a slow song, but it really didn't appeal to me.

I don't know. I guess at some point I'll be ready to move on from Cabe. Hell, I sure seemed ready in Paris, didn't I? But looking back on that, I think it was an escape. Grabbing onto something to keep from feeling. To keep from dealing. I don't know if Jack called tomorrow how I'd feel about him, or if I'd even want to see him again.

Definitely not ready to consider anyone else, though. Mel says I'm holding out waiting for Cabe to call. For him to come back. And maybe somewhere down inside, I am. But I think if he were going to, he would have. You either love someone or you don't. I may have been blind to it for a very long time, but once I became aware, I could no more deny my feelings for him than deny my own existence. So if he hasn't called back by now, he ain't calling.

So I'm sure someday I'll start watching the road for a new prince to arrive. But for now, I'm learning to be happy without one. Much less pain and stress that way.

Tuesday, April 8th

Melanie nearly tackled me before I could even put my bags down this morning. Chaz told her he turned in his resignation. I'm sure on some level I felt sad about Chaz leaving, but I couldn't focus on anything but the possibility of a senior position opening up.

I raced into Laura's office as soon as I heard.

"Is it true? Is Chaz leaving?"

"It would appear so." Laura answered me without ever looking up from her computer.

"So can I apply for his position?"

She looked at me then and removed her glasses, sliding them up on her head.

Lillian came over from her office and leaned against Laura's office door frame. "I recall mentioning you needed a degree. Have you somehow gotten one since we spoke?"

"Well, no, not yet, but-"

"No buts. The senior planner position requires a degree. Besides, your experience is limited to this office. We're looking for someone with varied experiences." She turned to go back to her office.

"But, but, yes, it's limited, but I don't see it as a bad thing. In fact, it's a benefit. You've both trained me. You know what I can do. Isn't your training the best experience I can have to do things the way you want them done?"

Laura sat back in her chair and answered me. "Actually, it's often better to have a mixture of backgrounds in an office to bring in best practices and fresh points of view."

I looked back and forth between them in disbelief. "So basically you're telling me I won't ever be considered for the senior position. Not even if I go back to school? Because I don't have outside experience?"

"I wouldn't say *never*, Lillian, would you?"

Lillian looked back at Laura as she spoke, then shrugged and raised her eyebrows in indifference. "Never is a strong word. But you're not ready now. Keep working." She turned and walked away. I had been dismissed.

I stopped on the way home and picked up fast food French fries, a whole tub of chocolate chip cookie dough ice cream, and two packs of wine spritzers. Then I took a bubble bath, put on my pajamas and preceded to have a self-pity party with a junk food feast. I wished I could call Cabe and talk it all over with him, but since he was also part of my misery, I was on my own.

So I ate and drank it all away. Cabe not calling (and thereby not loving me), Lillian not allowing me to advance, my job completely sucking, and my life being a waste in general. When I had eaten all the fries, drank all of the spritzers and put a heavy dent in the ice cream, I washed it all down with a good dose of salty tears and settled myself in front of my laptop. I was just across the border of being drunk, and the mixture I'd put in my stomach did absolutely nothing to get along with the roiling emotions that had taken up residence there.

But I was determined. I had a mission. A plan. I had research to do to back it up.

And now, two hours later, I have materials in hand to support my plan. I will walk into the office tomorrow and show them the newer, more confident Tyler. The one who can fly to Paris alone and make her way around the city. The one who left home and everyone she'd ever known to escape heartache and make a better life for herself. The one who gave up the man she loved to hold out for someone who could love her back in a healthy way. I'm going after what I want, and I'm not taking no for an answer. Something's gotta work out, for Pete's sake!

And who's Pete, by the way? Why are so many things done for his sake? What did he ever do for us?

Wednesday, April 9th

I brought in bagels and cream cheese and asked Laura and Lillian if I could speak with them for a moment in the conference room. I presented Lillian with a bagel I'd prepared just as she likes them, with her favorite chive cream cheese and crushed potato chips. She accepted the bagel and the request for a meeting, but she didn't look happy about either.

I laid out the handouts and timelines I had printed last night.

"What's all this?" Lillian asked, arching her eyebrows with a facial expression that would have struck fear in lesser women. I had a plan, though. I was mentally prepared for her disdain.

"While it certainly does not equate with a bachelor's degree, I found several nationally accredited certification programs for wedding consultants. I'd like to propose that I complete one of these programs, whichever you choose, and receive accreditation. The classes involved would further my education in our field, and with accreditation, I could obtain membership to be involved with local chapters of event management organizations. In the fall, I intend to register at the university to complete my studies and earn a degree in event management. This accreditation would serve in the meantime to show you my level of commitment and increase my qualifications for the senior position."

I had rehearsed the speech so many times last night and this morning that my words flowed together without pause or hesitation. It's possible I didn't even take a breath. I sounded like a recording being played back much faster than normal. But at least it didn't give them any time at all to interrupt.

"I realize this still leaves the issue of outside experience. I very much enjoy being a part of the Lillian and Laura team, so I don't want to quit my job here just to get experience somewhere else so I can come back here to get promoted. So, I was thinking maybe you could ask one of our fellow planners in the area to allow me to intern for an event. I could work on an entire wedding from start to finish to observe their processes, counsel with them to get best practices and feedback, and gain experience under different leadership."

I inhaled and sailed into the ending of my speech before they could protest.

"So I'd like to officially throw my hat in the ring for Chaz's position. I understand you'll be interviewing other candidates, but I feel my proven track record with the company, my desire for advancement, and my motivation to improve my qualifications should allow me the opportunity to interview."

I took a huge breath when I had finished, and I didn't know if I felt lightheaded from being so nervous, talking without breathing, or the slight hangover I had from drinking cheap wine spritzers.

Laura gave me a hesitant smile, and I could see I had a slight chance with her. I turned to meet Lillian's gaze, which was imperceptible as usual. That woman should have worked for the FBI. Or whatever the British equivalent is. I can't remember from the Bond movies what it's called. But you never know what she is thinking or feeling unless she chooses to share it.

Luckily for me, Laura asked her. "What do you say, Lillian? We'll be posting the position and asking for resumes. Tyler can submit hers, right?"

"Where are you going to find the time to take all this coursework, especially university classes, while interning for a competitor and managing a full wedding workload? Something will suffer." Lillian crossed her arms as she stared at me across the table, and I swear I saw a hint of glee twinkling in her eyes. She always enjoys playing Devil's Advocate in a challenge.

I had prepared for that too, though.

"Well, I've looked at the wedding schedule and found a block of time when I could complete the accreditation course with only two weddings being affected. Both of those are ceremony only, and the times do not conflict with another wedding, so I could ask Mel to cover them, or perhaps one of you."

"Why should we take on extra work for you?" Lillian took a slow bite of her bagel, much like a lioness casually toying with her prey.

"Because we're a team. Because it's the climate you've created in the office to jump in and help whenever needed. It's inherent in what we do every day and with every wedding. So I feel it's justified to extend it for a team member trying to improve her contribution to the team."

I swallowed and wished I had thought to bring in a bottle of water. My throat and mouth had gone dry.

"That may work for summer, but what about university this fall?

Ongoing courses will be much harder to work around."

I nodded and formed my words carefully. "Yes, true, but the efforts invested to help me achieve this will more than pay off in the long run. I can take some classes online around my schedule, and I will know what the classroom times are so we can work around that with scheduling. As far as interning, if it's only one event, it shouldn't equate to more than an hour or so a week other than attending planning sessions. Then of course I'd need the weekend of the actual event scheduled off here."

Lillian looked to Laura.

"I don't see any reason she can't apply. We'll weigh her against the other applicants and hire the best candidate for the job," Laura said.

Lillian nodded and stood, her bagel in hand.

"One more thing," I said, my voice crackling a bit as I almost lost my nerve.

Lillian looked back at me and frowned. "Yes?"

"The accreditation program requires a mentoring internship. However, that could be waived if you would both write a recommendation and summary of my experiences here. I'd like to ask if you'd do that for me."

Lillian nodded as Laura said, "Sure. No problem."

Laura and Lillian exchanged glances before Lillian left the room. Laura gave me a side hug as we walked out together and went our separate ways to our own offices.

I floated on a high the rest of the day. Almost giddy. I had taken charge of my own destiny. True, I can't control what Laura and Lillian decide or where they put me in the end, but I'm still proud of myself for making a decision to move me forward. I've spent entirely too much of my life making choices based on what other people wanted from me or reacting to what they did to me. It felt good to pursue the things I wanted.

Lillian walked out behind me when we left today, and she waited until just before I reached my car to speak.

"Nice to see you show up today."

"I'm sorry?" I turned back to face her, unsure of what she'd meant. She smiled at me then, a genuine smile that started in her eyes and transformed the rest of her face.

"I said it was nice to see you show up today. All feisty, fiery and prepared. I liked it. I admire backbone, and I've always thought you had one in there somewhere, hidden beneath the ingrained facade of politeness. I look forward to seeing more of it."

She walked past me as I stood momentarily stunned, but she turned back as she opened her car door.

"You should have asked for financial assistance, though. The company could have sponsored your accreditation as continuing education. Probably could have covered the whole cost."

She got in her car and drove away before I could think of a response.

What the hell? Why give me these little morsels of wisdom in the parking lot when it's too little, too late? Could she not mention some of this while we are in the meeting and it would actually be of benefit to me?

What is her deal? I drove away with the same feeling of not knowing whether she's trying to help me or taunt me.

Tuesday, April 15th

Tax day. Nothing like waiting to the last minute possible to deal with the devil.

I can organize someone's event like nobody's business, but my own life is a disarrayed shamble of papers and receipts stuck here and there with little scribbled notes in the margins. Every year I say I'm gonna do better, and every year at this time I'm scrambling to find everything and pull together an inventory.

It's a good idea to do an inventory, I think. To clean out and clear out and toss what's no longer needed.

I packed up all Cabe's photos today and put them back in the closet along with anything that reminded me of him. I took the stuffed dog and the frog out from under my bed and carried them down to the dumpster in a white trash bag. I couldn't resist one whiff of them before I tossed them in. It's been a month since I've seen him, but his scent still lingers ever so faintly. On the stuffed animals and on my heart, I suppose. But I have to move on. I even deleted our text history from my phone, along with all his contact information. I unfollowed him on every form of social media, too.

I can't believe he just walked out and never looked back. I mean, I told him to, I guess. But I didn't think he'd actually do it. I believed in my heart that he loved me. That I needed to force his hand. But now, I don't know. Which is the same conclusion he came to, is it not?

I've grieved enough. I've cried enough. I've waited enough. I'm tired of checking my phone multiple times a day just to see if I missed a call. Weary of scanning every store, every crowd, every intersection to see if I catch a glimpse of him. Tired of driving with no music playing because every song reminds me of him in some way. Done with avoiding any movie involving romance and sitting home alone in a funk.

I'm just done. Screw this.

It's time to accept the truth and move on.

I think I must be getting better at dealing with pain.

When my high school and college sweetheart Dwayne left me, it was crippling. Incapacitating. I couldn't move. Couldn't think. Couldn't breathe. I had to run as far as possible just to be able to live.

When Cabe left for Seattle, it was depressing. I stayed in bed for weeks. Any time I wasn't working, I slept. I lost weight. But I could breathe. I could live without running.

When Cabe disappeared in January, and then again in February, my hurt burned and ached and ate away at my insides. But I could still function. Still work.

This time, it's a numb, dull, ever-present emptiness that always feels like I'm hungry and can't be satisfied. Like someone tore out a piece of me and left behind a jagged hole. I mean, I'm okay. I'll be fine. I go through the motions of each day, and I engage in life without him. I'm even making plans for my future. So I'm doing better than just surviving.

But it doesn't mean it doesn't hurt every minute of every day. I think I've just grown so accustomed to hurting over Cabe that it's become a natural part of me. A function I do subconsciously, like breathing or blinking. The pain is just there, in the background, festering without ever truly healing.

Maybe cleaning out any sign of him will help the healing begin.

While I was at it, I packed away all the photos of Jack, too. Still disappointed he never called. Obviously easier to take than Cabe. What I felt for the two has absolutely no comparison, but there's still a sense of hurt and rejection there. Looking back on my time in Paris with Jack still seems surreal. Like something I watched or read, not something I lived. Completely removed from my actual life, almost as though it didn't happen. I find it hard to conjure up his face without concentrating and for the life of me I can't remember the sound of his voice.

I'm still grateful for him. Grateful for the experiences we shared. The way that weekend shaped me. I still think it changed who I am. I hate how it hurt Cabe, and I wish it could have turned out differently, but with all said and done, I can't say I regret Jack.

I just wish he had called. To validate it all somehow. I mean, if there's one advantage to getting involved with two men at the same time, it should be you're assured at least one of them is going to call? Right?

Maybe I should just burn this diary. Let go of all of it. I flip back through these pages and see so much of my life spent worrying about Dwayne. Cabe. Jack. My job. My bosses. My mother. Maybe I'll burn it and start fresh. A new diary. A clean slate. Fresh white pages not yet marred by the darkness the ink of life brings.

Thursday, April 17th

Yeah, so obviously I didn't burn it. Seemed a waste after I've put so much time and effort into documenting all this stuff. I'm sure there will come a day when I look back through it and laugh and say "Oh, wow. I remember that."

Not sure how far away that day is, though. It ain't today.

I came in this morning to find balloons and streamers filling my office. I fought my way through to my desk and stood there looking at the mess in bewilderment. Were they celebrating my birthday late? Like, way late?

"Congratulations," said Laura as they all piled into my tiny office. Laura, Lillian, Mel, Carmen, Chaz and Charlotte. The closest thing I have to family down here. "Ladies—"

"And Chaz," Lillian added with a grin.

"—and our gentleman," Laura continued, "please allow me to announce our newest senior planner, Tyler Warren."

"It's a temporary assignment," Lillian chimed in, ever the realistic party pooper. "Your permanent status will be contingent upon you acquiring the credentials we agreed to."

I nodded and grinned from ear to ear as happy tears filled my eyes. Just when I thought I'd run out of tears, I found I have a reserve supply. I guess I haven't been tapping into the happy ones so much lately.

Laura asked me to come to her office to sign the paperwork for the promotion contract, and Lillian followed me in.

"Now, as Lillian mentioned, we've made this a temporary six-month assignment. That should allow you enough time to get your accreditation in order. When you receive your official status, we will then sign a permanent agreement. However, if at the end of the six months you still haven't been certified, we would need to go back to your current contract as a ceremony manager."

I nodded my agreement as I looked over the contract wording.

"I don't see any mention of the bachelor's degree. This only mentions certification, and six months isn't long enough for me to get the degree."

Laura and Lillian exchanged glances, and I got the distinct impression they didn't agree on the topic.

Laura spoke first. "In the interest of setting precedent and taking into consideration those already in the position, we've decided to forgo that requirement. We would certainly encourage you and support you should you choose to pursue it. After all—," her eyes cut to Lillian's, "—my own degree is in interior design, Melanie's is in restaurant management, and Lillian doesn't even have a degree."

"All the more reason you should pursue yours, Tyler," Lillian said. "When I was a young woman such as yourself, I made choices which eliminated a degree as an option for me. It is one of the great regrets of my life. And yes, I've measured some success without it, but an education is invaluable. It's something you earn that no one can take away from you or rob you of. You will always have it, long after Laura and I are no longer with you. Wherever you may go from this point, having a degree will be an asset. So please, Tyler, do consider pursuing it even though we are not requiring one."

I left work feeling happy and accomplished, ready to celebrate my new future. I went and bought the comforter set and curtains I've been wanting since I saw it in the store months ago, and then I stopped by the paint store on a whim and picked up the most beautiful, tranquil lavender to match.

New me. New job. New bedroom. New life. I feel like I'm cutting loose the strings that have held me back and I'm ready to soar.

Friday, April 18th

I stayed up until almost three last night painting my room. With each brush stroke, I imagined myself painting over the past. Covering up old hurts and past heartaches with each stroke of my new life.

Tonight I made the bed with the new comforter set with its soft, dove gray background and beautiful watercolor flowers in varying shades of lavender and violet.

I added some new candles I'd purchased to match the bedding and hung the deep violet sheers from the new silver curtain rods and finials. I'd framed a couple of black and white architecture shots I'd taken in Paris on that first night alone, and they provided the final touches to make the room complete.

I stepped back to admire my handiwork and literally clasped my hands together and giggled. I love the way it turned out. The wall color is so peaceful and serene, and the bedding set is elegant yet whimsical. It completely transformed my bedroom.

Now the room is a welcoming sanctuary for me rather than an empty reminder of love lost. It reflects my state of mind, I think. I feel calmer. More confident. More at peace. But determined to move forward. Determined to choose a path of happiness for me.

Since I returned from Paris, I've tried to make choices and decisions to stand up for myself and seek what's best for me.

They didn't all turn out the way I'd hoped, but I feel good about the future. I'm excited about my job, and I have to believe there are more good things in store for me if I just keep moving forward and leaving the past behind.

Saturday, April 19th

Three observations on today.

1. British people are nice. If every wedding I did could be a British couple, I'd be fine with that. I've done many in my time here, and I've yet to encounter a nasty British bride or groom. Even their guests are nice. Just thrilled to fly across the pond on holiday and enjoy a lovely wedding. Definitely a great start to my day this morning, even if they did bring confetti after being told not to!

2. Insanely detailed itineraries do not work. Chaz's bride today (his last wedding with us—sad, not sad) had created an itinerary so freakin' to the minute that it was literally impossible to follow. Itineraries should be a *guideline*. Something to go by to keep things on track and in order, but adjusted as necessary throughout the day. Today's bride had typed absolutely everything by her stopwatch.

11:54 All guests have been seated. Parents and wedding party lined up outside doors.

12:00 Music starts. Doors open. Parents begin to walk.

12:02 Parents are seated and groomsmen return.

12:03 Groomsmen enter at lyric cues provided.

12:05 Groom enters on lyric cue provided.

12:06 Groom scratches his ass.

12:07 Music changes. Bridesmaids enter at lyric cues provided.

12:09 Random uncle coughs.

12:10 Flower girl enters. Scatters petals in two second intervals.

Okay, so she didn't have the groom scratching or the uncle coughing, but she did provide Chaz with the lyrics for each song marked as to which word each groomsman and bridesmaid needed to enter on. And she repeatedly told the six-year-old flower girl to count to two between each petal going down the aisle.

Chaz needed to tell her to chill a long time ago. I'm all about an organized bride, and one who runs on time when I have a wedding after hers? Yes, ma'am. Love it. Give me more. But talk about ridiculously excessive. No one can enjoy their day if they are micromanaging everything down to the second.

She even plotted the time for the kiss. Like, cue song and kiss begins on this word and lasts two minutes, thirty-seven seconds.

Do you have any idea how long two minutes and thirty-seven seconds is when an entire room of people is sitting there watching someone kiss? Interminably long. The kiss lasted longer than some people's wedding night! Guests shifted in their seats, fanned themselves with programs, and cleared their throats, but no matter what social cues they used to scream 'Awkward!', the bride and groom held to the schedule. I bet she choreographed it. Planned out turning their heads left and right at appointed times in the music. Moaning or sighing here and there for effect. I bet this chick literally made the poor dude rehearse the kiss over and over again until he got it right. For his sake, I'm hoping there's no music or itinerary involved for the honeymoon. Talk about pressure to perform!

3. Lastly, weddings are supposed to be about both people involved. I've always said the groom's wishes should be taken into consideration when planning a wedding. After all, it's his event, too. But it has to be a balance both ways. My final wedding today featured an ultimate Star Wars fanatic groom (Dale) and a considerate and giving bride (Keke), who had confided to me in the beginning how sweet it was that Dale wanted to incorporate his passion into their wedding. But as said passion took over her own plans, Keke had lost a bit of her enthusiasm. She readily agreed to him walking down the aisle to Darth Vader's Imperial March. He insisted she walk in to music from a Japanese Star Wars video game. She agreed to have Princess Leia and Han Solo figurines as a cake topper. He added toy Jedis and Stormtroopers standing shoulder to shoulder around every layer of the cake. She agreed to enter the reception carrying light sabers. He planned a light saber battle in lieu of a first dance.

When I saw the surprise Dale had planned for the ceremony, I suggested he discuss it with Keke first. Dale was adamant it should be a surprise, though, and one thing's for sure. His bride was definitely surprised.

When the pastor asked for the rings and neither the best man nor maid of honor had them, Keke began to panic and asked the maid of honor to loan hers. But when she heard the music start and looked up to see a seven-foot-tall, furry Chewbacca headed down the aisle carrying her rings on a pillow, she lost it. That girl said words I've only heard in Tarantino movies. The pastor blushed fifty shades of red, Chewbacca stepped back like his hair had been singed, and the groom went from euphoric glee to shocked disbelief.

It took about twenty minutes to calm her down and get her back inside the chapel, but I think Dale learned a valuable lesson today about his wife. The force may be powerful, but hell hath no fury like a bride on her wedding day. Needless to say, Chewbacca waited outside while rings were exchanged.

Tuesday, April 22nd

I truly had no idea what I was in for today. If only the Universe had sent me some kind of warning.

Chaz had a planning session booked today, which meant it became mine with the promotion. He'd called her to explain I'd be taking over, but we hadn't spoken before today.

I did a double-take when she walked in, certain Stevie Nicks had wandered in off the street in search of a wedding planner. Nadine's long blonde hair swung loose across her shoulders and down her back, except for where she'd randomly braided strands and tied them with brightly-colored ribbons. She wore layered skirts of white and ivory lace and linen, also adorned with multi-colored ribbons. She completed her gypsy ensemble with a long, black velvet shawl much too warm for April in Florida, and high-heeled brown suede boots with ribbons intertwined through the laces up the front.

Nadine's gentle, easy smile exuded kindness. Her eyes were a soft grey, crinkled around the edges, and twinkling with a bit of mischief. Every finger held a ring of different stones and rocks. Not diamonds, or sapphires, or rubies, mind you, but actual stones and rocks. Maybe a couple were crystals.

She greeted me with a huge smile and arms out-thrown like we were long-lost cousins seeing each other for the happiest of days.

"You must be Tyler!" she said as she wrapped me in a huge hug with her thin arms. She smelled of vanilla and ginger.

"I am. You must be Nadine."

"Wow. I have a good feeling about this," she said, nodding and smiling as if we shared some secret. I wondered what it was and if I was supposed to know about it. "Your aura is clearly defined in pale yellow. You must be excited about this new job opportunity. Your vibrations are elevated as

216

well."

"Well, that's good," I said, not sure what else to say. "Come on in, and let's get started. Would you like a coffee or perhaps a water?"

"Ooohhh, no coffee for me. It clouds my vision. Perhaps a Chai tea?"

"Um, we have Earl Grey?"

She scrunched her face tightly, shook her head quickly, and then broke into her smile again.

"No. Nothing English. I'll just take a water, thanks. Spring water."

"Sure." I opened the door to our larger planning room and motioned for her to have a seat at the rectangular table.

"Do you have any rooms with a round table? I find the angles of squares and rectangles interfere with my creativity."

"Oh. Okay. No problem." I led her to the smaller room with its round table. "How's this?"

"Too small. We need good energy flow so as not to confine our possibilities." She smiled again.

"Right. Well," I hesitated, my brain scrambling to find a solution that would be just right for Goldilocks. "I'll be right back."

I went to our kitchen break room, which was a little larger than the small planning salon and had a round table.

"Hate to break this up," I said to Lillian and Mel as they sat drinking their coffee, "but I need to use this room for planning."

"The break room?" Lillian asked with her signature eyebrow arch, her British accent strong in derisiveness.

"She needs a round table in a larger room so we don't confine our possibilities."

They looked at each other and back to me. Lillian rolled her eyes as Mel shrugged, then they both got up and left the room. I followed them out and back to Nadine.

"Okay, I think I found us a suitable room," I said with a smile. "Right this way."

I led her down the hallway and into the break room.

"No windows?" she asked with a look of horror. "No, no, no. This won't work *at all*. Let me look at the first room again."

So back to the first conference room, where she decided the rounded corners of the rectangular table would make it sufficient after all.

I nearly wore out my hand taking notes as she talked. I normally kind of guide clients through the planning session, asking questions in the order of our pre-printed sheet to ensure we cover the event from start to finish. Nadine had a very strong vision of what she wanted, though. By vision, I mean she closed her eyes, hummed for a few seconds, and then swayed back and forth in her chair, talking ninety miles an hour while I tried to keep up writing. She waved her hands in the air as she talked, as though she was drawing out the scene in her mind, stopping occasionally to clasp her hands together and hum.

"I see everything in pale, sky blue," she said. "Blue linens, blue drapes, blue chair covers. I see all the guests dressed in blue."

Humming.

"I see lilies, calla lilies. White, not blue." Thank goodness for that, since they don't come in blue.

More humming.

"We'll have fifteen bridesmaids and fifteen groomsmen," she said.

"Wow!" escaped my lips before I could catch it.

Nadine opened her eyes and smiled at me before closing them again as she swayed and hummed.

"They'll form an entire circle of love and support to envelop us and protect the start of our journey."

She pulled her legs up under her in the chair and clasped her hands together again, eyes closed the entire time.

The humming continued.

"Indoors. I'm seeing a nice chapel. Something very traditional."

Her eyelids fluttered for a moment, and then she stopped humming and stopped swaying. She just sat there motionless and silent. Forever.

Awkward.

Finally she opened her eyes and leaned forward to read what I'd written.

"So, did you have a date in mind?" I asked, pen poised above paper to start taking notes again.

"I'm waiting to hear back on that. I've put the question out there and haven't yet received an answer."

"Okay." I hesitated, not sure if the answer would come to her telepathically or via some other method of communication. Like perhaps a telephone or email.

She closed her eyes again and began to sway.

"I'd like to stop at fifty."

"Fifty guests? Okay, that's good. Not too large, not too small," I said, and her eyes flew open with frustration this time.

"No, fifty thousand. I want to cap my contribution at fifty thousand. I'm not sure how much my beloved will contribute."

"Oh, right, well, okay. You can just let us know the total budget when you've decided." Hearing the budget would be at least fifty grand was a relief. It certainly made my job a lot easier. I can do crazy if I have a budget to pay for it. "How many guests were you thinking?"

Her eyes stayed open this time. "It depends on who he invites. I probably have around seventy to eighty on my list."

"Well, to look at venues, we will need a good estimate of total guest count, just to make sure we're looking at the right size."

Her sharp intake of breath scared the crap out of me and nearly made me fall off my chair. She scrunched her eyes together, wrinkling her nose in what looked like mild pain.

"Are you alright?"

"Yes, just seeing fog for a moment." Her face relaxed, and she smiled again before she spoke. "Belly dancers. Fire eaters. A band who can play disco. Cake. Lots of cake. Four, no, maybe it's five different cakes."

"Okay." I wrote as fast as I could, my brain freaking out as much over our transcendental planning as where I was going to find belly dancers and a venue that would let someone eat fire.

Nadine leaned across the table and placed her hand on mine, stopping my pen immediately.

"I see concern on your face, and your vibrations have shifted. I'm not sure yet what my beloved may be bringing to the table, but don't worry. It will all work out. We'll have plenty of funds."

She reached for her purse to pull out a check and a pen.

"I've been saving a while, not knowing how much things might cost by the time I got to this point," Nadine said. "But I've always known it would be Orlando. I could see the city clearly. Just still foggy on the actual site. I can write you a deposit check now."

"Um, okay. We can just do a contract for our services, and then we can talk about venues and dates once you have more information."

She nodded. "I feel a harmony between us, Tyler, and I trust you to bring my vision to fruition."

"Well, if I could get you to fill out this profile with contact information for the two of you, I'll go and have Carmen, our office assistant, work up a contract."

Nadine closed her eyes and swayed, grabbing for the table to steady herself but missing it.

I reached to grab her instinctively, but she jerked away and stared up at me, her eyes unfocused for a moment.

"I seem to be experiencing a lot of interference," she said. "It's draining my energy rapidly. Could we get a steak?"

I thought I misunderstood her. "I'm sorry, what?"

"A steak. I need red meat to replenish my zinc levels."

Nope, I didn't misunderstand.

"Right. Well, we don't have any steak here..." Definitely the first time I'd ever gotten that request.

"Could you have someone go and fetch one? I'll need a few minutes to re-center before we continue." She closed her eyes again, and I almost felt shoved from the room.

"Sure. If I could just get you to fill this out? When you're centered?" I tiptoed from the office and went immediately to Lillian.

"She wants me to fetch her a steak," I told Lillian.

"Beg pardon?"

"She wants me—"

"Oh, I heard you. I just don't understand. Fetch? Fetch a steak? Does her highness want you cutting it up and feeding it to her, too?"

Carmen came in to drop off Lillian's mail. "Tell her to eat a granola bar. Who eats steak mid-morning?"

"Says her energy level is low. She needs zinc."

Lillian took off her glasses and twirled them between her fingers as she spoke. "We're not a diner. We don't do steak."

"She needs to take vitamins," Carmen said.

"What do I tell her?"

"Get a contract signed, and then we'll talk steak. No money, no meat," Carmen said, snapping her fingers and leaving the room. She'd been even more feisty than usual since returning from maternity leave.

I turned back to Lillian. "What do you want me to say? She's ready to pay a deposit and sign a contract, but she wants a steak. I have a banana in my office. Should I see if she wants it instead?"

Christ!" Lillian put her glasses back on and shook her head. "It's your call. Your client."

It was. My first client since the promotion. I'd be working with her start to finish all on my own. I didn't want to start off on a bad foot, so I told Carmen to call around and find a place to deliver a steak.

I came back into the room to find Nadine in a cross-legged position on the floor, head dropped forward with her eyes closed and both hands facing upward open-palmed on her knees. She opened her eyes and smiled up at me, nodding toward the table.

"I left you a check there with the information. I just need a few more minutes."

"Oh, okay. No problem."

She closed her eyes again, and I left with the paperwork and check to give Carmen.

Nadine's penmanship was impeccable, her letters in neat, even rows uniform enough to have been printed on a computer. Truly remarkable symmetry. So much so that it took me a couple of seconds down the hallway to realize she'd written no information regarding the groom. No name, occupation, phone number, address. Nothing.

I turned and went back into the conference room and cleared my throat. Nadine's eyes fluttered open and she stretched with a wide yawn, appearing to have just woken from a nap. She unfolded her legs and bent low over her knees as she flexed her toes before rising to a stand.

"Nadine? There's nothing on here about your groom. We can designate you as primary contact if he doesn't want to be involved in planning, but I have to put his information in the system."

She smiled sweetly and brushed her hair gently from her eyes.

"He's not here. The Universe has told me to prepare, so it won't be long now. I can feel it. He's on his way. He'll be here soon. We need to be ready."

"You mean he's on his way *here*?"

"No, silly!" She laughed like I'd said the funniest thing ever. "I haven't even met him yet! But he's coming, and when he gets here, I don't want to waste any time. I've waited thirty-seven years, so when he arrives, I need to get this show on the road."

"So you haven't met him yet, but you guys have talked online? On the phone?" I was so damned confused.

"No. I have no idea who he will be. The Universe has sent me signs to get ready because he's on his way. Isn't it exciting? My groom is on his way! I'm going to meet him soon!"

I thought maybe then the whole thing had been a joke. Like maybe I was on Candid Camera, and Carmen and Mel would bust in laughing and telling me how silly I looked. But no one came in. No cameras appeared.

So I had to give Nadine back her check and tell her we'd have to wait until she actually had a groom. I couldn't accept a contract signed by her and The Universe.

I offered to get her a steak anyway, but she graciously refused.

Carmen laughed about it all day, but I felt bad for Nadine. She's a nice lady. I hope her beloved does come along soon. I must confess I pity the poor guy already. Who wants to go on a first date and learn that the entire wedding is already planned and the deposit's been paid?

Hope he likes steak.

Thursday, April 24th

Mama called tonight. I've only talked to her once since I got back from Paris. I purposely haven't called her because I didn't want to get into the whole Cabe conversation. But she called tonight, and I figured it was as good a time as any to face the music.

"Hey Mama."

"Hey sugar. How you doin'?"

"Good. How's everybody up there?"

"Alright, I reckon. You remember Johnnie Lloyd?"

I don't know why she expects me to remember every random person who has ever lived in or passed through our county.

"No, I don't think I do."

"Sure you do. She married that boy your cousin Fred went to school with over in Louisiana. They lived in Bogalusa."

Oh great. Now she expects me to remember random people from other counties. In other states.

"I don't remember her, Mama. Did I ever meet her?"

"Yeah, we went to New Orleans with your Uncle Tommy when you were three and Johnnie came over and brought some clothes for Fred."

"I was three? No, ma'am. I don't remember her."

"Are you sure? Remember, she fell down the stairs at Luann's wedding and had to get stitches across her forehead? Remember? Her eyes were crossed for like a year after that."

I swear my entire family catalogs people by their infamy. Everyone is related in conversation by the illnesses they've had, the tragedies they've suffered, or the scandals they've caused. And the more bizarre the event, the better-known they become. Lose a foot in a tractor accident? Have a husband caught in bed with a choir member? Lose your family business on

222

a football bet gone wrong? Get ready for notoriety.

"Is there a point to this, or are you just testing my memory?"

"Well, Ms. Snippy, I was just gonna tell you her and Fred divorced and she ran off to Vegas to marry a politician."

Riveting information. Definitely life-changing news. Thank goodness she let me know.

"That's nice, Mama."

"What is the matter with you today? Did someone put sour milk in your oatmeal?"

"I'm just tired, I guess. Been working a lot." Okay, so I changed my mind. I wasn't up to facing any kind of music. She had this juicy morsel about Johnnie and Fred to chew on for a while. No need to tell her about me and Cabe. She'd be up all night calling people.

"Alright, well get some sleep. Oh, and before I forget, some guy called here for you. Jack somebody?"

My heart skipped a beat, and I jerked to attention.

"What? What did you say?"

"Some guy called here. Twice now. Says you met him in France? He wanted your number but I told him I don't give that out to just anybody. But then Tanya saw his name on the caller ID from when you called on your birthday, so I thought you may actually know him. Do you?"

"Yes! Did he leave a number?"

"He tried, but I told him you weren't interested."

"What? Why would you tell him that?"

"Because, hello? You have a boyfriend."

I squeezed my forehead with my fingers and tried not to yell at my dear mother.

"So you didn't give him my number?" I don't know why I even asked her. I already knew the answer.

"Well, of course not. I don't know this man from Adam. So who is he? Why'd you call here from his number, and why is he trying to get in touch with you?"

"We met in Paris. We kind of hung out together."

"So Gabe's okay with it? He's friends with him, too?"

"Cabe, Mama. His name's Cabe."

"What kind of name is that? Who names somebody Cabe? I bet his whole life he's been getting called Gabe. I mean, Gabe just makes more sense."

"Mama!"

"What? Why are you yelling?"

I took a deep breath and wished I knew more about meditation.

"I'm sorry. I'm just really tired. Can you please take his number if he calls again, or just give him mine?"

So wow. Wow. Wow. Wow. Why has Jack been calling my mama? Why doesn't he just call me? And can I be a silly girl for just a moment and run around my apartment squealing "He called! He called! He called!"?

'Cause that's what I just did.

Tuesday, April 29th

Charlotte came in the kitchen and told me I had a call from a groom. Of course, she didn't get his name or wedding date, which is typical. I started to send her back to ask, but figured it best to just go back to my desk so she could transfer him through.

"Please tell me this is the Tyler Warren who's scared of heights, loves smelly cheese, frequents cemeteries in Paris, and makes me laugh like no one I've ever met."

I couldn't speak for a moment as my brain processed the fact that it was Jack and not a groom, that he was actually on the phone talking to me, and that I made him laugh like no one he'd ever met.

When I recovered, I said, "Hello, stranger. Where've you been?"

"Where've I been? Where've you been? I've been trying to find you for over a month, and you are one difficult lady to track down."

"I gave you my number!"

"You wrote your number on a cocktail napkin like some bad scene in a cheesy romantic comedy. Don't you ever watch those things? The poor guy always loses the number and then has to go halfway around the world to find the girl, all while she's thinking the jerk didn't call."

"The thought had crossed my mind."

"See? You're not going to believe me, but I got into a conversation with a homeless man that night after you left. I got caught up in his story, and I ended up giving him my coat completely forgetting your number was in the pocket. I even went back to look for him, but he had gone."

"Ahhh. The old *I gave my coat to a homeless man* story. I think I've seen this movie."

He laughed. I'd struggled for weeks to recall his voice and suddenly there it was, amazingly familiar. He was real.

225

"I swear, you have no idea what I've been through to find you. I found your mom's number in my call log since you used my phone, but that was a complete dead end. She wouldn't even take my number."

I laughed. "Yeah, my mom is a definite dead end if she doesn't know you and you're trying to get in touch with one of her daughters."

"Duly noted. Do you realize in all our conversations you never actually said what town you live in? Only that you were from Florida. Which is kind of a big state. You did mention the theme parks a few times, so I assumed Orlando. I've called every wedding planner in Orlando and asked for Tyler Warren. I got down to the letter J when a kind lady told me you worked at Lillian and Laura's."

"A J? Must have been Felicia at Joyous Celebrations."

"That's the one."

We talked about the highlights of our lives since returning home. Well, minus my relationship issues. Since he didn't know about the story up until Paris, I saw no need to update him on recent developments.

"I'm so glad I finally found you," Jack said once we'd finished catching up. "I'm going to be in Tampa this weekend."

My heart fluttered, and my eyes immediately flashed to the wedding calendar on my wall. I had weddings Friday night and back-to-back morning to evening on Saturday.

"I'm working," I said, my voice dismal with disappointment.

"Well, that's not good. Just tell them you need to take off."

I laughed at the thought. "Um, yeah. Brides don't really like it when you ask them to postpone their wedding because you have weekend plans."

"I guess not. You're working the whole weekend?"

"Friday and Saturday. I'm off Sunday. What time do you leave?"

His flight was late afternoon, so we decided I would drive over to see him Sunday morning and spend a few hours together before he left.

So I guess this answers the question of how I'd feel if he called, huh? I feel excited, but I'm also nervous. It was one thing to see Jack half a world away in Paris. When we both were alone and on vacation, and thrown together in a whirlwind neither of us planned or thought out. What will it be like to see him here in the real world? So near my home turf?

I have to ask myself if I really want to see Jack again, or if I've just been so disappointed he hasn't called that hearing from him mends my wounded pride. Do I genuinely want to spend more time with him? Where will it lead? What does it mean? He's expended quite a bit of effort to track me down. Does he have feelings for me? In which case, what do I do with that? I enjoyed being with him, for sure. But my heart belongs to Cabe. Doesn't it? And should it if his heart doesn't belong to me?

What is it Scarlett says? Oh fiddle dee dee? I have to think about this tomorrow, because if I keep thinking about it tonight, I'll simply go mad.

May

Saturday, May 3rd

I'd been sitting on a bench staring into space when I heard the organ blaring the recessional music. I sprinted to the double doors to swing them wide open for the bride and groom, but they must have been in quite the rush to get back down the aisle. Just as I reached for the door handle, the groom shoved it open. The edge of the door clocked me right between the eyes and knocked me over. I landed on my butt with a thud and a groan before scrambling backwards out of their way on my elbows and heels like a drunken crab.

"Are you okay?" the bride exclaimed as the groom bent forward to pull me to my feet. The rest of the wedding party piled up behind them like an escalator blocked at the bottom, each couple trying to make their way out of the sanctuary but stopping when they saw me clutching my head.

"I'm fine," I said through clenched teeth. My vision flashed in alternating bright white bursts and dark spots as I stood. I half expected to see animated birds chirping around my head with swirling stars.

I rubbed my forehead gingerly and pasted on my best attempt at a smile. It must not have been too convincing, because the rest of the wedding guests kept giving me sympathetic smiles and stealing curious glances at my forehead. Not so long ago, I knocked myself out popping a champagne cork directly at my face. Now this. If I keep going, I'm going to have a permanent knot protruding from my forehead.

I've checked my face in the mirror about twenty times to make sure there's not a bruise or anything. The last thing I want is to show up to see Jack tomorrow with a big black lump in the middle of my forehead.

I'm so nervous. He's called a couple of times this week, and I've laughed and enjoyed the conversations. But I'm just not sure if it's a good idea to see him. I think in Paris I could separate him from reality and exist in our

229

alternate universe that helped me cope. Now he's really here.

What if I see him and I really like him? What if I want to see him again? He lives in Ohio. I think. I don't even remember for sure. How would that work out?

If I'm being honest, and I guess since I'm writing this to myself I have no reason not to be, I think I'm scared he may feel more for me than I'm prepared for. I mean, he went through quite a bit to find me. That says he feels something, right?

At any rate, I'm driving to Tampa first thing in the morning, and then we're going to Clearwater Beach. He asked about visiting Ybor City, but my heart tightened in my chest. No way could I go there. Too much Cabe all around me.

Oh Cabe. Why couldn't it have been you who called? It would be so much easier to know what to do and how to feel.

Monday, May 5th

Jack missed his flight yesterday. Well, technically he got bumped because we got to the airport late.

It turns out I enjoyed his company just as much in the 'real world' as I had in Paris. He was the same charming, funny, outgoing, interesting man I met there. It felt so good to laugh again after being sad for so long. It felt magnificent to be complimented and catered to. I soaked up his adoration like a sponge takes on water. I had the best time I've had since I left Paris.

Unfortunately, we lost track of time at the beach, and then an accident on the bridge back to Tampa backed up traffic to a slow crawl interspersed with complete stops.

I knew when I dropped him off at departures he'd never make the plane on time, so it didn't surprise me when he called to say they'd bumped him.

"They have a flight going out of Tampa tomorrow morning at six," he said, "but there's one from Orlando at nine. I was thinking I could get a room in Orlando, and we could spend the rest of the day together. Then I'll just take a car to the airport in the morning."

The melancholy feeling that had overtaken me when we parted lifted, and I smiled as I turned back to pick him up. I didn't want to stop feeling good, and Jack makes me feel good.

"Don't be ridiculous," I heard myself say to him. "Just stay with me." Wow. Where did that come from? Last night I felt all timid about even seeing the guy, and today I'm inviting him for a sleepover? What the hell?

"Are you sure?" he asked. "I don't want to impose."

"Of course! You're not imposing. I invited you." And there you have it. Even when he offered me an out, I still jumped in feet first. WTH.

It's not like Jack isn't a great catch. He is. He's smart. Funny. Handsome. He's got a great job. Seems to come from a stable, well-to-do family. He's interesting to talk to, and from what I sampled in kisses, he knows what he's doing in the intimacy department. Perhaps most importantly, he seems quite smitten with me. Attentive. Affectionate. No hesitation. No quandary. No morose conversations or holding back or torturous push and pull. No obvious abandonment issues. It's like Jack is Prince Charming. So now that he's here, and interested in me, I'm questioning whether or not I want Prince Charming.

Kind of ironic to consider I picked up Prince Charming at the airport and brought him home with me. I rescued Prince Charming. Go figure. I should have known if I got the chance to have a fairy tale it would be ass-backwards. Of course, to be fair, he'd rescued me first in Paris.

He asked again about visiting Ybor City, and I tossed the shadows to the wind and decided I could handle it. Not a wise choice on my part. It was like pouring water on a campfire. It dampened the day and brought Cabe to the forefront of my mind. Where he usually camps out anyway, but for the first half of the day, I'd been able to shove him to the back and enjoy Jack's company. Just like I did in Paris.

Ybor was harder, though. I could feel Cabe's presence as Jack and I wandered in and out of shops. Hear his voice in my head. Feel his touch on my skin. I shook my head to make him go away.

"You okay?" Jack asked.

"What? Yeah. Why?"

"I don't know. You just looked really sad. Haunted almost. Like you went somewhere else. Then you shook your head like you didn't want to be there."

I struggled to force a smile. "No, just thinking about work stuff. I have a busy week coming up."

"Am I keeping you? Do you need to be working today?" He placed his hand on my cheek and rubbed my temple with his thumb. Sweet, considerate Jack. Gentle Jack. Prince Jack.

"No, not at all. I can't think of anyplace I'd rather be." Not necessarily the truth. But if I couldn't be where I wanted to be, then by Jack's side was the next best place. Horrible, I know. I shouldn't say stuff like that to him when he doesn't know the rest of the story playing out in my head. But sometimes we do things to survive the moment we're in.

We'd been back at my place about an hour debating where to go for dinner when the doorbell rang. Jack had just excused himself to go to the restroom, and I walked to the door wondering who on earth would be ringing my doorbell on a Sunday night.

I never imagined I would see him standing there through the peephole.

I threw the door open to see if it was really him or if my eyes were playing tricks on me.

"What's up, Buttercup?" he asked.

I swallowed. Hard. Fighting the tears that automatically sprang to my eyes and willing myself not to run into his arms and cling to him. I also fought the desire to punch him in the face and kick him in the nuts. To say my emotions were running hot and wild was an understatement. How does he always do that to me?

"Cabe. What are you doing here?" I held onto the door to keep my knees from buckling.

His hair was longer. It fell over his eyebrows, and he shook his head to one side to flip it out of his eyes. He had on a green shirt I'd never seen before, and his hands were stuffed deep in his jeans pockets. He smiled as he greeted me, but then immediately the smile fell away and he moved to go past me into the apartment. His arm brushed against mine as he passed, and I jumped back like I'd been hit with an electrical shock.

He only took a couple of steps into the apartment before turning back to face me as he ran his hands through his hair. It stood wildly on end, and I resisted the urge to reach out and smooth it down.

"I apologize for just showing up like this, but there's so much I need to tell you. So much I should have told you long ago. I know that now, and I'm sorry. But I need you to know why my marriage to Monica ended."

He looked uneasy. Worried. Moisture glistened in his eyes, and although no tear fell on his cheek, I desperately wanted to rush forward and wrap him in my arms.

Part of the reason I didn't was because I was in shock. Frozen. I couldn't believe he was standing in front of me, and I couldn't process his words. They replayed in slow motion through my brain even as thoughts and emotions bounced back and forth at lightning speed. Everything rushing through me all at once, and yet all moving so slowly they came through like a tape player slowed down to a distorted setting.

Cabe. He's standing in my living room. He's here. He needs to tell me something. He's upset. Something he should have told me before. I wonder what it is. He's so handsome. God, I love his eyes. They're so blue. Is he going to cry? Wait. Did he say something about his marriage? Did I shut the door? I can't believe he's standing here. What a jackass. I haven't heard from him in over a month. Oh wow. What is he going to say to me? Why is he upset? Is this going to hurt?

Jack's voice cut through all the mental chatter and brought the tape playing in my head right back up to speed.

"Hello," Jack said, walking down the hall drying his hands on his jeans.

It occurred to me I had forgotten to put out a fresh hand towel about the same time it occurred to me that Jack and Cabe were both standing in my living room. At the same time. Together. And that Cabe had something he needed to say to me. Something important enough to upset him and make him drive over here to tell me in person after having no contact with me. After me telling him not to come back until he knew if he loved me. Something told me this wasn't a topic he'd want to discuss in front of Jack or anything Jack would care to hear.

"Oh, hello," Cabe said as he turned to face Jack. He looked back at me with a look I couldn't decipher. Shock? Embarrassment? Disappointment? Hurt? All of that. "I'm sorry. I didn't realize you weren't alone."

Jack rubbed his hand on his jean for one final drying swipe and then extended it to Cabe.

"Jackson Rainey."

I turned my head and looked at Jack, a bit surprised to hear the Jackson introduction, but then my eyes went straight back to Cabe.

Cabe held Jack's gaze for what seemed like forever and then shook the hand Jack offered.

"Cabe Shaw. Jack? Paris Jack?" His tone was accusatory, and I saw his eyes darken as they morphed from confusion to realization. He flicked a glare my way, and the vulnerability I had seen just moments before had gone.

"Um, I guess?" Jack said. "Not a title I go by, but I met Tyler in Paris, and I'm Jack." He looked back and forth between Cabe and me, searching my face for answers I couldn't give. I couldn't speak.

Cabe took a step back as he looked Jack up and down. I had never seen that expression on Cabe's face, and I never want to again. I honestly thought for a minute he was going to haul off and hit Jack. Jack must have thought so, too, because I saw a slight stiffening in his stance and an almost imperceptible flexing of his biceps.

Cabe gave Jack a quick nod, something I assumed to be some man-signal because Jack immediately released his stance and Cabe turned to face me.

"I'm sorry. I've caught you at a bad time. I should've called. Good night."

He nodded again toward Jack, and Jack nodded back. More man stuff, I suppose. Then Cabe was gone. Out the door and back out of my life, and I swear the oxygen left the room with him.

Shock held me in a place for a moment longer, but then the realization hit me that he was leaving without telling me what he came to say.

I flung open the door and ran out into the stairwell. "Cabe, wait!" But he was gone. The man had vanished down those stairs so quickly I think he may have actually jumped to the ground from the second floor landing. I heard his car start and the tires squeal as he pulled away.

I watched him drive out of sight before turning back to see Jack standing in my doorway.

"Do you need to go after him?" Jack asked.

I shook my head no and closed the door behind us. My legs wobbled a bit, and I plopped down in the nearest chair without the least bit of grace.

"Are you okay?"

I leaned my head back and closed my eyes, not sure how to answer him. How do I tell Prince Charming the man who just left has my heart, my soul, and my body all wrapped up inside him and I can't break free? Not even for someone as wonderful as Jack.

I felt the room spinning and couldn't get enough air. I took several huge, deep breaths as Jack knelt on the floor in front of me.

"Calm down. It's okay. Slow down. You're gonna hyperventilate. You gotta calm down. Here, put your head between your knees." He guided my head between my knees and calmly stroked my back, patting it as he murmured calming words over and over. The same way he did in Paris.

How embarrassing. I was falling apart in front of Jack again. Over Cabe this time.

I knew I needed to explain. To say something. Acknowledge what had happened. But I had no words.

What did Cabe want to tell me? What was so important that he came over out of the blue? Something about why his marriage ended. Didn't I already know?

The anxiety in his eyes. The look on his face when he saw Jack. When he realized who Jack was. Cabe would think we were together, Jack and me. Just like he thought we were together in Paris. I guess we were. I don't know. I don't know what the hell I was thinking. What I was doing.

I mean, Cabe left me, right? Yes, okay, I told him to. But I also told him I loved him and I chose him. So the ball was in his court. He ended our relationship—whatever it was—and he walked away. So I don't owe him anything, do I? I had no obligation to sit around waiting for him to show back up.

But he did show back up. He came back. I told him not to come back until he knew whether or not he loved me. And he came back. What was he going to tell me?

I felt so guilty. Like I'd betrayed Cabe. Again.

And Jack. What about Jack?

My eyes flew open as I realized how long I'd left him sitting there with no idea of what was happening. I sat up to face him as his concerned eyes searched mine, worry obvious in the lines across his forehead. I may not have owed Cabe anything, but I at least owed Jack an explanation.

"I'm sorry," I started, but wasn't sure what should come next.

Jack shook his head and shrugged. "For what? You don't owe me an apology."

"But I do, Jack. I do. I should have been more upfront with you, and I haven't been."

He rocked back onto his heels and looked away for a moment before meeting my gaze again. "Okay. You want to tell me now?"

I nodded and he stood to take a seat on the couch. "Okay. Let me hear it."

I started at the beginning. The coffee shop. The friendship. Dwayne. Monica. The divorce. New Year's Eve. Cabe's anniversary. Paris. Severing all ties. I laid all of it on the table.

He nodded here and there, patiently listening, never interrupting. His face wore a mask of intent attention, but he never showed a reaction to anything I told him.

"Jack, I know I should have told you. I should have been honest from the beginning. And I'm sorry. In Paris, we'd just met. I didn't want to go into everything, and I didn't understand enough of what had happened to even begin to tell you. Then when you called the other day, I felt like a lifeline had been thrown, and I just wanted to cling to it. To you. You were my bright spot. My happy place. I could be with you and escape again. I realize that was wrong of me, and I'm sorry. I didn't mean to use you or to hide things from you."

He nodded again, and if he hadn't been looking at me with such intensity, I might have thought he had tuned me out completely.

"I did want to be with you, Jack. I wanted to spend time with you." It was the truth, although I wasn't sure if I should be trying to convince him or if I should be just letting him go for his own good. Even now with all the cards on the table I wasn't willing to give him up entirely. My security blanket, I suppose.

"I wanted to be with you, too, Tyler. Still do. I definitely wish you had felt like you could talk to me. That you could tell me what was going on. But I guess I can understand why you didn't. I have to ask you, though. Are you still in love with him?"

I looked at Jack and wished I could say no. I wished I could turn my back on every memory of Cabe. Especially the look on his face tonight when he came through my door, and the much different look on his face when he left. I wished I could tell Jack my heart was free to explore whatever might come for us. But I couldn't look him in the eye and lie. I may have been dishonest by not disclosing everything along the way, but I wouldn't just outright lie.

"I think so. I wish I wasn't. I don't want to be. I want to be over him. To move past him. I want to be happy."

Jack nodded slowly as he stared at his hands. I wanted to ask his thoughts, but at the same time, I wasn't sure I wanted to know. I didn't think I could take them both walking out the same night.

Finally, he looked at me and extended his left hand in my direction. He patted the sofa beside him with his right. I got up and went to sit beside him, allowing him to hold me. To hold the tears at bay.

We sat that way for quite some time, completely in silence. I relaxed against him and tried not to think about what would come next.

From him. From me. From Cabe.

Anxiety and tension slowly ebbed away from me as he held me in his arms, safe for the moment from any pain or heartache. I have no idea what he was thinking. I can only imagine how he must have felt. But he just held me. No words. No pressure. Just comfort.

There is so much I could love about Jack. My Prince Charming. I curse myself for not being open to embrace that. To take it and make something solid and stable with it. Why, oh why, must I be so tangled up in Cabe's web when there is safety and security right beside me? Who would have ever thought when the prince finally showed up, I'd be pining for someone else?

I heard a light rumble in his stomach and pulled back to ask if he was hungry.

"I could eat. Do you still feel like going somewhere or do you want to just order in?"

I definitely wasn't up for a public appearance, so I ordered a pizza. We surfed the channels and watched mindless reality television, both of us muted by our own thought processes. I kept expecting him to bring it up again, to say what he was thinking, but he never did. He directed his focus and attention on me and making sure I was okay.

Attentive. Affectionate. Caring. Compassionate.

Guilt stabbed through me for every nice gesture he made. Because the constant dialog in the back of my head played a never-ending stream of "What was Cabe going to say? Why did he come here? Where is he now?"

I took my phone into the bedroom with me to change into my pajamas. I texted Cabe the moment the door closed, thankful I could remember his number since I'd deleted it from the phone.

I want to know what you were going to say. When can we talk?

I got no response.

Jack was standing in the living room staring out the sliding glass door when I came back. He turned and came to me, taking me in his arms and ever so softly planting the sweetest of kisses on my forehead before moving to my lips.

I couldn't refuse him. I didn't want to refuse him. I wanted his safety. His warmth. I had been honest. I had given him the truth. And if he still wanted to hold me, I wanted to be held. I allowed him to kiss me, to embrace me, to make me forget reality again.

I fell asleep like a rock curled against Jack with both his arms wrapped around me. When my alarm went off this morning, he was gone. I rolled over to find a note on my pillow, shocked that I hadn't heard a thing.

Tyler,

You looked so peaceful sleeping that I didn't want to wake you. I called a cab and am headed to the airport. I enjoyed our time together this weekend, and I'm relieved to finally know what haunts you and takes you away when we're together. I know I should probably bow out gracefully and leave you alone to figure out what's left between the two of you, but I'm a stubborn fool sometimes. I care for you deeply, and I'm not willing to let go so easily. Until you tell me I have no chance, I will stay in pursuit of the woman who has stolen my heart.

Yours completely, Jack

Holy Shit. What now?

Tuesday, May 6th

I texted Cabe three times yesterday and again this morning. No response. How can you just show up on my doorstep out of the blue and say you have all this stuff to tell me and then just disappear? What the hell? Typical freakin' Cabe.

It was driving me nuts. I couldn't think. I couldn't concentrate. I just wanted to know what he was going to say. I wanted him to respond to me.

It upset me so much I actually went to the gym at my apartment complex after work. Which I know should probably be a good thing in the overall scheme of life. But for me, that just shows how messed up my head was. I willingly went somewhere to sweat and put myself in pain to get out of pain. I had hoped the physical agony would outweigh the mental agony somehow. Tomorrow it probably will. I can't imagine it's a good idea to suddenly go lift a whole bunch of weights when the heaviest thing I've been lifting is my phone and a wine glass.

But for tonight, it did nothing but fuel the fire. I came out drenched in sweat, pissed at myself for not being able to lift the big ones, and furious with Cabe for making me go to the gym.

I showered and put on a sexy little black dress. I even applied eyeliner and attempted to put my hair up. Then I drove over to Maggie's intent on making him talk to me. Making him see me and give me answers.

No lights shone in the pool house, and his car wasn't in the driveway. I wasn't ready to give up so easily, so I rang Maggie's doorbell.

"Tyler? What a nice surprise! How are you? Come in, come in." Maggie backed up to let me in and went to the stereo to turn down her classical music. The room smelled faintly of garlic and red sauce. My stomach growled loudly in protest, and it dawned on me I had not eaten all day.

"I'm sorry to bother you, Maggie. I was just wondering if Cabe's

239

around?" A stupid question since he obviously wasn't there, but I didn't know what else to say.

Maggie turned to face me, her face a mixture of confusion and what I perceived to be pity.

"No, he's not," she said. "You do know Cabe doesn't live here anymore, don't you?"

I felt punched in the gut, but it may have been hunger. Whatever she'd had for dinner smelled incredible.

"Oh. No. I didn't. I'm sorry."

I was sure then her face held pity. I'd shown up all dolled up on her doorstep looking for her son. The son who had basically dumped me and left me heartbroken. Now she had to tell me he moved. I turned to go, but she put a hand on my arm and asked me to stay.

"Come in for a bit. I was just putting away dinner, and as usual, I've cooked way too much for just me. Could I fix you a plate?"

My stomach literally growled out loud in acceptance just as my mouth uttered, "No thanks. I appreciate the offer."

Maggie laughed. "Sounds like your stomach appreciates the offer. Have you eaten?"

Part of me wanted to stay and cry on her shoulder. To ask her what the hell was up with her son. To devour a plate full of whatever yummy goodness she was offering and seek comfort from someone who knows Cabe. Who loves him. Just to be near someone so close to him. Someone still connected to him. If she was still connected to him. I realized I had no idea if he was even talking to her after the mess with his dad. He had moved out, after all.

I wavered, but decided I couldn't stay. I knew I hovered on the verge of being a blubbering mess, and I didn't want to drag Maggie into my drama.

"I really need to go," I told her. "I just happened to be nearby, and I thought I'd say hi. I'm sorry."

Maggie wrapped her arms around me in an unexpected hug that almost broke down the shoddy dam holding back my emotions.

"Sweetie, you don't have to apologize. You're welcome to stop by here anytime." She released the hug but kept her hands on my arms. "Take care of yourself. Don't be a stranger."

I nodded and thanked her, barely making it to my car before the tears fell. I wanted to go back in there. To ask her where he was living now and how he was doing. But I didn't. If he wanted me to know, he'd tell me. He had come to tell me something. I just had to wait until he came again.

Thursday, May 8th

Jack sent an absolutely humongous bouquet of flowers to the office today. I seriously have never seen such a gorgeous arrangement, which is saying a lot considering I see flowers all the time in my profession. Everyone in the office swarmed around like bees to honey, oohing and aahing like they'd never seen a lily before.

They kept asking questions and grilling me mercilessly, except Lillian, who stood to the side and watched me with an eye that seemed to see right through me. I said as little as possible, not caring to get into any of the details.

The card simply read, *Just wanted you to know I'm thinking of you. And it makes me smile.*

I smiled. I mean, I'm a girl. A guy sends you a bouquet like that just because he's thinking of you, it's gonna make you smile. Especially when the guy is a prince.

But try as I might to just be happy about Jack, my thoughts were consumed with Cabe.

Why wouldn't he text me back? What did he want to tell me?

The immense size of the bouquet prevented me taking it to my own desk, so it sat on display in the reception area. Just as well since I didn't want to stare at them and be reminded of the mess I'd gotten myself into.

I've got one guy who can't get enough of me and one who finds walking away from me much easier than I'd like. I can't seem to let either of them go.

Tuesday, May 13th

It had to be done. I decided last night, and then I worked up my courage all day today.

Jack has called every night since he left a week ago. We texted back and forth during my weddings this past weekend, and he insisted I call and wake him up when I got home from work after midnight Saturday night.

Last night, we'd talked maybe twenty minutes when he invited me to meet his parents.

"I'm heading up to their lake house, and I'd love for you to come. We're looking at the first weekend in June, but if you've got weddings, it could be another weekend. I just need to let my sister know so she can arrange her flight. They're all excited to meet you."

Perspiration immediately popped out all over my body. Like one minute I was fine, listening to him talk while I munched on a handful of Cheetos, and the next, sweat drenched my body and I felt sick to my stomach.

Meet the parents? His sister flying in just to meet me? Oh boy. It all confirmed what I already knew but didn't want to face. Jack was serious. About me. About us.

I'd sort of allowed myself to enjoy talking to him each day. To enjoy his company across the lines. It felt nice to not be lonely. To have companionship, even if it was long distance.

It's not like I don't like Jack. Or that I don't care about him.

But I knew with all certainty when he asked me to meet his parents that I'm not invested in this.

The ugly truth is I've been using Jack to mask my anxiety and pain over Cabe. Much as I used Jack in Paris for the same purpose.

When did I become such a heartless person? When did I become one of those girls?

Leading him on. Dangling a carrot in front of him. Just to get what I needed. What I wanted. Just to be secure in the fact that someone adored me. Someone wanted to be with me. To talk to me. To see me. To introduce me to his parents.

I stammered a half-ass explanation about June being crazy with weddings, but he pointed out I'd already said June was slow for us due to the heat and overcrowded attractions in the area. So then I fell back on my accreditation and the time needed for coursework, and he immediately reminded me I hadn't booked the course yet and he was willing to work around it.

I sat in silence then, running out of reasons and not yet ready to state the truth.

"Tyler?" He paused after saying it, and I held my breath. "Tyler?" He said again, but without a pause this time. "If you don't want to meet my parents, I mean, if you're not ready, or if it's too soon or whatever, just tell me. Communicate, okay? I'm sensing something on the other end of the line, and I just want to know what it is."

I bit my lip and listened to my inner voice rant and rave about the importance of being honest and not leading him on. But my outer voice said, "I'm just tired. I don't know what my schedule looks like, and it's stressful to try and plan anything right now. Maybe another time?"

What a bitch. The guy deserved better. Here he was, asking for honesty and being the charming prince as always, and I couldn't give it to him. I wasn't ready to say goodbye. I wasn't ready to give up his phone calls, his laughter, and the way he made me feel.

It's weighed on me all day today that I'm not being fair to Jack. I do care about him. But I'm not in love with him. Not the way I was with Cabe. I don't know if I ever could be.

I'm not good for anyone right now, and I knew I owed it to Jack to 'fess up and set him free. It didn't mean it came easy, though.

I called tonight as soon as I got home, and we chatted back and forth about our workdays for a bit. Anxiety and dread twisted me in knots, and I finally decided the waiting was worse than the actual act.

"Jack, you're a great guy."

"Oh no. This sounds like the part of the movie where she kicks the great guy to the curb. I always hate this part, and I usually fast forward through it to get to where she realizes she made a mistake and comes back to him. Can we just skip to that?"

I smiled, and marveled again at the stupidity of my heart for not choosing to love this very special man.

"I'm not being fair to you, Jack. You deserve better."

"Isn't that up to me to decide? I can't think of anyone better for me, Tyler. You're amazing, and I feel like the luckiest man on earth for having the chance encounter we had in Paris. Like the universe was shining down on me that day. You can't tell me you didn't feel a connection."

I leaned my head back and looked at the ceiling, cursing the universe for sending me the guy who thinks I hung the moon and having me be hung up on a different guy at the time. Funny. Very funny. In a not at all funny way.

"Jack, I did. I felt a connection then, and I feel a connection now. I enjoy talking to you, laughing with you. I truly do. If we'd met another time, another place, a different phase in my life, I could easily see us together. See a future with you by my side. But I can't give you what you want right now. My heart still belongs to another, and it's not fair of me to keep taking from you without anything to give in return."

"Look, we don't have to go to my parents. Forget I asked. I didn't mean to freak you out or anything. I've just never felt this way about anyone before. I've always been wrapped up in my own needs and my own agenda, and I feel like all of the sudden the only thing I need is you. Nothing else matters."

We sat in silence as he waited for me to respond and I cursed my inability to be what he needed. When I didn't speak, he continued.

"I know I met you at a bad time. I know you and Cabe have a history, and there was a lot of ambiguity when I came along. But has anything come of it? Have you heard any more from him? I mean, are you really willing to keep sitting there waiting just in case he decides he wants you? I *know* I want you, Tyler. I have no doubts. I can't think about anything else. I know you feel something for me, too. Don't run from it."

I wavered, second-guessing myself. I've had no word from Cabe. No response to my attempts to contact him. So if he came to my apartment that night to say he had feelings for me, where is he now?

What would it hurt to keep talking to Jack? To keep enjoying his company? Why give him up when I may never hear from Cabe again?

I knew the answer, though. I didn't like it, but I knew it. Whether Cabe ever comes back or not, it wasn't fair to Jack to use him for my own selfish purposes. He is too great a guy to be a consolation prize.

So I closed my eyes and gritted my teeth together, steeling my resolve to put Jack's well-being ahead of my own need for security and companionship.

"Jack, I don't feel the same way about you as you feel about me. I don't know if I ever will. I do care about you, but I need to figure out what's going on in my life. You gotta stop calling."

He stayed quiet for a bit, and then he played the part of the prince right up until the end.

"I'll honor your wishes, but it's not what I want. So if you change your mind, you know where to find me. Please know no matter what the outcome is, I just want you to be happy. You deserve to be happy. You deserve to be loved. I'll always wish it was me."

I hung up and realized I felt more relief than sadness. Which says a lot, I suppose.

Now if only I could figure out how to untangle the rest of my twisted heartstrings and truly be free to move on.

Monday, May 19th

Saturday's wedding was a couple who dated in high school and then split up for forty years before reconnecting. They talked at the ceremony about true love never dying and how they never gave up on each other, even through each of their happy marriages to other people and raising children into adulthood. The flame never burned out, hidden away in a tiny little space in their hearts never to be forgotten. After each of their respective spouses passed away—both from lengthy battles with cancer—the two sought each other out. They'd been inseparable since then, and the wedding proved to be an emotional testament to the strength of their love and a true representation of a happy ending. They stood together with their grown children and grandchildren and prepared to live out their sunset together.

As blissful as they seemed, and as wonderful as the event was to experience, I felt melancholy settle over me with the whole thing. They missed out on their entire lives together. The children they would have had. The places they would have gone. The adventures they would have encountered. Yes, they had happy marriages and experienced love with other people. They each had incredible kids who had given them much joy and would continue to do so through grandchildren.

But I couldn't help but wonder if they mourn the loss of the lifetime together. Sure, they're closing out the final act on the same stage, but look at everything they missed. What if they hadn't split up? Would they have gone the distance and still be together all this time later? Do they ever wish it had turned out differently?

I'm ready to move on. I firmly believe I will have plenty of celebrations in my life. Promotions. Friendships. Travel. Accomplishments. And yes, relationships. Love.

This wedding touched me, though. It spoke to my heart about what can be lost along the way. I knew I didn't want to get to the end of my lifetime, however long that should be, and realize it was Cabe I missed all along.

I decided I couldn't truly put Cabe behind me without giving him one more chance to respond. In the days right after that night at my place with him and Jack, I texted and called several times, but got nothing but radio silence. It's been two weeks, so I made a deal with myself this morning. I would try one more time, and then I'd be done. If I reached out again and he didn't answer, I'd have no choice but to accept he is part of my past and I'd be free to move forward without him. To find my own lifetime free and clear.

My hands trembled a bit as I typed the message, and my thumbs hovered over the screen for several seconds before I finally got the nerve to hit send. I don't know if I was more nervous he would respond or he wouldn't.

Okay, Dude. I'm gonna try to reach you one more time, but this time you don't even have to text me back. I'll be at the lake at 4pm today. If I don't see you there, I'll leave you alone and stop trying to reach you. Please come.

I got there about a quarter til. So keyed up my hands were shaking, and I got the hiccups.

I heard his car park a couple minutes after the hour. Heard him walking up behind me, but I couldn't trust my emotions to stay calm if I turned to face him. I was determined not to go all to pieces.

"What's up, Buttercup?" He plopped down on the bench beside me, and I sneaked a sideways glance. He looked angry. Frustrated. Tired. The dark circles underneath his eyes only served to highlight the unbelievable clear depths of the blue irises. My breath caught in my throat at the sight of him, but then I hiccuped again, and it released. I decided to dive right in, not sure how long I could keep it together.

"You came to my house that night and told me you wanted me to know why your marriage ended."

He sat forward with his arms on his knees, his hands clasped together so tight his knuckles were white.

"It ended because there was a third person in the marriage from the beginning. I never wanted to acknowledge that, but I know now it's true."

"You mean Kristin? Was Monica seeing her all along?"

He laughed, but it came out ragged around the edges with no humor or joy.

"No, Buttercup. Monica did all she could to save our relationship. Kristen was her last resort."

I couldn't help but face him then, shocked to hear him say that. Monica had left him for Kristen, which broke his heart and devastated his life. How could he say now she had done all she could to save it?

"So, how's Jack?" His voice held a steel edge to it, sharpened and ready to strike. He didn't look at me, but instead gazed across the lake at the houses on the other side. The houses we used in our imaginary scenarios when we came here before. Long before our own lives became more drama-filled than the ones we made up for them.

"Good, I guess. Why do you ask?"

He looked at me then, only briefly, but long enough for me to see hurt and anger flaring almost out of control.

"Cabe, I'm not dating Jack."

"Really? Because I saw some photos of you in Paris that definitely seem to convey otherwise, and if I'm not mistaken, he stayed at your apartment that Sunday night and didn't leave until morning."

My mouth flew open in shock and indignation. "How do you know that? Were you watching us?"

He stood up. "I wanted to know. I needed to know. You see, I wanted to believe you when you told me there was nothing between you in Paris. Once I calmed down, I thought about it and realized you may be telling the truth. But then when I saw him there that night, the truth seemed to be staring me in the face and shaking my hand. I had to know. So yeah. I came back and waited in the parking lot to see when he left. Now why would he spend the night if you're not dating? Or do you guys just have something casual going on?"

"He missed his flight. He stayed with me so he didn't have to book another hotel room."

Cabe crossed his arms and glared down at me. "So you guys had a hotel room for the weekend?"

I stood then, crossing the space between us in two angry steps to stand toe to toe with him.

"No. He had a room in Tampa for a conference he was attending. But you know what? I don't owe you any of these answers. I told you I chose you. That I loved you. You walked away. You don't get to play the jealous lover. What I do and who I see is my business. You *chose* not be involved."

He looked down his nose at me, and I stood my ground just inches from him. I didn't see him move though, despite being so close. He reached out and wrapped me in his arms and crushed my lips beneath his before I even knew it was happening.

At first, I felt outraged. How dare he be such an ass and then expect that he could just kiss me! But any anger I felt stood no chance against my traitorous body. My very soul cried out for him and my body molded against him like we'd originally been one piece split apart by fire.

I wrapped my arms around his neck and pulled him to me, my hands submerged within the long curls at the nape of his neck. He plundered and searched and I offered myself up to him, completely open and receiving what only he could give me.

Jack may be sweet. He may be kind. Handsome and charming, too. But I don't think I could ever feel for him the passion I have for Cabe. The fire. The immediate combustion. Cabe ignites me in ways I never dreamed possible. Physically, emotionally, mentally.

I clung to him and pulled him tighter, our mouths smashed together so hard that it hurt, but I was unwilling to let go. He clung just as hard if not harder. He settled both hands across my ass and pulled me up into him, and I immediately knew how very excited he was to see me. Or to hold me and assault me with kisses, more accurately.

When he finally pulled back, he didn't release me. He just stood there and held me against him in a vice grip I had no desire to resist. He spoke in hushed, quiet whispers so close his lips almost moved against mine as he talked.

"I fell in love with you the first time I saw you. You were behind the counter at the coffee shop, and you were laughing and throwing water at some guy who worked with you."

"Rodney," I said, but then regretted speaking in case it made him stop talking. I so desperately wanted to hear what he had to say.

"I always thought we'd end up together. I just had this faith that you were the one and it was meant to be. We clicked so well. I'd never felt about a woman the way I felt about you. Hell, I'd never been as close to anyone as I was to you. You were the best friend I ever had. I kept thinking you'd see me eventually. When you got over Dwayne. When you got more comfortable being away from your family. When you found a job you enjoyed. When you saw how great we were together. But you never did."

He released me then and walked past me toward the lake. I felt cold air swirl around me, but the chill within me from his absence went deeper than any wind could cause. I started to interrupt him, to tell him I could finally see, but he wasn't finished.

"When Monica came along, it felt great. She saw me. She picked me. She wanted me. It was intoxicating. She made me laugh. She paid attention to me. Made me feel good inside. Made me feel like a man."

I nodded, even though he couldn't see me from where he stood. I understood all too well exactly how Monica made him feel. After all, wasn't that what Jack had provided me? Well, he didn't make me feel like a man, but he made me feel beautiful. Wanted. Adored.

"When she left to move back to Seattle, I was confused. On the one hand, I had this wonderful girl. Beautiful. Smart. Funny. Successful. And she wanted to be with me. It should have been perfect. But she wasn't who I wanted. I wanted you."

He turned to face me then, walking slowly back towards me but stopping just out of my reach. Purposefully, I'm sure.

"I came to you that night after she left for Seattle to tell you the truth.

To tell you I loved you and wanted to share the rest of my life with you. But before I could get the words out, you told me to follow Monica. You assumed I was talking about her when I tried to tell you I was in love. You told me to go after her. Pursue her. You said you thought that was where I needed to be."

"But wait. I didn't—"

"It's okay. I know you were only trying to help. I started off the conversation that night talking about loving someone and taking risks. Being vulnerable and willing to be hurt. You didn't realize I was talking about you."

I shook my head as the tears fell on my cheeks.

"So I moved to Seattle. I resolved to put you behind me and move on with my life. But it wasn't that easy. She had decided to move back there because she felt like I would never let you go. She thought it would be different when I came to Seattle, but you were too much a part of me. Your name came up in conversation, sometimes without me even noticing I'd brought you up. Five years of my life spent by your side, pretty much every day. So all my stories, all my memories of my adult life, were tangled up with you."

He looked toward the lake, and I wiped at my tears with the back of my sleeve.

"She gave me an ultimatum. To give you up and never mention you again or leave her and Seattle behind. You had made it clear there was nothing for me here. So I did what she asked. I severed all ties with you, even though it felt like cutting off a limb or tearing out a chunk of my heart. And you let me do it. Then she said if I truly loved her, I'd marry her to prove it. So I did. I married her. Pledged to love her the rest of my life and give her my name. I felt like I meant it when I said it, you know? Like I intended to follow through. I did mean to. I wanted to. I had the perfect girlfriend. The perfect wife. Why wouldn't I follow through?" He coughed and cleared away emotion from his throat.

"But the heart wants what it wants. She says I was sullen. Depressed. And I guess I was. I don't know. I felt adrift. Lost. Like I didn't know how I'd gotten there and wasn't sure where to go. I loved her. I did. But it wasn't enough. It wasn't the kind of love to sustain you through better or worse. It didn't have the roots for that. It couldn't. Because I was in love with *you*."

He kind of spit out the last part, and it occurred to me that loving me had mostly been a painful experience for Cabe. First dealing with my rejection, then with me sending him to Seattle oblivious to his feelings, and then being caught between Monica and a hard place. All the while without me returning the least bit of hope I would ever feel the same for him.

My tears poured, and I lifted my hand to touch him. He moved away.

"I used to call out your name in my sleep. Hell, for all I know I still do. It didn't happen all that often, maybe two or three times, but trust me when I say it wasn't a good thing to do with a wife lying in bed next to you. We were fighting a lot, both of us disillusioned and blaming each other for our misery. She started going out after work, to escape I suppose, but it left me lonely at home. Resentful. I'd been drinking one night, and I went to bed before she came home. She came in intoxicated and when she climbed in bed sans clothing, things got a little amorous. Something that hadn't been happening all that frequently. I was half asleep, still buzzing from going to bed drunk, and I guess at the worst possible time I called out your name. I don't even remember saying it. It wasn't a conscious thought. But that was it. She was done. Nothing I could do to make up for it. Nothing I could say."

He cleared his throat again and reached to pick a blade of grass, shredding it as he talked. "She pretty much never came home after that. I'd go days at a time without even seeing her. When she did come home to grab clothes or take a shower, Kristen was always with her. The two of them would laugh and giggle. Talk some secret language I couldn't decipher. Total bullshit. So I finally asked her if she wanted to be married to Kristen or me, and you know the rest of the story."

He moved toward the bench, but he didn't sit down. Instead he went around behind it to stand, almost as though he was putting a barrier between us.

"I just thought you should know the whole story," he said. "The parts I couldn't tell you before. I felt ashamed. Embarrassed. Too vulnerable to admit how I felt and what had happened because of it. But I've realized since we split up you deserved to know. I should have been honest with you."

I didn't know what to say. I mean, what on earth could I possibly say to all that?

He turned to walk away, and I called his name to stop him.

He paused, still facing the cars, but then he slowly turned and looked at me.

"Where are you going?" I asked.

"Home. I've said what I needed to say, and now I'll leave you to your life. I hope the two of you will be very happy together."

"Would you please listen to me? I'm not dating Jack."

Cabe laughed, or snorted, I guess I should say. I couldn't decipher whether it was derisive or if he actually thought my statement was funny.

"I've just been painfully honest with you, Tyler. The least you could do is not stand here and lie to me."

"Okay, you know what? Here's the truth. There *was* something between us in Paris. I did have feelings for Jack. A connection, I guess you could say.

I can't define it because I never understood it. I guess I got from Jack all those things you got from Monica. He made me laugh. He made me feel good. He let me know he wanted me around and that I was special to him. And yeah, I enjoyed his company."

"And his bed?" He crossed his arms again, his entire body rigid in defensiveness.

"What the hell? Why are you so hung up on that? I have never had sex with Jack Rainey, okay? Have I kissed him? Yes. Have I spent the night in his arms? Yes. Have I wanted to sleep with him? Yes, I guess I have. But you wanna know what stopped me? You. Because I don't love Jack Rainey, dumbass. I love you. And for the life of me, I can't understand how two people who say they love each other can screw something up so badly."

I walked past him to my car, praying the whole time for him to stop me, but he didn't.

I looked back at him as I stood there with one foot in my car, wondering if I was about to drive away from him for the last time.

"I'm glad you told me the truth, Cabe. Glad you came. But I don't know where we go from here. I think we've drug each other through so much mud at this point that I don't know if the water could ever run clear. Maybe we're just toxic to each other."

He didn't say anything. He just looked at me for what felt like forever and then turned to face the lake.

I drove home completely numb, but no more tears fell. I have none left to give. I replayed the whole conversation at least a million times since I left him there, astounded that our lives got so off track and we caused each other so much pain along the way. Not to mention the casualties who dared to fall in love with us without knowing we weren't available to love.

I said I would let go and move on if he didn't respond. He definitely responded, but then he let me leave. So what now?

Thursday, May 22nd

Cabe called this morning just as I got to work.

"Hey. You available for dinner this evening?"

I sat back in my chair and very carefully considered my response for probably all of, oh, I don't know, two seconds before blurting out yes. I could tell myself all I wanted that I needed to let him go, but the minute he offered, my heart had no response but to be with him.

He picked me up at six and took me to a restaurant near my place. Somehow he'd found one we hadn't been to.

At first, things moved at an awkward pace, both of us unsure of the other. Hesitant to say the wrong thing, and shy after so much time apart. But it didn't take long for the ice to break, and as my laughter came easier, my shoulders started to relax back down away from my ears.

I told him about my promotion, and he talked about how much he enjoyed being back in his old role. We danced around hot topics and didn't mention anything that might bring tension to the table.

Cabe seemed different to me. Older somehow. More serious. Still funny. Still Cabe. But not the same.

He echoed my thoughts as we walked to the car after dinner. "You're different, Ty. I don't know how to describe it, but you carry yourself differently. More confident. More sassy. Self-assured. It looks good on you."

When he opened the car door for me, he stood back and made no move to touch me. He hadn't held my hand or brushed against me the whole night, and my body buzzed with every nerve standing on end and starving for his touch. I was hyper-aware of him. His presence. His scent. His voice. I don't know why I ever thought I could just leave him behind. As though I could function without my heart.

Once we reached my place, I waited for him to come around the car and open my door. He took my hand to help me out, and it felt like electric shock waves passed down my arm and charged through my veins. We walked upstairs together, but he stayed outside when I unlocked the door.

I searched his face, uncertain where to go from there. He hesitated for a moment, but then he took my hand and pressed the back of it to his lips, holding it there for what seemed like forever as I trembled. My heart beat so loudly I feared he would hear it. I tried to take slow, steady breaths to make it calm down, but the proximity of him prevented that from happening.

Finally, he moved my hand away from his lips and clasped it against his chest.

"I'm sure," he said. "You told me not to come back until I was sure. I've always been sure I loved you. I've loved you for so long I can't remember what it feels like to not love you. I just wasn't sure I could make it work."

I attempted to swallow the huge lump in my throat, but it didn't budge. I opened my mouth to speak anyway and hoped it didn't come out as a croak. "And now?"

He smiled and reached up to cup my face in his hand. "I still don't know if we can make it work. I have my issues. You have yours. I have my fears. You have yours. I don't know if I can measure up to everything you need or want, but I know I can't deny my feelings any longer."

I opened my mouth to speak, but he put his finger gently against my lips. "Let me finish. I have a lot I need to say."

He smiled and I nodded as he released my lips and took my hand again.

"For all those years, I could pretend it was your fault. That we'd work if you'd give us a chance. Then when New Year's Eve happened and we seemed to finally be on the same page, I got a little freaked out by it all. It's one thing to love you from afar, but to actually try, to actually be in the relationship I wanted with you, was scary as hell. Because that meant I could fail. I'd failed before. I didn't intend to, but I did. I wasn't willing to fail with you. If we tried and it didn't work, you'd be lost to me forever. We couldn't go back to just being friends after that. A risk I couldn't take. I realize now it wasn't just you preventing 'us' all those years. I share the responsibility, too. My fears were just as much a part of it."

He cleared his throat, and I blinked to see him clearly through my tears.

"I love you, Tyler Warren. I want to give this a go. See where it can take us. I'm willing to give it all I've got. If you'll still have me."

He turned my hand over and kissed my palm, which of course immediately sent chills up my spine. I shivered and hoped I could get the words out without incoherently sobbing.

"I love you, too, Cabe Shaw. With every fiber of my being, I love you. And I'm sorry I didn't see it before. Sorry for the pain I put you through. I wish I could go back…" My voice broke off as a sob seized my throat and the tears flowed. I swear I think I could win some award for crying the most of any person on the planet. I should be in the book of world records or something.

He took my face in his hands, and despite the wet, sloppy, possibly snotty mess, he kissed me and took my breath away.

"We can't go back, Buttercup. But we can go forward."

"Okay, but now there's something I need to say."

Cabe bowed and swung his arm to the side in a gesture to give me the floor.

I swallowed hard against the lump in my throat. "I don't need you to be a prince or to measure up to some image you think I have in my head. You've mentioned that a couple of times now. I just need *you*. I need you to talk to me. Even when you're stressed or angry. Whatever. You can't just disappear on me." I shoved at him, probably only partly playful.

"I know, I know." He wrapped his arms around me and planted a kiss on my lips. "I just don't know what to do when it all goes south. That's why I steer clear of you."

"You can't, though. Life's gonna go south. If we're in this, we're in it. When it goes south, we figure it out together. So when I call you, you gotta call me back. If something happens, you gotta tell me."

"But that's just it. Sometimes, when shit's happening, I don't want to talk about it. I don't want to have to answer questions or put on some show trying to act like everything's okay when it's not. So it's easier sometimes just to stay away. I'm not trying to lock you out or anything. In my head, I'm trying to protect you from me being all screwed up."

"You're not protecting me from anything by ignoring me. If you don't want to talk, you tell me you don't want to talk, and that's on me to accept it. But tell me you need space. Don't just disappear. That hurts."

"Okay. No more disappearing acts. I promise." He held me closer and buried his face in my hair. "God, I love you, girl."

We kissed again, this time tender and slow, savoring each other before we said goodbye for the night.

Tuesday, May 27th

Having such an incredible night with Cabe Thursday and then working non-stop weddings for the Memorial Day weekend and not being able to see him for days equated to torture. We talked and texted every day, but I longed to hold him again. The clock moved at an excruciating pace, and I thought six o'clock never would get here.

He said he'd pick me up for dinner tonight, and I assumed he meant a restaurant. Instead, he drove me to our lake and pulled a picnic basket from his back seat. The sun had begun its descent, bathing the lake in golden ambers, deep pinks, and subtle blues. He laid a blanket on the grass in front of our bench and set the basket down on it.

"I hope there's no mosquitoes," Cabe said. "It's still been cool enough in the mornings to keep them at bay here during the day, but I haven't been out here at night in a while."

I looked at him, startled at the way he'd said it. "You come out here at night? Alone?" I wondered if he brought other girls here. To our place. I dreaded his answer.

"Yeah, I do. I come out here a lot actually. It helps me think. Clears my head. And it makes me feel connected to you."

I breathed a sigh of relief that it wasn't a hot date spot for him and relaxed on the blanket.

He poured us both a glass of wine and divvied out the sandwiches and fruit he'd packed. We ate in silence, each of us just happy to be together with no words needed between us.

Cabe plucked grapes from their stems and fed them to me, and I don't know if I've ever experienced anything more sensuous than eating from his hand as we sat there on the blanket. With each grape, his finger traced my lips and then I'd flick my tongue across his skin as I opened my mouth and he pushed the grape inside. It didn't take many grapes before he'd moved the basket out of the way and eased me onto my back on the blanket.

We got reacquainted, and I marveled anew at the effect his body had on mine. I arched toward him as he ravished my neck and laid open my shirt to explore further. His hands worked their magic beneath my skirt, and I didn't even care that we were laying in the middle of a public park in the midst of a neighborhood where any random stranger could come jogging by or casually pass us taking the family dog for a walk.

I think it's quite possible I would have let the man strip me down naked and take me right then and there, but unfortunately, we'll never know.

I don't know how much time had passed with us kissing, whispering, groping, pleasuring. Sharing words of love so long held constrained when he suddenly sat up and looked at his watch in a panic. Then he jumped to his feet and said, "We gotta go."

Picnic items went flying into the basket with no rhyme or reason, and he grabbed my hand and literally pulled me to standing as I struggled to button my shirt and adjust my skirt.

"What are you doing? Why are we in such a hurry?"

"I didn't realize it was so late. I have to be somewhere," he answered as he opened the passenger door for me and paused to toss the basket in the back seat. "Come on."

I hobbled up to the car with one shoe on and one shoe off, my body going through withdrawal and my brain trying to figure out what happened.

We drove about two blocks before pulling into the driveway of an adorable little cottage house. It sat nestled under tall, thick majestic oaks. A wide porch spanned the front of the house with a swing suspended on one end, and a vignette of table and chairs at the other.

"Whose house is this?"

He looked across the car at me and gave me a tentative smile. "Mine. Proud homeowner. There's someone I want you to meet."

My mind spun with the knowledge Cabe had bought a house that I knew nothing about. I tried to console myself with the thought that there would be plenty of time for us to share it now, but the nagging hurt didn't dissipate. My thoughts caught up with his words about meeting someone just as he opened the front door. A bundle of golden fur bounded out to greet us, rearing up on Cabe's legs and then immediately coming to run its nose up my skirt. I squealed and jumped away, covering my privates with my hands as Cabe admonished the dog.

"No, Deacon. That's not polite. The ladies don't like for you do that unless you buy them dinner first." He laughed at his own joke and reached inside the door to grab a leash, which he affixed to the dog's collar.

"You got a dog??" I asked, my mind completely blown. He bought a house? He got a dog? Who was this guy? And what had he done with Cabe?

"Come on, we gotta get him walking. He's good for about a four hour stretch before he pegs the rug." He adjusted the leash in one hand and grabbed my hand with the other, and we set off down the porch steps following Deacon.

"I can't believe you got a dog. What kind is he?"

"An absolute mutt. He came into the shelter about two weeks ago, and I don't know how it happened. He just spoke to me."

I cocked my head to the side to watch Deacon run. "Really? And what did he say?"

"He said, 'Cabe, I need a good home. And I heard you just bought a good home. Whaddya say?' So I took him up on the offer."

Deacon pulled at the leash as he sniffed each and every bush along our path. His face and body looked like a Labrador, but his short, stout legs were more like a beagle. If you took sculptures of both dogs and split them in half, then switched the top halves to sit upon the other's bottom half, the Labrador top half and Beagle bottom half would be Deacon. Bizarre looking, for sure, but Deacon walked with his head held high with confidence.

"I thought you didn't want a dog. Too much responsibility. Or a house. Same reason."

He chuckled softly and whistled to Deacon as he pulled him back from the street.

"Well, Buttercup, it's the funniest thing. All this thinking I been doing has made me realize the best things in life require a commitment. I've been working myself up to being able to make a pretty important commitment. I figured the house and Deacon here were good practice for me."

"And how's that working out for ya?"

"So far, so good. But Deacon and the house could use a woman's touch. So could I for that matter." He released my hand and slid his arm around my shoulders, leaning in to give me a kiss.

My mind jumped around so much I couldn't focus on one thought at a time.

I'm with Cabe. Cabe loves me. We're back together. Holy shit, he bought a house. He bought a house without me. I would have liked to buy one together. He said it needs a woman's touch. He wants to involve me. That is one bizarre looking dog. His legs disappear under his body when he runs. I can't believe he got a dog. Every four hours he needs to go out? Wow. That's a lot of responsibility. What now? Do we date? Are we dating? Are we still just friends? Do I ask? Will that push him away again? How do I know he's not going to leave?

I felt like a container of jumping beans had been let loose in my head, and the clatter of all those thoughts zipping around were deafening. Maddening. I couldn't clear my head. Couldn't turn it off. I finally just came to a dead stop in the middle of the sidewalk.

"What?" Cabe asked. "What is it? Is something wrong?"

Deacon tugged and pulled, unhappy to have suddenly stopped. He whimpered and whined as he danced in place, eager to be on his way.

"Are you okay?" Cabe bent down to look closer at me. We were between street lamps at the moment, and the shade of the towering tree above us made it hard to see.

I shook my head. "I don't know. This is all a little too much for me to take in. I think I need some answers."

"Okay. I'm an open book. What do you need?"

"What are we doing?"

He maneuvered Deacon back to where we stood and patted the dog's head when he sat. "We're walking the dog."

I gritted my teeth and tried to stay calm. "What are we doing?" I pointed back and forth between us. "You and me. Cabe and Tyler. What is this? I've made the mistake of assuming we were just friends when that was evidently not the case, and I've made the mistake of thinking we were dating when that was wrong, too. So no assumptions. What's going on between us?"

He shrugged as if the answer was no big deal. "I love you. You love me. We're going to see what happens."

"*See what happens?* What does that mean? Because I have to tell you, I'm a little wary at this point. There's a part of me, somewhere in this region," I pointed a circle around my heart, "that is jumping for joy. Screaming and squealing because you're back in my life and you're saying you love me. So that part's seeing all butterflies and rainbows. But this part," I pointed a circle around my stomach, "this part has been kicked around a whole bunch these last few months. Pardon my gut if it's feeling a bit more apprehensive about all this. Uncertain, if you will. How do I know you're not going to change your mind again tomorrow, or the next day? How do I know you're not going to bolt and run again?"

He turned Deacon back in the direction of the house and started walking again, extending his hand for me to take. I took it, annoyed at how his hands were so cool and calm while mine were sweating and shaking.

"I'm not going anywhere. I understand why you'd be hesitant to trust me with everything that's happened. But I love you, Tyler. I'm in. All in. I'm not going anywhere."

I stopped again. "You say that now, but how do you know what you'll feel the first time we get in an argument? Or the first time something difficult happens? A family member dies or one of us loses a job? How do you know for sure? Especially when your answer was '*I don't know*' not so long ago."

"My answer was '*I don't know*' because I didn't know if we could make it work. I still don't know if we can. I guess you're going to have to trust me, Ty. Just like I'm going to have to trust you. Neither one of us knows what the future brings. No guarantees. I can't promise you we won't fail. But I can promise to give you everything I have in making this work. I'm not going anywhere. You will be putting up with me for a very long time."

He kissed me then, and as usual, I lost all train of thought and got caught up in the physical sensations of his kiss. But I couldn't escape my thoughts on the drive home, and I can't shut them down long enough to get to sleep now.

I'm back to my old question, I suppose. How do I know if he's The One? How do I know I won't get hurt? How do I know I won't hurt him? And why, oh why, can't fairy tales be real and happily ever after be the norm and not the exception?

Saturday, May 31st

Cabe's come over every night this week. We've had dinner. We've watched movies. Shopped for groceries. Folded laundry. Hung out. He can only stay four hours at a time with Deacon waiting at home, but other than that, it's like we're back to normal. Well, except I don't even know what our normal is at this point.

Basically, we're back to talking and texting multiple times every day, hanging out every evening, and sharing all the details of our days. In addition, we're saying I love you morning, noon and night, and we can't seem to be in the same room without touching each other. We can't get anywhere near my couch and remain fully clothed. We've explored pretty much every option I'm aware of other than intercourse, but he still stops us. He keeps saying it's not the right time.

It makes me nervous. Scares me a little. I mean, not that I think we need to have sex for me to know he loves me, but I can't help but think about my conversation with Mel and her opinion about him holding back. The sex thing being the final claim. The last threshold. It's madness. Is it really his chivalrous idea of needing to wait? Needing it to be 'right?' Or is he holding back and keeping the most intimate part of himself safe?

I feel so weird even asking that as the girl. Stereotypically, I should be the one holding back and him the one all frustrated, but we've never conformed to the rules or the norms.

He invited me over to his house tomorrow night. It makes more sense, I suppose, because then he wouldn't have to leave for Deacon, but I still feel a little funny about the house. The dog. Like those are things he did without me. While we were apart. Like I don't belong there.

I know it's important to him, though, and it's not like I can stay away from his house forever. Right?

June

Sunday, June 1st

Deacon stayed on his best behavior tonight. I swear I think Cabe bribed him or something. He acted extremely well-behaved, and I have to admit I think he may have won me over. He really is an amazing dog.

As much as I hate to say it, Cabe's house was beautiful, too. Built in the 1920s and well-restored by the previous owner. Cabe hasn't hung a single thing on the walls or decorated in any way yet, so it feels a bit bare.

"I don't know, I just never got around to it," he said when I mentioned it. "I've only been here a month, and I've spent a lot of time training Deacon, so it hasn't really been a priority. I thought maybe we'd go shopping next weekend. You could help me figure out what to do with the place."

"I have the yacht wedding Saturday so I'll pretty much be gone out on the water all day. Then I fly out Sunday for my accreditation thing. I won't be back until Thursday night."

He led me to his sofa as I talked and pulled me into his lap as he sat. "Oh, right. I think I keep forgetting that on purpose. I'm a little nervous for you to go out of town again. It didn't turn out so well for me the last time."

I put my arms around his neck and pulled him close for a kiss. "You have nothing to worry about. You have my heart, Cabe Shaw. Besides, I don't think there's a lot of prospects at a wedding planner workshop."

He returned the kiss, deepening it beyond my light peck and stoking the inevitable fires between us.

"I just don't want anything else to come between us," he said as he pulled away. "Are you sure you can't pack me in your suitcase?"

"You'd probably miss the plane," I teased, but the look in his eyes said he didn't find it funny. "I'm sorry. Too soon?"

He shrugged. I kissed him again and rose up to straddle him, allowing

265

my body to reassure him that it belonged to him and him alone. We continued down the path together until he yet again put on the brakes.

"Why do you do that?" I asked. "And how do you do that? How do you just stop?"

"I don't know. I guess it's just important to me that we wait."

"Wait for what? I thought you were sure."

He laughed. "I am sure, silly girl. I've never been more sure than I am right now. But I'm also sure I want our first time to be special. To be memorable. I don't want it to be just sex. I want it to be different for us."

"Okay, you realize you're saying my lines right now, don't you?"

He shrugged. "Yeah, I guess. And believe me, there's been plenty of times—like every night this past week—where I questioned whether or not it matters. But it does matter to me. I have an idea in my head, and I want to see it through."

"Are you going to share this idea with me?"

He smiled and tugged me back closer to him. "Of course. You'll be the first to know when it happens." We kissed again, but I couldn't shake the little voice of doubt playing like a broken record in the back of my head.

"What's wrong?" he asked.

"I don't know."

"Bullshit. What's wrong? What's going on in that pretty head of yours? Are you thinking I don't want you? I don't find you attractive? What crazy thought process are you entertaining?"

I played with a button on his shirt and avoided eye contact. I wanted to avoid the conversation and tell him nothing was wrong, but we'd agreed from now on, we'd be open and upfront no matter how uncomfortable we felt. Hiding our thoughts and feelings had wreaked too much damage in the past.

"I just wonder if you're not holding back, you know? Like you're still making sure you hold onto something so you're not completely in."

"Completely in? Pardon the pun?"

I playfully slapped at his chest and rolled my eyes. "I'm serious. It's like that takes our relationship to another level. I feel like it's a deeper commitment for you, and it makes me nervous that you're hesitant to make the leap."

He placed his hands on either side of my face. "Tyler Lorraine—"

"Don't! You sound like my mother!"

"I told you I'm not going anywhere. I love you. I want to make love to you for the rest of my life. And I intend to. But there's a few things I want in place first. So could you please just trust me?"

"Yeah, I guess."

He laughed at me again and wrapped me up in a bear hug that made it impossible to be aggravated with him. I took a deep breath and resolved again to try and stop worrying. Now that we're actually together, the last thing I want to do is ruin it by constantly worrying about what might happen to tear us apart.

Friday, June 6th

Melanie called me at four o'clock and said she got tied up with a bride and groom and needed me to pick up a prescription for her before five. The pharmacy was quite a ways across town, so I left right away.

When I told the pharmacist I needed to pick up Mel's prescription, he handed me a card in an envelope. He smiled at my bewilderment and then told me to open it.

You are my drug. Without you in my life, I go through withdrawals. My body and my heart feel like they're dying. I feel sick. I can't sleep. But when I'm with you, I'm riding a high that's like no other. You make me dizzy. You make my head spin. You are a thirst within me no one else could ever quench. I'm addicted to you, and I don't ever want to recover.

What the hell? I looked back at the pharmacist and explained there must be some mistake. I was asked to pick up a prescription for my friend. He laughed and handed me an index card that said *Gimme Shelter.*

"I'm sorry. I don't understand what's going on."

"You will," he said. "Just follow the directions."

"But 'Gimme Shelter' is not a direction. It's a song title."

He nodded. "Sometimes we take directions from songs. Try to figure it out, Ms. Warren."

I didn't know how he knew my name or what was going on, but I began to suspect I knew who was behind it. I reread the drug passage on the way to the car, and called Cabe and Mel both when I got in. No answer.

I tossed the song title around in my head for a few minutes, and then I wondered if perhaps he meant the animal shelter. Where we'd worked together and where he'd gotten Deacon. I drove to the shelter and walked to the reception desk, hoping I didn't look like a complete idiot if I'd jumped to the wrong conclusion.

"My name is Tyler Warren. Did anyone leave something here for me?"

"Why, yes, they did." She handed me the card and gave me a huge smile as I opened it.

You are my shelter from any storm life can send me. With you, I feel safe. I feel secure. I have harbor. I will shelter you and protect you all the days of my life. I will never let anyone harm you as long as I am able to stop it.

I want to come home to you each night, sleep curled up next to you, and wake with you by my side. I promise to be your loyal and trustworthy companion, and I won't wet the carpet or run away during baths.

I laughed through my tears as I looked back to the receptionist, eager to find out what came next. She grinned as she handed me a card with the song title *Sanctuary.*

There were any number of options for that one, but only one true sanctuary. I got in the car and headed to Cabe's childhood church.

The pastor met me out front and suggested I walk through the gardens to the fountain. There I found the card leaned against the base of the fountain.

You are the answer to my prayers. The one my soul has searched for. God created woman to be a partner for man, and I could not ask for a better partner in life than you. You are more precious to me than any jewel on earth, and I promise before God to honor and cherish you for all my days. You can place your faith in me and trust I will be by your side.

The pastor waited for me at the exit to the garden, where he handed me the next song title, *Carnival.* I laughed out loud as I realized Fun Spot was only a few blocks away, Cabe's favorite place to spend a fortune playing those ridiculous carnival games. I tried his cell phone and Mel's on the way to Fun Spot, not at all surprised to get no answer. He'd put a lot of time and effort into this escapade. He would make sure it played out to the end.

The ticket lady at Fun Spot winked at me when she gave me the envelope, and I tore it in half in my haste to get it open.

Life is just more fun with you around. Your laughter is like music to my ears, and I love your sarcasm and your Southern sense of humor. I love being crazy with you, acting out our silly schemes and singing at the top of our lungs. I am my happiest and most free in your presence, and you bring out the best in me. I hope you'll consider your dance card filled for life.

Her card's title was *Love in the Library*.

We hadn't been to the library together in ages, but I knew exactly where to go. The librarian handed me a book of poetry with an envelope in it.

Roses are red, violets are blue. My heart sings poetry, when I think of you.

Okay, so I'm not a poet. But this I know. I could read every book in this library and still not know all there is to know about relationships, women, or you. Here's the deal. I'm willing to learn. I'm willing to try. I'm willing to own my mistakes and hold you accountable for yours, and to seek help when we can't find the answers.

I don't know what makes a relationship succeed, and I don't know how to keep one from failing. I can just tell you I love you, and I'll do all I can and learn more when that's spent.

The next card sent me to the bakery, where I had an entire box of chocolate chip cookies waiting for me.

I once tried to give you up, and in doing so, I compared you to being tempted by a chocolate chip cookie while dieting. Well, I'm officially off my diet. I intend to have chocolate chip cookies every single day for the rest of my life. You are the sweetest girl I know, and you are my single greatest temptation. Here's to giving in to temptation.

The bakery card led me to the lake, and I was a hot mess by the time I got there. Excited, yes. Elated, yes. But a hot, emotional mess.

I didn't see Cabe's car, but I could already see the telltale white envelope on the bench.

I read somewhere that a maiden should never desire a knight in shining armor, but one in tarnished armor instead. For it is the knight in tarnished armor who has been through battles and trials and proven himself able to overcome. It is the knight in tarnished armor who fought his way back to the maiden, and it is he who will protect her with his life.

I told you at the airport I don't know how to be Prince Charming, and I realize I'm no knight, but we've both been through some battles and come out battered but better for it. If you will be my lady, I will strive to be your knight. It may not be happily ever after since we're in real life and not a fairy tale, but I promise to start and end our days with love's true kiss.

The sound of a horse's whinny jerked my head up. Cabe sat astride a beautiful white stallion. They both looked a little terrified and totally out of place. Cabe caught my eye and smiled real big, like a child who has mastered a skill and realizes someone is watching. He sat up a little straighter and held himself a little more confidently, his grin plastered across his face from ear to ear. He looked so proud and so happy. My heart nearly burst with love for him, and my eyes filled with tears yet again. Bring on the world record.

He shifted in the saddle as they reached me, and I could see uncertainty in his eyes as he tried to dismount. Suddenly the horse bolted, and Cabe, who had let go in order to get off, went flying off and landed squarely on his rump in the grass.

"Oh my gosh! Cabe! Are you okay?" I ran to his side and knelt beside him and he sat up, laughing and brushing himself off.

"Well, Buttercup, I told you I'm not a knight or a prince. I guess that proves it."

I looked for the horse and saw him safely held underneath a tree by a man in jeans and a cowboy hat.

"How did you pull all this off?" I asked as the tears continued to wet my cheeks.

"I had a little help from some friends." He reached up and cupped the back of my head in his hand, pulling me toward him like steel to a magnet. He rolled me over his chest as we kissed, and then released me and set me back beside him.

Movement and a flash of white caught my eye across the lake, and I saw people lining the street in front of the houses we used for our imaginary scripts. White poster boards spelled out his proposal in bright purple letters.

Will you marry me?

I turned to face him, my mouth open and my eyes flowing. Of course!

He knelt beside me on one knee with an exquisite diamond ring between his finger and his thumb.

"You told me to come back to you when I was sure. This is how sure I am. You asked me how you could know I won't change my mind, and I guess there's no way to prove it other than time. But this is the strongest commitment I can give you. Will you be my wife?"

I nodded and extended a trembling left hand for him to slide on the ring. I felt its heaviness there, grounding me even as my heart took flight. "Yes, yes, yes! A million times yes. I love you, Cable Tucker Shaw."

"And I love you. Now, I know this probably all seems sudden, since we've never officially dated and all. But I wanted to make sure you knew I was serious about being all in. So take your time. However much time you need to process, to feel safe, to be sure of me." He twisted the ring around my finger and smiled. "I just wanted you to have this to remind you I'm not going anywhere."

He kissed me then.

Cabe, my best friend.

My fiance.

My love.

My life.

Wanna Know What Happens Next?

You can continue following Tyler & Cabe's journey in
Diary of an Engaged Wedding Planner,
Volume 3 in the Tales Behind the Veils series.
Now available at your favorite online book retailer.

Also available in Tales Behind the Veils:

Want to know about Cabe's beginnings? Volume 4 of the series explores his mother Maggie's disastrous choices at age nineteen, and her later in life chance at having true love at age forty-nine.

Love Romantic Suspense?

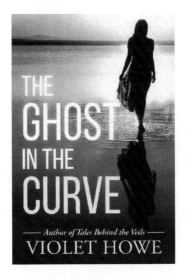

This lighthearted romantic suspense has a charming paranormal twist!
Sloane Reid never believed in ghosts before she met Chelsea. Now she's
trying to solve the mystery Chelsea has carried for thirteen years. But Sloane
can't solve it alone, and before local deputy Tristan Rogers will help her,
she'll have to convince him she's not crazy. Or a criminal. As they work
together to unlock the secrets of the past, Sloane soon discovers it may be
her own life that needs saving.
To purchase, visit your favorite online book retailer or
www.books2read.com/GhostintheCurve
or www.violethowe.com.

Photo Credit: Back Cover KLPS

About the Author

Violet Howe enjoys writing romance and mystery with humor. She lives in Florida with her husband—her knight in shining armor—and their two handsome sons. They share their home with three adorable but spoiled dogs. When she's not writing, Violet is usually watching movies, reading, or planning her next travel adventure. You can follow Violet's ramblings on her blog,
The Goddess Howe.

www.violethowe.com
Facebook.com/VioletHoweAuthor
@Violet_Howe
Instagram.com/VioletHowe

Sign up for the Newsletter

If you want to know what's coming next from Violet Howe, visit www.violethowe.com and sign up for Violet's newsletter. You'll get monthly updates on new releases, upcoming events, interesting tidbits, fun prize drawings, and more!

You'll also find out how to join Violet's Facebook reader group, the Ultra Violets, where you can get exclusive content, book discussions, contests, and you'll be in the know before anyone else on all things Violet.

Thank You

Thank you for taking the time to read this book.
I sincerely hope you enjoyed it! If you did, then please tell somebody! Tell
your friends. Tell your family. Tell a co-worker. Tell the person next to you
in line at the grocery store.

One of the best compliments you can give an author is to leave a review on
Amazon, Goodreads, or any other social media site you frequent.

Made in the USA
Middletown, DE
20 February 2020

85069771R00170